"TAKE ME WHERE YOU ARE . . ."

His lips brushed her throat as he pressed her down on the pillows. She lay soft, still under his hands, her heartbeat quickening at the catch of his breath. Her fingers found his hair as his lips brushed the cleft of her breasts . . . Her loins became warmly liquid, limbs weighted. This was surrender, this waiting, this need to be filled, be loved by this strange man who seemed to see into her soul as if it were his own . . .

Other Avon Books by
Christine Monson

STORMFIRE

Rangoon

Christine Monson

▲ AVON
PUBLISHERS OF BARD, CAMELOT, DISCUS AND FLARE BOOKS

AVON BOOKS
A division of
The Hearst Corporation
1790 Broadway
New York, New York 10019

First Avon Printing, September 1985

With love to my Bears
  For Bonnie and Jaya

And my thanks to
  Connie Rinehold and C. E. Miller

I owe a great debt to R. Talbot Kelly and E. D. Cuming, whose accounts of their turn-of-the-century travels in Burma allowed me to glimpse the past of that lovely land.

Rangoon

CHAPTER 1

Banned in Boston

Eternal Spirit of the Chainless Mind!
Brightest in dungeons, Liberty!
GEORGE GORDON, LORD BYRON

As she sharply surveyed the drowsy Rangoon wharves, the gleam in the young American's eye boded ill. Harry Armistead had seen that intrepid glint in Marseilles when she had persuaded the ship's cabin boy to take her ice skating; in Cairo where she had accepted their guide's sly wager and pelted up The Great Pyramid in less than four minutes; and in the Holy Land where she had irreverently announced, "Mr. Twain is right. I think it was not Joshua, but a horde of pilfering pilgrims who flattened Jericho for souvenirs."

In Calais, where she and her father had joined the British steamship *Robert Sydney*, Armistead paid slight attention when the pair plodded to the foot of the gangplank. As he leaned against the taffrail, he absently noted the young woman was as tall as her male companion. The purser cupped a mittened hand over his mouth, eyes squinting irritably at the shabby pair who huddled, backs to the gray, sharp-toothed wind. "So you'd be Dr. John Herriott"—his eyes dropped to the passenger list

1

tacked to his slate—"and daughter. We was about to weigh anchor without you."

"I gather we are the last to board, sir," the older man answered crisply. "Assuredly, we shall all be glad to remove ourselves from the cold. If you will have a man see to our luggage?"

With a derisive look at their ancient Gladstone bag and two worn portmanteaus, the purser spat briefly into the dirty dockside water. "That all? An't enough to break a man out for . . ."

The young woman cut him off in a tone clear and cool as a New England church bell. "Then you and my father can manage the three. I shall trip aboard with the steamer trunk." She stepped aside, her bonnet inclining a hair's breadth toward an ugly mammoth that completed the luggage.

With a slight flush, the purser shifted his tobacco plug. "Never mind, ma'am. I'll see to it." He waved to summon a crewman dockside.

Harry Armistead, amused at Miss Herriott's martial posture, strolled down the gangplank and doffed his hat to the Americans. "I am Leftenant Henry Armistead of Her Majesty's Coldstream Guards attached to the Burma Seventeenth Lancers. May I be of service? I've had no little difficulty with luggage myself in past travels."

The doctor's sharp eyes under silver-wired brows took his measure. At Harry's warm smile and square-jawed air of honesty, Dr. Herriott's tired, skeptical expression softened somewhat. "Thank you, Leftenant. I fear my daughter and I were too much taken with the Calais sights this morning to board when porters were about." The doctor looked like a man given to adept, swift decisiveness and a rueful awareness of the foibles of his fellowmen. In his mid-fifties, he was pale even for one from a northern clime and, but for his drawn expression, a handsome man.

Herriott's daughter, on the other hand, aside from inheritance of her father's eyes, a fine skin, and Slavic, oval face, had little to recommend her. Over sharp cheekbones, her skin was ruddy with cold; her rather long, slim nose blue and moist at the tip. Harry guessed her hair, concealed by an ugly bonnet, to be brown. Her lips were firmly pressed together as if she were used to having to hold her tongue and ill-resigned to it. She was too tall, and her figure threatened to be rawboned under her caped spencer. His glance flicked to her gloveless hands, which were long-fingered, but rough and crack-nailed as if she had been scrubbing floors. She did not even carry a reticule. She'll not see twenty again, Harry judged, and she's not likely to catch a husband, even in Burma.

Noting the direction of his assessment, level gray-green eyes took his measure. Look to yourself, you puffed-up prig, they seemed to say clearly. Mannishly shoving her hands into her spencer pockets, she gave him a curt nod when introduced by her father, then strode aboard ship.

In the days that followed, the *Robert Sydney*, a touring ship, skirted the coast of France, made brief stops at Gibraltar and Marseilles before reaching the Holy Land. Then the ship doubled back to Alexandria where its forty-five passengers transferred to overland rail along the Nile to Cairo and from there to Suez where they resumed a sea route to India. During those days, Harry gradually came to realize he had been both very right and very wrong about Miss Herriott.

The only thing dull about her was her attire. When her bonnet was discarded for the first evening's dinner with the other passengers, her heavy mass of burnished, bronze-gold hair torched the dim, mahogany salon. While not regular enough to be pretty, that pale, oval face with its faint air of ruthlessness might have belonged to a Khazar princess. She was bored with the social chatter of the women; they in turn resented her, for Harry had been also wrong about her inclination to hold her tongue. Miss Herriott said exactly what she thought on every subject with the sole avoidance of pleasantries. Her figure was not so bad as he had supposed, though he could tell little about it under the two overlarge, crow-black dresses she alternated every three days with monotonous regularity. If they had ever been fashionable, which was dubious, they were never intended to flatter the female anatomy. Where a bustle might be expected was a sagging wad of fabric—and she had not troubled to shorten the hem to accommodate the droop. Under those frayed hems briskly strode scuffed, cracked button-boots. Either Miss Herriott was in dilapidated mourning or she did not give a tinker's damn for her appearance.

And yet, there were moments after the *Robert Sydney* left the chill of France and approached The Holy Land where the heat became none of them, when he thought her very nearly attractive with that extraordinary blaze of hair. The other ladies who promenaded the sunny decks clung to parasols as tenaciously as tortoises to their shells. Miss Herriott, as ever, was eccentric. Not only did she not own a parasol, she donned smoked spectacles and tossed her bonnet over the stern off Capri. "It's better suited to a shark's stomach than a human head," she stated coolly at Harry's startled look.

He chuckled. "Indeed, Miss Herriott, a shark is likely to relish that pile of bugle beads as caviar."

A smile twitched her lips. "Burnt Boston baked beans may be more apropos." The interchange thawed some of the frigidity between them, and when Harry invited himself to a game of skittles, she did not object. After that, being fairly often in her and her father's company, he began to study her less idly. Without the bonnet, she tanned quickly and her hair became almost gilt rather than bronze. Her haggard look, which had made her appear more plain than she was, faded. Not so a certain look to her eyes, a guarded, sometimes bitter derision. Still, he found she had puckish charm when she chose to use it—or, rather, when she did not think to disguise it.

One day, she playfully flipped three fish from a galley-side salt barrel at the ship's napping cat; his scruffy hauteur evaporated as he exploded, round-eyed, claws stretched. Gales of laughter went up from crew and passengers as, in bewildered greed, he tried to scramble into the galley with all his windfall at once. While several ladies were unamused, Miss Herriott won an admirer so fervent he often lay across her feet at dinner; he presented her with a plump, lively rat as the ship entered Alexandria.

If some persons aboard thought her virtually unfit for polite company, Miss Herriott's father encouraged her unseemly behavior by treating her as he would a son. One suspected her outrageous opinions echoed his own and her colorful language was learned at his knee.

"Still, I daresay her conversation is quite sensible," one gentleman remarked to his wife as they played skittles on the aft deck.

"If only it did not issue from a *woman!*" the lady sputtered indignantly.

To top everything, the doctor had given his daughter the unlikely name of Lysistrata. "I was born in 1852 at the time of The Great Debate between Daniel Webster and Henry Clay over states' rights," she told Harry. "When Papa toasted my arrival with his friends, he said only a woman like Aristophanes' Lysistrata could prevent the American pot from boiling over into war. Unfortunately, I was no help." Other than that disclosure, she confided nothing of her background and made it clear that inquiries, however kindly meant, were unwelcome. Having met a scattering of American Southerners over the years, Harry could only surmise from her softly clipped accent that her entire life had not been spent in Boston. Her roguish, restlessly energetic father, while possibly the least stiff individual Harry had ever encountered, was as taciturn as his daughter on personal matters. Most passengers not plagued by seasickness whiled away their time in the salon and in deck chairs writing letters to relatives and friends; the Herriotts never publicly picked up a pen.

Each morning, the Herriotts rose before the sun; and for an hour and a half in the tolerable coolness of dawn, briskly walked the deck in a repeated circuit of several miles. They retired to the dining salon where they neatly wolfed an enormous breakfast, then returned to the after deck for noisily competitive skittles and skeet-shooting. Afterward, they went to their cabin and no one saw them until they reappeared to demolish a hefty lunch. They then began several rounds of chess in the after cabin. Chess lasted until four o'clock in the afternoon. Another promenade and a deck game occupied them until dinner, which was given the assiduous attention of the first two meals. As all meals were included in the passage fare, Harry concluded the Herriotts were making the most of them.

The farther east the *Robert Sydney* progressed, the more relaxed Lysistrata seemed, although her clothing appeared more dismal as the other women donned pale-colored lawns and muslins in the Holy Land. In Alexandria, where they all disembarked the *Robert Sydney* and boarded a sweltering train for Suez, she packed a cooling wet cloth into the crown of a jaunty fez bought in Jerusalem. Fine white dust covered everyone like sugared cakes, the more obviously in the folds and tucks of Lysistrata's black dresses. She unbuttoned at the throat as far as she dared, but the heat must have been unbearable in her serge. Still, when they periodically left the train to view the monumental remains of Egypt, she rode her flea-bitten donkey through ancient rubble with a mounting elation that had nothing to do with veneration for the past. She was particularly unawed by the stony hulk of Karnak. "Those columns are so ostentatious, they appear about to burst. Lend one of them your collar, Harry, and see if it turns blue."

By the time they boarded the HMS *Mayfield* in Suez, Lysistrata's excitement was pitched high. From Aden to Bombay to Madras, she paced the decks as if she were a caged lioness. Harry had the impression Lysistrata Herriott expected a great deal of Burma. When at last he stood beside her at the bowrail of the *Mayfield* while it cut through the drab dawn and muddy Rangoon River, Lysistrata's prospects, like his own, lacked promise. The river was as fat and placid as a sleepy brown crocodile burrowed into mud, and was seamed by elephant grass and monotonous, stunted jungle with only an occasional slow-rising waterfowl and the screech of kites and gulls to break the humid silence. Still, with her hands white and taut on the rail, Lysistrata's stance was expectant.

After the *Mayfield* passed Elephant Point, tamarind and palms rose from the scrub to shelter Rangoon's outlying, palmetto-topped villages and modest pagodas. Then, beyond Poozoodoung where the dawn paled the hills, soared the Midas-touched dome of the great Shwe Dagon Pagoda, its golden tiers flaming into the sunrise. "It doesn't seem to touch the earth," Lysistrata breathed.

She and Harry were still enthralled by Shwe Dagon when they rounded Hastings shoal, and a sleek, sharp-hulled schooner cut past them, outward bound. Eyes alight, Lysistrata intently watched it. To a Bostonian, no ship could be a novelty, but this one with its snowy sides was a marked change from the dug-out catamarans and Chinese paddy boats that plied the river mouth. Like a

Himalayan hawk, it seemed bent on freedom, only in an opposite direction from herself. The name *Rani* flashed across the schooner's stern, then faded into the growing glare of morning light off the river.

The *Mayfield* neared Rangoon, her bow looming over a drift of fanciful little galleons steered by Burmese who waved as they veered past to bounce in her wake. Unimpressed by steam launches hooting for right-of-way and ponderous teak rafts turtling toward the harbor mouth, henna-sailed sampans, paddy skiffs, and spider-rigged catamarans scurried through the churning water. The *Mayfield* steamed under the Monkey Point Battery guns into the harbor, then slowed to glide through ranks of high-riding, cargoless shipping of the British East India Company, Bibby, and other international lines that filled most of the slips. Beyond them, bleaching under a cloudless sky, the city of Rangoon was strung like dingy laundry across the dun and khaki hills below Shwe Dagon. Along its waterfront jumbled quay-bordered shipping offices, chandleries, mills, and docks bare of cargo except for a few stacks of square-cut teak. In the shade of the teak lazed idle coolies.

The harbor's Dallah side was a whining haze of imported coal soot and native sawdust that dulled its offshore water. Tamil and Cingalese *mahouts* sat with the calmness of leeches on the great, gray necks of mud-caked elephants that waded through the shallows scum to pluck waterlogged teak from bank-butted rafts. Reflected in the water, rusty metal godowns with roofs mirroring the early sun seemed to semaphore the distant monsoons to fill their empty shells with sugarcane, rice, and fruit for shipping.

"The whole place is bound to be sprightlier after a good rain," Harry consoled Lysistrata, then saw he need not have bothered: she was hardly aware of his existence as she watched the *Mayfield*'s anchors plummet over the side. The decks crowded as servants scurried about, loaded with their masters' baggage. The customs boat pulled alongside. The harbormaster, customs inspectors, and port medical officer climbed aboard to be greeted by the captain, the ship's doctor, and Dr. Herriott, whose assistance had been asked in certifying the passengers' health, particularly on the point of yellow fever.

Lysistrata leaned against the rail. "Look, someone else is putting out to greet us." Two narrow, palmetto-canopied canoes, each manned by oarsmen in bow and stern, nosed out from a jetty. Single, stern-mounted oars flashed, then cut the river's turbid surface. They drew near, their crews competing with each other in execrable English for the privilege of selling melons, birdcages, raffia-strapped pottery, carved wooden panels, and miscellany that included a monkey on one man's shoulder. They were generally ignored by the passengers preoccupied with customs. When Harry laughingly declined their goods, they grinned and shrugged philosophically, then began to back water preparatory to returning whence they came. "Wait!" Lysistrata called. "You can ferry me in!"

A gasp of horror went up from a New York matron behind them as Lysistrata darted for the starboard side opposite the customs boat.

Harry darted after her. "Lysistrata!" He caught her arm. "Miss Herriott. You cannot possibly go ashore with these men!" He flicked an unhappy eye over the fellow already grabbing for the rope ladder she was shoving over the side. A Chino-Burmese Karen, he was dressed in a sun-faded black tunic and knee breeches. The other man was a Madrassee. A brawny, sweat-polished specimen with a villainous cast to one eye, he was bare except for loincloth and turban.

Lysistrata politely but firmly put Harry's hand off. "Why ever not?"

Wondering how much English the pair in the canoe comprehended, Harry said loudly, "The port authorities haven't cleared you." In an undertone, he remonstrated, "They look unsavory, Miss Herriott. That one in the prow has twenty inches of steel at his waist."

Lysistrata gave the weapon in question an appraising glance as she eased up onto the rail. "If they pose any difficulty, I shall jump into the river. I swim quite well, and help is not far away, after all. As for customs, they will take until Kingdom Come to complete their business. Papa has charge of our luggage and can verify my goatish good health to his local colleague."

Harry hurriedly looked around for the aforesaid senior Herriott to gainsay his headstrong daughter. When he turned back, that young woman was over the side and ducking under the canoe's tunneled canopy. "I'll accompany you," he called hastily, and, cursing the rubbery ladder under his breath, clambered down after her. His defection without clearance was bound to cause trouble with his colonel. Also, he had a pair of field glasses and several hunting weapons in his baggage, which were bound to be questioned and perhaps confiscated by the inspectors. The British authorities took care to see potential military equipment did not find its way to possible insurrectionists and bandits among the natives.

Trouble, Harry did not need. He entertained some very ill thoughts indeed of Miss Herriott as he scowled at her black-clad back perched ahead of him in the wobbly canoe slopping through swirling eddies. Still, as they disembarked without incident on the quay, he quickly dug in his breeches for coins to pay the canoemen, for he was sure Lysistrata had no money and he wished to save her the embarrassment of an argument with them. Lysistrata forestalled him by unfastening a cameo brooch from her bodice and with a smile giving it to the Madrassee. "Thank you. You are very strong oarsmen." Highly pleased with their trophy, they hastily *shikkohed* and hurried off chattering about the jewelry's prospective value, as Lysistrata, with the air of an enchanted child, slowly looked about at the rusty, sunbaked tin sheds and godowns. Harry wrinkled his nose at the dock stench of spiced sweat and sewage. If this seemed so marvelous, what could her prior life have been?

He was playing protective sheepdog again, he thought ruefully. How his sisters would laugh if they could see the resigned look he knew was upon his face. He had kept a soft spot for strays, no matter how irascible or unlovely, since he had been old enough to toddle. The stables of Weslingham, the family manor in Kent, had housed a menagerie of his "collectibles," as Jane, the youngest, called them. He was not, however, as susceptible to the feminine gender as he grew older. Though he doted on his sisters, Harry saw through the wiles they practiced on his sex, for those wiles had been well-honed upon him.

Ruddy-cheeked, sandy-haired, he had grown into a handsome young man, particularly adept at athletics. He was bright, affable, and rich enough to be one of the most eligible bachelors in England. His plush-bear appeal and sunny manner belied his perspicacity; many a young lady discovered to her rue that Harry was a more elusive catch than he looked. All might have gone well with his military career in the prestigious Coldstream Guards if one of those young ladies, more determined and reckless than her sisters, had not thrown herself into his arms and bed. Had he not been mellow with port, he might have thought better of the encounter, but as it was, his refusal to patch the girl's long-departed maidenhood at the altar led to a duel with her brother, then posthaste to Burma.

Harry had waxed first bitter, then philosophic, about exile. After all, aside from the brilliant society of London and the glorious countryside of England in all its radiant seasons, his military skills could hardly be said to be sharpened by pheasant shooting in the Cotswalds, and he wanted the adventure of being a soldier. Shepherding the family acres might be a pleasant enough life, but a bleating dull one. Harry thought he had sufficient courage for the military. He'd never balked a jump, and though bullet-scarred at the hairline, he had handled himself decently, albeit too accurately, in his one affair of honor. Burma, rich in teak, rice, and jewels, was the new frontier of the Empire and the gateway to the coveted China Trade. A man could make a fortune and a new life for himself in Burma, and a new life Harry required, for there was no going back to England for many a year.

By the eagerness of his departure to a summoned ricksha, Lysistrata Herriott sensed Lieutenant Armistead felt well rid of her. He had lingered only long enough to explain to her father and several irritated port officials the circumstances of her headlong dash for shore. Then he collected his baggage, called for conveyance, and bid her a hasty good-bye, with belated assurance they would meet again in Rangoon's small European society. He also contributed some brief advice. "I've heard the cart drivers don't speak a word of English and can scarcely locate the chief hotels. You'd best let the captain instruct one of the fellows where to take you." While her pride could sometimes be easily pricked, she was little perturbed at his desertion. Men did not usually take to her, and although Armistead had—in a purely platonic way— she was prepared to do without male assistance other than her father's in Burma.

If Lysistrata had learned nothing else since her family moved north from Charleston, South Carolina, just before the war, she had learned self-reliance. She had been nine when Fort Sumter was fired upon. Southerners treated her and her three brothers like mange-ridden alleycats because of their Yankee father; the Bostonians did likewise because of their Rebel mother. In the following four years, the war took her older brothers; typhus the youngest; and grief her mother, not three months after Lincoln's assassination. That was the coldest winter she remembered, until Frank Wyatt had come along. After Frank, she had discovered just how frozen hell could be.

Well, my girl, she thought, dismissing the past, Burma's hot enough to toast you properly. Seeing her father still in conference with the port medical officer, she strode up to the captain who stood with his purser at the gangplank. "Captain, where might Loo Gow Street be found?"

"Why, it's in a native residential quarter, only a little way from the harbor."

"If you will be so good as to direct one of these cart drivers"—she nodded to the assortment of rickshas and rustic, horse-drawn cabs that had magically assembled—"my father and I should like our baggage conveyed there at once."

The captain frowned slightly as other passengers without native servants for interpreters clustered behind her to ask the same assistance. "But Miss Herriott, Europeans do not—"

Dr. Herriott, coming up behind Lysistrata, quietly intervened. "I asked to be quartered near Queen Anne's Hospital rather than in the cantonments. Dr. Thomas Lighter, the chief surgeon, has arranged for our lodging, which I am certain is entirely suitable."

"Very well, sir," the captain replied, "but I believe you will shortly want a change of residence. The native sectors of the city offer few amenities, and during monsoon season, the harbor area is in danger of flooding; however, for the moment, you should do well enough until you are better acquainted with the manner of life here." He waved toward the closest driver. "Hi, you! *Gharry-wallah!*"

Shortly, Lysistrata and Dr. Herriott tagged on foot after their baggage-laden *tikka gharry* pulled by a runt pony whose tail dusted the ground. As they threaded through narrow harbor streets, she stared with confused fascination at Cingalese paddy workers, wiry Chittagonian coolies from the northwest border, frock-coated Madrassee clerks, veiled Kashmini women: slit-skirted, black-eyed wisps from Shanghai, Canton, and Kowloon. Almost nowhere did she see Burmese, who seemed to have left their city to foreigners. Everywhere were laborers from East India and China, and seafarers from the far reaches of the globe in masses of color and racket. Roll-gaited, leather-faced American and European sailors boldly eyed her as she squeezed by them—until her gimlet-eyed father clamped her hand on his coattail and took the lead. Dodging *gharries*, they nearly stumbled into a drifting, houri-eyed ox. Under faded shop canopies, beggars, carts of strange produce, and sagging baskets of rice— along with stalls of imported gimcracks—were piled against the walls. Underfoot, crows hopped after scraps.

When her father asked directions at the corner of Capricorn Street, a strapping Sikh policeman impatiently jutted his rolled beard at the stream of traffic moving toward a business district fluttering with Chinese signs. As they fell in with the traffic to wind through streets cloistered by trade, Lysistrata craned under wide verandah roofs to watch the flash of loom shuttles and spin of potters' wheels. Catching sight of a dusty display of European food in an Indian shop window, she joked to her father, "Look, Papa, bonbons only a mummy could love!"

More and more as they neared the major boulevards, they saw British colonial construction jammed in with pagodas, Indian temples, and Chinese josshouses. Shaking his head, Dr. Herriott surveyed the sun-blasted, flat-roofed houses that rambled among the potpourri of architecture. "Those crumbling boxes are probably as sweltering as bakery ovens most of the year."

"They look miserable *now,* and *now* is the dead of Burma's winter, but fortunately"—Lysistrata glanced overhead at a padouk among the shade trees lining the main streets—"we are not likely to get heatstroke out of doors." With a grin, she readjusted the wet rag in her cocky fez. "At least, for another ten minutes."

Eventually, the *gharry* led them into the fringes of a quiet, residential quarter where houses with palmyra mat walls were perched on stilts. Ladders led to living quarters above stock pens where chickens, pigs, cattle, and an occasional naked child dozed in the heat. Few people were out of doors in the sandy, scrub-edged road when the sun was high; and the Herriotts, with perspiration dripping from their fingertips, looked enviously at the *gharry* driver slouched in the swaying shadow of his calico parasol. What if their lodging was one of these flimsy cages, Lysistrata wondered, spirits sagging. She had been forced to face many another unpleasant situation during the last years.

Then, from one of the houses appeared a man in a white jacket and ankle-length skirt so vivid even her smoked glasses could not mute its bold-patterned orange and purple. His hair was swept into a topknot, and he waved a floozy's pink fan. This, she realized with some awe, must represent the male of the elusive Burmese species. Oddly enough, his attire—far less his broad-jawed, Mongol face and brisk, bandy-legged stride—did not appear effeminate, although she noticed her father's startled look. Behind the man trotted his wife, virtually his twin except for an orchid tucked in her hair. She might have been comely to Western eyes, but for one thing. "My God," whispered Dr. Herriott, "did the woman shove her face into a bucket of whitewash?"

The Herriotts soon saw that although a few men and

children went about in loincloths, most men dressed like
the women who, fortunately, did not all daub their faces
with paint. Lysistrata was intrigued, for after stolid Boston, she found the Burmese's deft, uninhibited use of
color, their gay flowers and fans wonderfully appealing.
She ventured a tentative smile as a rose-clad woman with
a yellow umbrella passed them. To her delighted surprise, the woman flashed a row of betel-stained teeth,
squatted in a polite *shikkoh,* hands pressed together before her face. Lysistrata curtsied; her father bowed with a
dip of his hat. A small head poked out from behind the
woman's skirt and another flash of teeth emitted from a
black-banged three-year-old male. As the trek resumed
behind the driver, who had patiently halted for amenities
to be exchanged, Lysistrata breathed a sigh of relief. The
natives were friendly.

The house on Loo Gow Street proved vastly better and
vastly worse than Lysistrata had anticipated. The section
was a well-to-do Chinese-dominated area of the city
sprinkled with josshouses, scarlet-emblazoned pawn-
shops, and elaborate houses with lantern-hung eaves.
Seeing the pale rose tiled roof of their dwelling tower
over its high, palm-fringed wall, Lysistrata wondered
how Dr. Lighter had ever thought they would require so
much living space. Still, she was impressed, despite her
New England–acquired frugality.

Dr. Herriott rapped smartly on the heavily carved teak
gate, then they waited. The only answering sound was
the dry rattle of palm fronds. Blankly, they stared at the
lavish relief of peacocks, devils, and gnomish *nats* that
covered the gate. Colored glass eyes goggled back. At
length, their driver leaned from his perch, gave the gate a
couple of loud thwacks with his split bamboo goad, and
yelled something in Burman. Again they waited. Lysistrata longed to climb one of the palms and assail the cap
of the wall, so desperate was she for a cool bath. Perspi-

ration pasted her clothing to her body like papier-mâché. Wiping wet hair from her eyes, she squinted at the sun with some anxiety. If there was a mistake about the address, they would have to continue to the hospital on foot, for they had only been able to afford the single cart for their luggage. She began to calculate how many more precious coins would be required to pay the driver to the hospital and from there to . . . wherever.

She might have known this imposing place could not be the residence of an ordinary doctor. Too, this heat could be doing her father no good. He was not so young as he used to be. "There's no one here, Papa." She sighed. "We had better—"

"Wait." He held up a hand. "I think I hear someone coming." Moments later, she too heard a slow pad of footsteps. A peephole partition lifted, then clacked shut. A heavy bar shifted across the interior side of the gate. The gate swung back, and a topknot stabbed in their direction.

"Welcome, *Tuan* doctor! Welcome, *Ma* . . . Herrot!" The topknot belonged to a wizened little man, his wide grin only slightly dimmed by betel nut and several gaps. His white jacket was immaculately clean. This, Lysistrata was soon to discover as the man led them along a wide, pebbled path, was virtually the only well-scrubbed item about the place. The house was as large as promised, a two-storied bungalow with a wide, double-tiered, teak-beamed verandah that framed its bulk. The path led perhaps fifty feet to shallow steps that joined the verandah in front of the main door. Long, glass-paned windows and Venetian doors festooned with bedraggled, red *joss* papers for luck ranked both tiers of the house. The place was a curious blend of East and West, comfortable-looking if its whitewash had not faded in gray sheets streaked with bird dung like the surrounding garden walls. The garden had grown wild, its variety of palms, padouk, and tamarind thrusting from a riot of bougainvillea, trumpet vines, and Spanish bayonet. The grounds, once grassed, were now bare except for thickets of weeds and young cactus.

A pair of brown faces blurred behind a dusty window flanking the richly carved main door, then plummeted from sight. Lysistrata heard a faint giggle as they crossed the verandah. When their guide held the door open, the two faces were actually three, all belonging to females identically dressed except for varying multicolored prints in their long skirts. The eldest was perhaps in her early forties, with a smooth, handsome face and intelligent eyes. She was nearly of a height with Lysistrata, which was, as the Herriotts were to learn, extremely tall for a Burmese. Her serene smile seemed unlikely to dissolve into a giggle. The middle one was a lovely sylph with long-lashed almond eyes, which she used to lavish effect, Lysistrata was startled to notice, even upon Dr. Herriott, who gave her a disconcertingly benevolent grin. The youngest was about six. She bobbed a neat English curtsy despite her slim skirt and flashed up a perfect smile in a dainty flower of a face, her huge, nearly hazel eyes eclipsing her elder sister's. Stars of yellow jasmine aureoled her sleek little head.

The old man, with many smiles and gestures toward the three female Burmese, began to rattle in Burman. The three waited patiently for him to cease, then the tall one, with a graceful gesture of her hand, said in studied English, "My father-in-law, U Pho, bids you welcome and wishes to name us. I am Ma Saw. These are my daughters, Sein"—eyelashes swooped—"and San-hla." The little one smiled absently, her eyes rounded on Dr. Herriott's luxuriant mustache and side whiskers. The old man interrupted her scrutiny with a swift, eager speech, and Ma Saw began again. "My father-in-law is . . . buttle of this house for five years"—holding up appropriate fingers, she ignored the old man's insistent show of seven digits—"under old master and a most good man. I am housekeeper, Sein is maid, and San-hla help in kitchen and garden. Sein speaks English some, French much from Sisters of Saint Martin. She very smart, learn quick." Seeming to read Lysistrata's mind concerning her lissome daughter's availability to Dr. Herriott, she added smoothly, "U Pho lives in garden house. Sein and San-hla live with me in own house in Green Orchid Street." Then ambivalently, "You need nighttime, you send."

"I'm sure it won't be necessary to trouble you," was Lysistrata's firm reply, eyes narrowed on Sein, whose lips continued to curve meltingly. Lysistrata noticed Ma Saw's eyes flick almost imperceptibly from her father to her as in appraisal.

The doctor gave his daughter a quizzical smile as he completed the Herriotts' side of the introductions with a courtly manner that softened his daughter's bluntness. "This seems to be a very fine house," he remarked pleasantly, professional nose taking in a strong odor of carbolic; the very walls seemed to have been washed in the stuff. Lysistrata noticed it too; also that the long room in which they were standing, probably the parlor, was devoid of furniture. Shutters were closed on the east and west, but the bare teak floors were unnaturally bleached in water-stained patches that caught sunlight from the few windows that were open. Had the floors too been scrubbed with carbolic?

Ma Saw inclined her head as she replied to Dr. Herriott. "Yes, very fine. Belong merchant, Ho Lung Chi. Have Burmese mother, Chinese father. He die cholera."

That explained the carbolic.

"You like see house?" Ma Saw asked.

"Yes, but we should like to bathe first," Lysistrata replied briskly, shunning euphemisms about toilette, "and lunch in an hour."

Ma Saw gave her a slight look, then said something to her father-in-law. He nodded, grinned, bowed to the Herriotts, then seesawed off down a shadowy central hallway that led to the rear of the house. Ma Saw's two daughters waited with expectant looks at Lysistrata, but when she strode toward the stair, they shrugged at each other and, like a pair of alert cockatoos, turned instead to watch Dr. Herriott go outside to collect the luggage.

To tell the truth, as Lysistrata mounted the stair with Ma Saw quietly following, she was unsure how to deal with servants. She disapproved of servitude, considering it akin to slavery and pointless unless one was lazy and excessive about one's manner of living. Employing someone to brush her hair and dress her seemed preposterous, but she was reluctant to abruptly dismiss U Pho's family from their accustomed livelihood. The squalid horrors of the streets of Bombay and Madras had shown that to be poor in an Eastern country was worse than in America. Still, she did not know how these servants were to be paid, for she and her father had scarcely enough money to feed themselves until he received his first salary.

For the moment, she supposed firmness was the wise course. The dockworkers in Indian ports seemed excitable and prone to much discussion of the task at hand. Observation led her to believe U Pho might be of this sort, but Ma Saw appeared intelligent and coolheaded. No doubt the woman and her family had a far better idea of what was expected of them than she did.

As they reached the second floor, Lysistrata discarded that idea. Though not precisely dirty, the wide, barren hallway had an air of neglect. The walls needed fresh whitewash, and she heard scuttling among the beams overhead. A two-storied, arched window that banked the

stairwell showed a rear courtyard and garden as overgrown as the front grounds. Two windowpanes were
cracked; none showed signs of washing in recent history.

Her bedroom, enormous compared to her pinched
room in Boston, was surprisingly pleasant; it took up half
the rear of the house, with a view of the garden from Venetian doors which opened onto the upper verandah.
Neighboring rooftops of terra cotta, rose, and pale mauve
showed behind the heavy leaves of a banyan which af-
forded privacy. A large, four-poster bed with legs set in
water pots to discourage vermin, a black-lacquered armoire, and peeling gilt Empire dressing table with a native cane chair made up the furnishings. That the bed's
lace canopy was rotting and mildewed, the mosquito-
netted bed devoid of linen, and the dressing-table mirror
blackened in spots made little difference to Lysistrata, so
relieved was she to see furniture at all. One corner was
tiled in a pretty blue, yellow, and white motif of birds and
flowers faded by grime. On the tile sat a copper tub green
for want of polishing and a blue pottery toilet jar she was
glad to see was merely dusty. The walls were white-
washed tabby and teak like the rest of the house—which
was probably for the better, she thought, for the climate
must take a quick toll of wallpaper. There were no draperies.

"I bring bed linen," Ma Saw told her, "also linen for
bath. Dr. Lighter send from hospital for you and Dr.
John. Perhaps you wish sleep till sunset? Eat when
cool?"

Reviewing the odd assortment of furniture, Lysistrata
suddenly wondered just how many basic furnishings Dr.
Lighter had been obliged to supply. He probably felt his
new surgeon should have brought his own household ne-
cessities and sedately installed them in a cantonment
among respectable Europeans.

As if reading her mind, Ma Saw said, "I send message

Dr. Lighter, tell you are here. He not busy, perhaps he come see.''

Lysistrata bridled, then realized the woman had not meant to imply condescension on Dr. Lighter's part, only that his duties as hospital administrator were demanding. Still, she did not wish her father and herself to be once again viewed as charity cases, for she had become heartily sick of the smug tolerance of their relatives and acquaintances in Boston. Burma meant a new life that, with energy and intelligence, might be shaped into a reasonably happy pattern. She could hardly wait to dispense with bath and dinner in order to begin. ''Thank you, Ma Saw. I shall make up the bed after I bathe.'' Ignoring Ma Saw's startled look, she went on. ''As my father and I did not dine aboard ship and I am not in the habit of lying abed during the day, I would like luncheon as soon as possible''; then added with some alarm, for she was ravenous, ''There *is* food in the house?''

''Oh, yes,'' Ma Saw replied. ''Plenty fruit, *ngapi*, plenty rice and curry.'' Then waited, clearly expecting an order to go to market and purchase fare customary to a Western palate; it was not forthcoming.

Lysistrata sighed inwardly. Not only were she and her father unable to pay servants, they were unable to feed them; and she had no intention of dining on poultry and fish denied her household. ''Curried rice, *ngapi*, and fruit sound delightful,'' she replied, hoping *ngapi* was not some kind of clammy squid. Then another unpleasant thought occurred to her. ''It is not your supper we are to eat, is it?''

''No, come with house.'' Ma Saw's reply had a new note of friendliness, as well as one of amusement.

Lysistrata cursed at having betrayed her anxiety, for the woman had perceived more than she wished.

Ma Saw seemed to sense her discomfort. ''I see all is prepared.'' She disappeared.

Lysistrata wandered about the room, gazing at each lovely view framed by the Venetian doors. After a while, she began to think U Pho exceedingly slow with the bathwater. Surely he was not troubling to heat it in this climate? As if in answer to her query, the old Burman arrived with a pottery crock containing perhaps a gallon of water. With a flourish, he dumped it into the tub. For a moment, he studied the film of dust and scattered insects that rose to the surface of the inch-deep water, said something jovial in Burmese, then drifted out again.

After a half hour passed, Lysistrata began to simmer. She stalked out onto the verandah and stared at the cistern where U Pho dreamily watched a butterfly play among jasmine that cloaked its rim. A huge white cheroot was stuffed in his mouth. "U Pho," she yelled. He looked up, startled. "More water, please!" Her voice rose a note higher as she forked two fingers at him. "Carry two potfuls this time!" He nodded peacefully and dipped the crock. When he appeared at the doorway with yet again his single container, Lysistrata jabbed her fingers under his nose. "Two, two! At this rate, I shall grow gray before water is sufficient to cover my knees." Reference to intimate anatomy did not matter in the face of U Pho's sweet, uncomprehending smile. He held out the pot, his head cocked. Wearily, she took the pot and waved him out.

Taking no chances on U Pho's dim understanding, Lysistrata locked the door before discarding her clothes. The lithe body reflected in the dusty mirror would have amazed Harry Armistead. Matter-of-factly, she skimmed her scanty water supply of its undesirable wildlife with a banyan leaf from the unswept verandah. After placing the crock in the tub, she stood on the tile and splashed herself, then rinsed her hair. If not the luxurious soak she longed for, it was refreshing.

Reluctantly, she eyed her perspiration-soaked dress;

then with a muttered expletive, doused it in the tub. After wringing the soggy mass nearly dry, she donned it, combed out the worst wrinkles with her hands, then ran her fingers through the tangles in her hair before winding it up again in its usual careless knot. Upon leaving the room, she found her portmanteau by the door, the steamer trunk at the stairtop.

Her father greeted her downstairs. He noticed her glance at the whiskey flask raised to his lips. "Down, girl. I've a need to wet my whistle. That trunk not only looks like a dead rhinoceros, it's as heavy as one."

She frowned. "Surely U Pho could have helped with it."

"And have him drop dead of heart failure?" He took another swig and popped in the stopper with the heel of his hand.

"I suppose you don't think that could happen to you?" Her voice lowered. "Papa, I really don't think U Pho will be much use. We cannot afford—"

He crooked a finger. "In here. I've been touring myself about."

She followed him into a side room lined with large panels of teak carved in scenes from the life of Buddha. Bright lacquered colors and gilt gave the room a gay look despite its dimness. Slits of sunlight through louvers along two sides of the room streamed across a long, heavy table supported by huge, carved lotus blooms entwined with tendrils. The lotus petals were inlaid with broad expanses of ivory. Lysistrata's face lit. "How wonderful!" She wonderingly ran her fingers across the intricate inlay of plants and animals on the table surface. "Even the birds' beaks and monkeys' eyes are gilded. Here's an elephant with real ivory tusks. And a gilded leopard."

Her father smiled oddly. "That isn't gilt."

Her fingers stilled abruptly. "You don't mean . . . ?"

He nodded. "On the walls, too. With a wee bit of mining with my penknife, I could make us comfortable for several years."

She whirled fiercely. "Papa, you're not thinking . . ."

The odd, wry smile appeared again. "Of course I'm thinking . . . but while I'm a doctor and perhaps a beggarman, I'm not yet a thief."

Her smile matched his, then she went to him and clasped her arms about his neck. "And not likely to be," she murmured softly, "but if ever that day comes, I'll carry the swag, mate."

He held her tightly, then swatted her bottom. "You owe enough bad habits to me, miss." He gently pushed her toward a scarlet lacquer chair, one of five that remained of what probably had been a set of eight or twelve. "Dinner should be served shortly. I saw San-hla picking it in the garden." Seeing Lysistrata's face become a trifle glum, he lifted an eyebrow. "Come, fresh fruit after weeks at sea shouldn't be half bad."

She propped her chin on one hand. "Oh, I'm not complaining, Papa. We're lucky the place has a back-door larder, but I doubt it can support six people for a month; and even if it can, our digestive systems would rebel."

Herriott gave her a whimsical look. "San-hla is only a third of a person, and the digestions of her family do not seem to suffer unduly. Of course, they must have ample choice of simple, cheap foods in their markets. If we eat native fare, we should fare as well as the natives; once we get used to it."

The affordable chickens in Madras must have been hatched in the infancy of Kublai Khan, she wanted to protest; nothing was left of them but beady eyes and bone. But she kept her silence. Dr. Herriott was a patient believer in providence and the inevitable turn of cards at poker. Sometimes, that dogged assurance was all they had to go on, and she was careful of it. "What about U Pho?" she asked. "Do you think we should keep him?"

Whatever he would have answered was cut off by Ma Saw's appearance in the doorway. In each hand was expertly curved a banyan leaf laden with peeled fruit, fish, and rice. Behind her followed Sein with a yellow porcelain teapot and two mismatched, cheap pottery tea bowls. As Ma Saw arranged the makeshift plates and Sein poured tea, Lysistrata could not help wondering if their appearance had been calculated to forestall a decision about U Pho.

"You wish she stay, you need more?" Ma Saw gestured toward her daughter and Sein looked demurely at Dr. Herriott.

He caught his daughter's eye. "That won't be necessary, thank you, Ma Saw"—he twirled his mustache—"though Sein's loveliness is an ornament to any room."

Aware the last was added out of mischief, Lysistrata studied the teapot glaze.

After the Burmese made their exit, Dr. Herriott glanced at his daughter's rapt expression of concentration as she sipped her tea. "What are you thinking, Lysistrata?"

"Oh, only that I've seen this type of porcelain in the Boston Athenaeum. The guide said it was made exclusively for the emperors of China." Her lips quirked. "This is marvelously genteel poverty, Papa."

He grinned. "Perhaps we should invite your Aunt Agatha to dinner."

Lysistrata thought of Agatha, that haughty dowager of Beacon Street enthroned at the head of her table laid out with enough calla lilies for Lincoln's wake. Mercifully, she and her father had been grudgingly included at only a few clan dinners to preserve appearances. She pictured Agatha wolfishly chopsticking salted *ngapi* fish paste off a leaf with her fingers. In mid-giggle she caught her fa-

ther's look of disappointment at Ma Saw's reappearance
at the door. She had not often laughed after the war, and
he sometimes went to elaborate lengths to make her do
so. Despite their loneliness in Boston, they were accustomed to privacy. She had not realized it was a luxury.

"Yes, Ma Saw?" Herriott inquired. .

"Dr. Lighter send message." She handed him a
folded paper. "He sorry not meet you."

Herriott scanned it. "Dr. Lighter sends his regards and
regrets he was unable to leave the hospital to welcome
us. He wishes to do so this evening. We are invited to
dinner. A conveyance will be sent for us at sunset." He
looked up. "It seems we must do without Aunt Agatha
tonight."

Dr. Lighter's modest bungalow adjoining Queen
Anne's large, three-storied hospital compound was only
a brief ride from the Herriotts' new residence. The man
himself was a short, stout Irishman with a face red as his
unkempt stock of hair. He was sharp-eyed, sharp-witted.
While his native eloquence flowered with the vinegary
dinner wine, he accorded only perfunctory attention to
Lysistrata, and unabashedly grilled Dr. Herriott about his
experience. The meal was a meager, ill-prepared selection of vaguely European-style dishes Lysistrata assumed
were planned to suit palates wary of local cuisine. The
linen was threadbare, the rooms as poorly appointed as
their own had been in America. The Herriotts exchanged
resigned looks over the stale trifle served as dessert. If
the hospital chief-of-staff lived so modestly, they could
only presume him to be either ill-paid or a miser, which
did not bode well for their own prospects.

Lysistrata decided no moment would likely prove better to make a proposition to the Irishman. Upon hearing
it, Lighter reacted as if she had suggested she ride naked

through the streets. "You? Nurse? Whatever for?" he ejaculated.

"I am an active person, Dr. Lighter, and accustomed to hospital procedures. I have a letter of recommendation from Boston General Hospital, where I served as nurse for the past three years."

"Begging your pardon, Miss Herriott, I'm sure you mean well, but there's more to medicine than emptying bedpans," Lighter replied bluntly. "I have enough people who don't know a catheter from a syringe."

"I'm not likely to approach the wrong end of a patient with a catheter, Dr. Lighter. I nearly completed the nursing course at—"

"Nearly completed." He gave her a weary look. "I shall tell you my opinion plainly. I should be rich enough to retire if I collected a pittance from every bored, evangelical young lady who vows to be a 'nearly' nurse. Florence Nightingale and her lot should meet a martyr's end: grilled like Saint Lawrence over a slow fire, remembered in our prayers and never heard from again. That woman's devotees have descended upon the medical profession like locusts. I hope never to see one in my hospital." He lifted a hand to ward off her protest. "Admittedly your service in Boston gives you considerably more experience than most, but Rangoon is the East, Miss Herriott, and you will soon discover it to be vastly different from the West." He cocked his head. "Some Westerners attempt to ignore that fact; some contrive to change it. Very few completely succeed at the former, and none have succeeded in the latter to more than a superficial degree.

"Asiatics contend with the most devastating pestilences of mankind as commonly as we take tea. Cholera, typhus, leprosy, dysentery, malaria, elephantiasis, and a horde of jungle diseases you've never heard of nor possibly imagined. Ho Lung Chi, the merchant who owned your house, died with two-thirds of his household in the space of two weeks due to cholera. Having no heirs, he donated his property to the hospital, a rare act of gratitude pitiably ill rewarded by nearly worthless care.'' Hardily, he took a swig of his dreadful wine. "Nearly the whole country suffers from malnutrition, and more than a third of the children never see their first birthday. I do not mean to frighten you, Miss Herriott, but this part of the world has hazards you would be wise to recognize."

"As you say, I have never encountered most of the diseases you mention, but I have endured typhus, diphtheria, and scarlet fever epidemics. No disease is pretty, Dr. Lighter, and had I wished to live in Boston, I should have remained there. Well, sir, as you admit, you need trained personnel, and I am trained more than most; certainly, I wager, more than most of the native population." She paused, then stated flatly, "I need the money."

He viewed her wrinkled serge unsympathetically. "I take it you feel your father's income as surgeon will be insufficient to your needs." He frowned. "I had assumed when he agreed—"

"I am completely satisfied with my salary, doctor," Herriott put in quickly. "My daughter did not mean to imply we are ungrateful for your efforts in our behalf." He smiled wryly. "But, you see, we did not expect to be supplied with a staff of servants, and we are unprepared . . ."

"Ah." Lighter's face lightened. "That poses no difficulty. They will cost you no more than a few *kyat.*"

Herriott made a face. "Unfortunately, this month that is a few *kyat* more than we can afford."

Lighter sobered. "That tight, is it?"

"Will they have any difficulty finding new employment if we dismiss them?" Lysistrata asked. "I am used to managing a household alone and unused to servants."

Lighter shook his head. "You would find it nearly impossible to keep a house decently without help in this climate. Simply keeping a garden from reverting to jungle can be a full-time proposition. Why, the sheer size of Chi's bungalow would occupy all your time in the drudgery of cleaning. The windows, for instance . . ."

"Perhaps we could simply close off some rooms."

Lighter shook his head emphatically. "Mildew, vermin, and woodrot plague buildings here. As the property of the hospital, the house must be maintained."

Face set, Lysistrata stared at him. So, the old skinflint had purchased himself a housekeeper along with a surgeon at no extra cost. No self-respecting Western woman would allow her residence to deteriorate as an easygoing Eastern woman might do. She was hardly in a position to argue. At least he did not expect her to do the work herself, but still she was furious.

Lighter seemed to read her mind. "Of course, you will wish to occasionally entertain. The small European community here is close-knit. You will receive invitations and be expected to reciprocate." He paused and added succinctly, "Women, in particular, find living in the East lonely without such diversions."

"I would find nursing," Lysistrata retaliated, "extremely diverting and a great deal more useful."

Lighter's mouth set stubbornly. "I'm sorry; that is completely out of the question. After you have lived here a time, you will thank me for refusing you." He pushed his chair back and rose. "Dr. Herriott, will you join me in the study for brandy and a cigar?" He glanced offhandedly at Lysistrata. "You will find a fairly recent copy of *The Tatler* in the parlor interesting, Miss Herriott. My syce will bring you tea."

Thus cavalierly discarded, Lysistrata glared hot pokers through Lighter's back as he led her father from the room. Abruptly she rose and went to the sideboard, where she found, as she expected, what she was looking for.

Sometime later, the doctors, still engrossed in conversation about the latest surgical techniques in Boston, strolled into the parlor. Lighter's jaw dropped in mid-sentence. Lysistrata, with one of his fattest cigars perched between forefinger and second, blew a smoke ring into the air. Her nose was buried in a medical gazette, her crossed feet propped up on an overstuffed chair. She glanced up casually. "A tolerable Havana, Dr. Lighter, but I must say my maiden Aunt Agatha brews a cherry cordial with more snort than this brandy." She took a deft draught from the snifter at her elbow. "Papa, we shall have to build a good Savannah-style still in the garden."

"Lysistrata," Herriott sighed as the carriage rolled back toward Loo Gow Street, "do you wish to see me dismissed before I've begun?"

She laughed mirthlessly. "Lighter won't dismiss you, Papa. He's already paid our passage. I'll warrant he wouldn't spend so much as an additional penny for a stamp to advertise for a replacement. To be dismissed, you would probably have to mistakenly stuff a patient's innards in his ears, but you're too good a doctor to give him any excuse to be rid of you."

"They didn't need any excuse in Boston."

"You were married to a Rebel, and your eldest son was a Rebel. Lighter's an Irishman. He could care less about American squabbles." She squeezed his hand. "If he is prejudiced, he probably hired you because he thought *you* were a Rebel."

He laughed wryly. "You may have a point there. While we were in the study, he did agree to advance a portion of my first month's pay."

Her hand tightened on his. "Thank heaven . . . what about plates? Did you remember to ask . . . ?"

"A set of dishes by lunchtime. He was most embarrassed to have forgotten."

"I daresay," Lysistrata replied dryly. "Imagine my inviting the local ladies to sip tea from coconut shells."

Herriott laughed and patted her pale green cheek. "How was the cigar?"

She smiled crookedly. "I suspect I should have been better off smoking an umbrella."

CHAPTER 2

East Meets West

But on her forehead sits a fire,
She sets her forward countenance
And leaps into the future chance,
Submitting all things to desire.
ALFRED, LORD TENNYSON

As Dr. Lighter had predicted, the Herriotts' first social engagement was not long in coming; Lysistrata, while absorbed in organizing her household, was not sorry for it. She suspected the invitation, which came from the British commissioner's wife, stemmed as much from curiosity as official courtesy. After two weeks in Rangoon, she had already learned Lighter had accurately described a woman's position in local European society. If anything, it was more cloistered than in Boston. Any new face, even hers, among its members must be a relief; and if not eventually welcome, at least a fresh topic of gossip.

She learned this from several occurrences. For one, she created a stir in a marketplace near Merchant Street where she accompanied Ma Saw to buy food. When upon hearing her intention, Lighter informed her European women sent servants to do the marketing, and even stylish Fytche Square shopkeepers were often summoned to European homes to display fabrics, jewels, and objets d'art in private. She scoffed, "How particular of them to shun 'contamination' by the natives, yet invite dysentery and cholera to their dinner parties." To her father she privately conceded she was less interested in sanitation than diversion.

On the morrow, surrounded by the lively color and banter of the rambling marketplace, she was not disappointed. After descending from the ricksha amid ox-drawn *gharries* piled with bananas, pineapples, bael, and papaya, she stood fascinated. Like a beckoning incense, baskets of saffron, betel nut, and turmeric displayed under bright parasols spiced the air. Following her nose, she began to dreamily wander the bazaar with Ma Saw tolerantly trailing behind. Ah, yes; this was a genie's lair where she might be happily lost for a thousand years.

A pity the genie was not about to dole out wishes. Fingering the familiar flatness of her reticule with its tiny hoard of *kyat*, she philosophically eyed a fluttering fairyland of superb Burmese, Siamese, and India silks; they would have been a great bargain in Boston. The thriving trade of neighboring stalls selling simple European goods was less understandable. Browsing through their wares, she picked up a book. German grammar. She tried on spectacles. Ordinary window glass.

A few shops later, when Lysistrata was drawn into a stall by the flash of an exquisite silverwork mirror among some flamboyant carvings, Ma Saw cocked her head. "We Burmese make pretty things, yes?"

"Like San-hla?" Lysistrata teased. "Yes."

With a smile, Ma Saw waved a coin at a basket of ornamental combs. "You mind I buy for her?"

After Ma Saw selected a white wooden comb, Lysistrata sharply listened to her energetic dickering with the well-dressed, *chanakka*-painted proprietress. When Ma

Saw had made her purchase, the painted Burmese offered an ivory comb to Lysistrata. "She says perfect for your hair," Ma Saw contributed.

Regretfully, Lysistrata shook her head. "It's lovely, but I'm afraid . . . perhaps another day."

Smiling, the proprietress exchanged a few words with Ma Saw. "She say you take now, perhaps another day pay. She never see such hair before. Not right it hide like Hindu."

Lysistrata was taken aback for a moment, then said softly, "Please tell her I cannot buy the comb. I shall always cherish the gift of her kindness."

Upon hearing Ma Saw's translation, the Burwoman reluctantly returned the comb to the basket, then extended a little sheaf of jasmine. "She say this cost her nothing. Besides, she rich; she eighth cousin of king."

With a shy smile hiding her skepticism about the Burwoman's lineage, Lysistrata let her fasten the flowers in her hair. All agreed its effect was "more better."

Lysistrata and Ma Saw wandered on until they were lured by a Cingalese bakery's sweetmeats and spicy whirlwind cakes. Several children ceased scampering after scrawny dogs to hover hopefully about Lysistrata's skirts. While she could ill afford the sweets, she could not resist the urchins' wistful eyes. Shortly, with cries of delight, the children received their precisely divided booty. Lysistrata absently licked toddypalm sugar from her fingers as they scampered off. "Come"—Ma Saw tugged her into the crowd—"soon they bring every child in market and we eat cactus tonight."

On the next corner, she introduced Lysistrata to a native-style restaurant. Squatting in the dust, three Burmese dined casually under a sagging orange canopy where fish in sesame seeds and lemon simmered over a charcoal fire. "Much better than cactus," Ma Saw cheerfully advised. "You want, I cook." In the next bamboo lean-to, native shish kebab was being devoured with rice plugs cooked in bamboo tubes. "This your papa maybe like."

With a rising appetite for lunch, Lysistrata was ready to dine on the spot, then noticed the aging chef dump a concoction of flowers and red ants into a bowl of curry. Hooking the housekeeper's arm, she retreated.

Deciding she had better start the household shopping, Lysistrata armed Ma Saw and herself with new shopping baskets in the heart of the market. She was recounting her change when, over the hum and chatter of trade, came the calm, insistent beat of a gong as saffron-clad Theravada monks trailed through the crowd to collect food offerings. Ma Saw directed a questioning look at her mistress. Resignedly, Lysistrata nodded. With a reverent *shikkoh,* Ma Saw distributed yams in the monks' vermilion bowls. Eyes averted, they blandly smiled and passed on. "You revere priests, missy?" the Burwoman questioned.

"Only skinny ones, provided they don't feed on brimstone," Lysistrata replied dryly as she paid for the yams. "The Boston variety are invariably a plump lot who envision the dove of peace as roast duck."

Ma Saw, although initially surprised by Lysistrata's disregard for Western habits, readily adapted. Charity aside, Lysistrata had made up her supply list with a New Englander's narrow eye and had no intention of letting Ma Saw add unnecessary frills to it. She firmly directed Ma Saw away from the smelly, fly-ridden meat stalls where the mostly Buddhist and Hindu crowd, though forbidden to destroy life, were anxious to purchase the *fait accompli,* particularly the pork. But when a flock of vendors waving more appealing foodstuffs pressed about her, Ma Saw was quietly amused when the tantalized Lysistrata capitulated. Now eager to sample every unfamiliar food she discovered while rooting through the carts, she had to be cautioned not to eat more than one exotic fruit at a time. "Very rich." Ma Saw gently retrieved a papaya. "You be sick." She waved a maternal finger. "Later, you have with dinner."

"You're right," Lysistrata sighed with a sticky grin. "I'm behaving like a greedy child."

Ma Saw smiled. "Not bad to be curious about what is new, but maybe good to poke with stick first."

Lysistrata quickly and literally became adept at stick-poking. She had never been afraid of insects, but the Loo Gow bungalow hosted an army of leggy pests in sizes ranging from near-microscopic to a baby's fist. The garden was their nursery. As soon as an insect was able to walk, it invariably marched into the house. When Lysistrata suggested U Pho, who had proven as useless as she feared, exterminate them, he and his Buddhist family were appalled. Every living thing had a right to its place in the sun, they declared. And *out* of it, Lysistrata thought as she nervously scanned the eaves in expectation of some tiny pilgrim's dropping into her hair.

At one invader, she drew the line. As she drowsed into sleep one night, a scuttle heavier than usual instantly put her on the alert. Actually, she decided with an involuntary shiver, it sounded like a slither. Though she had not seen one, Burma must have its generous share of poisonous snakes. Why those snakes should neglect her garden when virtually nothing else had seemed a redundant question.

Cautiously, she lit a candle and slid out of bed, her toes curling at the thought of touching the floor and whatever might be coiled on it.

A swift, dark movement in a ceiling corner snatched her attention. The shadow it painted was at least the size of a snake. From it extended a long, licking tail; a blunt, narrow head. Throat almost closed from fright, she backed toward the door. When the creature sprouted legs and darted diagonally across the wall, she bolted.

Ignoring her father's door, for he was still at the hospital, she scrambled down the stair, yelling, "U Pho, U Pho! Come quickly!" Needless to say, he did not come quickly. She found him still nakedly curled up on his cot in the small garden house, his withered buttocks two small, quiet moons in the light of her gyrating candle. Belatedly noticing he was flamboyantly tattooed from neck to knee, she stamped her foot. "U Pho!"

He jerked slightly. Betel-dark eyes blinked, then peered sleepily at her over his shoulder.

"A huge lizard. In my bedroom." Impatiently, she made a slithering movement with her hand. He blankly stared at her. She wanted to throttle him. The Burmese, she had learned, did not believe in too much efficiency. As Ma Saw spoke English, U Pho saw no need to duplicate her effort. On the other hand, Lysistrata's scant vocabulary of Burmese had not yet encountered reptiles. She snatched up his *pasoh*, or loincloth, threw it at him, and jerked her thumb toward the house. "Come! You know *that* much, don't you!" Her angry tone stimulated him to movement. With no affectation of modesty, he bound up his *pasoh* and followed her.

Candle advanced, she pointed out the lizard. U Pho studied it, smiled, shrugged, and looked at her like a dog commanded to retrieve a nonexistent bone. Clearly, he wondered why she had troubled him.

And just as clearly, she thought he must be an imbecile as well as worthless. With a muttered expletive, she went for her father's Colt .45. She should have done so in the first place, she thought angrily, if she hadn't been such a startled ninny. Upon returning to the bedroom, she leveled the gun at the serpent, now nearly obscured by the bulk of a beam. Candle glow picked up the reptilian glint of eyes that looked flatly into the pistol's bore. To her amazement, U Pho showed his first energy of the evening by thrusting the gun aside with a sharp exclamation. At her confounded stare, he began a flurry of gesticulation, eyes pleading, mouth pouring out a torrent of Burmese. All she could catch was Buddha, Buddha, Buddha.

Temper rising, Lysistrata ignored him and shifted a few steps to one side to draw another bead on her quarry, which had discreetly retired to the opposite side of the beam. U Pho tugged at her arm, half-firmly, half-timidly, uncertain about the wisdom of defiance, especially when her hand was filled with a Colt .45. "Stop it!" Lysistrata tried to shake him off. "Dammit, U Pho!"

Realizing her implacability and throwing his fate to the winds, the old man clung like a leech. With a low growl of exasperation, Lysistrata shoved him away with all her strength. She was no weakling, the man no heavyweight. He skidded backward, lost his balance, and landed sharply on his backside. Lysistrata took quick aim and fired at the ceiling, but the quarry had been urged to retreat by the struggle below. With an extraordinary, blasting bellow that echoed the revolver, he streaked across the ceiling. He was as long as her forearm and nearly as full-bodied as an iguana. With a departing flick of his tail, he exited through a broken louver in a verandah door. Lysistrata stared almost stupidly at the vacant chink of moonlight as she waited for her heartbeat to return to normal.

Finally, she turned to U Pho, who had scrambled to his feet. He flinched slightly as she began to hurl her store of anger, nerves, and frustration at him. But shortly, she began to dimly realize his reaction was not one of apology. His face grew colder as she reprimanded him. Finally, with a look that bordered on contempt, he turned his back and left the room. A few minutes later, she heard the

scrape of the gate bar being removed, then the squeal as
its doors swung back and kept swinging.

The dignified message of resignation Ma Saw bore
from her father-in-law when she and her daughters
arrived in the morning was not unexpected, and from Lysistrata's viewpoint, not unwelcome; still, she felt
uncomfortably that she had mishandled the situation.
Though she expected the defection of U Pho's family as
well, it was not forthcoming. Ma Saw's manner was reserved, but not accusatory. It seemed U Pho was not only
offended by Lysistrata's dressing-down, but her handling
of his *pasoh*. In Burma, a woman not a man's wife did
not damage his *pon*, male power, by touching his personal belongings. Even his wife did not touch his things
and his bed with her lower garments. She could not touch
his head or pass her possessions over it.

Lysistrata, though baffled and amused by this quirkish
relationship of Burmese male and female, had learned
enough from the confrontation with U Pho not to ridi-
cule it. "Will your father-in-law's age give him difficulty
in obtaining a new position?" she asked quietly.

Ma Saw's expression softened at her concern. "He
does not need to work. Sein, San-hla, and I make enough
to supply his few wants. If he has a full belly, enough
money for toddy, and a little *gungah* to smoke with his
friends, he is happy. It is time for him to sit in the
shade."

Lysistrata noticed the sudden improvement in Saw's
grasp of English. The Burwoman could not have increased her vocabulary so much in a fortnight. Had Ma
Saw considered it prudent not to appear too clever in
English language and customs so her new employers
might not feel threatened and would behave more freely?

Aloud, she asked, "Why was he so determined to protect a common pest? With all respect, isn't that carrying religion to an extreme?''

"According to Buddha, *all* life is sacred, even that of a mosquito.'' Ma Saw smiled faintly. "U Pho would perhaps not have tried *quite* so hard to stop you from killing a mosquito. The *tuk-too* you saw last night is a friend. He lives here. If he did not, the house would be overrun by insects.''

"He eats them,'' chirped San-hla, also demonstrating an unexpected command of English. "He's the biggest *tuk-too* on Loo Gow Street.''

"He has a wife, too,'' added Sein with a coy giggle.

"Any children?'' Lysistrata asked warily.

"Not that I have seen,'' Ma Saw replied. "If he has, he sends them away. No more than one pair *tuk-toos* to a house.''

"Ah,'' said Lysistrata vaguely. Housecats. She had a pair of scaled housecats.

As Lysistrata brushed her hair in preparation for the commissioner's party that evening, she was glad she had no illusions about her looks. Illusions brought nothing but disappointments, particularly when it came to men. Besides Frank, few men had noticed her as a woman, and for that she was profoundly grateful. Frank Wyatt. Her cousin. Her love. Her liar. He had taken so much, given only misery. Her heart could still feel scalded in her breast if she let memory seep into her mind. She had armored pain in steel plate, rivet by hard rivet. Aside from its debilitating effects, she thought she might welcome age. No one expected anything of an old woman. Her skin might be flawless, but no man would ever caress it, and eventually it would wither into part of her armor.

Without the distraction of an ugly dress, her hair was more than passable; eyes fine behind their sharp, steady regard. "My sister Eden's hair and eyes,'' her mother used to say; but Lysistrata judged her mother's remembrance more fond than factual. Eden, the beauty of Savannah, had died young; so had her mother.

She felt some deep, indefinable part of *her*, likely the woman part, had been killed by Frank; she wanted no resurrection. And judging from past experience at parties, she would be in no danger of it tonight, she thought grimly as she parted, then twisted her hair up into a tight knot at the nape of her neck. The humidity kept the tendrils she usually pinned flat from obedience, but they would be plastered with perspiration to her forehead by the time she was escorted to dinner.

She pulled on her mother's aged gray silk, then applied a dab of perfume to her wrists to help dispel its faint odor of camphor. The bodice was too small, as her mother had been slight, and too scantily cut for Lysistrata's taste, but her black merino shawl would dispatch that problem. The skirt, designed for antebellum crinolines, was caught up into a semblance of a Worth-style cascade at the back and carelessly basted into position. She would not have bothered, if the ladies she encountered at rare social engagements in Boston had not pointedly reviewed her dragging skirts and harassed her with boring lectures on fashion, offers to lend her their seamstresses, and even more obnoxious suggestions of sewing lessons.

She did not bother with jewelry. After giving the cameo, a parting present from Aunt Agatha, to the boatmen, she owned none. She threw the shawl about her shoulders, then went downstairs to join her father.

Dr. Lighter, also one of the commissioner's guests, called for them in his carriage. Lysistrata thought slightly better of him for doing so, for she hated to waste any part of their small livelihood on a conveyance.

"If you don't mind," he told them as Herriott helped Lysistrata into the carriage, "I need to stop by the harbor. I'm expecting a drug shipment today."

The errand was quickly run. As the carriage waited, Dr. Lighter went to complete the necessary transactions in a handsome shipping office at the east end of the dock area. He returned, followed by a pair of armed Chinese coolies bearing four wooden boxes stamped with red Chinese *chop* characters. Instead of putting them in the luggage box, he had them placed inside the carriage on the floor, which cramped its passengers considerably once he reclaimed his seat. The two coolies climbed on topside.

"Sorry for the delay," he apologized as the carriage bumped along the quay. He gave the top box a slap and smiled at Herriott. "This is the opium we've been waiting for, John."

"There's a great deal of it," Lysistrata observed.

"Yes, Richard Harley knows how to get what he wants. And there's no faster carrier than his *Rani.*"

"The *Rani?*" she echoed. "We saw her leaving the harbor when we arrived on the *Mayfield.*"

"Bound for Tennasserim and the South China Sea."

Herriott frowned. "I seem to vaguely remember her. She looked like a pleasure craft, certainly not armed for venturing into pirate waters."

Lighter laughed. "Harley's a bit of a pirate himself, and the *Rani*'s pretty portholes have cannon and gatlings enough behind 'em." He took out a cigar case, then looked half-mockingly at Lysistrata. "May I?"

"Of course, doctor," she replied coolly.

"Would you care for one?"

A stifled chuckle issued from Herriott as she retorted, "Not before dinner, doctor. I find it spoils the palate."

When he offered the case to her father, Herriott asked, "Who is this Harley? A Yankee trader?"

"Actually, he's a local character," Lighter answered between puffs as he lit his cigar. "Stays a step ahead of the law." He applied his lighted cheroot to Herriott's.

"His father was an English officer in the Punjab and his mother a Rajput princess. Half-castes are common enough in these parts, but Harley's a rare one in that he's been clever enough to turn it to his advantage. Has a foot in both worlds. The British don't usually tolerate mixed bloods socially, but Harley has made himself valuable to them. He has contacts in the China Trade they won't accomplish in the next decade. The Indians won't have anything to do with him, but the Burmese are usually tolerant." He tapped his cigar ash into the street. "You'll probably see him at the boss-*wallah*'s tonight."

Only half-listening to the conversation, Lysistrata hoped the boss-*wallah* would serve *hilsa* fish with curried rice. Ma Saw's was superb.

Gaslight from the Government House windows spilled across a lawn already whitened by a tropic moon and jewel-colored paper lanterns poised motionless in the close night air. The great white bungalow, its gingerbread trim carved in fanciful Indian motifs of monkeys and elephants, stood at the end of a crushed-shell drive lined by palankeens, carriages, and rickshas attended by drivers lounging in groups according to nationality. On the east side of the drive, decorative patterns of magnolias and bougainvillea on the lawn obscured, then disclosed perhaps sixty guests. Almost all were European, the men in black cutaways and uniforms; the ladies in rich Asian silks adapted to the previous year's Parisian styles. Many women wore opulent jewels Lysistrata critically thought would have been considered vulgar in Boston. The few native guests were a mixture of Chinese in silks and brocades; Burmese in patterned *longyi* skirts; several Indians, one a plump Indian in a fabulously jeweled turban and peacock-embroidered purple coat, and an assortment of Asiatics: all were males. White-jacketed Indian servants circulated among the throng with champagne punches and hors d'oeuvres. The Herriotts sampled everything within reach as Lighter steered them through the crowd.

The commissioner, Sir Anthony Bartly, and his wife, Lady Mary, were holding court under a lion-embroidered green-and-gold pavilion that faced a reflecting pool at the rear of the house. Water lilies and jasmine chains floated upon the water dotted with tiny candle-bearing paper boats. Sir Anthony was a distinguished, silver-haired former Calcutta nabob in his fifties. His civilities to the Herriotts were precise, his manner impersonally polite. His wife was fortyish. Her manner, aquiline good looks, and frosty blue eyes so much resembled her husband's, she might have been his sister rather than his wife. Her gaze swiftly raked Herriott in his frayed black suit, then Lysistrata in her clumsy dress. To Lady Mary's credit —or perhaps practice—Lysistrata noticed, the English-woman's gracious manner did not alter in the slightest. "I am so glad you and your daughter could join us this evening, doctor. We are a small society and always glad of newcomers." Her attention returned to Lysistrata. "Do you play bridge, my dear? Perhaps you could make a fourth at my afternoon gathering this coming Thursday."

"I have never really learned the game, ma'am. I am rather better at poker."

"Poker?" Lady Mary paused. "I fear I—"

"It's an American game, Mary," murmured a striking brunette who stood just behind Lady Mary's chair. She had been introduced as Mrs. Evelyn Chilton. Her beautiful face was composed except for a curious smile which suggested Lysistrata's reply had delighted a sense of mischief. Her dress was a claret silk by Worth; her pendant necklace of diamonds, emeralds, and opals with a dove-colored, baroque pearl hung between beautiful breasts. Her figure was superb, her violet eyes fringed by heavy, black lashes that Lysistrata suspected were touched by mascara.

"Indeed?" Lady Mary replied. "Excellent. You must demonstrate your American game, Miss Herriott. The diversion will be welcome. This Thursday for tea, then, at four?" Noting a balky look entering Lysistrata's eyes, she added shrewdly, "Lady Pan-byu of the Royal Court at Mandalay will read from her translation of *The Glass Palace Chronicles*. It is a formal play not often experienced by Westerners, and Lady Pan-byu is considered to be a remarkable scholar."

She well judged Lysistrata's weak point.

"I should be delighted to come, ma'am." Lysistrata inclined her head slightly to the Bartlys, then took her father's arm and, between the two doctors, walked off toward the house.

"That's a dowdy bird for your taste, Mary," Evelyn Chilton drawled, her tone now openly amused, "and she's on the sullen side. Why bother with her?"

"I'm inclined to pluck those dingy feathers and see what she's made of." An enigmatic smile crossed her ladyship's aristocratic face. "Besides, I haven't encountered a stiff hand at poker since Tony and I hunted in the Rockies with Lord Gore."

Two scarlet-clad Sikhs in white puttees flanked massive teak doors of the mansion reception room, which blazed with the light of six Burmese rock-crystal chandeliers. Perhaps another eighty guests roamed the room lined by lacquered Coromandel screens. The screens were fronted by settees upholstered in luxurious Indian brocades and leopard skins. A Bengal tiger hide stretched its glorious length before the porphyry fireplace, which could never have been used. Rhino, various deer and big-game heads were interspersed among oil paintings depicting the exploits of the British forces in subduing

India. Under them, Madrassees waved peacock *punkahs* in a vain attempt to circulate air which entered through ivory filigree window screens. Another pair of Sikhs guarded the dining room door framed by towering elephant tusks mounted in bases of ebony and gold. The British lived well off the land.

As he escorted the Herriotts about the drawing room, Lighter kept up a running commentary on the guests over the light hum of conversation and laughter. "That peacock-coated Kashmiri is here to confer about the China trade, I'll wager. His name is Gopal Prasad. He's a greasy sort, particularly about women." After the cigar incident, Lighter did not trouble to mince words around Lysistrata. "That bewhiskered gentleman there is General Nigel Chilton. You met his wife earlier."

Lysistrata was startled by the man's age. The portly, self-important-looking little man with muttonchops was at least thirty years his wife's senior. Evelyn Chilton might have a streak of mischief, but she was no romantic.

"Ah, there's the fellow I described to you, John," Lighter remarked. "Richard Harley. If you'll excuse me for a moment, I owe him a word of thanks for that last opium run." He strode off through the crowd. The man he spoke of leaned slightly against a mahogany column, where he was in conversation with a Chinese richly clad in green silk.

If General Chilton had been unexpected, Richard Harley was more so. Lysistrata had thought to see a moon-faced, soft-bodied Indian of medium height with the grayish pallor and oddly colored eyes of an Asian mixed-blood. Harley, taller than Lord Anthony, might easily have passed for a European. Though his coloring was dark, his features were aquiline and his slim body carried Savile Row black as if born to it. She would have guessed him to be a Spaniard or Italian. Still, something was indefinably different about him. No European male had that slow, subtle smile, that liquid ease. Even to Lysistrata's jaundiced eye, he was extraordinarily attractive.

When Lighter joined him, Richard Harley glanced automatically in the direction from which the doctor had come. Obsidian eyes looked directly into Lysistrata's. Surprised in open scrutiny, she flushed scarlet. She whipped around to face the other way, then belatedly realized that reaction made her faux pas even worse. Taking a deep breath, she turned to face the man. And found him amused. Anger replaced her embarrassment. To be blatantly mocked was intolerable, particularly when she had not meant to be rude. Her eyes flat, she kept them locked to his. The sensation was that of trying to outstare a cat. Though only a few seconds passed, she began to feel foolish. Then, as if she were a bird too spare to be pounced on, he casually turned his back and resumed his conversation with the Chinese and Dr. Lighter.

Lysistrata felt as if she had been slapped; and for one swift, hot moment, wished she were stark naked with a fat, baroque pearl swinging between her breasts. He'd not ignore her then, the bastard!

Seeing her tight, white face, Herriott put his hand on her arm. "Lysistrata, what's wrong?"

"I . . ." She bit back the words, and for a moment covered his hand with her own. "Nothing. Nothing, Papa, I—"

"Miss Herriott?" came a male voice behind her.

Breath caught in her throat, she spun. Then exhaled in relief. "Leftenant Armistead. How nice to see you again."

Harry nodded to Herriott. "I confess I did not know the two of you were here, sir, until Lady Mary informed me I was to have the honor of taking Miss Herriott in to dinner."

As Lysistrata silently thanked Lady Mary, Herriott remarked, "She appears to be an accomplished hostess. I daresay she discovered we were fellow passengers."

Poor Harry probably wishes he were dead, thought Lysistrata, but she was glad to see him. She liked Harry, but she was more relieved to have a dinner companion with whom she could be at ease. Her composure had not been so rattled in some time, if one discounted the *tuk-too* affair.

Under wafting *punkah* fans, the heavy English dinner served on Wedgwood porcelain seemed to go on interminably. Lysistrata wondered if the guests would so blandly consume the beef and mutton if they knew its flyblown origins. Richard Harley reserved his attention for his pretty, blond dinner companion and the couples near him; he did not once look at her. Though glad he had apparently forgotten her existence, she was also a trifle irritated. Harry, however, soothed her ruffled feathers with his usual good-humored charm. Indeed, he seemed to enjoy her company; and she responded with spirit that stopped just short of flirtation.

All the same, Lysistrata found herself left to her devices after dinner, for Harry excused himself and, with her father and Dr. Lighter, joined the gentlemen for brandy and cigars. She wandered about the grounds, then returned to the verandah where she watched the musicians set up their instruments by the portable dance floor spread on the grass. When they began to play, she retreated to a secluded niche so her partnerless state would be less noticeable.

She loved to dance and did occasionally with her father, but the opportunity had not often presented itself since the war. Following the first dignified Strauss waltz was a polka. As she sat on a windowsill, her toes patted irrepressibly in time to the music as she watched the dancers.

Then she heard a muted, erratic click from the room behind her. Peering through the louvers, she saw several men playing billiards; along with two British officers, one of them was Sir Anthony, another was Chilton. Over their heads hung a pall of cigar smoke humming with insects. Someone she could not see was speaking perfect English, the accent strangely sibilant. "I assure you, gentlemen, if you employ great care, the road to Yünnan may be opened, but negotiations must not be hurried. Chang Yin is a difficult man to approach."

One of the British officers spoke up. "Chang's power may work to our advantage. If he were less sure of himself, he would never allow us past his borders."

"Forgive me"—with a glitter of jewels, Gopal spread his plump hands—"but Wa Sing expects us to put a great faith in his word alone, as well as his avenues of influence, to accomplish this matter. I fear my master, the Maharaja of Kashmir, will wish greater assurance if he is to finance any part of an expedition to Yünnan. His promised share of the profits is very handsome." His tone, faintly sneering before, was now oily. "However, the investment asked of him is also . . . very handsome. In such a circumstance, I cannot authorize so large a sum to be given. Surely you all understand my position."

"Indeed, I am sure everyone sympathizes with your difficulty, Honored Gopal Prasad," came the whispery voice of the Chinese. "Unfortunately, I cannot vouch for the predictability of my countrymen when dealing with a foreign representative."

Lysistrata caught a flicker of his black fan beyond a dwarf palm which blocked her view. Sir Anthony, who had been quietly listening while he prepared his billiard shot, made it precisely, then straightened. "Still, Mr. Prasad has a point, Mr. Sing. You ask a great deal of money. A number of British merchants will be ruined if the expedition should come to mischief."

"A great many will become rich if it does not," the Chinese replied imperturbably.

"What do you think, Harley?" one of the officers asked. "You know that country. Rumor has it you've dealt with Chang himself." He turned to Harley, who sat on an arm of a massive teak chair, his chin on hands folded over the end of his billiard stick.

Lysistrata leaned forward with heightened interest, for she had not noticed Harley, silent in the shadows.

He answered simply, without moving. "It's possible." His soft English was lulling.

Gopal Prasad's lips curled dubiously. "With all respect, is that all you have to say?"

Sir Anthony gave the Indian a cool look. "For Mr. Harley, it is a great deal. I have myself attempted to negotiate with petty officials of Chinese border provinces. Only a liar or a fool would offer guarantees. We cannot even be sure an expedition could reach the Yünnan border. After all, we do not control the Shan States. They are still under the mandate of King Mindon."

"That difficulty is easily eliminated," said General Chilton bluntly. "We ought to seize that corridor and be done with it. Mindon will simply tuck his head under his skirts and groan with his priests."

"The corridor might not be so easy to take as you think, General," Harley said quietly, "and priests are not necessarily cowards."

"He's right," inserted Sir Anthony. "Persuasion assures the better route. King Mindon has proven accommodating in the past. We have no reason to suppose he will be less so in this matter. Even a small war would take time and money we need not expend at this point."

"Perhaps you could assist in persuading King Mindon, Mr. Harley," Prasad interposed, his smile insinuating. "I have heard you have friends at court."

"One cannot have too many friends, if one does not

rely too heavily on them," was the easy reply. "You must give my regards to *your* friend, Mr. Endicott, the British envoy at Mandalay. Perhaps you might persuade him to head the expedition."

Prasad's eyes narrowed, though his smile did not alter. "Perhaps. Mr. Endicott and I rarely meet." He bowed to Sir Anthony, then to the other men. "If you will excuse me, gentlemen, I will retire. My master, the Maharaja, will study your proposal; however, like Mr. Sing and Mr. Harley"—his eyes cut toward them—"I fear I can promise little."

After Prasad left, Chilton said glumly to Sir Anthony, "Well, there goes thirty percent of our money."

"We do not depend on Prasad for financing, General," Sir Anthony replied. "Money is our least difficulty. Intelligence is what we require." He inclined his head to Harley. "That *you* will provide, I hope, Richard."

"As well as I can, sir." Harley eased off the chair and moved to the table. "I think you need not worry about Gopal Prasad, General. He has not grown fat from lack of greed." He lined up his shot, made it, then lined up another. Methodically, he scored several shots before one veered a fraction wide of its mark.

"Aha, misjudged that one, sir!" Chilton assumed his position, elbows flexing.

"Why is it, Richard, I always feel your misses are deliberate?" Sir Anthony murmured.

"I make mistakes, sir, like anyone else."

"Do you? I wonder . . ."

"For the love of heaven," Chilton protested, "will you fellows be quiet? I'm trying to concentrate."

Judging from his heated fox-and-hounds style of play, Lysistrata observed, the general would have difficulty thinking coherently, much less with concentration. As the game progressed another round and Chilton's exasperation grew, Sir Anthony suggested they adjourn to rejoin the ladies.

"If you don't mind, sir, I've not finished my brandy," Harley said. "I'll join you shortly." In a few moments, he was left alone with Wa Sing.

The Chinese's fan moved slowly. "Do you believe they will really attempt this?"

"They are no different from Prasad. They are simple people, these British." Harley lifted the brandy to his lips. "It seems to have occurred to none of them Chang has not become warlord of Yünnan through stupidity."

Lysistrata thought Harley's statement odd, considering his role in the coming negotiations. She still pondered it as the conversation between the two men shifted to Chinese. She listened for a few minutes, then became restless with incomprehension. Deciding to look for her father, she rose. Her movement was careful but a faint rustle of silk was enough. With dismay, she noticed Harley looking at her window. Swiftly, she headed for the verandah steps.

He met her inches before she reached them. Her heart sank, for she was still too near the billiard-room window for him to have any doubt she had eavesdropped.

"Good evening." That velvet voice unnerved her like a phantom fingertip trailing along her spine.

"Good evening," she replied; then added lamely, "We haven't been introduced."

"Then it is convenient that we meet." His lips curved slightly. "I was just this moment wondering who you were."

She straightened with a trace of defiance. "My name is Lysistrata Herriott. My father is chief surgeon at Queen Anne's."

"Lighter's new assistant," he mused, "fresh from America. I do not know the custom in Boston, Miss Herriott, but in Rangoon it is thought not only impolite, but unwise to listen to private conversations uninvited.''

"The conversation was less than fascinating," she feinted, becoming angry, "as I do not speak Chinese." After all, he could not know how long she had been at the window. "As for being foolish," she continued, "don't you think it unwise to threaten me under the commissioner's nose? You see, I have heard of *you*, too!" She moved to brush past him, then tensely halted when he blocked her.

"Then you have also heard it is not my habit to cut young ladies' throats, even outside the realm of the commissioner's nose." He smiled. "I assure you, you are quite safe."

Looking into his black, penetrating eyes, Lysistrata was not quite sure of that. With those high-raked cheekbones, he appeared to be more predator than pet of the English. A whisper of sound made her suspect the Chinese was at her back. She whirled. To see no one.

"Miss Herriott," Harley repeated gently, "you have nothing to fear. May I escort you to your father?" When she turned uncertainly to face him, he added lightly, "You need not be seen with such a notorious character. I shall leave you at the acacias behind the orchestra."

She relaxed a trifle, then felt foolish. "I *am* sorry, Mr. Harley. Truly, I had no deliberate intention of eavesdropping. I simply wanted to find a convenient seat in order to listen to the music." At his quizzical smile, she wished she had chosen a more apt word. The billiard-room window was hardly convenient to the dance floor. "Private" was no better; it fairly moaned wallflower.

He shrugged. "It is fortunate you do not speak Chinese. You would have been even more bored. We tradesmen are a dry lot when we discuss business."

You're the least dry-looking lot I ever saw, Lysistrata

thought. "Tradesman? Is that what they're calling pirates these days?" she countered wickedly.

He laughed. "Every third man here tonight is a pirate if you're particular." He offered his arm. "Are you particular, Miss Herriott?"

As she laid her hand on his arm, her answering grin was impish. "One of my uncles was a pirate."

They strolled along a hedgewalk that angled toward the stand of acacias at the edge of the crowd. "And was your uncle the source of your family fortune?" he teased.

Thinking he was deriding her shabby dress, she replied tartly, "Obviously not. He was hanged penniless at Charleston." She drew away. "You need not escort me further, thank you. I can find my own way."

As she started toward the hedge bend, he said something in swift Chinese. Ignoring him, she almost broke into a run. He followed and caught her arm. "There is a Russell's viper on the path, Miss Herriott."

She froze. "Where?!"

He studied the ground. "It seems to be gone."

She let out her breath, then had a quick suspicion. "Did you just warn me in *Chinese!*"

His lips quirked. "You must forgive me. Sometimes I think in Chinese."

"You were testing me!" she hissed. "You ought to be hanged!"

He laughed. "Undoubtedly."

Her eyes narrowed. "Your private discussion must have been important."

"Not very," he replied calmly. "Secrecy is a habit in the East."

She planted her hands on her hips. "Well, is your habit satisfied?"

"I did not think you could really be a spy, Miss Herriott. A competent one would not have been so red-faced."

"I don't think I like you," she told him flatly.

"Would you like me better if I cut your throat?"

Her sense of humor won over. She lifted a shoulder. "Perhaps." Then added, on reckless impulse, "I usually make my most fortunate decisions while dancing."

His smile took a formal slant. "I'm sorry, my religion forbids me to dance in public, Miss Herriott."

"Oh." The embarrassment of being caught on the verandah did not compare with being considered a forward fool.

"I *am* sorry," he repeated softly.

Without being aware of it, she put a hand to her flaming cheek, then felt its heat. Red-faced, he had called her. "I . . . really must find my father. Will you excuse me?" Without waiting for his answer, she fled.

From the shadows of the bougainvillea behind Harley stepped a wispy figure. A needle resembling a hat pin disappeared into Wa Sing's emerald sleeve, then his fan flicked from its recesses. He watched Lysistrata's fading figure. "Miss Herriott is not so much a sparrow as she looks. Are you sure letting her go is wise, my friend? If she were to drown in the reflecting pool, the accident would be attributed to the effects of champagne; no one would look for a needle mark under that marvelous hair." The fan waved as Wa Sing shrewdly eyed Harley. "She would not be much missed."

"You are undoubtedly correct as to her importance. I think the tempestuous Miss Herriott would not be much use to anyone as a spy," answered Harley softly. "Only one old man would likely feel her loss."

"One old man cannot be weighed against all Burma."

"And will not be," was the quiet reply, "without proven cause. If I am mistaken in Miss Herriot, I will see to her silence quickly enough."

The Chinese bowed like a breeze-ruffled reed. "I defer to your skill." His lazy purr became gently mocking. "Is it true you can kill with a kiss?"

The black, opaque eyes of the half-caste studied him. "Surely an exaggeration, don't you think?" Harley drifted into the darkness.

Lysistrata searched the grounds for nearly an hour without finding a trace of her father. Lighter must have dragged him into a smoking room where they were either thrashing out a surgical procedure or conversing with other men. When engrossed in talk, her father was likely to lose track of time. She was strongly disinclined to return to the house in search of him, for fear of encountering Wa Sing. Too, like her, her father had not had many friends in Boston; to begrudge him an opportunity to make new ones was selfish. Still, she was not far from tears. Thus far, the evening had been disastrous.

She turned to a waiter, chose a glass of champagne, and morosely drank it as she watched the dancers. She felt doomed to a dim netherlife while others loved and laughed in the light. Well, she decided grimly, wasn't she what she had chosen to be?

At that moment, a waiter skimming through the crowd carelessly let his tray dip and let a splatter of champagne down the side of Lysistrata's dress. For a moment she stared at the stain in disbelief. Though she was not fond of the dress, it was the last thing she had of her mother's; now it was ruined. The oblivious waiter had disappeared into the crowd.

Slowly, mechanically, she retreated into one of the hedgewalks that led to the deserted reflecting pool. Upon reaching it, she looked down at the pale, perfect water lilies drifting on its candlelit surface, the yellow jasmine chains floating in effortlessly graceful patterns. Tears began to flow: a dry, squeezed trickle at first, then a heavy, salty stream. She knelt and raised a hand. As if it were a hateful face she slapped at a lily, hit it again and again until it shattered, then sank fragment by fragment into the inky water. Breast heaving, she stared at the empty darkness where the lily had been, then felt a stab of remorse. Growing bitterness had led only to this: a mindless desire to seize and destroy what she envied.

Her breathing slowly evened. She removed her shawl and soaked it to scrub the worst of the skirt stain. She wasn't likely to need the thing in a sweltering climate, and its ugliness was now intolerable. Carefully, she washed her face, then after dropping the shawl into the pool, rose and looked again at the spot where the lily had been. "I *am* sorry," she whispered softly.

Aimlessly, she wandered back into the hedgewalk, but after a few turns, realized it was not the one that led back to the main group of guests. In trying to retrace her steps, she became lost. Unthinkingly, she had entered an elaborate bougainvillea maze that bordered the pool. At each turn was another high, hedge wall. Oh well, she thought in resignation, at least exploring the thing was something to do. Undoubtedly, she would trip over a pair of lovers only too happy to point the way out.

For a time, she used the moon as a guidepoint, but as she was no navigator, had little luck. The music led her deeper into the maze. At length, her feet began to ache in their stiff New England shoes, and she paused at a stone bench to drag them off. Despite the predicament, she felt more cheerful with each garment discarded. Wriggling bare toes, she threw her head back. She must get sandals to wear about the house. The East certainly seemed to have a saner notion of footgear than the West. Her feet began to swing in time to Strauss's Emperor Waltz. Pom, pom, pa pa pom . . .

She rose and began to move to the waltz's rhythm with a gracefulness uninhibited by a partner's formal constraint. The basting in her dress collapsed as she whirled, bare feet skimming. With a little growl of a laugh, she tugged her hair from its knot and let it fall free. Deeper,

deeper into the labyrinth she danced, carelessly, defiantly.

She virtually spun into a pair of dancers. Harley had not lied when he said he did not dance in public. He danced in private. And with reason—for in his arms, as if she were long used to being there, was Evelyn Chilton. Appalled, Lysistrata breathlessly stumbled to a halt, her hair hanging over one eye. She turned to bolt, anywhere, away from this . . .

Before she had taken two steps, Harley's hand clamped with harsh strength on her arm and spun her about. "We meet again, Miss Herriott." His voice was quiet, controlled, but she was more afraid of him now than when he had caught her on the verandah.

Evelyn Chilton did not seem at all upset. "You've discovered our little secret, Miss Herriott," she said with an amused laugh. "My husband, as you may have observed this evening, is no dancer. Mr. Harley was kind enough to save me from neglect."

This particular bald, impudent lie sparked mounting rage in Lysistrata, neither hypocritical nor urbane enough to accept it casually. "You seem to have accumulated very little dust for a neglected woman, Mrs. Chilton," she snapped.

Evelyn looked startled, then laughed as if delighted. "My dear, I have rarely been more uniquely complimented." Her tone became intimately conspiratorial, "I realize how this must appear to you, but I assure you, it's quite innocent. Under such a lovely moon, a woman can be tempted to forget strict propriety for a few moments." She waved a gay hand at Lysistrata's dishevelment. "I see you must sympathize. Surely I may trust your discretion?"

"Your affairs are your affairs, Mrs. Chilton," Lysistrata said coldly. "I want no part of them." She gave Harley a scathing look. "May I leave, or must I scream?"

"Richard," Evelyn cut in softly, "I think you had better see Miss Herriott from the maze. In her nervous state, she may choose the wrong path."

"I am *not* nervous," Lysistrata shot back, "and I am perfectly capable of finding my own way out!"

"It may take you some time," Harley said, then more quietly, "Are you sure you want to linger longer than you must?"

Chastened, she recognized his point. They must know that as a stranger, she had to be completely lost. "Very well," she replied tightly. Harley offered his arm, and she glared at it as if she wished she had an ax. With a faint smile and a languid gesture, he stood back and indicated the way. Dimly aware she was leaving her only pair of shoes behind, she marched off ahead of him.

"You've had an eventful evening, Miss Herriott," Harley observed after they had gone a little way.

"You think I *followed* you?" she spat. "Don't flatter yourself!"

"What other reason could you have for removing your shoes?" he countered lightly. "You're quite a bloodhound, running around in bare feet."

"Oh, will you shut up, you horrible man!"

He turned. "I'm afraid it is *your* silence that must be ensured."

Alarmed now, she backed away.

"You would do well not to run," he advised mildly. "I know the maze; you do not. And the longer you are in here, the worse it will be for you."

"What do you mean?" she demanded, voice shaking. "If you touch me, I'll scream!"

"That would be unwise. If you do, or even whisper that you saw Evelyn alone with me, she will simply say you were the one *in flagrante delicto.*" He studied her low bodice, her unbound hair, her bare feet. "In your present condition, you are not in a position to refute the point.''

"You'd protect one woman by compromising another —one totally innocent?'' She was stunned.

"Evelyn *is* a general's wife,'' he reminded softly.

"And I'm no one,'' she spat. "Expendable.''

"Miss Herriott,'' he replied patiently, "as I told you before, this is not Boston. For a Western man and woman to be linked in questionable circumstances is bad enough, but when the man is of color . . .'' He shrugged.

"But your father was English,'' she protested.

After a long silence, he sighed. "Lysistrata Herriott, your naïveté is stunning.''

Her jaw stuck out mutinously. "I'm not naive enough to be bullied by a liar and libertine!''

There was another long silence. "Ah, Lysistrata, you should not have come to Rangoon,'' he said wearily, then moved toward her. She shrank away, but like a cornered bird, could find no voice to cry out. He was right. If she screamed, no one would believe her. The ostracism, the hate, and contempt would begin again just as it had in Boston. Her father might lose his position, and they would be stranded. Even when Harley's hands slipped over her bare shoulders she could not move. His dark eyes seemed to have the quiet certainty of a cobra's as his arms tightened about her. His mouth closed on hers, skilled, unhurried. She trembled, her hands making a fluttering futile struggle against his back. Then the moon turned molten. The frozen wastes of her body softened, heated, molded to the sinuous fire of his. As if tempted by the possibility of his own immolation, his fingers grazed the curve of her, the arch of her nape, then wove into the bright blaze of her hair. They whispered through its forbidden silk, tangled, tightened. Then brought her back to awareness as they brushed her lips.

"There, now you are compromised," he murmured huskily. "Which of us will be the liar, Lysistrata?"

"I hate you," she whispered, tears of humiliation beginning to trickle down her face.

His hands left her shoulders, then he motioned to a turn in the hedge. "The ball floor is just beyond there. Don't forget to put up your hair." Then he disappeared back into the maze, leaving her with throat choked, hands clenched.

"Was that kiss absolutely necessary?" Evelyn teased.

Harley thought of Lysistrata's slim, bare shoulders, the rich weight of her hair, and her softness in his arms. He remembered the hand that went to her cheek when he would not dance with her . . . that uncertain, heated mouth under his.

"Yes," he answered simply.

She looked at him speculatively, then stroked his sleeve. "Will she talk?"

"No. She has little to lose, but it's all she has."

"I think you're sorry for her," she purred against his throat.

"Shouldn't I be? She has you for an enemy."

As Harley promised, the maze opened some fifty feet from the musicians' chairs. Dazedly, Lysistrata saw the dancing had been interrupted by a ceremony. Sir Anthony, with Lady Mary at his side, was giving a speech to the guests encircling the dance floor. A few hesitant steps beyond the bougainvillea, Lysistrata encountered Harry Armistead. He stared at her disheveled appearance. "Lysistrata, where have you been?! Your father has been looking for you for the past half hour. He and Dr. Lighter are covering the pool grounds now."

"I became lost in the maze," she answered unsteadily. "My feet hurt, so . . . I lost my shoes, too." Her slight laugh held a note of hysteria. "I'm such a fool, Harry. You've no idea."

"I've some idea, Lysistrata," he replied quietly. "I saw him."

She whitened and he pitied her. "Don't worry, I won't say anything. But God, why Harley? He's little more than a renegade and a half-caste as well." He paused. "I'm sorry. I suppose you didn't know."

"I know enough." Her lips trembled. "But Harry, it's not at all what you think . . . he—"

He caught her shoulders. "Did he attack you?"

"No," she whispered. Harley's kiss had been a kind of attack, but she had not fought. She would not have fought even if he had wanted more than that kiss. And it all could have meant nothing to him. Nothing. "No, Harry, he didn't have to use force."

"Look"—his hands tightened—"you don't owe *me* any explanation, but you'd better have one for your father. If he sees you like this, he'll call Harley out, and Harley has a nasty reputation as a duelist." He shot a look over his shoulder at the crowd. "Our timing's lucky. Sir Anthony's doling out a decoration . . . Bearer of a Silver Sword or whatever, to the Honorable Wa Sing, but I'd better get you out of here before someone notices us. Come on. No one can tell if you're barefoot if you're careful how you walk. Sweep your skirts back a bit."

"What about this?" Her hand brushed at bare shoulders.

"Very becoming," he observed puckishly.

"Oh, Harry . . ." Stabilized by his matter-of-factness, she gave him a look of mock reproach, then added as he steered her away from the party, "Where are we going?"

"To Lighter's carriage. Then I'll collect him and your father."

* * *

Harry was startled and impressed when the two coolies mounted fore and aft of Lighter's coach box challenged him with Remington rifle and shotgun respectively. Lysistrata explained to them what seemed necessary, and the shotgun waved Harry to help her into the carriage. "Well, it appears you'll be safe enough," he observed cheerfully, his head thrust through the carriage window.

"How fortunate they understand English," Lysistrata replied ironically.

"Are you all right now?" He became serious.

"Yes. Perhaps someday I can offer an explanation for tonight. Just now, I don't quite understand myself what happened." She touched his hand on the sill. "But thank you, Harry. You've been a friend."

"Thank me by staying out of trouble." He tapped her nose.

CHAPTER 3

A Game of Chameleons

. . . dream of her beauty with tender dread
From the delicate Arab arch of her feet
To the grace that, bright and light as the crest
of a peacock, sits on her shining head,
and she knows it not: O, if she knew it,
To know her beauty might half undo it.
                          ALFRED, LORD TENNYSON

Lysistrata would have given much to have forgone Lady
Bartly's tea the following week, for Evelyn Chilton was
sure to be present. But she had to face the woman. The
day, as had the other days in the interim, dawned
sunny, and Lysistrata put on her serge with particular
loathing, aware Evelyn would not have been caught
dead in it.

As she was driven in a hired *gharry* through the cantonment, she found its spacious serenity more to her lik-
ing than she had expected. Gone was the bustle of the
city, the smell of too many people. Nestled between
copses of banyan and bamboo, the European bungalows
stretching toward Prome Road were inviting, their teak
beams shawled by convolvulus and fringed palms. On
broad verandahs, barefoot house servants padded about

laying tea things and arranging filigreed wrought-iron
furniture—while, under sweeping shade trees, children
played games of croquet and blindman's bluff with their
spaniels racing underfoot. In a gazebo banked by Medi-
terranean shrubs, an old, white-clad Madrassee tuned a
violin. On one lawn, the Renaissance velvet of roses and
pansies were daintily clustered about bold yellow clumps
of blooming cactus and pink and red geraniums. Across
another, marigolds appeared in great yellow and orange
carpets. Home is where the heart is, Lysistrata thought.
These people have brought home with them and written it
upon the earth, yet I wonder if their hearts linger in another place.

As mine does not. How easy it would be to love this
land. With an unfamiliar feeling of peace, she gazed
down the wide, sandy road shaded by palms and lovely
bronze mohur drifting above canopies of banyan and
padouk. Through their broad, still shadows trotted Indian
and Chinese laborers, tiny sari-clad Indian ladies with
crimson flashes of hennaed fingers and toes, and brightly
clad Burmese with giggling children scampering through
the dust at their skirts. Upswept *gharries* passed like
wheelbound ships loaded with Burmese, their umbrellas
rainbow sails; the plump, pampered bullocks in scarlet
traces gaily jingling with brass bells. If I do not belong in
this place, Lysistrata thought as she watched them, I belong nowhere.

After the charm of the *gharries*, Lysistrata felt no
qualms about her own little cart when its driver pulled up
between the sleek victorias and landaus parked along the
Government House drive. By daylight, the Government
House grounds were a patchwork blaze of flowering
shrubs on bright green grass set with white wicker tea
tables and chairs. Even so, the place had lost its moonlit
glamour. Lysistrata hoped the light of day would also reveal some flaw in Evelyn Chilton's beauty, but Evelyn,

like the flowers, looked even better twirling a lacy parasol over her perfect self in a pale froth of yellow organza. Lysistrata, in her audacious little fez, returned the brunette's subtly mocking smile as if greeting her fondest friend.

She'd had time to think in the last week. Hideous black serge *did* give one a sense of proportion. She had been caught off balance at the ball, but her feet were firmly planted now. Let Evelyn smile; if she attempted more, she would get a nasty surprise. And so would Richard Harley.

Madame Pan-byu's recitation from *The Glass Palace Chronicles* was all that was promised. She was a slight woman, plain but for a vivid smile. In the course of her narrative under a purple-flowering padouk tree circled by tea tables of pastel-clad ladies, her hands gestured with delicately precise symbolism to color the interpretation. As she watched the willow-shifting of Lady Pan-byu's body, Lysistrata supposed her to be trained dancer.

When Lady Pan-byu was done, Lysistrata waited until guests ceased to flutter about her with compliments; many ladies had been bored, but did not wish to incur Lady Bartly's disfavor by slighting her guest of honor. Lysistrata greeted the noblewoman in simple, formal Burmese that she had asked Ma Saw to teach her for the occasion. Ma Saw was most happy to do so, for Lady Pan-byu, she told her mistress, was highly regarded in Burma. "Lady Pan-byu has written down many poems and plays which have been told one person to another for thousands of years. Now they will not change or be lost." Lady Pan-byu was surprised and pleased to be addressed in her native language, for Westerners rarely troubled to study it. Her replies, though, left Lysistrata at a loss. *"Nah mah lay boo . . .* I do not understand," she confessed, adding she had only a little store of Burmese but hoped to learn more.

Lady Mary smiled approvingly. "So you shall, my dear. We'll practice together. My Hindustani is rather good, but my Burmese is deplorable. Anthony and I have only been here for two years, you see."

Evelyn cut Lysistrata a glance under the confection of tulle and straw that was her hat. "You do have a tolerable ear, Miss Herriott." She turned to Lady Pan-byu and said something in swift, fluent Burmese. "Don't you think so, Lady Pan-byu?"

"Miss Herriott will do very well," the Burmese lady replied.

"Evelyn is the expert here, Miss Herriot," Lady Mary said. "She and Nigel have been stationed in Rangoon since '64. She's been giving me instruction. You wouldn't mind taking on Miss Herriott, too, would you, Evie?"

Cool amethyst eyes studied Lysistrata. "I should be delighted. There must be so many things you would like to learn about Burma, Miss Herriott."

"I'm sure you would be the ideal teacher, Mrs. Chilton, but Ma Saw, my housekeeper, has already undertaken my instruction." Lysistrata's head tilted. "You must concede, her ear is perfect."

"Possibly for servant jargon, but how you speak is, of course, up to you. Also, spoken and written Burmese are completely different forms."

"As I do not often have the honor of meeting Burmese nobility as I have today"—Lysistrata curtsied lightly to Lady Pan-byu—"I have no pretension to your intimacy with native custom."

Lady Mary, who caught a whisper of sharpening sabers, linked an arm of each of the two women with hers. "Why don't we have a lovely squabble about Burmese dialects? Lady Pan-byu shall be arbitrator." Firmly, she steered the group toward the house. "In a country with so little distinction between its classes, are social levels of vernacular really so greatly different, Lady Pan-byu . . . ?''

"Will you linger a few moments, Miss Herriott?" Lady Mary whispered conspiratorially an hour later as she saw her guests off.

Startled, Lysistrata replied, "Yes, of course, if you like."

Evelyn was last to leave. When she saw Lysistrata was to remain, she dallied pointedly until it became evident Lady Mary did not intend to include her. Finally, with an exasperated sweep of her parasol, she descended the verandah steps to her landau.

"Now." Lady Mary took both Lysistrata's hands in hers. "I have a proposition for you. Let me show you something." She led her upstairs to a handsome bedroom where she flung open the doors of a massive armoire; in it hung dresses sealed in gauze with camphor sachets. "My daughter Louise's waistline expanded past recovery with her first child. She wouldn't admit it then, but she's come around now the second one's due." She pulled out a peach silk and held it up to Lysistrata. "I thought so. You're just about right. A bit tall, but the hems can be let down." She raked through the dresses. "I'm going to give you the lot"—she shot a pointed look over her shoulder—"but only if you have them rehemmed properly. They're too expensive to be botched."

"Lady Mary," Lysistrata began firmly, "I don't need—"

"Bother. What have you got on under that dust-catcher?"

Lysistrata flinched. "What do you mean?"

"I am referring to your feet, miss."

"Sandals. They're quite comfortable," Lysistrata asserted stoutly.

"I daresay, but they're suited to a native's *longyi* skirt, not that shroud."

"Lady Mary . . ." Lysistrata began angrily.

"If you continue to wear heavy clothes in this climate, you'll attract every ailment under the sun. And," the Englishwoman added grimly, "Burma has them all."

"Then I'll sew—"

"Oh no, that would *really* be unbearable."

Lysistrata stiffened. "My state of fortune may be evident, but that does not mean I require charity, particularly when doled out with insults. If my manner of dress does not suit your society, then I shall have to forgo it."

Lady Mary clapped her hands. "Bravo, my girl! I confess I was misled. I had not realized you were so fond of your own company. Your usual appearance does not suggest that sort of vanity."

Lysistrata flushed, unable to reply.

"You've a superb figure, a remarkable face, and magnificent hair, yet you make every effort to obliterate them," Lady Mary stated bluntly. "Oh, yes, I've an eye for good looks. I had more than my share once upon a time." Her voice softened at Lysistrata's dumbfounded expression. "Poor girl, you don't even recognize your possibilities. How on earth can anyone else?" She took Lysistrata's shoulders. "You should really try to like yourself a bit. You might be pleasantly surprised."

"Why are you taking so much trouble with me?"

The Englishwoman laughed. "Perhaps I'm fascinated by someone who might beat me at poker."

"But you—"

"It was Evie who suggested I'd never heard of it." She began to sort through silk-covered boxes of shoes. "She doesn't like you. That's unusual for Evie. She rarely bothers to dislike anyone."

"Particularly a nobody," Lysistrata replied dryly.

"Do you know why she dislikes you?"

Lysistrata said nothing.

"I'll tell you. Evie doesn't brook rivals."

Lysistrata was startled. "How could I be her rival?"

"You couldn't, not now. Shortly, she may even decide you wear those widow's weeds because you mourn some man. I suppose she might even learn to pity you, in her distant fashion."

"Now you're being transparent, Lady Mary," Lysistrata retorted

Lady Mary grinned wickedly. "Which dress would you prefer to try first, Lysistrata?"

"The peach."

"Miss Herriott."

Looking up from the melons she was weighing, Lysistrata squinted in the blinding sun which probed under the market-stall canopy. Evelyn Chilton prodded open the polished door of her gray landau with her closed parasol. "Will you join me for a drive? I've been hoping we might meet again."

"I'm not finished shopping," Lysistrata said flatly and turned back to the melons.

Evelyn studied Lysistrata's blue cotton dress and leghorn hat, then glanced about China Street's marketplace under Shwe Dagon's ornate looming temple. "I gather you come here quite often."

"My household enjoys eating regularly."

"Miss Herriott," Evelyn said gently, "you may not be aware white women do not frequent the markets in Burma."

Lysistrata dropped a melon into her shopping basket. "Then their snobbery costs them a great entertainment."

Evelyn laughed. "I daresay you are right. I think I shall join you. The heat has given me a taste for a mango." Gracefully, she dismounted the landau.

Lysistrata regarded her coldly. "You must be aware, Mrs. Chilton, that your company is unwelcome."

"But we should talk, don't you think?"

Lysistrata strode on to a raffia mat piled with rusty orange yams. "What could we possibly have to discuss?"

"Our common interest in Richard Harley."

Lysistrata laughed mirthlessly. "Your hedge Lothario? You're joking. Besides, why should you care? If you loved him, you couldn't continue to live with Nigel Chilton."

Evelyn lifted an eyebrow. "You *are* direct, even for an American. You might make an effort to be civil, you know, in your position."

Lysistrata flipped several yams into the basket. "Just what is my position?"

"Fragile." Evelyn shot open her parasol. "Dr. Lighter is inclined to be stuffy. He thinks Florence Nightingale is a common whore." The parasol slowly twirled. "And Lady Mary is particular about the reputations of those she befriends when they reflect upon her judgment. She *is* a trifle vain."

"Then she has a good friend in you," Lysistrata replied lightly. "You're vain indeed if you think you and Richard Harley can continue to intimidate me. We are not a cozy threesome in the moonlight now. No one saw me leave that maze, so now it is just my word against yours." She poked through a stack of yellow, green, and scarlet peppers under a turquoise paper umbrella and, ignoring the vendor's effort to barter, handed him a fair price for several of them. "Everyone is familiar with Harley's questionable reputation, and I doubt if yours would stand much scrutiny. I daresay he's not the first lover you've acquired in your many years of Burmese experience. More than one woman in Rangoon must be jealous of you. They'd love to pounce, so I'd be wary of purring about shredded reputations."

The parasol had long stopped. "My dear Miss Herriott," Evelyn breathed, "are you threatening me?"

"Just warning you to retract your claws." Lysistrata left her standing there.

Late that afternoon, Lysistrata, with a sarong-style *tamein* hiked up about her thighs, swabbed doggedly at a bungalow entry window. When only women were in the house she dressed as she pleased, finding Burmese clothing sensible for the humid climate. Still, the heat glued down the cotton garments like a second skin, and her hair, piled atop her head, to her forehead and neck. Dunking the brush in a bucket of soapy water, she reattacked the window.

At the moment, she could cheerfully have scrubbed the glass with Lighter's tongue. So she could not do without servants! Ma Saw was the only one of any use. Sein, *la coquette*, her face often daubed with dreadful white *chanakka* paste, always seemed to be gone on "errands" that kept her giggling with the young men outside the toddyshops. Of course, San-hla was too small, though she tried.

Lysistrata rarely thought of the little Burmese without a smile. The child's charm had stolen her heart from the first. In the evenings, she taught Lysistrata her simple dances and songs and how to rattle coconuts from the palms by U Pho's old quarters. She also taught her to weave flowers into her hair and wrap a *longyi* skirt properly. Missy was not to wear certain unlucky shades of green, but pink was always a good choice, particularly with her wonderful sunset hair. She was puzzled by Missy's adamant refusal to try *chanakka* paste.

Ma Saw observed Lysistrata's instruction, but other than language, rarely offered advice. While she was a diligent, steady worker, the two women were hard put to manage the bungalow alone. Although Dr. Herriott helped whenever he could, his time was usurped by the hospital.

Oh yes, Lysistrata thought vehemently, Dr. Lighter has made himself a good bargain! Angrily, she dumped the remains of the water over the floor, which also needed washing, and kicked the bucket after it with a clatter. Her feet skidding on the slippery floor, she went down with a smack on her bottom. As she let out a screech of pure frustration, the front door opened and her father quizzically watched the bucket roll across the room. Behind him stood Richard Harley. Her jaw dropped, her hands shot to her skimpy *tamein*. *Why*, she railed, did Harley always have to see her looking as if she had just climbed out of someone's bed or was bound for his? It was well her father could not see the amused interest on Harley's face as he studied her legs before the *tamein* dropped into place. But only to the knees for that was as far as it went. With as much dignity as she could retrieve, she stood, bare shoulders squared.

"My daughter Lysistrata, Mr. Harley," said Herriott dryly.

"Miss Herriott."

So that was his game, was it? she thought in contempt. You don't know me, I don't know you. Evelyn must have sent him to try blackmail.

"Dr. Lighter has given me responsibility for ordering drugs from Singapore, so I've asked Mr. Harley to join us for dinner in order to discuss scheduling. I hope we've something special to offer him?"

As a matter of fact, we haven't, she thought. As a matter of fact, I should like to offer Mr. Harley an asp-wrapped fig. "Yes, of course. I'll see to it," she replied sweetly.

Dinner, though simple, was well prepared, for Lysis-

trata had learned something about cooking from Ma Saw.
Dr. Herriott purchased wines from a canny Frenchman;
while the evening's vintage was not fine, it was better
than Dr. Lighter's. Candlelight soothed the absence of
furniture and crystal. Lysistrata was not a little proud of
herself when she recalled the tasteless messes she had
foisted on her father's rare guests in Boston. Though she
had had no time to change, she hurriedly smoothed her
hair. Ma Saw insisted on weaving tiny orchids into the
coil at her nape. "Only men do not wear flowers. Mr.
Harley will think it odd to see you without them."

I do look rather pretty tonight, certainly not like a
woman a man would regret kissing, Lysistrata thought
with mounting confidence as she glanced at her reflection
in the kitchen water chattie.

At dinner, she studied Harley over her wineglass as he
and Herriott discussed the *Rani*'s schedules. Utterly unlike her father's open, honest, bluffly American face,
Harley's vulpine features belonged to a Borgia courtier,
clever at back-room and bedroom intrigue. While the
satyr slant to his eyes and full-curved underlip were sensual, the severe cheekbones and hard jawline suggested a
plains-bred, hard-riding Rajput. His irises were actually
the color of tea, so dark under thick lashes they seemed
black. He was not past his middle twenties, but seemed
older with the smooth, hard polish and containment of
jade.

He must be aware she was scrutinizing him as if dis-
secting a bug, but he did not seem uncomfortable, only
patient. When he had kissed her in the maze she had reacted to him with a passion Frank Wyatt had never
touched, that lay beyond her comprehension. Unwillingly, she still reacted to him: a possible traitor, unscrupulous blackmailer, an adulterer, and God knows
what else. *Why?* From her brief experience of him, he appeared to have royally earned his unsavory reputation.

"How do you find Rangoon, Miss Herriott?"

"Full of surprises, Mr. Harley."

"Pleasant ones, I hope."

"Most of them. The disagreeable ones seem to be associated with the difficulty of being rid of vermin." With her napkin, she delicately dispatched a large ant aiming toward the sugar bowl, then picked up her wineglass.

"Ah yes," he agreed gravely as she sipped. "They are tenacious. They appear to be most persistent when one wishes to go to bed."

She choked. With fond innocence, Dr. Herriott patted her back. "My daughter hasn't my familiarity with the grape, Mr. Harley."

"A very pleasant vintage this is, sir," Harley complimented him. "You are fortunate Miss Herriott is a sensible young woman. Far too intelligent not to realize . . . intoxication has its dangers."

"And its pleasures," quoth the doctor, not seeing the livid glare Lysistrata directed at her suave tormentor.

Forcefully, she changed the subject. "Papa, perhaps Mr. Harley would like dessert."

"Something sweet?" Harley cocked a brow at her. "Thank you, Miss Herriott, but I shouldn't want to put you to so much effort."

"Ma Saw made dessert, Mr. Harley. I've gone to more trouble for the garden monkeys when I've tossed them bananas."

Though Harley's few conversational exchanges with her thereafter were impeccably polite, her responses were curt, her expression stony. Dr. Herriott, at last noticing the danger signs, attempted to forestall unpleasantness. "Lysistrata, why don't you and San-hla show Mr. Harley the dance you learned the other day?" He turned to Harley. "You really must see it. San-hla is a charming child. She's taught Lysistrata—"

"Not tonight, Papa," Lysistrata cut in quickly. "I've

had a long day.'' Her gray-green eyes held Harley's.
"Mr. Harley will understand, I'm sure. I gather his many
interests occupy him day *and* night.''

Harley smiled slowly. "Just as you say, Miss Herriott.
At any rate, I must see my head clerk tonight to check a
cargo inventory. Doctor, I hope you will both forgive
me.''

"Of course.'' Herriott slid his daughter a searching
look, then said cheerfully, "Lysistrata and I look forward to seeing you this Sunday.''

Lysistrata sat up straight. "What is happening this
Sunday?''

"Mr. Harley has kindly invited us to attend a *pwe.*"
Her father added firmly, "I told him we would be delighted.''

There were times even Lysistrata did not argue with
her father. "Yes, indeed''—she glared at Harley—"delighted.''

Harley inclined his head, then rose. "Until Sunday,
then, doctor.''

After Harley left, Herriott waved Lysistrata to linger
on the verandah. He studied the tropic moon's huge,
white disk slit by slender, whispering palms. Cactus and
Spanish bayonet cast fantastic shadows across sand
patches to a great padouk nearly choked by creamy cyclamen. Herriott's deep breath of the strange perfumes of
musky humus and unknown flowers that filled the night
air sounded like a sigh. "Lovely night, isn't it?''

"Lovely.'' She plopped down on the verandah steps.

"Mr. Harley seems to be a pleasant young fellow,
don't you think?'' The American-style porch swing, one
of U Pho's leisurely projects, began to rock as Herriott lit
his pipe.

She shrugged. "So-so.''

As the match guttered, he swore, then struck another

against his boot sole. "Why do you dislike every unmarried man I bring home?"

"I don't. Neither do I feel like performing tricks for them."

"And particularly not for Harley." His voice had an edge never applied to her before. "You were eyeing him as if he were an unexploded torpedo."

"Why do you say that?"

He gave his pipe a long pull. "You're not a bigot, are you, Lysistrata?"

"No." She shifted uncomfortably on the stone step. "No, I don't think I am. I simply don't relish entertaining a man with Harley's unsavory reputation in my home."

"The commissioner is less particular. So, it appears, is the rest of the community. Tom says Harley is invaluable to the operation of the hospital." He paused. "You might remember, Lysistrata, your home is mine as well." Pipe clamped in his teeth, he left her on the verandah.

Shortly, she tracked him to his makeshift study where he sat thumbing through dog-eared medical journals. "I'm sorry, Papa," she apologized contritely. "If Harley's important to Dr. Lighter, I suppose he's important to you. I'll be civil to him."

"That's good of you," he replied dryly.

Stung, she protested, "What do you want of me? I hardly know the man!"

"You refuse to know *any* man. You treat each of them as if he were personally responsible for—" He stopped as if debating the wisdom of continuing, then plunged on. "I don't know what happened between you and Frank Wyatt back in Boston, but in my opinion, Frank wasn't worth a tenth of the remembrance you give him." He stabbed out the pipe to ward off argument. "If I'd known you'd leap into Agatha's shoes the day he married, I'd have given him the toe of my boot!''

"You're right, Papa,'' she said simply. "Frank wasn't much.''

At his dumbfounded stare, her lips quirked. "Haven't you noticed I've lost my shoes?'' She displayed sandaled toes.

He broke into a broad grin. "If I weren't your father, I'd nibble 'em.''

Lysistrata laughed in delight as Hanuman, the monkey king, scampered atop a stone pedestal and mimed a perfect simian grimace at his flea-scratching, capering minions. Around him the actors spun, turning flips, linking arms two by two and cartwheeling in midair. About them was a pretended feast which they and Hanuman greedily gobbled with quick, spidery snatches. The background was a simple drop of red and yellow cotton, the music energetically provided by drums, gongs, and bamboo clappers.

"So you like the *pwe,* Miss Herriott?'' Harley's softly modulated voice came over her shoulder.

"Very much!'' she replied without reservation. *Comédie Française* performances must be something like this.''

"Oh, why do you say that?''

"Because of the boisterousness, the wonderful artificiality. The West hasn't employed mimes so well in centuries. It's a great loss, for everyone responds to mimics; they're so—'' She hesitated, realizing she must be running on.

"Fundamental?''

She eyed him warily. He looked perfectly serious.

"You may be right.'' His eyes turned to the brilliantly costumed actors with their painted faces and masks. "*Pwes* are not so far from Molière's false noses and exaggerated makeup. Or the European 'masques' of medieval times.''

"I confess I know little about medieval theater.''

As Harley described the masques, he and Lysistrata sat on portable campaign chairs directly in front of the *pwe* arena. The sand of the surrounding streets was hardly visible under the chattering, cheroot-smoking audience. A mule could not have pushed through them; even the rooftops were covered. Her father had disappeared during the second act to sample the local liquor in one of the toddyshops whose awnings shaded gossiping, drinking men. Everyone chatted freely, as there was no speech to hear, only music.

"So the masques began Western theater,'' Harley continued, ''but the East moves at a different pace. Here, you will find drama practiced in its purest form. Plays are often performed by life-size puppets.''

She laughed, feeling at ease in one of pregnant Louisa's most feminine frocks. ''Artificiality in its purest form.''

"Artificiality in both East and West is a form of self-protection. People crowded together as they are in Asia develop elaborate methods of preserving their privacy.''

Instantly, she was on guard. ''Artificiality is also a form of concealment.''

His hand made an easy gesture. ''As you like. Quite often, there is nothing to conceal. It is merely a way of life.''

"I think I see what you mean,'' she observed levelly. ''Pearls are made up of pretty layers; under them is just a bit of dirt.''

His eyes narrowed a fraction. ''Pearl-diving is a hazardous occupation, particularly for amateurs who rarely recognize what they are looking for.''

"I don't care much for pearls, Mr. Harley,'' she retorted. ''They carry a tradition of bad luck.''

"A wise decision." He smiled as if privately amused. His attention went back to the players. "In this case, Evelyn has decided to forgo her pearl and return to being a simple oyster."

Lysistrata stared at him a moment, then as comprehension dawned, she threw back her head and laughed. "I don't believe it! Why should she?"

"The union between oyster and pearl is more parasitic than affectionate."

She gave him a derisive look. "Next you'll be telling me it's nothing but an irritation."

A smile played about his mouth. "One can become accustomed to most things."

Lysistrata found she did not want to know how long he and Evelyn had taken to grow accustomed to each other. She dropped her bantering attitude. "Mr. Harley, I can easily guess who suggested to Dr. Lighter that my father assume the Singapore requisitions. If you are currying favor with my father or seeking to put him in your debt to keep me silent, you can save yourself the trouble. I want only to forget the night of the ball, and you and Evelyn Chilton in particular. What you do is your own business." She disliked the intent way his eyes searched hers, but knew he had no more reason to believe her than she him.

"Very well," he said at last.

No more was said on the subject. Silently, they watched Hanuman and the villain battle with long, clashing sticks. Dr. Herriott emerged from the toddyshop during Hanuman's victory dance. "I watched from a window. Right brisk stuff, this monkey business," he observed cheerily, handing them paper cones of salted *zithee* plums.

The next play, a romance between a commoner and a princess, was anything but brisk. Two hours passed with no indication that the plot was progressing beyond the exchange of love poems between the protagonists until Dr. Herriott shifted restlessly and leaned across to Harley's chair. "Just how long is this one?"

"It should end sometime after midnight."

Herriott drew back. "That's another seven hours!"

Harley laughed. "In Burmese theater, the path of love is never smooth."

"But apparently eternal," Lysistrata quipped.

Harley made one of his liquid gestures. "We will miss very little if we leave for a time. As you see, many people come and go during a performance. They even take naps. *Pwes* are mostly excuses to drink and gossip. The denouement won't begin to build until nine."

"Then I should like to try some palm toddy," Lysistrata announced.

Herriott and Harley exchanged looks over her head. Harley rose from his chair. "I'll bring you some jaggery, Miss Herriott. Doctor, why don't the two of you walk toward Dalhousie Park. I'll meet you there and Miss Herriott can taste her jaggery while I show you the grounds and Victoria Lake."

Lysistrata eyed him. "You wouldn't be afraid I'll become inebriated and prove an embarrassment, would you, Mr. Harley?"

"Not due to jaggery, Miss Herriott."

"Is it that mild?" she asked in some disappointment.

Harley gave her an enigmatic smile.

Dalhousie Park at dusk was lovely, not only because of its luxuriant gardens that now seemed customary to the Herriotts, but because of its human flowers. Among Europeans on the carriage paths were Burmese with troops of happy-go-lucky children, native nannies leading more decorous charges, and bangled Indians pattering after their men. A British army band softly played "I Dream of Jeannie" from a cupolaed pavilion as skiffs and sail-

boats from the Boat Club on Lake Victoria's opposite
shore glided across distant Shwe Dagon's rippled golden
reflection. Among the waxy water lilies, swans dined,
occasionally startling a glimmering fish after skimming
dragonflies. Over all floated scores of paper kites, dip-
ping and fragile in the still dusk.

The Herriotts were watching an ancient Burmese gentleman explain the intricacies of kite-flying to his two-
year-old grandson when Harley walked toward them.
With the mischief of Pan, he presented a cheap white
crockery cup to Lysistrata. After one sip of milky-
colored jaggery, she whirled and spat it into a flowerbed.
"How horrid! It tastes like chalk!" Her father handed her
his handkerchief to blot her mouth. Through the cambric,
she protested, "How can you drink that, Papa?"

"My palate is somewhat more sophisticated than
yours, my dear. After all"—Herriott tipped his hat jauntily forward on his brow—"it's been refined in Boston's
lowest establishments."

"Do you suppose"—he waved at the kites—"we
could do a bit of that?"

Harley laughed. "Of course. Miss Herriott?"

"No, thank you." She would have loved to fly a kite,
but was not about to scamper after it for Harley's amusement.

He summoned a tribe of young Burmans and, after a
few words, held up a rupee. With alacrity, the children
handed over the handsomest kite and bolted with their
booty. He handed the kite to Herriott, who had shrugged
out of his jacket and rolled up his sleeves. Moments later,
the doctor was gaily running across the park in hot pursuit of his winging bit of paper. Ready to kick him if he
appeared to find her father foolish, Lysistrata shot a hard
look toward Harley. He gazed after the kite with a sadness, almost a tenderness, that startled her more than the
jaggery. Though the impression vanished swiftly as an il-

lusion, that—more than his indefatigable charm—disarmed her. After the kite-flying, the rest of the evening with Harley turned out to be unexpectedly pleasant. By the time the *pwe* reached its end, she could almost forget how unpleasant he could be.

By next morning, she was reminded. The door-knocker clacked. On her doorstep stood an Indian, more accurately a Pathan, of forbidding stature and more forbidding face swept by giant mustachios. "I am Ali Masjid, Miss Herriott." He bowed. "I am to be your houseman."

She blinked. "I beg your pardon?"

"Mr. Harley sent me," he said briefly as if that explained everything.

To Lysistrata, it explained enough. If Harley thought to plant a spy in her household, he was much mistaken. "I am sorry for your trouble, Mr. Masjid, but we do not require an additional servant." Much less one who takes his orders from someone else, she thought grimly.

"Your father has already agreed," he said solemnly. "Here are my letters of recommendation."

Seething, she read them. All proclaimed Ali Masjid to be a superlative fellow. Probably forged. She handed him back the letters. A Brussels carpetbag was precisely aligned with Masjid's large feet. The Pathan had come to stay. For the day only, Lysistrata decided firmly, and he would do more work in that day than he bargained for in three. Her finger crooked. "Follow me, Mr. Masjid."

"What do you think of Masjid?" Easing comfortably back in his chair, Herriott smiled beatifically at his empty dinner plate.

"I've been wanting to talk to you about him, Papa." Lysistrata carefully placed her coffee cup in its saucer.

"Oh?" Herriott sounded surprised. "Isn't he up to snuff?"

"It's not that. He can work an elephant into the ground," she reluctantly admitted, "but, Papa, we just can't afford him."

"Yes, we can." He smiled benevolently. "I had a raise in salary today."

Had Harley gotten to Lighter as well? Her mind was going dull. "But we have no savings, and Ma Saw and I can manage—"

"That's just the point. You can't manage. I didn't bring you to Burma to be a drudge, Lysistrata." He sat forward. "Masjid is accustomed to running large households. Besides, we can not only afford him, but a gardener as well." He noticed her expression. "*And* save money."

Defeated, she subsided. At least she had the slight satisfaction of knowing Harley was paying an inordinate amount for a useless watchdog. One she would not allow to grow fat.

CHAPTER 4

Tuan Cupid

And shall I take a thing so blind
Embrace her as my natural good;
Or crush her, like a vice of blood
Upon the threshold of the mind?
ALFRED, LORD TENNYSON

Harry Armistead did not encounter Richard Harley again until over a month after the commissioner's ball when he was invited with several officers to a plantation north of Rangoon for bird-shooting. Harry had met Claus Bettenheim, the plantation owner, at the Green Monkey Club shortly after he arrived in the city. Bettenheim was a blunt-headed, heavy-shouldered German in his early forties. He informed Harry he had systematically enjoyed the vice of the city as a form of calisthenics since his wife's death. Most of his time went into managing his three large plantations. When he had not the time to go into Rangoon for entertainment, he set up weekend bachelor parties. "Working plantations are a lonely life at best," he confided in tipsy melancholia to Harry. "Nothing but wogs to talk to for months."

Harry did not particularly like the man, but the hunting invitation offered a chance to increase his acquaintances,

As the cauldron sun glimmered on the
bile, listening to the ... , Harry and th...
flat rice paddies, Harry and h...
ing symb...

marsh...
dozen Ka...
game bags.

Harry, out of cu...
chant named Arthur W. ...
ted after them. Originally, ... an
Indian as well; but the man, up... atly
refused to attend them. The Karen ... ently,
jaws working betel, as the Indian, sha... is head,
broke into a flood of Hindustani and sawed at the air with
his arms. His eye-whites showed in fright as Bettenheim
loudly berated him in front of the other hunters, but he remained adamant. Finally, the German was forced to give
up. "I'm sorry"—he turned to Harley—"but you see
how it is . . ."

Harley shrugged carelessly. "It's unimportant. I prefer a good dog to a Tamil."

With an abrupt change of manner, the Tamil turned as
if he meant to attack Harley. Bettenheim cuffed him.
"None of that, you offal! Get back to your work. I'll see
to you later." As the Indian sullenly retreated, the German spread his arms and said in a helpless tone, "I really don't know what gets into these fools. They're
more trouble than they're worth. I'll beat this one myself."

"Don't bother," Harley drawled. "When one pays
them eight rupees a month, one can afford to be generous
in other ways."

Bettenheim's eyes narrowed piggishly for an instant,
then he smiled tightly. "Yes, patience is often rewarded,
isn't it?"

edge of the vast, ... the three men stood immo- ... birds begin tentative calls like a tun- ... phony across the marshland. Frogs added bass notes as they leaped and plopped through bands of water between earthwork bunds and rows of rice. Slowly, night melted into an apricot dawn, and one by one, doves, hoopoos, and geese were silhouetted against the sky; then, in a blur of wings they plummeted to frogs, lizards, and bugs lavishly spread among the rice rows and on the distant, glimmering lake.

"It seems a pity to shoot, doesn't it?" Harry murmured to no one in particular, then heard Harley's soft laugh.

"Such audible mourning may relieve us of the burden."

"Sorry."

"Don't be. It *is* a pity to shoot."

"Oh, for God's sake," Wilton growled, and opened fire. He missed.

Within a heartbeat after Wilton's first shot, Harley's Martini-Henry rifle sprang up. Swiftly, exactly, he shot a bird, reloaded and downed another. Reloading again, he nodded to the Karen. To Harry's surprise, the man splashed into the water to retrieve the birds as if he were a trained dog. Wilton, red-faced, his jowl pressed against his stock, emptied his shotgun, then swore because the Karen was not there to hand him another gun. Fumbling and furious, he hastily reloaded while Harry took two birds. Wading among the paddy rows, the Burmese bagged his catch and Wilton's single wood duck.

Harley lit a cheroot as he waited for the man to return. "That does it for me. What about you, Leftenant?"

Harry fished for his own cigars. "Um. I was just after dinner."

Wilton looked at them disgustedly and shoved his gun under his arm. "What the hell did you rotters come out here for! You ruin a man's chance, then pick off a piddling handful and scare off the rest." His florid face assumed a sneer. "If it's all right with you, I'll take the wog here and bag my share."

"Go ahead," Harley said mildly. "The leftenant and I can carry our own catch."

Without regret, the two men watched the merchant stamp off through the field toward a bamboo stand on the jeel with the Karen behind him.

The sun still floated low on the horizon, its rim nebulous along the necklaces of water that curved the steaming earth. About the field's edges crept shadowed jungle as if it were an inevitable dusk. Absolute stillness held the land except for a spatter of distant gunfire like stones tossed in a still stream. Mammoth lavender and gold clouds lay motionless with houri languor, their opulence reflected in the marsh. And across it marched Wilton's stubborn, antlike form.

Harry glanced at Harley, whose attention was still on Wilton. On his face was detached distaste, as if he were studying an animal dropping.

"Do you hunt with Bettenheim often?" Harry asked.

"Not often."

With feigned innocence, Harry puffed thoughtfully at his cigar. "He seems rather an unpleasant fellow. That bit back at the house with the . . . Tamil, was it? It seemed deliberately planned, along with his yelps of apology."

"Do you think so?" was the mild rejoinder.

Harry puffed. "Why do you suppose he'd do a thing like that?"

Harley shrugged. "Perhaps he doesn't like me."

"But to invite you . . ." Harry shook his head as if

perplexed. "Why did the Tamil make such a fuss anyway?"

"Because he was asked not only to serve a half-caste, but one defiled," Harley explained patiently, though clearly aware he was being baited. "I eat pork, you see."

"You are not a practicing Hindu, then."

"Neither am I a practicing Englishman."

Harry smiled sweetly. "I'm sorry, I must seem unbearably inquisitive, but I've seen you before and been curious."

"Oh? Why?"

For all Harley's easy manner, Harry suspected he was meddling with an attractive, but possibly poisonous snake. He prodded the coil. "You were with Lysistrata Herriott at the Bartly ball, weren't you?"

Harley smiled, but Harry heard the rustle of moving scales.

"Perhaps, Leftenant, it is Miss Herriott, not myself, who arouses your interest."

"She is a friend." Harry's heedless adolescent guise disappeared. "I would not care to see her hurt and her father obliged to take up an uneven quarrel."

Harley drew upon his cheroot and strolled off in the direction of the plantation house. "Just how far does your interest in Miss Herriott go?"

Harry, with the game bag slung over his shoulder, fell into step beside him. "As I said, I am her friend." He paused, then added with a touch of anger, "I escorted her from the maze to her carriage. I cannot pretend to sainthood, but you did not do well by her, sir."

"No, Leftenant," Harley said slowly, "I did not. I am in your debt, both for Miss Herriott's protection and your discretion." He studied Harry's sunburnt, boyish face under its solar topee. "Did Miss Herriott describe to you the nature of our encounter?"

"She was far too upset," Harry replied grimly, "and I did not feel it my place to question her."

"You show no such reticence with me today."

"You do not appear to be upset," Harry retorted.

Harley smiled faintly. "I assure you, Leftenant, I am not unconcerned about Miss Herriott. Someday I hope to repay you for your assistance to her."

"That will not be necessary, sir. You may thank me by staying away from her. She has had, I think, enough difficulty in her life."

"I shall decide the manner of my gratitude, if you don't mind, Leftenant," Harley replied coolly, then continued gently, "If you are concerned about Miss Herriott, perhaps you should convey that fact to her."

"Are you proposing to play Cupid?" Harry asked sharply.

Harley laughed as if the idea were intriguing. "I simply suggest that if you wish to be a friend to Miss Herriott, you would do well to let her know she has one."

'Perhaps I shall do that," Harry retorted.

Harley's gaze drifted over the field as if he had lost interest in the conversation. "The sun's getting high. We ought to just make the house for a punch before the others return."

Harry glanced toward the bamboo stand. "Odd we haven't heard any shooting from Wilton. I should have thought he'd have spotted a bird or two by now."

"He may be a while," Harley said briefly.

Harley was accurate. The other hunters drifted back to the house by the time he and Harry finished a milk punch and sat down to a second, elaborate breakfast. Wilton came in about noon. Jauntily, he entered the gathering. "Well, I bagged my share. I shouldn't doubt if I haven't taken the day's record."

Bettenheim swung his feet off the table. "Well, why

don't we have a look. Five pounds of my best tobacco for the high man.''

When the game bags were emptied, the array was sickening. Loose-limbed masses of bloody plumage lay stiffening with glassy eyes. The hunters averaged a slaughter of nine birds apiece, but Wilton had taken nearly twenty. He was carried into the dining room on the shoulders of the others amid raucous shouts of praise.

With disgust, Harry viewed Wilton's mangled heap. "I didn't think he was that much of a shot."

"He's not." Harley took down a fan from a wall hook. With a flick of his wrist, he drove away the flies, then raked back the feathers on one of the lax necks. A hairline band of blood oozed in the underdown. "He had the *shikkar* set silk snares. They work like a garrote." He prodded the bird with his boot. "The bullets came later."

Harry frowned. "If you knew, why didn't you say something?"

"Bettenheim knows about snares. His workers wouldn't waste bullets on small game even if they had them." Harley rehung the fan. "If he wants to let his guests feel like fools, he'll see to it."

"Yes," Harry said slowly, "I think I see now, too." Harley could hardly choose a simpler, more pointless way of making enemies than exposing Wilton. The Europeans would not thank a half-caste for enlightening them on their lack of perspicacity. "I suppose Bettenheim does business with Wilton?"

Harley smile quizzically. "Why not ask *him?*"

As it turned out, Harry had little further conversation with either his host or Richard Harley, for Bettenheim and his cronies cornered Harley to elicit information about the Yünnan scheme, whatever that was.

In one sense, Harley conceded to Harry Armistead's request that he avoid Lysistrata Herriott, though he had not intended to see her again in any case. He was sufficiently satisfied she was neither spy nor gossip. Certainly she was not fool enough to involve her father in her adventure at the commissioner's. Masjid's services would help repay the damage to her pride and free her to explore local society. Like a girl playing at being grown-up in a woman's frock, she had been remarkably appealing in her lilac muslin at the *pwe*. While the dress was contrived, she would soon perfect her veneer with Lady Mary's guidance. In the narrow world of the cantonments, her clear-eyed intelligence and lack of affectation would turn to calculation and be tapped by mediocrity. With sharp regret, he knew the untrammeled, lovely Lysistrata in her simple *tamein* would be gone. He did not need Harry Armistead's warning to realize he must tear her from his mind. An involvement with her could bring her only unhappiness and wreck his precarious, hard-won position with the British. She was too naive, too impetuous to entertain an affair and for him to do more than bed her was out of the question. Yet to stay near her and not bed her . . .

When the *Rani* left for Singapore, he was aboard.

Harry, in turn, held up his end by calling on Lysistrata, first on point of obligation, then because he began to prefer her company to the other women he knew and he already knew several intimately. She had no artifice, she was not coy, she could talk about anything from the price of Pacific copra to Keats. And he had to admit she seemed lovely at times: in the garden twilight when shadows dappled her face, in a graceful *longyi* with magnolia blossoms in her bronze-gold hair. From playful San-hla, she learned to release her natural grace, from Lady Mary to use a more polished manner. Unable to forget the old Lysistrata in hoary black, he was slow to accept the gradual transformation.

Lysistrata's adjustment was even slower, for she mistrusted its direction. Despite bonhomie with Harry, she was disinclined to flirt, though he occasionally tried to lure her into it. He was not quite sure why he tried, perhaps because he either thought the practice might do her good or that his well-founded confidence in his appeal was piqued by her intense reaction to Harley. Fairly sure of rejection, he did not quite dare attempt a forthright approach.

Still, he squired her about the city until speculation arose about an engagement. Lady Mary advised her protegée not to allow him such exclusive right to her company. "He's a marvelous catch, my dear," the Englishwoman remarked one afternoon as they played cards under umbrellaed shade at the Gymkhana Club, "but he cannot go back to England for ages, and you may not wish to stay in the colonies. His father's a stubborn old boar who'd disown him before he accepted a penniless American as the next Lady Wilbur." The Englishwoman dexterously shuffled the deck. "Besides, several young men will gladly take Armistead's place. You may easily become a belle."

Lysistrata glanced at the cricket field now scattered with children, nannies, and club members at tea. They looked as comfortably domestic as a yawn. With a little smile, she tapped the shuffled deck. "I've no intention of 'catching' Harry, and I've neither the social position nor dowry for being a belle any more than tilting at the peerage. Most men tend to be practical when they marry."

"And well they might. Being a gentleman is not always a profitable occupation." Lady Mary cut and dealt. "You may have to settle for less than a nabob, but if you're clever, a great many bucks about Rangoon will think themselves privileged to support you. Just be careful of John Company men. Half of them are stuck here out of dissipation and debt. Some, though, are as well-bred as Harry Armistead; they've simply the misfortune to have been born on the wrong side of the blanket. Dynasties, mind you"—she tapped Lysistra's cards with her own—"have been founded on a good deal less. You just need confidence."

Lysistrata arranged her hand, then discarded two. "Marriage seems to always tally down to trade, doesn't it? Buying and selling. Support. Repayment."

"Love and loyalty are still extant, my girl. I loved a man in England, but I am loyal to Anthony." Lady Mary's lips quirked. "Life is only as dull as you make it. In the end you must play with what you are dealt. If you're not a fool, you play to win." She slid the ace of hearts from the pack, palmed it in her glove, then made it reappear in the deck. "And sometimes cheat."

Lysistrata took Lady Mary's advice, solely because she had to deal with the world and evolve new armor more impervious to pain than the old. Chinkless armor, finely wrought as jewelry, with a sheen that could blind the eye.

When the next weekly tea dance was given at the Gymkhana Club, Lysistrata went. For the occasion, Harry playfully hired a *tum-tum* dogcart, in which they rode around the Switchback at sunset with the usual congregation of carriages. Like pups, they tried to tease the laughing drivers into a race. Failing with the carriage drivers, Lysistrata, face flushed and aqua muslin fluttering, clung to the wicker cart side as she offered challenges in lowbrow Burmese to grinning Burmen in *gharries*. Amid cheers from the carriages, a clumsy but determined race eventually ensued between the *gharries* and *tum-tum,* which ended in the midst of a cricket match with a *gharry* overturned. The driver, fortunately unhurt, was generously if inaccurately declared the winner and presented by the cricketers with a bottle of Scotch. The Scotch was shared all around; the *gharry-wallahs* went away mellow while Harry and Lysistrata, accompanied by several cricketers, abandoned the *tum-tum* for the tennis courts. In impossibly dim light, Lysistrata had her first tennis lesson from six competing instructors and succeeded in swatting more droning insects than balls. Upon hearing players from a local regiment band strike up a martial polka in the clubhouse, Lysistrata's instructors gaily insisted she take a "Tennis Court Oath" to grant a dance to each of them.

As a half of the men at the dance were bachelors grateful for any Western woman's companionship, they were pathetically eager to be introduced to a pretty one. Although at first Lysistrata, unsure of how to deal with the sudden attention, clung tightly to his arm, Harry soon faced keen competition for a turn about the dance floor with her. While bright-eyed lizards frolicked about the walls, she learned to flirt. Her uncertainty was generously ignored; she was declared delightfully shy, deliciously innocent. The men courted her as inevitably as moths courted the gaslights and lizards courted the moths. She accompanied Harry home in the *tum-tum* with a childish air of dazed anticipation.

When he called two days later in expectation of taking her to tea and shopping in Fytche Square, Sein archly told him Missy had gone to play *chinlon* with a fishnet! He drove to the Gymkhana Club where he found Lysistrata in the company of a Lieutenant Smith-Deckers on the tennis court. As he might have expected, she had become quickly bored with sedately pacing about in her hampering skirts of peppermint-striped silk and giving the ball tepid swats. As a beginner, she missed the ball more often than she connected with it, but not for lack of effort. When, pink and perspiring from scampering after the ball, she succeeded in returning it to the amused lieutenant, he occasionally had to duck.

As Harry's wave caught her attention, her mouth formed a dismayed O. Prodding a straw chip hat out of her face as she ran toward him, she panted, "Harry, I am sorry! I became so involved in the game, I forgot the time . . . you've met Leftenant Smith-Deckers?"

"Of course, the other night at the dance."

The lieutenants studied each other.

"Nice to see you again, Armistead," Smith-Deckers observed without enthusiasm. "I gather you have an engagement with Miss Herriott this afternoon. Sorry about the delay. My fault, I assure you."

"Think nothing of it." Harry grinned wickedly. "I'm sure Lysistrata will make it up to me."

"Harry!" Lysistrata protested after leaving the lieutenant irritably pounding balls off the backboard. "He probably thinks I'll be kissing you over the teapot!"

"Won't you?" Intrigued by the notion, Harry feigned disappointment.

Her eyes widened in teasing reproof, then she affectionately squeezed his arm. "I'll tell your fortune instead. San-hla is teaching me to read tea leaves."

He laughed as he handed her into the *tum-tum*. "You're the last person I should have thought to be superstitious."

"I'm not. I just like explanations for things." She retied the hat ribbon just under her ear as he mounted the *tum-tum*. "Then again, perhaps nomads like Papa and me become superstitious. Maybe it's just the East, being near the jungle where Eden must once have been. Near the beginning of life. It's easy to see why the natives believe in spirits of nature. They're as close to creation as butterflies."

Squinting against the lowering sun, he lazed against the wicker seat. "Speaking of butterflies, you're about to become the social sort, it seems."

"You disapprove?"

"Good God, I'm not your maiden aunt, though I admit being spoiled to having you to myself."

"Am I good company, Harry?" she asked earnestly.
"The best."

For a moment, she gazed out at the glassy sheet of lake with its cricket-chirping reeds and drifting boats with bleached white sails. Then she kissed his cheek. Before he could react, she said briskly, "Where are we having tea?"

"Stratton's." Slapping the reins over the pony's back, he grinned happily. "They've a new pastry chef who's going to make you too fat to play tennis."

Stratton's was just off the greensward of fashionable, European-styled Fytche Square near the graceful Sulay Pagoda. On the restaurant's yellow-brocaded walls were gaslights illuminating watercolors by Constable and Turner. Hanging with the watercolors were Browning's overblown verses and Fitzgerald's doggereled *Rubaiyat*. Several seasons of mildew were temporarily dormant under the richly framed glass. Brass rails separated English oak tables with chairs of citron brocade.

Stratton's was crowded at tea hour, and the Chinese maître d', because of Harry's lateness, was about to forgo his reservation. With the quick smoothness of a squid, he saw them to their table and summoned a waiter. The confections the Chinese waiter displayed from a glass-domed cart looked delectable on lace-lined silver dishes. Harry was chagrined when Lysistrata selected only a small chocolate torte and declined his urging of a plump strawberry delicacy heaped with custard. The waiter transferred the pastries to Wedgwood porcelain, poured Javanese tea from a heavy silver teapot, and departed. Harry sadly shook his head. "Things will never be the same between us, Lysistrata."

She giggled. "Harry, if you're so determined to tow a tub about, you should call on Masjid's sister. She's enormous!"

"Masjid, eh?" Solemn now, he dug into his pastry. "Seen anything of his former boss-*wallah* of late?"

Guardedly, she glanced up from her plate. "Harley? No, why should I? Isn't he off to Singapore or somewhere?"

He grinned wryly. "Trust a woman to rebuff a question with three more. You've all the conversational instincts of Gatling guns."

She nibbled a morsel of chocolate. "Employing a Gatling gun on a ferret does seem excessive."

He winced. "You're right. It's none of my affair."

Smiling sweetly, she poured him another cup of tea. "Drink up, Leftenant Ferret. I want to play gypsy."

Before surrendering his cup, Harry insisted, "No fibs now, pretty gypsy, or I shall dub you a fake."

Ignoring him, Lysistrata studied the arrangement of tea leaves. After a long silence, he teased, "Well, isn't a beautiful, mysterious lady waiting in my future?"

"Several."

"Adventure?"

"Rather more than you might expect."

"Hurrah!" He leaned back in his chair. "Long life?"

She looked up as if startled; then with a worried frown brushed the leaves aside with a spoon. "This is silly. Destinies aren't written in tea leaves."

He became curious. "What did you see? Aren't I going to grow old and creaky?"

"It seems not," she said unwillingly, then with firmness: "It's rot, Harry."

He firmly caught her hand as she swiftly started to rise. "You wouldn't be so upset if you didn't believe it a little. You've been hanging about the bazaars too much. Listening to all that mumbo jumbo Ma Saw and San-hla go on about. It's time you came back to your own world" —he grimaced—"to playing tennis with flat-footed leftenants."

"Harry, you . . .'"

"Predict your own future."

"What?"

"It's nonsense, isn't it? So what does it matter?"

She tried to withdraw her hand. "San-hla says I'm not supposed to—"

"Read your own destiny? Why should that make a difference if the whole lot is just a game?"

Her chin lifted. "All right. Why not?" Lifting the cup, she looked steadily at its inner curve, rather than the dregs, and calmly observed, "I'm to have a dull husband and six children. I shall live to be ninety." She replaced the cup in its saucer. "Satisfied?"

He studied her. "If you are." His hand lifted to summon the waiter. "Shall we go shopping now?"

While Lysistrata admired the magnificent jades, jewels, and art objects in Fytche Square's stylish shops, she did not linger over them, and Harry presumed she was irritated by his insistence about the fortune-telling. Because she was not easily ruled, he was uncertain of her mood. "Still angry with me, gypsy?" he murmured as they left a brocade shop and headed across the green.

She looked startled. "Whatever for?"

"You don't seem to be enjoying yourself. I just wondered."

"I'm sorry. The shops are wonderful. Even," she teased in an effort to placate him, "very nearly English."

He smiled faintly. "But not as fascinating as the bazaars."

He received a mock-doleful look. "Harry, you sound as if you were jilted."

He grunted, feeling as if he were.

In effect, he was. In the fortnight that followed, if he wanted to see Lysistrata, he was forced to do so over the shoulders of the gentlemen who accompanied her to the races on the maidan, to cricket, to sculling at the Boat Club, to dinner at the Pegu Club. To have a chance of being included in the group, the most enterprising directed their morning rides toward the Chinese quarter and left their cards at the Herriott residence at dawn. Lysistrata's ''delightful shyness'' soon developed into tantalizing elusiveness. ''Artful'' might have been the better term—in Harry's understandably jaundiced opinion.

''Well, the *Rani* has returned from Singapore,'' John Herriot announced at dinner one evening.

Dr. Lighter tested his brandy. ''She's always in port for the spring regatta. Harley usually makes a pretty penny off it.''

Herriott shot a look at Lysistrata. The only sign of interest was a slight lift of her head.

Lighter took another sip. ''This brandy is very fine, John . . . the dinner as well.'' He nodded hastily to Lysistrata. ''But the brandy''—he sipped again and sighed—''is really something special.''

''Naturally,'' Lysistrata murmured. ''It's Richard Harley's brandy.''

Regatta Day shone fine, and small craft loaded with spectators bobbed in the harbor. Bright parasols of East and West bloomed from decks and docks. The chop from the boat traffic was raw, the heat beginning to build weight that would reduce the spectators to sweaty resignation. The yachtsmen stood patiently with the race officials and their guests on the committee boat dock as General Chilton droned the rules of the Royal Burma Yacht Club with the minutiae of yearly adjustments. Her blue eyes restless, Lady Mary stood beside her husband and Evelyn Chilton. When she saw what she was looking for, her gloved hand waved a summons.

A young English naval officer pried a path through the dock crowd, then stood back to let Lysistrata Herriott through. Evelyn Chilton's lips tightened. Lysistrata was dressed in a crisp, white linen suit with straw boater perched over her brow. The suit discreetly but admirably showed her figure to perfection; the boater complimented her flawless jaw.

From his vantage among the entrants, Richard Harley glimpsed a glint of burnished gold beneath the hat, a linen-molded length of leg that recalled Lysistrata Herriot half-clad with her hair an unruly cloud as she panted in anger over a hurled bucket. He remembered taut, bare thighs and stormy gray-green eyes and a powerful urge to take her on that slippery floor. The eyes were the same, only they met his with a kind of insolence as she glanced around the dock.

Lady Mary threw an amused look at Evelyn, who, determined not to be upstaged, strode away with her own entourage to another part of the dock. Mary waved again. A good-looking naval captain and a middle-aged civilian squirmed out of the crowd that closed behind Lysistrata. With male flotilla in tow, Lysistrata strolled up to Lady Mary. Her parasol dipped as she leaned to listen to the Englishwoman's whisper behind the white silk shield.

At length, Chilton finished his spiel. The dock observers crowded around the contenders to offer wagers and wishes of good luck. Lysistrata made the rounds with the Bartlys. One of the favored contenders was Bettenheim, who, Harley noticed, spent an inordinate amount of time hovering over her hand. Her escorts had begun to fix the German with severe looks when she drifted on to Harley.

"Mr. Harley." The hand kissed by Bettenheim and twenty others democratically extended to him.

He brushed it with his lips. "Miss Herriott."

Gracefully, she waved at her escorts. "May I present Captain Highman, Leftenant William Manley, and Mr. Benton Adams. Gentlemen, Mr. Richard Harley." The men bowed. Lysistrata smiled up at Highman. "Captain, will you all excuse me for a moment? I wish to place a wager with Mr. Harley, and I perceive he may give considerable argument about the terms."

"No gentleman could fail to be persuaded by you, Miss Herriott," Adams burbled, eyes dreamy with sheeplike lust.

"Everyone does not dote on me as you do, Mr. Adams." The umbrella delicately blocked his moist gaze. "Be good, boys, won't you, and secure me a place in the committee boat? It will be fearfully crowded and I should be sorry not to have you all by my side for the race." They scurried off.

She turned back to Harley, her head cocked a little inquisitively to one side, eyes challenging.

"You seem to be enjoying your success, Miss Herriott," he murmured, "though it is a trifle sickening."

She laughed, thinking he looked princely even in white Dacca cotton breeches and open-throated shirt. "Yes, I sometimes wonder if my sense of humor will endure the season. You had a successful voyage, I hope."

"As ever."

"Then I trust I shall not dent your complacency by wagering against you?"

"Not at all," he retorted lightly. "I rest upon my record."

"Good. If I win, I should like a sail on the *Rani*. I saw her leaving the harbor when I first arrived in Rangoon. She has a sentimental significance." Seeing a wary flicker in his eyes, she added, "My father would accompany me, of course."

"And if you lose?"

"A private dancing lesson, perhaps?" Narrowed, tawny green eyes belied the insinuation.

"Only a child plays with fire." His dark eyes held both lure and warning.

"I am not a child, Mr. Harley," she replied coolly.

"Perhaps not." His expression altered to lazy detachment. "Shall we see?"

Adams checked his fob watch for the third time as he shifted restlessly by the committee boat rail. "Do you not find the eternal zig zagging of those boats tedious, Miss Herriott? We have been waiting three-quarters of an hour, and they have not yet settled in their starting places."

The naval officers gave him tolerant looks laced with disgust. Lysistrata laughed. "I'm a Boston lass, sir. Few things delight me as much as racing yachts vying for the starting advantage. I fear you are spoiled to steam. Sail requires a deal of patience."

"I daresay," mumbled the merchant, furtively snatching at the rail as the boat rolled. After a time, the starter's first flare whistled in a rosy stroke across the sky, followed in exactly three minutes by the second. Thirty yachts heeled against the wind as sails snapped taut and keels sliced the harbor chop toward the first buoy on the harbor mouth's lee side; two more buoys marked the triangular course about which six circuits were to be made.

Amid the general hubbub and binocular-waving over the boat rail, Adams remained mute. Glassy-eyed and green-tinted, he clutched the rail as if it held him from the devil's jaws. Lysistrata had hoped the water's roughness would discourage his vacuous but tenacious determination to follow her about, but at length she took pity on him. "Dear Mr. Adams, you must be wretched. Let Leftenant Manley help you to a deck chair."

Lips clamped, Adams nodded. With a sigh, Manley supported him to one of the green-and-yellow canvas sling chairs scattered about the deck, then returned to Lysistrata and Captain Hillman with a significant shake of his head. Less than two minutes later, Adams furrowed through the crowd to the rail astern and emptied his belly into the brine. There, retching weakly, he hung for the rest of the race.

The *Rani* and Bettenheim's *Marlene* led the pack, neither gaining a significant advantage until rounding the last buoy for the run to the finish with three-quarters of a mile to go. The *Rani* was a half-length ahead, downwind of the *Marlene*. With the wind slightly ahead of abeam, Harley had nicely placed himself with no fear of being caught in the German's wind shadow. Because both boats were well matched, Bettenheim could do little to come abreast. With one hundred yards to go to the imaginary line between a clanging bell buoy and the committee boat, the German began to head downwind, picking up speed on a collision course. *"Marlene!"* Harley hailed through a bullhorn. "Head off!"

"Make way!" Bettenheim bellowed back, his brawny, blazered torso hunched over his starboard side.

"The hell you say! Point up and follow me in!" Harley snapped.

"New rules," truculently roared Bettenheim. "Windward boat . . . right-of-way! Fall off!" Appearing intent to ram, *Marlene* bore down on the *Rani*.

The German's bowsprit was dancing over her rival's gunnels when Harley finally gave way, deciding risk of damage to the *Rani* was pointless when a protest would affirm his win; nonetheless, his cold anger mounted, for the German continued to push him downwind until *Marlene* was just inside the committee boat; the *Rani* on a collision course, with pale faces gaping at her knifing bow. Harley did the only thing possible: he swerved outside the anchored committee boat and allowed *Marlene* to cross the line alone. By the time he came about and correctly crossed the finish line, two other boats had preceded him. *Rani* came in fourth. Eyes narrowed as he gazed sternward, he noted with grim satisfaction that the protest flag was up on the committee boat in reply to his own.

Two hours later, under the stuccoed porticoes of the Yacht Club, Harley inwardly seethed as the race steward confirmed the judgment. "Sorry, old chap, but the new rules clearly state the windward boat has the right-of-way." The steward wanted to add that for Bettenheim to take advantage of the rule when so obviously beaten was a damn poor show, but racial contempt and respect for rules kept him silent.

Lysistrata heard the race results with a curious feeling of defeat. She had named a wager she felt she could not lose, whatever the results, yet *had* lost . . . something she could not name. An open confrontation with Harley, perhaps. Or perhaps a childish illusion of perfect felicity that *Rani* suggested.

With stubby husband in tow, Evelyn Chilton arrived at the Regatta Ball at the Edward Hotel that night smashingly girded to do battle with rumors of a pretender to her throne. Clad in scarlet satin by Worth and a fortune in rubies, emeralds, and diamonds, she had crowned the whole with a diamond-and-pearl-mounted aigrette in her jet hair.

"I do declare, Evie," Lady Mary chuckled as Evelyn arrived at her chair, "you practically clank. Who's the unfortunate?"

"Does it matter? After tonight, no one will remember her." Evelyn's amethyst eyes watched the toffee marble columned entrance of the ballroom with a patient, feline stare.

"Poor little bird," Lady Mary murmured. "Fresh out of her cage into the jaws of an overfed housecat."

Evelyn's head whipped around. "I beg your pardon?"

"Nothing, Evie," Lady Mary replied mildly. "Only that the victim has arrived."

The victim was in a Doucet satin de crème that showed off a lustrous skin and blaze of hair misted in pearls. She wore no other jewelry. Evelyn had enjoyed audible admiration, and the vacuum of silence that greeted Lysistrata as she and her father crossed the shining floor gave her savage pleasure—until she realized the crowd was not apathetic, but stunned. She could have bedecked herself with diamonds from head to foot, but neither her looks nor jewels were a novelty to Rangoon. Lysistrata could have been less attractive and still achieved a success. As it was, the simplicity of her gown set off a beauty that was the breath of dreams. She was not just a success but a sensation. And Evelyn suspected she had been used as a foil. Her taste for magnificent array was well known, and the contrast was stunning.

"Those pearl studs seem familiar," she stated coldly into space.

"Yes," Lady Mary mused, "my hair was a credit to them in my Calcutta days." She patted Evelyn's hand. "But time takes toll of us all."

The hand snatched away. "I haven't let go the clapper yet, Mary," la Chilton breathed sweetly, "and you'll kiss the devil before I do."

"Pride goeth . . . and so forth, Evie. Your landing should spread your backside from here to Tibet," Lady Mary retorted ironically; then her eyes turned glacial. "For the moment, you'd best remember your manners or I'll grease that clapper for you."

Lord Anthony himself requested Lysistrata for the first dance. She dipped a graceful curtsy. "If you don't mind, sir, I should like to open the ball with my father. This is a special night for me."

Bartly smiled. "So it should be, my dear. You look lovely." He bowed to Herriott. "I envy you, doctor. I have not had the privilege of dancing with my own daughter in some years.''

Herriott laughed. ''Then, sir, we share a complaint.''

Aimlessly strolling about the periphery of the ball floor, Harry Armistead glanced at the swirling dancers, then at the few women who remained on their gilt chairs in gappy parade ranks against the walls. As usual, turbaned, white-jacketed panjandrums waved huge *punkahs* to create an illusion of fresh air. His ears were assaulted by music like a single note which beat against the palpable, ponderous heat of what must be one of the last nights before the monsoons.

Harry did not much like the tropics. The flies and mosquitoes bit savagely and on days when the wind blew out to sea, the land's stench seeped into the nostrils like a harlot's foul perfume. Frequenting the bordellos guaranteed syphilis, yet the few eligible women of his own kind . . . His gaze quickly dodged that of a particularly intent, hatchet-faced miss and wistfully returned to the distant, flawless profile of Lysistrata Herriott. Most colonies offered dreary marriage prospects, and Australia—with the majority of its area a barren outback—left him cold. Even America had its hostile Indians. Eyes still on Lysistrata, he sighed and contemplated a cigar.

''You're looking dismal, Leftenant,'' a familiar voice observed at his elbow. ''I take it the lady's card is filled.''

Harry smiled crookedly at Richard Harley. ''Oh, Lysistrata's a good egg. She wrote me in for a polka and the last quadrille. If she hadn't, I might as well have gone home. There's no getting near her now that she's 'rani' of Rangoon.''

''Is that what they're calling her?''

Harry gave a slight laugh. ''No, it's what I call her. Anything to give her a tickle. She thinks all the fuss is silly, but I suspect she likes it. Can't blame her. After all,'' he muttered as if to himself, ''she's got a right to marry as well as she can.''

''Any serious contenders?''

Harry made a long face. ''Adams proposes daily at teatime. Hillman gives it a shot a week. Behind them, a long line's forming—mostly for a flirt, of course.'' His eyes narrowed. ''I don't know what Bettenheim's after. He's formal as hell—flowers, all the pretty words— but . . .'' Harry shoved his hands in his pockets. ''He doesn't strike me as the sort to pay serious court to a penniless woman . . . I say!'' He turned on Harley. ''What do you mean, 'contender'? I'm not after her, you know.''

''Just a careless choice of phrase, Leftenant,'' rejoined Harley mildly. He reviewed the occupants of the gilt chairs. ''Why should you want her? Rangoon has so many ladies of means more than eager to be your life's companion.'' His smile grew a trifle wolfish. ''With no contenders for their attentions other than lapdogs.''

Harry fixed him with jaundiced eye. ''Ply your bow and arrows elsewhere, Cupid. You're aiming at the wrong posterior.'' His head cocked. ''You show a remarkable interest in the lady. Careful you don't get pricked with one of your own arrows.''

''Particularly if it's poison tipped,'' murmured Harley.

Harry shot a suspicious look at Harley's closed face, then remembered the Tamil incident that demonstrated some men's hunger to see another—their superior in many ways—humiliated. ''Yes,'' he said slowly, ''I suppose . . .'' Then he broke off when the lady-in-question and her dancing partner walked toward them.

''Gentlemen, may I present Mr. John Forbes. Mr. Forbes, I'd like you to meet Leftenant Harry Armistead and Mr. Richard Harley. Leftenant Armistead is a cricket enthusiast like yourself, Mr. Forbes. Perhaps the two of you would like to become acquainted while I settle the terms of a race wager with Mr. Harley.'' When Forbes and Harry made no sign of moving, she gave them a brilliant smile, linked her arm with Harley's, and, to the ballroom crowd's keen interest, led him away toward the terrace.

''Miss Herriott,'' Harley said curtly as they walked into the palm-broken moonlight, ''I despair of your learning discretion.''

She glanced up from the city's shimmering carpet of lights beyond the balustrade, then her lips curved wickedly. ''So you *can* be angry. I'd begun to wonder whether you were quite human.''

''Is that why you brought me out here for a solitary tête-à-tête, to see if I'm human?'' His voice became husky and a trifle menacing. ''I should think you would know better.''

Lysistrata sidled away. To cover unease, she said brightly, ''We're hardly alone.'' Her ostrich fan flicked toward several couples strolling about the potted palms and calendulas. ''And as for that kiss you forced on me in the maze, why pretend it meant anything to you?'' She longed to add, ''Or to me? '' but was uncomfortably aware he knew better. Just now, after months of separation, his nearness was particularly disturbing. That sleek head and black cutaway suggested less civilization than the ease with which he could discard it. Under their curved lashes, his eyes were darker than the night; and not a star, not a light, averted her sense of plummeting into dangerous mystery. Yet she could not have looked away from those shadowed eyes, that compelling mouth that had claimed hers as if he had waited centuries for her. But he had not waited, logic sharply reminded. He had not even wanted. She forced a casual shrug. ''If you like, we can demurely argue in front of the punchbowls. I simply thought this to be the best place to settle our wager. We should be constantly interrupted in the ball-room."

"Isn't this a rather blatant way to remind me you're not begging for dances now?" he said cruelly.

She did not move, did not speak. Finally, he heard her low, choked voice. "You're right. I want my pride back. I want it more than all the dances in the world. You trampled it so you and Evelyn Chilton could have a moment's . . ." Stiffly, she turned away. "You're absolved of your wager." Then whispered as she started toward the ballroom's lighted door, "The *Rani* isn't what she once was to me, anyway."

Harley thought of letting her go. Her pain now was nothing compared to what it might be if he did not. Then he touched her shoulder without knowing why, almost out of an impulse—though he rarely allowed himself the luxury, and never in situations like this. "Lysistrata, I keep my wagers and I don't indulge in cheap amusements. I was pointlessly rude before; I apologize." Then he added softly, "Does that satisfy you?"

She stood silently, then turned slowly, wistfully. "I think I shall always be sorry we did not dance together."

"Why should that matter when so many men are fighting for the chance?"

"Perhaps because they remind me of Boston . . . and you do not," she replied simply.

"That's not a good enough reason, is it?"

"No," she murmured, and returned to the ballroom.

As he gave Ma Saw his hat the evening after the ball, Dr. Herriott looked askance at the overflowing salver of calling cards. "My daughter has had a busy day, I see."

She chuckled. "Missy had the gentlemen recite her translations of Burmese plays, then take a dancing lesson with San-hla, which she says will help them not to behave like walking sticks. She even tucked an orchid behind Mr. Bettenheim's ear.''

Herriott sighed. "How did he take it?"

"Like a walking stick." She hung up the hat. "Missy made eyes while he turned red, so he was not sure if she flirted or made a fool of him. Missy is getting rather clever that way."

"I wonder," Missy's father replied skeptically.

Several days of putting prim, paunchy merchants, stiff bureaucrats, ardent sailors, and glory-and-guts soldiers through dramatic and terpsichorean paces began to bore Lysistrata. Aside from seeking relief from the flowery monotony of their wooing, she had hoped a few of them might enjoy Burmese arts. Less kindly, as her father suspected, she diverted herself by seeing how foolish they were prepared to be to gain favor with a woman they had once ignored.

Harry flatly refused to take part. "I'm an Englishman, not a windblown willow." Lysistrata was unsurprised; he knew her ironic bent too well to play the fool.

"Why don't you show them the door?" he muttered as they watched two grinning Australian ensigns weave and bob like boxing gibbons about San-hla's delicate form. "You're not at your best as ringmistress."

She gave him a sidelong look. "Are you criticizing me, Harry?"

"I am."

He heard a relieved sigh. "How refreshing. I knew I liked you for some reason." She took his arm. "Unfortunately, I must marry one of them."

"One of *them?*"

"New ships arrive every day."

Lysistrata was not at home to callers the next day. The gentlemen were sent on goose chases. Miss Herriott had

gone shopping. To view Shwe Dagon. To gig crocodiles.
To men newly encountering Miss Herriott's independent
and presumably glamorous habits, San-hla's wildest im-
provisations were accepted whole. Lysistrata narrowly
missed being run over as the Australian ensigns' carriage
raced through the neighboring Burmese quarter en route
to the harbor. Their lady fair had supposedly taken a
steamer upriver to view tigers. Presuming her to be
somebody's maid loaded with market baskets, they did
not give her a second glance. Calmly doffing the leghorn
hat, she fanned away the sandy street dust in the ensigns'
wake.

Her presumption of safety was premature. A few steps
later, she was forced to duck a cascade of water dashed
from a high, palmetto doorway. A dripping Burman,
laughing and yelling protests, darted from the door onto
the platformed porch, where he was pursued by a gnomish old woman who gleefully doused him again as he
slithered down the ladder. Lysistrata giggled, dancing
through alarmed pigs who squealed underfoot as they
streamed from under the old woman's house.

Eager to see the outcome of the comic battle, Lysistrata, with her baskets batting against each other, ran after the combatants. On Merchant Street, the entire
neighborhood was having a water fight. Adults and children merrily pelted each other, slipped, slid, and rolled
through the mud. Even dogs did not escape; they ran
drop-tailed and barking amid scrambling legs and livestock. Drenched, spitting cats had taken to the rooftops to
sulk like small gargoyles. Laughing as she had not in
years, Lysistrata, a basket held over her head, dodged
through the melee. Mud-spattered, out of breath, she
shortly arrived on her kitchen doorstep. She had no more
than lowered the makeshift umbrella when the door
banged open and a dishpan of water dashed in her face.
Ma Saw and San-hla shrieked with laughter as she sput-

tered, "What in blazes is going on? Has everyone lost his mind?"

"When monsoon season is about to begin, we have *Thingyan*, our water festival to celebrate the New Year," Ma Saw explained with a wide grin. "The rain is Buddha's blessing and promise of good fortune."

Another panload cascaded over Lysistrata's head. "Buddha's blessing on you, Missy!" crowed San-hla.

Lysistrata swatted the culprits with the ruined hat, then swept them close in a sodden hug. She had come halfway around the world to find sweet acceptance. Boston could go hang.

The next morning, a Chinese brought a message. The *Rani* was to make a day-long sail in the Gulf of Martaban on Friday. Dr. Herriott and his daughter were invited to join her.

After brief dockside exchanges, Harley and Lysistrata said little to each other after the *Rani* entered the Rangoon River. Each realized the short sail was a formal farewell, a decent ending to an impossible beginning. Under the hypnotic monotony of the river and the thrum of the *Rani*'s auxiliary steam engine, even Dr. Herriott, intermittently dozing in the steamy heat, sat silently with feet propped as he blinked at passing scrub jungle. In the Gulf of Martaban, things livened. Harley handed the Herriotts cork vests as the auxiliary shut down and sails were hoisted with a rattle of halyards against the masts. "Aren't you wearing one, Captain Harley?" Lysistrata inquired impudently.

"I lead a charmed life, Miss Herriott," was the mild reply, "but if I didn't, I wouldn't tie those vest straps in bows."

The day was bright, breeze brisk, and swell moderate; but on a vessel the *Rani*'s size, the last two seemed considerably exaggerated to the Herriotts, who had little experience with sailing other than observation and their voyage to Rangoon. The bow thwacked the troughs and leaped the caps while the *Rani* heeled sharply, port gunnels nearly awash. Lysistrata soon lost her insouciance and remaining romantic nostalgia about the *Rani* as she clung to a cabin roof gunnel. Her father valiantly tried to make himself useful to the crew at first, then meekly subsided to a position similar to his daughter's. They were just as well relegated to ballast. Harley's crew was so accustomed to his command that a ghost seemed to direct the ship. At length, all feeling left her hands and went to her stomach. Miserably, she regretted her cavalier dismissal of Adams to the committee boat stern during the regatta.

"Miss Herriott." A hard hand gripped her arm. "Are you feeling unwell?"

Mute with misery, she nodded.

Dr. Herriott's sickly voice came over a crash of spray, "She looks like the devil. Perhaps she should go below . . ."

"She's better off here," Harley replied. "The lack of horizon below exaggerates the sensation of motion."

Minutes later, Harley held her head over the rail. Never had she been so happy to see dirt as when land showed off the port bow.

But as the longboat lowered over the side, Dr. Herriott refused to accompany her and Harley ashore. "If you think I'm climbing into that bouncing cockleshell, sir, you're mistaken. Whatever the consequences, I'm going below for a whiskey."

"Then I'll stay with you, Papa," Lysistrata asserted instantly.

"Don't be a ninny. You need a brisk walk on solid land, and as for a chaperon, you're not idiots." He lurched toward the cabin. "Off with you. I want out of this infernal sun."

His defection exasperated Lysistrata and Harley; each for different reasons did not want to be alone with the other. After the dinghy touched the narrow, jungle-backed beach, however, Harley sent the Madagascar oarsman back to the *Rani*. At Lysistrata's startled look, he said ironically, "No man has any love for chaperons, particularly useless ones. If I did molest you, he wouldn't stop me; if I didn't, no one would take his word for it. He'll be back for us in a couple of hours."

Not altogether reassured, Lysistrata watched the dinghy dwindle toward the *Rani,* which rode at anchor in the jade gulf beyond a shielding spit of jungle. Behind her came a low laugh. "If your father isn't worried, why should you be?"

She turned, eyes mischievous. "He doesn't know you as well as I do, but I wouldn't put it past him to provide me with a bit of practice."

"Practice?"

"At dealing with a lone man. He suspects managing strings of them in public is giving me a false sense of confidence."

"Oh, I see." His white teeth gleamed. "Is your father always so sensible?"

"Oh, no. Once, he lost his temper and shot a married man who flirted with Mama." She scuffed carelessly at the powdery white sand. "He's an expert with pistol and saber, you know. He survived Antietam."

"And you."

She laughed. "Never fear. After today, each of us can go his merry way."

"Then let's not spoil today with hints about whose gore is going to soak the sand if he doesn't behave." And that, Harley realized, might be more of a trial than Lysistrata imagined. He had long recognized he shared a predilection of some Eastern males for blond women, and Lysistrata's hair glinted almost white in the sun.

Open-throated yellow chambray was wind-molded to her lithe, high-breasted body, and he knew more than she how easily he might persuade that body to yield to his. But he must not think of it and neither must Lysistrata. He kicked off his boots, caught them up, and held out a hand. "Come, let's walk."

"That seems chaste enough." She doffed her own sandals and took his hand, but with a certain carefulness.

She's like a butterfly, he thought as they wandered barefoot through the tide run, too fragile to dare more than a brush of contact. "How is your seasickness now?" he asked, thinking small talk might put her at ease.

"Fading. Particularly when I don't look at the water." Perplexed, she frowned. "How odd. I came all the way from Boston without a trace of seasickness."

"It's unpredictable. Certain foods seem to have something to do with it, but Admiral Horatio Nelson was nauseated every day of his naval career."

"I think that rather pleases you." She affected a sonorous tone. "A Britisher on whose realm the sun never sets, sick in his own self-seeking scuppers."

"Why do you say that?" His grip tightened and she winced, regretting the slip. She was not supposed to have overheard his remark to Wa Sing, the Chinese.

"How couldn't anyone whose nation has been reduced to a colony like them?" she countered. If he were sufficiently provoked, she might learn something of what lay behind his ironclad reserve. "Aren't they thieves, after all?"

"You showed no reluctance to deck yourself in the products of their efforts at the Regatta Ball," he observed dryly. "Those pearls in your hair were part of the Jansi estate. It was 'appropriated' due to lack of a direct male heir. Perhaps next time you borrow Lady Mary's jewelry, you should express your views. Her reaction should be scintillating.''

Neatly parried, she conceded. Harley was used to dealing with more wily adversaries than her.

''You seem thoughtful,'' he remarked ironically. ''Or are you merely offended?''

''Perhaps I'm phrasing my remarks to Lady Mary,'' she retorted lightly, ''or my apologies to India. You are Indian? Perhaps I should direct them to you.''

''I'm a Rajput. Sardines in a tin may look much the same to one who opens them, but to sardines the differences are less vague. That inclination to niggle sometimes leads to bloodshed, but it does reduce overcrowding.''

''To the benefit of the opener or the openees?''

He stopped and studied her thoughtfully. ''It's just possible I've overestimated your naïveté, Miss Herriott.''

''Is that a compliment or a prelude to something else?'' she teased.

''Possibly both; I haven't decided yet—Shall we eat? I'm starved.'' Without waiting for an answer, he pulled her after him to a palmetto grove up the beach where a few wizened fruit trees persisted in the dry soil among sawtooth spears of palm. He picked pomegranates and mangoes, and hacked down spiny jackfruit with a boot knife, then, monkey-agile, ascended a bowed palm to shake down coconuts. While she collected the booty, he dug up thick, hand-size roots among papery debris at the palm base.

She prodded one. ''The regional truffle?''

''Arrowroot. Pure starch, for queasiness.'' He raked through the pile of coconuts and fruits, then tossed several items into her lap. ''Eat those, too.''

''I haven't the capacity of an elephant,'' she complained halfheartedly, then squinted at an unfamiliar green pod. "For all I know, this could be a convenient way to eliminate a pest."

His teeth glinted unpleasantly. "If I wanted to do that, I'd have let you pick your own fruit." He nodded toward the palmetto thicket. "Several pretty plants in there are poisonous."

Speculatively, she began to peel a mango. "But you do think I'm troublesome, don't you?"

"Yes." Expertly, he cracked a coconut and caught the milk in the larger half.

"Because you have what is crudely termed a touch of the tar brush." Expression bland, she nibbled mango. "So you avoid white women because they're bad for business."

"I avoid *single* women, but otherwise you're crudely correct." Lips curving mirthlessly, he tossed her a chunk of coconut. "Front doors may not always be open to me; back doors and bedrooms are less guarded."

"Why only married women?"

"They have as much to lose as I do." He bit into a pomegranate. "That guarantees discretion."

"Which I lack," she rejoined. "On the other hand, I shouldn't want a cold-blooded lover."

"No?" His gaze lazed over her. "Tell me what cold thoughts I am thinking now, Lysistrata."

She stiffened; uncertain, wary.

"You needn't be afraid. Dr. Herriott entrusted your honor to me for today, but tomorrow . . . you must decide what you want of me and what you are willing to pay for it." He tipped her chin up. "I have no use for a child, Lysistrata, and I will not treat you like one. I will not turn away from other women for you. Whatever we take from each other must one day be relinquished; then we must go our separate ways. Until that time, we will not be seen together and will meet only on my terms."

Her eyes brightened with a flicker of anger. "I think

this exaggerated need for secrecy allows you to manipulate your lovers. It's convenient, isn't it?''

He sighed. ''How can anyone who lived through your civil war be so blind? Nearly a decade has passed since your slaves were freed. Have you seen them in your government, other than a few pathetic puppets? Seen them in your universities, your places of religion, your marriage beds?''

''It's not the same thing. You were never a slave. Your father was a titled officer, your mother of royal blood. Dr. Lighter says you went to an English military school in Bombay. You are accepted in British society, and judging from your concern over what I am supposed to have overheard at Lord Anthony's, included in their councils.'' Gray-green eyes glinted. ''You admit yourself, you are not denied their beds, so one might be forgiven for thinking you have little to complain about.'' She began to eat the arrowroot.

''That's all true as far as it goes and it goes as far as my usefulness to the English''—he smiled faintly—''in their councils and in their beds. That is a slavery of sorts.''

Lysistrata's appetite faded, particularly for flavorless arrowroot. Her eyes turned pensive. ''Then we *are* worlds apart, for I must marry. I cannot settle for less. I owe responsibility to Papa, both for his welfare and his self-respect. I have been selfish for a good many years, too much a coward to face myself, much less the world. I will not hide again.''

''Nor should you,'' he said softly, fingers brushing the shining coils of her hair. ''Here we will say good-bye, but first . . .'' He tugged loose ivory combs until a torrent of pale silk spilled about her shoulders. For a long moment, he silently gazed at her, then rose and took her hand. ''Come, at last we have a ballroom to ourselves.''

For a man who did not dance, Lysistrata thought as he skimmed her across the packed sand, Harley waltzed as deftly as a hawk flew. Then surf rushing across their bare feet made them laugh like children. She taught him *Camptown Ladies,* and spinning like a single dervish under the sun, they stamped and splashed with each exuberant "do, dah." With a mischievous grin, he steered her into the breakers until soaked skirts tangled in her legs. Yelling protests, she shoved at his chest, only to lose her footing in the breaker wash. As he hauled her up, she threw a leg behind his knees, shoved again, then tumbled atop him as he went down. He dragged her to shore, where they flopped down laughing, sprawled in the tide.

Rolling onto her side, Lysistrata looked down at her unlikely playmate. His black hair was stuck to his head, and under seawater-spiked lashes, the elusive, primeval tint of his eyes caught the sun's fire. In moments, she saw those eyes lose their laughter, grow intent. In them now was the naked lure of desire, danger. Spray glistened on smooth olive skin where, half-bared by the open cambric shirt, his chest quickly rose and fell, nipples outlined by soaked cloth.

Suddenly, her eyes widened as she remembered the condition of her own clothes. When her hands flew to cover herself, he caught them and she stiffened as he pulled her down to him. "Ah, the linnet born within the cage," he whispered, "that never knew the summer woods . . ."

His lips, at first cold-wet, became warm and searching. Lysistrata felt a moment of fright, then a tightening knot of need as he gently probed her mouth. The shadow of a hawk seemed to veer across her mind, yet she felt it meant her no harm, only to guide her to a high, tranquil place she had been long seeking. All were one: the hawk, the *Rani,* Harley, who without words was telling her she should once fly unfettered, that her understanding of herself as a woman should go beyond stale duty, that she should have one soaring moment of freedom. Richard

Harley held the key to her restless, yearning spirit. Why, she did not know, only that if he made love to her, she could never return to a cage.

Somehow, her hands no longer strained between them, but tangled in his sand-rough hair, her breasts soft against his hard chest. His lips brushed against her throat, down the wet cotton stretched taut against the roused peaks of her nipples. Demandingly, his body covered her on the wet sand, and the gathering heat of his mouth on hers dissolved her will. The sensitive, seductive mouth began to explore the wet, transparent skin of chambray, sweetly torturing until the ache of her breasts, the burning between her thighs made her arch against him. Reveling in the catch of his breath, the hardness at his groin, she felt a dawning wonder that his need was as intense as her own. Suddenly, fiercely, she wanted nothing between them, not their sodden garments, not suspicion, not even flesh. Let all barriers end here. Let him . . .

Dimly, she felt a sharp tug at her scalp, heard his voice, harsh and taut. "Damnation, you'd make a monk forget his vows . . ." Abruptly he pulled away and got to his feet. "It's time to go, Lysistrata. The sun's low."

Startled as if water had been dashed in her face, she sat up thinking that because the tropic sun set quickly, the dinghy must have put out from the *Rani*. Then she saw the sun would linger yet two hours. And she understood. Harley saw her cage as a Pandora's box.

"It cannot be, linnet," he murmured. "I'm sorry. I never meant to touch you. It's a fault of mine, stealing things . . . moments, kisses"—he smiled crookedly—"even whole women from time to time."

She looked up at him with sad irony. "But you always give them back, of course."

His eyes became enigmatic, his voice a caress. "Of course." He gently pulled her up. "Besides, I'm not the only pirate in these waters. They don't hang about off Rangoon by the day, but the night is theirs.''

Feeling close to tears, she laughed unevenly. "If you were as wicked as some suggest, *this* night might have been yours. You're less hypocrite than I.''

"A hypocrite would have denied what she felt.'' He caught her head hard between his hands, and for one moment she thought he would not let her go. Then his hands dropped as if weighted. "In time you will learn that art, but I will not be the one to teach you. Good-bye, Lysistrata Herriott.''

CHAPTER 5

The *Nats'* Reign

Imp that dances, imp that flits . . .
Maddest! Whirl with imp o' the pits
GEORGE MEREDITH

The next morning, the western monsoon began its sweep of Burma. Lysistrata awoke to torrential rain that flooded the house gutters before it spilled in silver-green sheets to the parched garden. She sighed. Now, she would have to wait until the rain let up in order to do shopping put off the day before. And shopping was the last thing on her mind. For most of the night, her thoughts had reluctantly, relentlessly followed Richard Harley to one conclusion. If he did not care a little, he would not have said good-bye; and if tempted to seduce her as strongly as female instinct predicted, he would return. Years later, she was to remember of her first monsoon that she was to make two major errors before even getting out of bed: one was thinking the rains would stop; the other, that Harley would choose to see her again.

The rain descended as if Noah had been recalled to rebuild the ark. The garden flooded within inches of the house's floorboards, and a raised plank walkway had to be strung from verandah to gate. Aside from relieving a

124

fire hazard, the reason for the covered passageway from the house to the kitchen and stable became obvious. If one cared to eat, one did not drown the cook. One also minced about the countless puddles on the floor until the heat-dried roof swelled sufficiently to cease dripping. Bedding and clothes were perpetually damp. Insects and lizards invaded the house, not in twos or their usual congregations, but hordes that floated, scuttled, and expired on every available surface, most particularly food.

Outside, sullen birds sat silent. Bedraggled junks slopped in the harbor, pedestrians waded to the waist in low-lying streets, the Gymkhana Club cricket field and the army parade ground turned to lakes. Only pigs and frogs oozed happily through the mud, yet Lysistrata's gentlemen callers, swathed in rain gear, indomitably braved the muck and, for her sake, called it trifling—to some advantage, for she was not heartless enough to have Ma Saw turn the doughty knights back into the pounding rain. Richard Harley was not one of them.

As sodden weeks came and went, the Herriott house became a prison for Lysistrata. Masjid and the Burmese were used to the seemingly endless monsoons, but Lysistrata had become too fond of newfound freedom to be confined to the house. Also, realization that Harley really had no intention of seeing her again hurt far more than she would admit. He had probably holed up in his shipping offices with his clerks—the chatter of abacus and scrape of the pen to blot out the incessant rain. He appeared to balance emotion as meticulously as a tally book; yet, while she would not let herself hope love existed between them, desire there was, and he felt it too. Her armor, impervious to Rangoon's most attractive men, had burned away like paper with Harley. For a dingy, once-singed moth, she had thrown herself at him as if he had some mysterious incandescence she would not live without . . . or live with, if one believed his blunt warnings about Eurasian relations. He *was* capable of lying, she learned from Masjid, whose innocent answers to questions about the Hindu religion revealed that it in no way prevented males from dancing publicly or otherwise. Harley's "otherwise" with Evelyn still grated, even more because she knew instinctively he was still seeing the woman. With the blandishments of suitors and flirts at daily tea a mounting ordeal, once again she began to depend on Harry Armistead's company.

A month after the advent of the monsoons, the tedium was sharply, terribly broken. Adams barged into tea without removing his dripping hat and slicker. "Cholera's in the city!" he blurted, then stammered as he saw Bettenheim's bludgeon face. "It may not enter the cantonment, but . . . it's spreading in the harbor area. Lysistrata—Miss Herriott, may I offer you and your father the shelter of my home? It's high in the hills, and everyone says that's the safest—"

Bettenheim cut him off. "That's rot. Where did you hear about cholera, anyway?"

"The docks," Adams answered nervously. "Why aren't the hills safe?"

Bettenheim ignored him. "If you'll excuse me, Miss Herriott, I have to get to my godowns. Cholera shows up every year with the monsoons. Usually it's not too serious, but sometimes riots break out in an epidemic. At any rate, the jigs will use any excuse for thievery." He paused, then added, "I advise you to stay put until I can send over food and whatever you need."

"You're very kind, Mr. Bettenheim," Lysistrata said, rising from the settee, "and you as well, Mr. Adams, but I cannot do as either of you suggest. Additional nurses will be needed at the hospital." She rang for Masjid.

Bettenheim caught her wrist. "You're not going anywhere. You're safest here unless"—he shot a forbidding look toward Adams—"this idiot has brought it in off the streets."

Adams looked down at his slicker as if it had suddenly come alive with deadly organisms. His head jerked up; his hat jacked up and down in his hand. "Pardon me, Miss Herriott, I've got to get home!" He fled.

"Kindly release Miss Herriott, Mr. Bettenheim," said Harry quietly. He moved from the corner where he had been silently suffering through Bettenheim's tales of his feats in pioneering Burma.

Bettenheim turned, fists bunching, then spotted Masjid's massive form filling the doorway. "No offense meant, Miss Herriott," he said smoothly. "I'm afraid I was too concerned about you to think properly."

"No offense taken, Mr. Bettenheim," she replied lightly. "Masjid will show you to your carriage."

"Are you serious about going to the hospital?" Harry asked when Bettenheim had left.

"Oh, Harry, don't *you* start."

"From what I hear, cholera's a nasty business. You're asking for it in a hospital."

"Where are you planning to go?" she dodged.

"My club, I suppose. It's as good as anywhere else . . . *except* the hospital."

"My father's there, Harry," she gently reminded him.

"And he'd be happier with you here."

"Undoubtedly," was the quiet reply, "but he wouldn't like me as much and neither would I."

"Orderly, fetch me another pan, dammit!" Lighter snapped over his shoulder. "This one's already full." A clean pan presented itself at his elbow. He snatched it and bent over the retching male patient again. "Where the hell's Herriott anyway? This place is filling as fast as the blasted pans."

"Still in surgery, I believe, doctor," answered a calm voice.

He whirled. "Lysistrata! What the—"

"Hell am I doing here," she supplied evenly, "particularly when you doughtily forbade me to set foot within Queen Anne's hallowed halls?" She gave the dingy surroundings a jaundiced look. "This place is grim enough to hold *your* martyr's bones, all right." She relieved him of the pan. "I'll take this. You've more important things to do"—she arched an ironic brow—"haven't you?"

He glowered, then enunciated succinctly, "The first time you spill puke on my shoes, out you go, you presumptuous bitch."

Cholera, or *kala na* as the natives called it, was a great deal grimmer than the gray, dungeon-like stone walls of Queen Anne's hospital, and Lighter's single order was less simple to obey than it sounded. The beds filled, then the pans filled with relentless vomitus and defecation until the patients dehydrated, suffered either heart or kidney failure in half the cases, and died. It was a simple process of devastation. Replacement of fluids was the only treatment, but attempts to get sufficient water down a choking, convulsing patient were rarely successful. Children succumbed within a matter of hours. To make matters worse, a deadly strain of Chinese cholera threaded through the milder cholera that usually visited the Asian subcontinent. As weeks wore on, the epidemic showed no signs of lifting. People collapsed in the streets, but as no one wanted to touch them, they lay where they fell until a relative, friend, or British-organized *gurkha* troops removed them. Everywhere was the din of Burmese who wandered the streets and climbed to their high porches to whack with bamboo sticks at pots; play trumpets, gongs, clappers, and drums as they shrieked to drive away the *nat sohs*, the evil spirits.

Lysistrata thinned until her cheekbones jutted and

dresses hung slack, but she worked steadily without complaint and little recompense other than Lighter's grudging approval. Her quiet confidence reassured the patients, and her father noted with relief she seemed content. If she had been prickly before budding into a belle, she had been more so after weeks of being cooped up with gushing swains. Now, she seemed to have burned out some hidden frustration and regret.

As a result of the epidemic, Richard Harley found the Green Monkey Club deserted. Sir Anthony Bartly had arranged to meet him in the club room, but he saw only two men stalwart enough to be seated at the tables as if death were not stealing through the outside streets. More accurately, one was seated facing the street windows as he reviewed a newspaper; the other was folded over on a snowy linen tablecloth as if he had drunk his luncheon. Harley turned to summon the club maître d' when he recognized the unconscious one as Harry Armistead. Swiftly, he went to the table and tugged Harry's head up. A taffy pool seeped about the crystal base of a vase of roses. Without waiting for the commissioner, Harley heaved the young Englishman over his shoulder and headed for the door.

"Lysistrata."

At the tired, familiar voice, Lysistrata whirled to see Harley with the slack Armistead in the stone-arched aisle between the hospital beds. "Harry! Oh Lord, not Harry!"

Harley felt an unexpected surge of jealousy at her anxiety. He was also irritable in his rain-soaked clothes. "Where can I unload him?" he said briefly.

"Over here." She quickly led the way to a bed in a corner of the ward. Over the barren room hung cholera's pall of silence, broken only by the muffled grieving of huddled figures at the bedsides of dying loved ones. Here and there came an iron bed's skeletal rattle as its ruined occupant shook grotesquely in a parched seizure. As if combating the fearfulness, Lysistrata became matter-of-fact. "If you had come twenty minutes ago, we would have had to make a place on the floor." She pulled down the sheets, and Harley dumped his burden on the bed with a relieved grunt.

As they undressed the Englishman, Harley crooked an eyebrow at her efficient removal of Harry's under-clothes. "Aren't there orderlies for this sort of thing?" He flipped up the covers as she scooped up Harry's soiled clothing off the floor.

"Orderlies? You mean men?" Her eyes glinted with amusement. "Come now, who ever heard of a priggish pirate."

He laughed faintly and rubbed absently at his forehead. Because no *tikka-gharry* would take a cholera victim, he'd had to carry Harry nearly six blocks. His temples had begun to throb as he neared the hospital. Harry was not tall, but rock-solid. "Point well taken, Miss Herriott. I'm glad to see the leftenant will be left in capable hands."

She shook Harry's clothes at him. "How tactful of you not to say 'practiced.' I would have hit you with a bed-pan."

He jerked an arm up as if to fend her off. "That won't be necessary. I'll leave peacefully."

Lysistrata, wondering at the nervous gesture, handed Harry's clothes to a passing orderly. She turned back to Harley. "Thank you for bringing Harry. Most men would have sent for the *gurkhas.*"

He shrugged. "I owed him a favor. Good-bye, Miss Herriott."

Bleakly, Lysistrata watched him head down the line of narrow beds toward the door. This time she would not delude herself that she would see him again. Odd, the small things one noticed when the soul was shivering. Despite his purposeful stride, he walked as if the floor were uneven. Then, in her mind minutely gaped the missed stitches in the knitting she had taken from her mother's dead hand; her brother Teddy's nose that needed wiping after his breath had stopped. Eyes stinging with tears, she turned away and bent to sponge Harry's flushed face. Until she remembered the peculiar cast to Harley's olive coloring. The sponge slowed. Surely, he was just overheated. After all, he'd carried Harry . . . Wait. Harley's walk. His awkward gait triggered memories of more than loss; it suggested grievous illness. After a moment's debate, she went after him. In the next ward, she asked the male nurse to see to Harry, then hurried into the hospital's back corridor to see Harley's dark head as he disappeared down a stair beyond a pair of incoming stretcher-bearers. When, from the top of the stair, she saw how clumsily he managed the last few steps, she called out, "Mr. Harley, wait!"

Squinting nearsightedly, he looked up, then sagged against the stair rail. "What now, Miss Herriott? Has dear Harry got the heaves again?"

Snatching up her skirts, she hurried down the steps, then clamped a hand against his forehead. He jerked away. "Don't do that. This place is as public as the China Street Market."

Her heart wrenched with fear, she ignored him. "You're burning up. Harry's not the only one with cholera."

"The hell I have cholera. These epidemics come around every year and I've never caught it."

"I'd never been seasick before the *Rani* cruise," she reminded him as a distraught woman with a sick child hurried by them on the stair. "Come back upstairs. Dr. Lighter will want a look at you." As the woman began to wail through the wards for a doctor, Lysistrata summoned a hollow effort to make light of Harley's condition. "Come on, I'll anchor you on the floor next to Harry and keep you afloat in fruit juice." At the flat look in his dark eyes and the rising of the frantic mother's voice, she lost patience. "Feel your forehead yourself if you don't believe me. Your skin is the color of clay and you're adrift on your feet."

He loosely saluted. "Then I'll sail straight home like a good scow."

The woman was screaming by now. "The only place you're going is to see Lighter," Lysistrata said tautly, "then a hospital bed."

"Lysistrata," he replied tiredly, scarcely audible over the orderly now remonstrating with the woman, "surely you've noticed this is a Caucasian hospital."

"So?"

"So," he went on patiently as the voices upstairs quieted, "Lighter couldn't admit me if he wanted to."

"That's ridiculous! We're not barbarians," she retorted angrily.

"Suit yourself. This is a hospital with rules for barbarians only, and because none of us is a barbarian . . ." He lurched out of the door into the rain of the rear courtyard.

She ran after him. Hampered by sodden skirts as she struggled through nearly knee-deep water vibrating with splash rings as if pelted by stones, she nearly stumbled against him. Grabbing at his jacket, she babbled in desperation, "You can't go to a native hospital. They're not even clean!"

He swayed, peering through the rain. "I'm not completely out of my head yet, Lysistrata. I'm going home. The servants will look after me."

"Just how will you get there? There isn't a *gharry wallah* in sight." She pushed him out of the rain into an alcove and pressed him against the wall to steady him. "Where's *your* carriage?"

"I sent it on to my shipping office with some ledgers." He shook his head as if to clear it. "Had a meeting with Bartly at club where I found Harry. Just around the corner. Should tell him I can't—" He tried to head out into the rain again.

She held on to him. "I'll see that Sir Anthony gets word. Can you hang on to a horse?"

He smiled mirthlessly. "More or less."

"Stay here." She shoved him deeper into the alcove.

Shortly, Lysistrata, wearing a yellow slicker, returned with a rawboned nag. A second slicker hung over the saddle. "This is my Marian. She isn't much to look at, but she won't shy on you." She helped him into the slicker, then laboriously into the saddle. "Where do you live?" Her face shining in the rain, she caught the reins to lead the horse from the hospital yard.

"You're not taking me there," he said with quiet implacability. When she turned to argue again, he abruptly jerked the reins from her with surprising strength. Seeing her face flood with worry and fear, he added gently, "Thank you for the horse."

She made an effort to scowl. "See you get where you're going then! I want that nag returned! She's a great deal brighter than you."

"That's a relief to me, I'm sure." His hand flicked from the folds of the borrowed slicker and he twitched Marian toward the gate. Heads down, horse and man slowly disappeared behind a blinding gray wall of rain.

In a high temper, Lighter was waiting for Lysistrata when she returned to her ward. "Where the hell have you been?" he bellowed. "Two new patients have come through with nobody to look after them! The *gurkhas* just dumped *that* one in his muck on the floor there!"

"I was seeing to another patient," she replied coldly. "One it seems this holy British shrine of healing is too sanctimonious to accept. Mr. Richard Harley."

His anger instantly vanished. He jabbed a finger at her. "Come with me."

She jerked a finger at the man on the floor. "What about him?"

"Orderly!" he trumpeted. A small, nervous Indian appeared. "See to that *wallah* over there!" He stalked off toward his dingy office.

Once they were inside, Lysistrata demanded, "Harley said you wouldn't take him. Is that true?"

"Stop squawking! Yes, it's true." With an unhappy, irritable look, he settled like a potato in a sack on the desktop. "I don't like it any better than you do"—a hand chopped at the air—"but there's nothing I can do about it. I have *a* say in the rules of this place, not *the* say."

"Richard Harley is half English! This is an epidemic!"

"He could be English as Queen Victoria, but if Vicky had an Indian great-aunt thrice removed, she'd be out in the rain—mumps, measles, or plague."

"That's loathsome! I thought at least the west wing was reserved for nationals!"

"Wherever did you hear that?" he returned.

She advanced on him. "Then this place is *absurdly* huge. It could accommodate most of the cantonments. What's in the west wing? It couldn't be patients!"

"Lumber," he said glumly. "Lumber and rice and silk. Overflow from the godowns of the hospital board of regents, most of whom just happen to be merchants."

"Like Bettenheim?"

"Like Bettenheim."

She dropped into a chair and glared at the opposite wall as if it were the German entrepreneur.

"Where's Harley now?" ventured Lighter.

"At home, if he hasn't fallen off my horse."

He frowned. "That's not good. His servants won't want to touch him. It's a damned shame. He's a good man."

"What's so good about him?" she asked with scathing irony. "He's a jig, isn't he?"

"He can get drugs where and when no one else can, and he sells them to Queen Anne's at a fraction of what they would bring on the open market." His eyes glinted wickedly. "I gather he gives them to the native medics for a deal less. The ones who try reselling them disappear."

She sat up. "Disappear?"

His fingers snapped. "Poof." His smile matched the touch of malice in his eyes. "He's not an *entirely* good man."

"But useful," she bit the word out.

"That describes him well."

"I've always thought you were a bastard."

"I know."

"I'm not going to do double duty tonight," she said coldly as he picked up pen and paper and began to scribble. "I'm going home."

His grin was knowledgeable. "Where you go is up to you."

"Bastard."

He threw back his head and laughed, then tossed her Harley's address.

The Muslim syce who opened the door at Harley's Georgian town house goggled before he plunged into a hasty bow. "How may I help you, miss?"

"I've come to help Mr. Harley. I'm a nurse."

His gaze flicked beyond her to the street, which like Loo Gow Street, was situated in a wealthy Chinese quarter. Relieved not to see anyone who might be curious about a lone American female at his master's door, he wavered, perplexed. "Who shall I say . . . ?"

She cut him off. "Never mind. Mr. Harley knows me." She determinedly moved past him into the foyer, dim in the rain-dulled dusk but for his candle. The few shield-back chairs against the walls were golden mahogany Hepplewhite; the refined commode and side tables by Adam. Several fine landscapes of Burma hung on the cream walls, and through the open library door she noticed a large portrait of a handsome, tawny-mustached British colonel, presumably Harley's father, William. The only hints of Harley's Eastern ancestry were a golden statue of Rama on the commode and several Ch'ing-pai and Kuan porcelains from the Sung Dynasty in the library. A Saxon tapestry of the same century dominated the dining room opposite the library. Despite the excellent taste of their furnishings, the rooms had a spare, temporary look. "Where is he?"

"The sahib's room is at the top of the stair," the servant answered hesitantly, then as if finally making up his mind, hastily thrust the candlestick into her hand and retreated to the kitchen and a sherry bottle.

Holding the candle well in front, Lysistrata mounted the curving stair. A turbaned Hindu squatted beside the designated bedroom door. He stared at her, then slowly rose, hand on pommel of a wide-bladed sword in his sash. His eyes were cold and expressionless as an adder's, and diagonally across his face from jaw to hairline jagged a saber scar. Lysistrata tried to quell a shiver of fear. "I'm a nurse . . . I've come to see Mr. Harley."

His eyes narrowed, then he jerked off her slicker hat. Heart in her throat, she backed against the wall. He studied her face and hair, then opened the door and waved her inside. Bowstring-taut, she stepped into the room and, in utter disbelief, saw Sein sitting lotus-style on the floor beside Harley's bed. Beside her was a wizened *sayah* clad in turban and *pasoh* loincloth. Spread on a cloth between them were his cures: everything from rhino horn to herbal concoctions to fetishes. Sein's eyes widened in dismay, then jealousy. "What you do here?" she demanded angrily.

"I might ask you the same thing," Lysistrata retorted.

The scarred Hindu behind her said something in swift Burmese to the native girl. She regarded him sullenly, then gave a grudging nod. He bowed slightly to Lysistrata and left the room.

"Well"—Lysistrata folded her arms—"what *are* you doing here?"

"I take care of *Tuan* Harley," replied the girl proudly, with a significant arch of her brows. She waited with the patience of proprietorship as Lysistrata, trying to hide her anger and anxiety, quickly moved to the restlessly unconscious figure on the narrow, silk-draped Regency bed. Though his color was frighteningly pale, Harley was breathing. Her own breath unknotted. Unconsciously, she straightened the pillow, gripped it to stop her hands from shaking. Her mind jigged to and fro from joy that he was alive to jealousy hot as Sein's. From the bed's hard, Spartan appearance, Harley seemed to prefer the closest thing to a floor for sleeping. It did not look like a bed that often accommodated a woman.

"Exactly what are you doing for him?"

"I bathe him." Sein gave her a knowing smile. "I change bed linens and bowls. I wait. Nothing else to do except watch old U Ba make charms." She waved a contemptuous hand at the door. "Everybody else but the syce and Scarface Naswral run away. He only stay because he untouchable. Got no place to go."

Lysistrata's lips tightened as she took Harley's pulse. It was faint. His skin was cold. The second phase of the cholera had already begun, but whether the disease was the fatal Chinese variety, she had no way of knowing. The old *sayah* began to mumble to himself in Burmese as she pulled off the slicker. "Dare I ask how you met Mr. Harley?"

"He have lunch one day your father." Unfooled by Lysistrata's clinical calm, the girl smiled archly. "You gone out." She watched Lysistrata check the whitish-clear fluid in the bowl by the bed, then thumb back Harley's eyelids. "Why you not go home? I know what to do."

"What have you been giving him?"

"What you mean?" Sein countered warily.

"His pupils are dilated by narcotics." Lysistrata stared her down. "Well?"

"I give opium," the girl said defiantly. "Keep him quiet so not sick so much, help when shakes come." She leaned forward belligerently. "What *you* do?"

Not much, Lysistrata thought grimly. You've covered about all of it, you and that bone-rattling quack, you little trollop, but I won't kill him with opium. "What you have not," she retorted aloud. "Drugged, he may strangle if he goes on retching." She picked up the empty water pitcher by the bedside table. "We'll start giving him water, as much as we can get down him . . . until it's over." She thrust the pitcher into Sein's hands. "Fill this, then get a few hours' sleep. I'll call you. Tonight and tomorrow morning will be the worst times."

Jumping to her feet, Sein started to argue. Lysistrata cut her off. "Don't be stupid. You need me as much as I need you. I must be back at the hospital tomorrow and you'll have to watch him. You have to rest sometime." She jerked her head toward the door. "Harley's watch-dog doesn't look like the sort to empty bedpans, and this old man wouldn't know one if it was shoved under him."

"I don't like," Sein replied angrily. "You go!"

Lysistrata towered over her. "I don't give a damn

what you like. You'll do as I say or leave. Naswral will see to it. He knows which side his bread is buttered on.''

With a look that said she'd like to paste the pitcher across Lysistrata's mouth, Sein went after the water.

Lysistrata returned to the bed to stare down at Harley's drawn features. "Live," she whispered. Then fiercely, "Damn you, live. Live to love me or make me miserable again. But if you leave me dangling this way, I'll hate you all the way to hell." She touched the still face that told her nothing, that now might hold its secrets forever. "No compromises, even now, Mr. Harley?" She smiled crookedly. "But why should you bargain now? Am I not the girl who thought it better to marry than burn?" Yet I do not marry, and I cannot damp the fire. When you are gone to ash, my heart will be mixed withal, a single cinder in the mass.''

Dimly hearing Sein arguing with someone downstairs, Lysistrata lifted her head. The strange voice was a woman's. "Ah, my sweet"—she touched Harley's cheek with gentle irony—"you should be followed with a broom." Leaving him, she went by the curiously incurious Naswral to the head of the stair. At the bottom stood Evelyn Chilton, wrapped in a hooded evening cloak. Sensing another presence, she looked up and saw Lysistrata. She said something in Burmese to Sein too swiftly for Lysistrata to understand.

Sein gave Evelyn a glare even more venomous than the one she had given Lysistrata. "Meddling *kala* bitches." she snapped succinctly, then stalked off to complete her errand for water.

"Have you come to stay with Harley?" Lysistrata asked quietly, wondering if Evelyn could see the tear streaks on her face. If Evelyn meant to help, she was welcome; otherwise, she could climb right back on her . . . broom.

For an instant, Evelyn appeared nonplussed, then uncomfortable. "No, I . . . my husband expects me. I simply wished to inquire—"

"He isn't dead yet. Does that satisfy your curiosity?"

Evelyn's eyes narrowed. "I am not curious. I *am* concerned. Mr. Harley and I are old friends."

"He could use a friend just now." Lysistrata came slowly down the stairs. "Why not send your husband an excuse? I'm sure you've been 'detained' in the past. He appears to be *most* understanding."

"We're attending the theater tonight with the Bartlys," Evelyn replied curtly. "Ostensibly, I have a headache; but if I do not shortly return to our box, the Bartlys are even more understanding than my husband."

"If you were Harley's friend, the Bartlys' understanding wouldn't matter, would it?" Lysistrata faced Evelyn. "I think you're aware Lady Mary probably knows already. So it's the cholera, isn't it? A nasty disease, cholera, even if you don't contract it. You just keep changing the sheets until your back breaks, but you don't really suffer until the patient stops soiling them. If you care, that is. And you don't"

"You smug idiot," Evelyn snarled. "Try crawling under your self-righteousness if anyone finds out *you're* here. Sein can have a *very* big mouth."

"Not when her family's livelihood depends on her keeping it shut. And if anyone hears it from you, he will hear how you found out about it." Lysistrata smiled sweetly. "I'm not sure my self-righteousness can accommodate us both."

Evelyn's face grew stony. "You'll regret this." With a sweep of cape, she left.

The night was long for Sein and Lysistrata, who had little to do but wait for Harley's few semiconscious moments to give him water. And, as Sein had said, listen to the old *sayah* mumble. Most of the time, Harley lay inert, a bluish cast about the eyes and lips, his skin increasingly cold until he shook despite the blankets they put about him. At last, he ceased to pass fluid and his pulse disappeared. Only the faint rise and fall of his chest indicated life.

Lysistrata felt as if she were being suffocated with Harley. Terror crushed her until she dimly realized she was bent over like the droning *sayah*. His nagging mumble made her want to scream, yet she sat huddled, stifled.

"His butterfly spirit will fly away soon," predicted Sein in a mournful tone.

"We'll know shortly," was the tight reply. Lysistrata tried to tear her mind from Harley to Harry at Queen Anne's, but the path it found was no less bleak. Harry must have entered the crisis just before Harley. If so, he might already be dead.

"Maybe *tuan* not strong enough to fight *nats* because I give him opium," Sein went on dismally.

Lysistrata looked at the girl. The perky flame hibiscus in her black hair had wilted and she with it. "Perhaps the opium has allowed him enough rest to fight them." She gently touched Sein's hand. "If he dies, it does not mean you killed him. He is very clever; the *nats* will not find it easy to win against him."

A flicker of gratitude appeared in Sein's eyes, then the old suspicion. "He get well, you make him not keep me anymore?"

For a moment, Lysistrata sat silent, then murmured, "Your going or staying with Mr. Harley is your choice, and your mother's."

Just after dawn, Lysistrata saw Harley's bedding was wet, his color somewhat improved. He stirred slightly as she felt his forehead and pulse. "What you feel?" Sein asked anxiously.

How to describe the indescribable? The tremor of a hovering hawk, its slow, winging strain for the sky? Her own pivot in blue ether? "His heartbeat," Lysistrata said softly. "He's going to live."

Sein dropped to the floor and clutched at the side of the bed, then let out a startling series of whooping sobs. "He not die! You stupid *nats!* He too smart for you!"

Harley flinched at the sudden noise, and his eyes opened. Gradually, they focused on Lysistrata's gaunt face, then narrowed with a fury she would not have believed possible in so contained a man. "You fool!" he whispered harshly. *"Damn* you, get out of here!"

Lysistrata's soaring joy exploded as if by a hunter's gun. The blast seemed to splinter her skull. For a moment, she stood stunned with pain, then turned and fled. Behind her, Sein's almond eyes filled with pity and triumph.

Lysistrata did not run far. She was too tired. In too many pieces to pursue any of them. By the time she reached the main street of the quarter, she had slowed to a stumble. He's right, she thought starkly, I'm a fool. But better that than to see him dead. She sagged against a wall. Perhaps I'm still being a fool. Perhaps staying with him made no difference.

"Mem?" A Madrassee beggarwoman with a glaucomaed baby held out a tentative hand. "A few coins, *mem,* for my unhappy son?"

Lysistrata gazed blankly at the child for a moment, then held out her empty hands. "I have nothing, nothing more to give."

The woman looked solemnly at her nursing dress, stained but in one piece. At the shoes that were whole. At the tiny Queen Anne's insignia pin at her collar.

Lysistrata touched the insignia. "Can you sell it?"

The woman shrugged. "It's pretty."

Lysistrata pinned the bit of enameled silver to the

child's ragged swaddling clothes, then stroked his dark head. "Better fortune, my son of India."

The Madrassee watched the *feringhi* woman out of sight, then scrubbed the baby's skull with a handful of dirt.

When Lysistrata at last reached Queen Anne's, she went directly to Harry's cot. Having passed the crisis, he was in somewhat better shape than Harley. Wearily, she tousled his hair. "How's Queen Vicky's best boy?"

"Wrung out," he muttered, then managed a weak grin. "Guess I'll be goldbricking for a week or so."

"A good deal longer, if you don't keep quiet. Your heart's sustained quite a strain." She paused, then added softly, "I'm sorry I wasn't here, Harry."

"Not much you could have done, I guess." His head shifted slightly on the pillow. "Lighter says Harley brought me in."

"Yes. He's ill as well."

He studied her face. "That's where you were?"

She smiled faintly. "One of his mistresses was dosing him with opium. It's a wonder he's still alive."

He took her hand. "I'm sorry, Lysistrata."

She shook her head. "He warned me. He warned me about a great many things, but I wouldn't listen." Fingers tightened on his, she smiled down at him. "You'd better get some rest. I'll be back to see you before I leave."

Lighter was busily scribbling away at his desk when Lysistrata entered his office. He glanced up. "Well, how did it go?"

"He'll be all right." She told him about the opium.

"Good God, talk about being hoisted by your own petard!" He leaned forward and flipped open his humidor. "Lysistrata, my girl, have a cigar."

"No, thank you," she replied without rancor. "What I would really like is your resignation."

Lightning did not crack about the ceiling when she told him why, along with several other suggestions; but of course, neither did he resign. Still, forty-two hours later, a twelve-man team of coolies, at the various owners' expense, delivered several tons of lumber, rice, and silk to their appropriate godowns to settle like mammoth swine in the mud and rain.

One morning, six days later, the monsoon let up for several hours. Almost as the sun broke through the sullen clouds, Masjid knocked on his mistress's bedroom door. Lysistrata, exhausted after her harsh experience with Harley, weeks of overwork, and violent argument with hospital officials over racial policies, was heavily asleep. Groggily, she wandered to the door. "What is it?"

"A man was here to return a horse."

Instantly, she came alert. "Accept the horse and thank the gentleman, but tell him I am not at home."

There was a silence. "He has gone, but perhaps you should see the animal, *mem.*"

She flung on a robe and wrenched open the door. "Is something wrong with Marian?"

"Most definitely not," he answered quickly. "That is . . . perhaps I should say, the horse in the courtyard is no Marian."

Something snapped. She charged down the stair. "Damn that buccaneering bastard! I want my Marian!" Still yelling, she tore out of the front door. Only to hear a startled whinny as a vision of a horse shied at the racket. The Arabian stallion who restlessly danced in the court was a dream of white so pristine the sun on his damp coat seemed to reflect rainbow prisms. Dark, intelligent eyes wary, he tossed his narrow head with a flow of creamy silk, tail drifting across the pebbled ground. As she cautiously approached, he backed slightly, his nostrils flaring at her scent. "Oh, you beauty. You're too glorious to be real!" she breathed, hardly daring to put out a hand to touch him for fear he might disappear. The dark eyes watched her, watched until her fingers brushed skin that rippled ever so slightly, but the stallion did not move. Then, as if he were some unicorn lured by a maiden in Persian myth, his head lowered to nuzzle her bright hair.

"Is he not splendid, *mem?*" came Masjid's admiring voice behind her. "Such a one is worth his first foal's weight in pearls."

For Lysistrata, the reality of the stallion's worth ended the dream. Reluctantly, she withdrew her hand from the satin hide. "Send him back, Masjid. I cannot accept such a gift."

The Pathan frowned. "It is right to refuse gifts, *mem,* from those men who come here to flatter you and persuade you to accept their courtship for it is their gifts and not themselves they wish you to see. But it is wrong and prideful to refuse the gift of a man who owes you his life, for he does not give it lightly. Better to have let him die than trample his honor."

Lysistrata stood silent a moment, then said quietly, "I shall name the stallion *Fleche du Soleil.* Arrow of the Sun."

While Soleil was a luxury fit for a monarch, Lysistrata felt he could not have been bestowed on anyone more powerless than she. The sullen regents were adamant: Queen Anne's doors remained closed to natives. Those same regents first wheedled, then pressed Dr. Herriott to silence her protests. His refusal sparked a rash of complaints about his work.

"Lysistrata," he announced after a particularly unpleasant day, "I'm going to resign."

Miserably, she gazed at his tired face. "No, Papa. I'll be quiet now; after all, no one's listening." She laid her head in his lap. "I'll be the one to resign. This isn't your fight."

"Bigotry is every man's fight, honey. To let a lone girl take it on for the rest is as shameful as the deliberate, pig-minded hate itself." He smoothed her hair. "You're also wrong about no one listening. You don't get squeals from deaf hogs."

Her lips quirked. "Unless you twist their tails."

He twirled a strand in his fingers. "Two can twist harder than one. Just be ready to quick-step over the wallow fence. Hogs have a mean bite."

"Even the nips are difficult to ignore," she observed ruefully. "I'm not likely to marry us a prosperous young mister now. My beaux have begun to run squealing."

"You'd have sold yourself off to one of those posturing . . ." He shook his head impatiently. "Not with my blessing. No doubt you'd have stoically tried to make your unlucky choice happy, but I've never known a female less suited to a marriage of convenience. I'd have been on the first boat out rather than see you turn into a false, miserable—"

She touched his lips. "I love you, Papa."

He laughed. "Naturally. You've more brains than sense."

The next day, the Herriotts hopped the fence. While the spot where they landed smelled worse than Queen Anne's, it was a comparative bed of roses in regard to human decency. The Royal Burmese Hospital, which eagerly accepted their services, was a combined monastery and medical unit. Mysticism, nonsense, and wishful thinking played as much a part as practical medicine—most of it ancient, some wildly bizarre to Western practitioners. The death rate was high due to ignorance, poor sanitation, and the population's general malnutrition. Also, despite the low fees, the natives customarily avoided the hospital until mortally ill.

Still, after a single week, the Herriotts ceased to be complacent about their own medical knowledge. Dr. Herriott, obliged to perform brutal field surgery without anesthetics during the war, was confounded when he saw a conscious patient smile through removal of kidney stones, the only painkiller a network of needles implanted in his skin. Often medicines he and Lysistrata would have viewed as lethal or appropriate to the pot of a witch proved effective.

Whatever its virtues and faults, the hospital turned no one away who requested help. Because of the Royal's charity, need, and contribution to their medical learning, the Herriotts joined the staff despite long hours for ruinous pay. Marian and the new carriage had to be sold, the gardener let go. Fortunately, Masjid, who claimed private investments, stayed; otherwise, Lysistrata might have collapsed from handling bungalow housework as well as the hospital schedule. She was right in suspecting Masjid's income issued from Harley, wrong in supposing Masjid did not predigest the information purchased.

As soon as he was able, Harry called on Harley, who was still convalescing. Harry sat in a rattan planter's chair with Harley on a long chair in a glassed arbor room at the rear of the town house. "I wanted to thank you," Harry said earnestly. "You saved my life."

"Don't bother," was the easy reply. "If I hadn't owed you a favor, I'd have left you draped over the table. You were quite decorative among the roses."

"I daresay." Harry grimaced. "At any rate, I'm in your debt. I'm afraid I cannot repay you as handsomely as you did Lysistrata . . ." He saw Harley's eyes narrow sharply. "She didn't have to tell me. Even Bettenheim isn't *that* liberal with the gifts he's been pushing at her." He smiled wryly. "She's turned them all down, of course, but she's not likely to have the opportunity again in future. He's mad as Tophet.''

''Oh?'' The dark eyes flickered with interest. ''Did she show him the door?''

Harry laughed. ''Worse than that. Haven't you heard?'' He related the tale of Queen Anne's Warehouse. ''Our butterfly persuaded Lighter to dump all those stores the board was keeping free of charge onto their muddy doorsteps. Lighter said if one of the board members came down with cholera, he'd be glad to trade places with a rice bag. Then he sent around a letter to local churchmen asking for a petition to open the wing to nationals, also for a list of parishioners who contracted cholera.'' He sighed. ''Only Father Cassetti of Saint Mary's and Rabbi Solomon gave him what he asked.''

Harley smiled faintly. ''Father Cassetti isn't responsible to his parishioners and Jews sympathize with underdogs; they've been on the bottom of the pack often enough themselves.'' His head dropped back on the chair pillows. ''All that must have gone down the community throat like a dose of asafetida.''

''Lysistrata and her father jumped ahead of demands for their resignations by joining the staff at the Royal Burmese Hospital established by Mindon. That's fine with the Queen Anne regents, of course, but Lighter is threatening to do the same unless adjustments are made in hospital policy. That isn't so fine. Lighter isn't easily replaced, and the regents are puffing like grampuses . . .'' He paused. ''You don't look precisely pleased.''

''We civilized pirates prefer to lead quiet lives,'' said Harley dryly.

Harry lifted an eyebrow as he leaned back in his chair. ''Ah, well, your name *was* mentioned a time or two.''

Harley stared thoughtfully into space. ''Lysistrata, Lysistrata, what shall I do with you?''

* * *

Harley had a second caller that day: Sir Anthony Bartly. The visit was expected, but Harley was not quite sure which way it might go in view of Lysistrata's recent bent for social reform. She had stirred up more of a hornet's nest than she knew. When Sir Anthony began with a somewhat stiff apology for Harley's reception, or rather the lack of it, at Queen Anne's, Harley relaxed; with his usual skill he put Sir Anthony at ease. Sir Anthony accepted a glass of arrack with visible relief. "I confess I was not only concerned for you as a friend, Richard, I was afraid this incident might jeopardize the expedition. That's putting it baldly, I know, but you are of inestimable importance to this venture. It will be a remarkable achievement for Britain and the sponsors who make it possible."

"I am more concerned with profits than wounded pride, Sir Anthony," Harley replied lightly. "The glory of Britain I leave to you and your associates."

Sir Anthony laughed. "I think I would trust you less if you presented your position otherwise." As he drew a thick letter out of a leather folio, his voice became grave. "This is the proposition we have drawn up for Chang Yin. I need not remind you of the lives and fortunes that rely on your and Mr. Sing's abilities to safely relay it to his eyes alone." He sat back. "How long do you think negotiations will take?"

"That is difficult to say. Months, at best. Perhaps years."

The Englishman sighed. "I regret echoing Prasad, but, Richard, you are maddeningly vague."

"Surely that is no worse than being specifically incorrect."

Sir Anthony gave a philosophical grunt. "I suppose I shall never understand the Asian carelessness about time."

After being civilized for a few thousand years more,

you may understand better, Harley thought, for what I require from you is time. Aloud he replied, "The road to the Christian heaven is brief compared to that of the Buddhist; therefore a Buddhist is less pressed to achieve what he must."

"An advantage, I'm sure, but one that leads to little progress."

"That depends on whose progress it is," Harley countered. "Also, heedless progress may be worse than none."

Sir Anthony lifted an eyebrow. "That's not your father talking."

"My father was passionately progressive. I am more conservative." Harley grinned. "You will note I am not risking my neck in this venture."

"Bosh!" Sir Anthony scoffed. "I pity the man who openly questions *your* nerve."

"The Naga who last questioned my father's is still collecting heads in the upper Arakans. It does not pay to be overconfident."

"Yes"—Sir Anthony absently fingered the side of his nose—"that is a pity." He was silent a moment, then spoke. "Richard, this is none of my personal business, of course, but . . . are you and Lysistrata Herriott connected in some way? I mean, she has gone to a great deal of trouble in your behalf."

"You mean she has *caused* a great deal of trouble in my behalf, I think, for some idealistic whim. Possibly you and Lady Mary are more familiar with her than I, but she seems impetuous and easily bored. Now she has a new diversion. Probably she would have pounced on a sick coolie if he had been convenient. By the end of the season, she will forget about reforming the hospitals and petition you to replant Dalhousie Gardens."

The Englishman looked relieved. "Well, I am glad she is not your particular friend. I fear her boredom may lead her into difficulty." He rose and patted the letter on the table. "You will see to this as soon as possible, I hope."

"Of course, Sir Anthony. It will be on its way before you reach Government House."

Sir Anthony shook his hand. "Thank you, Richard, on behalf of England as well as myself."

"I'm happy to be of service, sir."

When Sir Anthony had gone, Harley slit open the letter and read it twice. After dropping the envelope into an ashtray, he lit a cheroot, applied it to the envelope, then fed the letter's pages one by one to the blaze.

CHAPTER 6

The Reformer

And it was but a dream, yet it lightened my despair
  When I thought that a war would arise in defense
  of the right,
  That an iron tyranny now should bend or cease,
  The glory of manhood stand on his ancient
  height,
  Nor Britain's sole God be the millionaire.
                    ALFRED, LORD TENNYSON

"Has Lysistrata seen Shwe Dagon?" Harley asked Harry as they rode together in the Cantonment Gardens during the last week of October. The monsoons had swept on their way to China and the Pacific, taking the worst of the cholera with them. The Burma they left behind was glossy with fat, flowering buds and chattering birds who, like the populace, were glad to be dry for days at a time.

"Well, as she's preoccupied with bazaars and hasn't much interest in formal religions, I think it's one of the few things she hasn't explored. She hasn't had time of late," Harry said. "She's been up to her ears helping her father at the Royal." He nudged his horse into an easy trot. "Are you suggesting I take her there?"

"Why not?"

"Well, Shwe Dagon's spectacular enough from the outside, but inside . . ." He grimaced. "Enough human refuse is about to turn one's stomach, particularly a woman's. Even if she's a nurse."

"That's the point, Harry," drawled Harley.

"You mean—" Harry swiveled in the saddle. "You really don't think much of her reforms, do you? That surprises me a bit."

"What I think of them doesn't matter." Harley's voice hardened. "If she keeps at it, she'll run into trouble. Some of the people she's irritating can be dangerous." His dark eyes fixed Harry's. "I'm one of them."

Harry's eyes narrowed. "Is that a threat?"

"Call it what you will. She has to stop, Harry."

A mass of white towers slashed with green and scarlet, Shwe Dagon's glittering, gold-leafed dome belled against the cobalt sky. At its base crouched gigantic lions lacquered with more green, scarlet, and gold. Bulbous black eyes glared over jaws that sounded a silent roar at the city and crowd of chattering human monkeys with umbrellas, candles, flowers, and joss papers who milled about their great frozen claws. Vendors of souvenirs, sweets, flowers, and prayer flags scampered among the pilgrims who walked between rows of stalls along the terraced ascent to the temple entrance. Lysistrata sniffed the incense Harry bought and wrinkled her nose with a laugh. "I suppose it has to be strong to reach Buddha, but we had better beat a hasty retreat after we light it."

"You'll get used to it in a hurry inside the temple. You'll be glad of any perfume." Harry paid the vendor an extra few *kyat* for a packet of gold leaf, then adroitly dodged Lysistrata past a vendor slung with bamboo poles which rhythmically bounced cages of screeching parakeets and cockatoos.

"Wait, Harry." She dragged at his arm. "Look at that cheeky little green one! He has muttonchops just like my Uncle Claudius." She whistled at the bird, who cocked its yellow head and whistled back. "Let's buy him, Harry. I've always wanted a pet."

Harry looked at her eager face. This was her first outing in weeks and she was in need of it. Pale and drawn from overwork, she wore, as usual now, a plain, dark *longyi* skirt like the Burmese staff members at the Royal Hospital. When he had asked teasingly if she could not have donned a fetching European frock for the excursion, she had laughed. "Dear Harry, I don't need them. Except for you, my knights have all deserted me for damsels who cause less fuss. Besides, I haven't any frocks. Lady Mary gave me a ferocious dressing-down for ungrateful rabble-rousing and refused to vouch for my social position if I continued. I told her I couldn't see the point of dressing a gap in society, so I gave all her daughter's clothes back. She hasn't spoken to me since."

"Lysistrata, you haven't time for a pet," Harry said quietly. "Don't you think it would be unfair?"

Her face fell, and he wanted to stuff a handful of money in the vendor's hand, take the cageful of parakeets, and haul her as far as they could get from the pagoda. "I suppose you're right," she said slowly, then clicked her tongue lightly at the bars of the parakeet cage. "Good-bye, Claudius." The bird danced back and forth, his beady eyes bright, then jumped to his swing. The last they saw of him, he was swinging madly to and fro, trilling and squawking.

After they pasted their offering of gold leaf to the bulk of the temple dome, Harry led Lysistrata inside to where the gold ended and the beggars began. Every loathsome and pitiful infirmity of man crawled about floors and against the walls which seemed to move as with vermin: all ages, all sexes; but with many, the definition of age,

even humanity, was virtually obliterated. Leprosy rotted
by ethereal candlelight. Elephantiasis swelled ponderously across narrow stairways. Limbs of deities painted
on walls offered illusions of limbs on living stumps
placed in front of them. The stench was unbelievable. A
hand covering her nose and mouth, Lysistrata stumbled
against him in an involuntary instinct to return to the sunlight. He stepped back to let her pass, but she stood motionless. Then stepped forward. And kept walking on
into the bowels of the place. Among the beggars glided
pilgrims who might have been suspended on celestial
clouds so far removed were they in health and felicity
from the wretched inhabitants of this netherworld of disease and starvation. At the dank core reclined a huge,
eternally dreaming Buddha which floated above them all
in a halo of light radiated by a thousand candles. The
light was blotted here and there by a praying suppliant, a
saffron priest, a singing child.

Lysistrata placed a candle among the others and knelt.
When she finally rose, Harry saw her face in the candlelight
was wet with tears that seemed leafed upon it in gold. She
looked back into the shadows where crouched and moved
the abandoned. "There are so many of them."

"It's as though she has furled her life into a torch and
set it ablaze. It's like being around some bloody saint,"
Harry growled at Harley in his house the day after visit-
ing the pagoda. "I can hardly bear the sight of her. She's
too bright, too intense, too bloody self-destructive." He
picked up his drink and flung himself into a chair. "Now
the bitch is taking to the streets. Whether she's heaven-
or hell-bound is just a fall of the cards."

Lysistrata might have been amused by Harry's dramat-
ics had any sense of humor remained about the misery at
Shwe Dagon. She was not self-destructive, only preoccu-

pied. If the natives would not come to the hospital, someone must go to them. As the doctors were busy, the priests disinclined, the understaff unwilling to add to their duties without remuneration, she was presented with the hideous responsibility. And the difficulties.

In a city filled with medical deprivation, she had to prowl for patients. The Indians were repelled by a shamelessly unveiled woman who invaded their privacy. For a few weeks, they politely invented every possible excuse to avoid admitting her to their homes; only her position of authority sometimes pried open doors. Once they discovered she was out of favor with the English, the doors sealed shut. Pathans were flatly hostile. The Chinese coolly announced they had their own doctors. Only the Burmese welcomed her and the Buddhist acolyte who sometimes followed, at Dr. Herriott's request, amid the worst sections of the city.

Unfortunately, the Burmese rarely troubled to follow the medical advice she left; and when dispensing medicine, she tried to see it contained enough alcohol to encourage consumption, but not enough to pickle the patient if he drank it at a sitting. Gradually, she made a little progress. While Burmese adults might be casual with their ailments, they were less so about their children. She could sometimes count on the mothers' diligence if not their understanding. In turn, the practical parents could count on her working for free, unlike the *sayahs*. As the number of patients increased, the weary acolyte, protesting mildly that he was first a priest, then a medical student, became less available. More and more often when summoned for a emergency, she went alone on Soleil without disturbing Dr. Herriott. Often, she suspected the ever-discreet Masjid followed.

Restlessly stirring, Lysistrata flung a hand across the bed. She heard the quiet rustle again. Her eyes opened, then heavily closed. Tick-Tock the *tuk-too* must be on his nightly chase after dinner. Or Wili, Masjid's lively new contribution to the household. She flopped over, face burrowed into the pillows.

Claudius uneasily hopped again to his swing. He felt a tremor, no more than a vibration on his senses. It came again rhythmically with increasing strength. Nervously, the bird transferred to one side of the hanging cage, then the other, making it sway.

Lysistrata sighed. Harry had been a dear to relent and buy Claudius. Thrilled, she had even listened to him lecture about keeping more civilized hours so the new pet would not be neglected. His reason for purchasing Claudius was transparent, but she had laughingly agreed that, collapsed in a heap, she would be no good to anyone. But just now she needed sleep that Claudius too clearly did not. She stuffed a pillow over her head.

At the sound from the bed, the vibration abruptly stopped. When silence fell, it resumed. Frightened, the bird chittered as like a dark, night-blooming flower, a goblet shape rose from the darkness. Moonlight shaped slits of eyes like death's own. Claudius let out a string of terrified screeches, then quieted, distracted by the creature's unhurried sway. His head cocked, round eye of victim fixed on narrow eye of killer. The bird blinked. The goblet swelled and struck. Hung silently, patiently poised . . . until claws and fangs sank together into its tail. With a malevolent hiss, it jerked in a convulsive spasm, then drove down to combat its attacker. The pole which held the cage and cobra crashed to the floor.

Lysistrata bolted upright. "Who's there?!" For an instant, there was stark silence, then a bloodcurdling duet of hiss and yowl. Afraid Wili had gone after Claudius, she lit the lamp. Then shrank back with a muffled scream. Its head reared and fangs gaping, a cobra was wrapped around Wili. Both creatures' heads were covered with blood. Lysistrata jumped out of bed with a shriek. "Masjid! Masjid! Help!" At her voice, the cobra reconsidered the odds. The decision was fatal. The instant of diversion gave Wili his chance; his sharp teeth ripped at the cobra's throat. He was still worrying the corpse when Masjid burst into the room. The Pathan halted, pistol in hand as the mongoose mauled its victim. "Can't you stop it?" Lysistrata said tightly, sickened.

"I should have to kill the mongoose, *mem,*" Masjid answered quietly.

"No . . . he may have saved my life." Lips trembling, her eyes went to the lump of bright feathers that lay under a still lightly swaying swing. "The cobra went for Claudius first. He must have entered through that broken louver in the verandah shutter."

"I repaired the louver some time ago, *mem.*"

"But that leaves only the door. Isn't that uncommon?"

"Most."

She was silent a moment. "Masjid, is this why you brought in Wili just after I circulated those petitions?"

He shrugged. "Rodents are common in Burma; so are cobras."

"I see." They watched Wili, ears flat to his head, drag his catch out of the room. Lysistrata went to the overturned cage to withdraw the tiny corpse; its fluff barely filled her hand. "Oh, Masjid," she whispered, "he was so harmless. He couldn't even fly away."

"Cobras have strange power, *mem.* The bird may not have flown, even if free to do so." He paused. "We must take care. Next time, we may have to contend with a danger more sure than a serpent."

"You think there will be a next time?"

"Most assuredly, *mem.* Petitions are not so harmless as parakeets."

* * *

A few days later, Lysistrata and Dr. Herriott were presented with an invitation by San-hla and her mother, who, dressed in fine shot silk and gold-set, ruby necklaces that would have pleased a queen, entered the dining room during breakfast. Though familiar with Burmese methods of investment, the Herriotts were hard put not to gape at the expensive jewelry. After formal *shikkohs,* Ma Saw announced San-hla was to have her *natwin,* a coming-of-age party. She and the family would be greatly honored if Lysistrata, as their esteemed friend, would perform the *natwin* ceremony. They would be pleased if the doctor would also attend. Lysistrata *shikkohed* in turn, and accepted with all the happy dignity merited. After the pair left, she wondered whether Ma Saw and her daughters had refrained from wearing jewelry during working hours out of shrewd realization their salaries might be affected or a tactful effort not to appear more prosperous than their employers.

That Ma Saw had gone to considerable expense to celebrate the *natwin* was evident on the appointed day. Though the house on Green Orchid Street seemed painfully simple, it was beautifully decorated with flowers, colored kites, and San-hla's marvelously woven birds of straw which hung from the thatched ceiling. A single red lacquer Chinese chair headed a low dining table laden with delicacies on pretty Chinese dishes for the crowd of relatives and friends. Beyond a bright blue *purdah* cloth was the bedroom with rolled-up palmyra pallets and a carved teak chest for storage. By the kitchen was a plank with battered metal pots, a large salt-crazed porcelain water jar, and charcoal fire where two female cousins made tea and kept the rice kettle boiling. Dr. Herriott was given the chair, Lysistrata the place on his right. Ma Saw was on his left, San-hla facing them from the end of the table.

Unlike the monkish ceremony of the boys, *natwin* was

a secular affair with only family and friends present. Even so, Ma Saw had given several expensive gifts to the neighboring Buddhist monastery and the city's major temples. As nobody had to worry with the presence of dignified priests, soon all were giddy from the doctor's gift of Kentucky bourbon and had sticky faces and fingers from the feast. Everyone seemed delighted by the Herriotts' presence. Except for Sein. She sulked, face lighting only when she looked at her sister and the pickled ginger hors d'oeuvres. Even Ma Saw seemed to be in Sein's bad graces; from this, Lysistrata gathered she had been chosen for the *natwin* only after a flaming row.

Little San-hla was exquisite in a costume and gilt headdress that emulated the court ladies of Mandalay. When the moment for the *natwin* came, Ma Saw had everyone sit in a circle; then after appropriate speeches by the senior males and ladies, gave Lysistrata a tiny brocaded box. In it were a gold needle and a dainty pair of gold earrings. Lysistrata, fearing she might hurt San-hla at the piercing, blew unobtrusively in her ear as a distraction at each jab. Such diversion was unnecessary, for surreptitious sips from an undiluted cup of bourbon had rendered the limpid-eyed young lady oblivious. The ceremony complete, she turned to Lysistrata with elaborate dignity. Her body began to descend with excruciating slowness into a *shikkoh*. Dr. Herriott, when he saw Lysistrata's eyes widen, suddenly guessed San-hla's condition and held his breath. To forestall her small friend from falling on her bottom, Lysistrata hastily dropped into a *shikkoh*, firmly pressing San-hla upward as if meaning to pay her homage. Dreamily, San-hla inclined her regal little head to accept her due. Then gave Lysistrata a small, woven parakeet of green straw. "Claudius," she said simply. Lysistrata carefully took the little bird; then, her eyes filling with tears, buried her head against the child's soft neck.

* * *

Impatiently, Lysistrata picked her way along narrow planks suspended above refuse-littered water between moored sampans and paddy boats in the harbor. With little time before sunset, she had no great eagerness to perform a Caesarean by lanternlight in a rocking boat. She arrived to find the patient had delivered a previous child by clumsy Caesarean; scar tissue had retorn at the rupture point. After quickly cleaning and chloroforming the woman, she made a quick incision. Minutes later, to the delight of his fisherman father, a hefty, red-faced boy squirmed into the world.

By the time she left the fishing junk, the sun had set and the lights of Rangoon seeped through the river mist. Boats squeaked against one another with only a few lights dully gleaming through their stern openings; the water people usually went to bed shortly after sunset. Lysistrata, precariously balanced on the footbridge, gave a muffled gasp as it suddenly bowed under a heavy weight. Silhouetted against the moon-pale mist, a palmetto-hatted hulk spoke gutturally, "You nurse?"

"Yes." She tried not to sound frightened out of her wits.

She could not count on Masjid tonight. He was bedridden with the flare-up of a stomach ulcer—no doubt from having to keep track of her.

"My son, foot hurt. You come see." The last was more order than request, but Lysistrata had learned to reserve judgments about the Burmese. While they rarely followed advice about medication, they cheerfully accepted help, invariably offered dinner, and freely spread the word that she was a little crazy but a very nice lady.

"Yes, of course. Where is he?"

His forefinger hooked toward a junk tethered at the end of the quay adjoining the footbridge. She sighed. It was a long way, but the boy's cut could easily become infected, particularly around the waterfront.

As if he had the night sense of a bat, the man walked swiftly along the footbridge. Expecting a dousing, she followed him as best she could. After an impatient wait on the quay until she reached solid ground, he trotted off toward the junk, leaving her to catch up her skirt and run after him.

With a curious half-smile, the Burman stood back to let her enter the cabin of his dilapidated junk; except for a rough palm mat and some dirty crockery, it was empty. Her mouth went dry. She whirled, the heavy instrument bag aimed at the side of his head. With a mirthless grin, he blocked it, then wrenched it away and threw it into a pile of rotting vegetables. She backed, eyes flicking toward his eating utensils to find a possible weapon. Before she could even define a bowl, he launched himself. She smelled fetid breath as he wrenched at the shoulder of her shirtwaist, then heard a sharp thud. The Burman's eyes rolled back as his head jerked back on the vertebrae. Blood seeped from his skull orifices; he was dead before he struck the deck. She felt terror rise, then saw Harley's taut, angry face where the thug's had been.

"Don't scream, dammit! You've caused enough trouble!" He dragged her after him off the boat, then past several wharves down the quay to the *Rani*'s mooring. He shoved her aboard, then into the cabin. "What the hell are you doing alone on the waterfront at night?"

"I was delivering a baby—"

"On Lop Ear's junk!" He was white-lipped with anger.

"What business is it of yours?" she cried, close to hysteria with belated reaction and confusion. "How did you know I was there anyway?" Legs beginning to tremble, she abruptly sat down on his bunk. "You killed him . . . how?"

"Never mind," he snapped. "If the Kanaka hadn't seen you board Lop Ear's rattrap, you'd be at the bottom of the harbor now"—sardonically, he flicked the torn shirtwaist—"with a few fond memories of Burma." With a taut-wire tension she had never seen in him, he began to pace restlessly about the small cabin, then turned on her again, face rigid. "Lop Ear's a fine hand at carving teak . . . and other things. Your own mother wouldn't have known you by the time you hit the river." He seized her shoulders. "Do you understand what I'm saying? Get off the streets! Go home and mind your damned business! Rangoon is rotten with Lop Ear's kind, and they don't all have slit noses and chew betel. I could tell you things about Bettenheim—" He broke off, then released her and went to a brandy decanter. "Pretty women disappear every week in Rangoon, whether to Lop Ear's sort or the slave trade . . . Oh yes, it exists." He poured two snifters and gave her one, then leaned back against the timbrel desk and took a hard swig from his own. "Lately, the count has picked up, even by official standards. Some influential men in Rangoon deal in the trade: men you've been making uncomfortable. Your messianic zeal"—the phrase was a sneer—"in providing house calls at night practically begs them to scotch their problem."

Lysistrata held the brandy untouched. She knew her almost unnatural calmness was due to shock, but her mind was clear, filled with sadness and realization of the inevitable. "Harley," she said quietly, "you said once that no one who lived through the War between the States could be as abysmally naive as I, and you may be right. We've never discussed my personal beliefs. My oldest brother died because he believed it was wrong for one man to own another; the middle one, Jason, died because he thought it was wrong for one man to dictate how another thinks. My mother and youngest brother died because that conflict broke them with sorrow and deprivation. My father lost his career because of it, and I lost . . . perhaps I lost my womanhood.

"Everyone in the family, even Jason, was against slavery. And when the slaves were freed, we all would have rejoiced—and did, those who were alive. Then we forgot about it. After the war, we assumed the freedmen had the same chance to build happy, prosperous lives as anybody else. Only, they didn't." She absently fingered the snifter. "It's easy to forget a man penned behind a wall. When I came to Rangoon, you made me look over the wall. Walls allow one to feel safe and superior. You can build on another man's achievements and never have to see the rubble of his life piling up or the deadness in your own if you never look down." She smiled faintly. "I'm rambling. I suppose I'm still shaky." Her eyes met his and she was startled by a flicker of naked pain in them, yet also saw something else less apparent—a sadness, a longing.

"You aren't going to go home," he murmured, "are you, Lysistrata?"

She smiled faintly. "I'm tired and afraid. If home existed, I would give anything to go there."

He put down the brandy, and in one fluid movement took her head in his hands and kissed her with a lingering sweetness that melted her against his breast as if she were a weary child. For a long time he held her, stroking her hair. As his fingers brushed the nape, her head fell back against his arm; and as if unable to help himself, he found her mouth again with slow hunger. "Eve, Eve," he whispered, "you would know too much, and that way leads from Eden. You do not want to come where I am."

His lips brushed her throat as he pressed her down on the pillows. She lay soft, still under his hands as he unfastened the shirtwaist, her heartbeat quickening at the catch of his breath. Her fingers found his hair as his lips brushed the cleft of her breasts, then drifted to their peaks. Her loins became warmly liquid, limbs weighted. This was surrender, this waiting, this need to be filled, be loved by this strange man who seemed to see into her soul as if it were his own. Feeling the hard, quick thud of his heart, she touched his cheek. ''Take me to where you are. I was not made for Eden.''

He hesitated, his eyes seemingly blinded by a storm of struggle; a perilous night of loneliness and desire. His mouth poised over hers, then plunged down. And in his kiss, Lysistrata knew the Fall. In his touch was the beauty of Adam, the lure of the serpent and all that lay beyond innocence. As if she had been formed from his flesh, he reclaimed her, his body slipping into hers with sweet ease. In his potency was the flush of earth's first dawn, in her the glimmering flower of its life. And where Eden was, remained one lost, lucent star briefly emblazoned on the night, the passing of its brilliant, singing light left to a silent drift of firefly sparks.

Harley dreaded that unearthly silence, its gathering, waiting cold. He lay enveloped in the warmth of Lysistrata's still peace, all the while feeling the chill creep over him. He had been insane, not with transient lust, but with the slow, burning need that could obliterate him. And her. This mating could breed only destruction; that ending had already found its ashen course.

He looked down into the luminous clarity of her eyes, lambent as if with the exaltation of a miracle. He had not hoped to find her like in a thousand lifetimes. In her was a rare, childlike glory that humbled him. Yet if he loved her, if that glory was not blackened, she would be destroyed and perhaps a nation with her.

His fingers tracing her features as if he would never see them again, he buried his face in her throat. How could he cast her alone into the void that he roamed like a restless ghost? Was it better to see her damned than dead?

The inevitable answer snaked through his mind. He was to be cheated of this choice like so many others. He must make her see him as damnation black and certain. She must flee him and all his kind, all those who were not of the narrow world she must inhabit. If she fled, she might live. In hatred. His shining innocent. He coiled about her in futile yearning to protect her, his shoulders curved against the needling chill.

"What is it?" she whispered, the radiance of her eyes dimming. "What's wrong?"

His voice came harsh and muffled, as if it emerged from another man, one he ached to destroy at this moment: the assassin, the cipher, the cold, calculating result of all those unavoidable, inflexible choices. "Nothing. You're quite promising for an amateur." His eyes shielded: hard, flat, impenetrable. "You'll not lack opportunities to polish your skills." With seeming carelessness, he flicked the discarded *longyi* twisted beneath her bare body. "Every man in Rangoon must know you wear nothing beneath this saintly uniform."

He saw confusion fill her eyes, then stunned pain like corrosive acid wash away her desire. Her face went a frightening white, and his hatred for the assassin went murderous.

"Stop it." Her lips moved stiffly. "Don't—"

His hand moved to her breast, closed hard, without tenderness. "You should be more careful in choosing your next lover beyond the pale, Lysistrata. Eastern males aren't accustomed to women so blatantly eager. We think of them as whores."

When she fought to get out from under him, he smiled tightly. "Did you think we would share a bed unto eternity?"

"Please," she whispered, "don't do this. Don't do this to me."

"Don't worry. After all, you're not just another bored

white woman, but the joke of Rangoon, particularly among the native population; I haven't ceased to be amused just yet.'' He gave a short laugh as shame and disillusionment transformed her face. "So now your taste of the Tree of Knowledge has gone bitter. Shall I salve your discontent?'' As if to seal her humiliation, his lips brushed the bare shoulder where Lop Ear had ripped the shirtwaist. Hate for him filled her eyes as love, throttled at birth, never had. When his weight moved away, she twisted like a cat, and with taloned nails roweled his face.

He touched his cheek and studied with detachment the bloody fingers that came away from it. "Impulsive,'' he murmured. "Right into the jaws of hell.''

Her tear-glazed green eyes slanted ferally. "I'd like to send you down the throat of the devil himself!'' Grabbing the *longyi*, she flung herself from the bunk.

He watched her wrench on her clothes and head for the door. "If you're thinking of taking a tale of offended virtue to the authorities, you may have trouble explaining what you were doing here in the first place. They're sure to believe you; after all, you're popular with them now. Even the Burmese officials adore you for causing so much trouble for them with the British. Dr. Herriott should enjoy the recital more than anyone.''

She turned, face stiff with loathing. "I should have let you die of cholera!'' The door slammed behind her.

Into Harley's eyes seeped a bleak shadow of terrible isolation. He had accomplished his purpose. One more rebel radiance was extinguished, the world a blacker haven for hatred. For assassins. At length, he summoned the Kanaka. "See to the woman who just left. Make it quick. We sail for Sumatra tonight.'' The Kanaka disappeared. As his footsteps died away on the planking, Harley lay back on the bunk, put the brandy decanter to his lips, and upended it.

* * *

Lysistrata, wild with pain and impotent rage, gave little thought to route while darting through harbor alleys toward the Royal Hospital. She only wanted to get as far as possible from the *Rani* and the monster she had begun to love. Love! Love had the cold eyes of a cobra. It lied and mocked and destroyed. Like a silly bird, she had been fascinated by Harley as if he had been a pretty bit of string. Now he had wound himself about her neck. Coldly, he had debased her in the worst possible fashion. All the wonder she had felt in their lovemaking had been a delusion. He had turned splendor into sin, low and mean and miserable. She felt defiled, dirtied as if she had been immersed in sewage.

Everything had changed. Before Lop Ear and Harley, the people she helped had responded with warmth and casual affection. She had felt protected, as if even the worst of them must know she meant only to ease their lives. Now every shadow mocked and threatened. Where was busy Water Street with its shops? As in the maze that had hidden Harley, one alley only entered another. Perhaps unpaved dirt muffled the following footsteps, for she heard them too late. As she broke into a run and turned a corner, a hand snapped over her mouth, another clamped her arms to her sides. Frantically, she kicked the attacker, but the soft sandals were useless. Briefly, she glimpsed a Chinese face before a chloroform pad flattened across her nose. I shouldn't have warned him, she thought in panic as it stifled her. Neatly, her unconscious body was slipped into a scarlet and black coffin for priestly cremations.

CHAPTER 7

Havoc

Here play'd a tiger, rolling to and fro
The heads and crowns of kings
ALFRED, LORD TENNYSON

"I don't know what to do, Harry." Distractedly running his fingers through his hair, Herriott paced about his study. "I've been everywhere, seen everyone. The Burmese officials are as sympathetic as the British and as useless." He plummeted into a chair. "I'd swear they're all glad to see her gone and unable to stir up more controversy. Mindon and his inane compromises and collaboration! He'll compromise his throne from under his bottom and plant it under Victoria's—" He caught himself. "Sorry, Harry, but I'm frantic. She's all I've got."

"I know very nearly how you feel, sir," Harry replied quietly. "I've talked to my commandant about a search, but he insists the case is civil business. If we just had a clue . . . It would be nice to say Lysistrata hadn't an enemy in the world, but the *Mayfield* couldn't carry all the people she rubbed raw. I'm afraid several of them are capable of having her out out of the way."

"I'm glad you don't say 'killed,' Harry," Herriott muttered dryly. "It's so much more bearable."

"Sorry, sir."

Ma Saw appeared at the open doorway. "I beg your pardon, doctor, but may I come in?"

"Of course, Ma Saw," Herriott said wearily.

"I could not help hearing your talk," she said hesitantly. "I know you are worried about Missy, so I did not say anything, but . . . my Sein, I think she is gone, too."

Herriott's head lifted. "What do you say? How long?"

"Over a month ago, she went to the house of *Tuan* Harley." She paused, then plunged on. "I know she stayed with him when he was sick . . . also before, but always she came home sometimes. She is foolish, but not bad. For two weeks now, nobody has seen her."

"Harley, eh," Herriott said thoughtfully. "I don't know that I'd worry too much, Ma Saw. He may have taken her with him to Sumatra. The *Rani* sailed about two weeks ago."

"And Lysistrata disappeared about that time, too," Harry muttered. "Ma Saw may have something. Harley told me he was displeased with Lysistrata's social agitation. He even threatened to do something about it . . . but *abduction?*" He shook his head. "I don't believe he'd resort to that."

"Rumors around the toddyshops and waterfront say he is a dream merchant and in the slave trade," Ma Saw put in. "Maybe he took Sein and Missy for slaves."

"Bosh!" Harry retorted. "That's damned chancy for a man as careful as Harley. Why, he almost lives like a Puritan—"

"In Rangoon," Herriott said slowly. "He may be less particular elsewhere. Perhaps we'd better see Bartly."

The Chiltons were at dinner with the Bartlys when Harry and Dr. Herriott arrived. Grudgingly, Sir Anthony

received them in the dining room when informed they
had a possible clue to Lysistrata's whereabouts; however, upon hearing it as the butler brought them coffee,
he snorted. "Richard Harley! Good God, I'd as soon suspect my mother! Do you take him for an imbecile?"

"Dunno, Tony," General Chilton said into his wine.
"I've never trusted the rummy blackguard. None of
those jigs has any moral sense."

Sir Anthony shot him an impatient look. "Nonsense,
Nigel; he's always been reliable. All this is the thinnest
speculation."

"Perhaps not, Tony." With a speculative frown,
Evelyn laid a hand on his sleeve. "My maid, Anne, has
not returned from her day off—that was two days ago.
She has also been most reliable."

"Perhaps she has an unreliable beau," suggested Lady
Mary, with a shrewd glance at Evelyn.

"Perhaps," Evelyn returned coolly, "but I have seen
Harley look her over once or twice. Haven't you, Nigel?"

"Dear me, he'd be hard put to do anything else. She's
a fetching little trollop." Chilton chuckled with a ribald
gleam in his eye.

"It *is* odd that all these young ladies have been acquainted with Richard Harley," Harry mused.

"Well, we shall wait a week to give the ladies a chance
to return before we jump to conclusions," Sir Anthony
stated firmly. "For the moment, I don't wish to hear any
more wild speculation."

That night, Lady Mary sat thoughtfully brushing her
hair as her husband reclined on a chaise with a three-
month-old *Times*. "Tony, you don't suppose Richard
Harley *could* have anything to do with these disappear-
ances, do you?"

"Didn't I make my opinion patently clear at dinner?"
he replied irritably.

"I suppose it *would* be most awkward for the Yünnan project if Harley should prove to be involved . . ."

Bartly threw down the paper. "Do you suppose I would knowingly thwart justice just to avoid an unpleasant piece of information?"

"If Harley cannot be trusted, the expedition may prove disastrous."

"I'm aware of that."

"His friend, Wa Sing, dabbles in the slave trade, doesn't he?"

"I daresay half the merchants in Kowloon have a hand in."

She swiveled on the dressing stool. "Tony, I wouldn't lend credence to much Evelyn has to say about all this; after all, she has a private ax to grind. But don't you think you should make some discreet inquiries about Harley's affairs? We have a good deal of money at stake in this expedition and your reputation as well."

He sighed. "Very well. You're usually right."

Three days later, a discreet inquiry was out of the question. On his way to work, a Madrassee clerk passing the *Star of Calcutta*, one of Harley's cargo ships, noticed a woman's bloodstained petticoat dangling from a porthole. Taking to his heels in fright, he probably would have said nothing about the discovery only he ran headlong into a port customs officer. His white face and fumbling excuses aroused the officer's suspicion; to keep from being taken into the customs office, the clerk described the petticoat.

Directly, the officer, the clerk, and a port security man went to the *Star* and demanded access to the hold. The captain was startled but agreeable. The section they described, he said, had been loaded with bags of rice nearly a week before, and no one had gone there since. Not that the crew kept captive women, he joked.

The first man into the hold was Portman, the customs man; behind him was the clerk. Portman began to paw through the mound of bags, then froze. The Madrassee clerk peered over his shoulder, turned and retched on the policeman's tunic. Disgusted, the policeman thrust him aside, only to pale himself. Grotesquely strewn among the sacks were three female bodies: a Burmese and two Europeans. One was nude and dead; the other two still partly clothed and alive but unconscious. All three had their tongues cut out. The dead woman's throat had been slit. Dried blood was everywhere. All had been bound, but the surviving European had managed to work free. When Portman bent over her, she roused and came at his face like a cornered wolf. Foam and blood flecked her mouth as she grunted obscenely in an effort to howl outrage and fury as they subdued her. "She's mad," muttered Portman, holding a sleeve against his slashed face. "Stark, raving mad."

The madwoman was identified as Anne O'Shaunessy, Evelyn Chilton's maid. The other European was a Portuguese prostitute; the Burmese was unknown. Immediately after the identification, three police officers were sent to Harley's house. In the master bedroom, which appeared to have been closed for some time, they found Sein. Nude, she was bound to the bed where she had been raped. In her mouth was stuffed a handful of sour tamarinds. A single bullet had been fired through her ear. The body was bloated, the stench horrible. The stench that surrounded Harley's name was far worse.

Harley returned the next night. As the *Rani* entered the port mouth, the helmsman stiffened and quickly turned to Harley, who was marking a coastal map. "Looks like trouble, sir. A godown fire on the east side of the harbor. Might be your section."

Harley looked up. "Hard a starboard. Let's have a look." The words were barely out of his mouth when a gaslight searchbeam raked the *Rani*'s side, flicked back and framed the cockpit.

"You there, *Rani!* This is the port authority. Cut your engines and heave to," sounded a megaphone hollowly over the water.

"What's the trouble?" shouted Harley, easing back to the oilskin-sheathed Winchester '73 rifle kept in the cockpit.

"You're under arrest, Mr. Harley. Prepare to be boarded."

"On what charges?"

"The authorities have some questions about your connections with Miss Lysistrata Herriott and some other women."

"Oh, all right," Harley replied calmly. In a smooth sweep, he shot out the harbor-patrol reflector, then his own binnacle light. As the startled patrol captain yelled, "Damnation, he's got one of those new American repeaters!" Harley leaned across his helmsman's arm, goosed one screw and reversed the other to pivot the *Rani* sharply on her stern.

In answer, the patrol sent a shot across his bow. It chunked up a spray that splattered the foresail.

"Get this scow moving!" Harley snapped in Chinese to his pilot. "We'll have a shell up our stern in a minute!"

Like a wraith, the *Rani* wove through the mist as shells grossly pocked the river on both sides of her. A flare arced the night sky. As soon as the water swallowed it, Harley ordered, "Hard aport!"

A moment later, the water exploded where the *Rani* had been. The next ten minutes were tense as Russian roulette: flares spotting the *Rani*'s position, her dodging, each captain trying to outguess the other. Harley was fatalistic. The patrol would dog him all the way downriver, which put the odds in their favor that he would be hit by a shell. She might run out of flares or plow into an obstruction in the dark, but he wouldn't trust to luck for that. So, he ordered the *Rani*'s extra spars and sails buoyed by floats strewn in her wake. Shortly, upriver sounded a series of dull thuds, the brief, sharp complaint of a damaged engine, then silence nicked by curses. The *Rani* disappeared into the darkness.

"That damned witch!" Harley was white-lipped with fury. He had hidden at Hsta Island in the maze of Irrawaddy delta creeks while awaiting return of a crewman sent to Rangoon. The man brought details of his supposed crimes, also the news that everything he had built in a lifetime was gone. The godowns had been mobbed and burned; his ships, their records, and his bank accounts seized; the house and shipping offices confiscated. Millions in pounds sterling might as well have been torched. Apparently, a competitor had snatched a chance to ruin him and used murder to insure his inability to recoup. That chance had been offered by Lysistrata Herriott. With the expedition at stake, Sir Anthony would never have begun an investigation without serious reason, which Lysistrata must have given him. Hell hath no fury like a woman scorned. He smiled tightly. This time, she had opened her mouth once too often; and someone, perhaps the same someone who had scotched him, had seen a golden opportunity to close it and let him take the blame. She might be dead, but he doubted it. The murders pointed to the slave trade where a bright-haired woman was too valuable to waste. He leaned against the *Rani*'s taffrail, and with eyes the color of cold steel, studied the cirrus clouds banked on the eastern horizon. He knew just where he might find Miss Herriott. She owed him a very large debt—which he would take out of her beautiful, bitchy hide.

* * *

With a bare foot, Lysistrata kicked disgustedly at the torn, dirty rags that trailed from the remains of her *longyi*. The Bangkok hole the slave-traders had kept her in for weeks was even filthier than the sweltering shiphold where she had spent several days and nights. At least the air here was breathable, though the stench of unwashed bodies and refuse on the straw-covered floor was horrible. Besides herself, fourteen women from the Asian subcontinent were packed into the cell. A menu of females for every palate was accumulated for the monthly auction floor. Her teeth gritted. Any man stupid enough to buy her would regret it! She would rather die than be degraded again. If a batch of drooling lechers thought she would perform on a leash, she'd give a show they'd never forget!

That afternoon, two guards herded the women into a bathing room. Lysistrata debated rebellion when ordered to disrobe, but decided whatever happened, she preferred to meet fate clean. With outward insouciance, she tossed off the rags and entered the already crowded pool, briskly soaped, then submerged. She came up to meet the appreciative stares of the guards. Grinning at her icy eyes, one gestured to a pile of clothing where some of the other women were already dressing. Gold bangles, earrings, and hair ornaments were scattered among the gauzy silks, and the women pounced on them like bandit monkeys bickering over who was to have the best. Noticing Lysistrata's contemptuous look, a delicately featured Siamese said sarcastically, "You want good owner, or pig?"

"'All men who buy women are pigs. One does not have to wear silk to please a pig." Glancing up at one of the guards, she drawled in Burmese, "Have you something in black?"

He was puzzled, unable to understand, then caught the word *black*. He looked questioningly at the other guard, who shrugged. The first one left to return with a black swath of silk. She wound it sari-style, then strode past the few remaining bangles without looking back.

Habib, the fat trader, took one look at Lysistrata and placed her last, the best position on the bidding order. Quickly, he sent flunkies dressed as clients from the curtained anteroom to tout his wares among the potential buyers. At length, a flunky sidled up to a black-eyed, white-robed Arab who lounged among several Chinese at the rear of the room. "I hear Habib has a rarity among his beauties this evening," the tout murmured. "A golden one with skin of mountain snow and eyes of jade. Her hair blazes like a temple flame." He discarded any idea of extolling the golden one's innocence. No male past the age of ten would take her for a virgin in that clinging black. "It is said she knows as many ways to please a man as there are—"

"Stars," finished the Arab dryly behind the draped *haik* which only revealed unimpressed eyes. "No doubt she is as cold as one. Prattle to yonder Kashmiri; he is a stranger to Bangkok."

Unintimidated as a cockroach, the tout scuttled off. Shortly, he and his companions accomplished their purpose. Knowing they could not afford the golden one, yet titillated by the description, the more modest patrons bid over their usual limit on the other females. The rich ones, the specialty and international merchants, bid on the best of the list, then bided their time and reserved their largest coins for the *pièce de résistance*.

Finally, most of the women had been distributed to their new owners. Only Lysistrata and a lovely Siamese were left. Aware her own value must be high, the Siamese sneered at Lysistrata. "You and your black! You will make more of a whore than any of us!"

Without malice, Lysistrata slapped the girl's face, then with a detached smile at her surprise, slapped it again. As she expected, the Siamese let out a screech of rage that echoed beyond the anteroom curtains. Spitting, clawing, the girl threw herself at Lysistrata. "Bitch! Witch!" she shrieked. "I'll tear your eyes out!" Lysistrata met the attack with a foot planted in her stomach that thrust her backward across the room. She crashed into servants assembled with trays of fruit, sweetmeats, and wine flagons to refresh the assembled males who sat with ears pricked at the yowls and clatter. The guards pounced on the Siamese, now dripping with food-flecked wine and ready to do murder.

Habib sharply gestured Lysistrata to the block. "If you don't bring her price as well," he hissed, "I'll beat it out of you!"

"Only if you still own me." With a sweep of the hips that would have daunted Cleopatra, Lysistrata sauntered before the crowd.

The Arab's black eyes narrowed. He had to give the "golden one" credit. Bronze-gold hair torched about her extraordinary face, she stood poised on the dais as if she were desire incarnate. The black silk gauzed the ivory of a body whose lush richness appealed straight to his loins. The high, ripe breasts and gilt pelt between her thighs beckoned, challenged him. Yet she was all an alluring lie. Sardonically, he noted her eyes' Arctic glitter.

When bidding began, Lysistrata stood motionless, as if impervious to it all. At length, a plump Indian silkily suggested the assemblage might like to examine the merchandise more closely. The Indian, one of the high bidders, was Gopal Prasad. The Arab cut in. "Three hundred gold *dinars* for the girl if she is not disrobed. I do not care to purchase 'examined' merchandise."

Gopal Prasad smiled ironically. "Unfortunately, the rest of us are unwilling to buy possibly damaged goods."

"I can afford the luxury of surprise," the Arab returned casually. "Offhand, I should say she looks distinctly undamaged."

Prasad studied the Arab's eyes, then his own narrowed. "Perhaps you have had the unfair advantage of having seen this girl before."

The Arab shrugged. "Perhaps. Zanzibar is full of blondes, but if I remembered her, I would not bid. Women peddled too often must be thrashed with boring regularity."

The eyes of the woman in question cooled noticeably. She said, "Why not ask the merchandise if she objects to being examined?" Her arms lifted invitingly to Prasad. "Perhaps you, my eager one?"

Prasad wasted no time crossing to the dais, and the Arab's lips tightened. If that toad's what she wants, I'll get revenge without having to lift a finger . . . or anything else.

Licking his lips, Prasad reached for the shoulder of the sari. "You still haven't asked me if I object." Lysistrata kneed him viciously in the groin. "I damned well do."

Yelling imprecations, the crowd rose as Prasad dropped, still grasping the sari. It ripped as she caught at it, exposing much of the curve of a breast and flank. The Arab darted onto the block as she recovered the sari and with her free hand flamboyantly made an international gesture, her eyes snapping with malice. With an air of resignation, he decked her with a right and swung her limp body over a shoulder. "I retract my offer," he told Habib. "It's half or nothing."

Habib gave Lysistrata's inert form a murderous look. "Done. Get that bitch out of here before I reconsider."

The Arab tossed him a small bag of coins. "May I ask where you got her?" At Habib's flat look, he flashed a smile. "I only wondered. Two like this one might be really remarkable, mightn't they?" With a *salaam*, he quickly departed before the moaning Prasad uncurled.

* * *

Lysistrata awoke with jaw bruised from chin to ear and a headache that barred description. She lay not wanting to move, not wanting to know in what wretched sty or lewd bed she had landed. It felt like a bed: one that faintly bore the uneasily familiar scent of sandalwood. Her eyes snapped open, took one look at the surrounding ship's master cabin, and clamped shut. As she contemplated setting fire to the ship and the unfortunately final pleasure of sending its owner to the bottom of the sea, the cabin door opened and the tall Arab who had flattened her ducked in. "That bruise is singularly unattractive," he observed judiciously.

"A man trying to talk with a curtain about his mouth is singularly unintelligible," she retorted acidly. "You'll forgive me if I ignore you."

Lazily, he unfurled the *haik*.

She gave his dark face a jaundiced look. "I thought it was you. You'll never get away with it."

"Perhaps not, but you will never see Rangoon again," Harley replied softly. "You may count on it."

"Dammit!" She sat up too quickly, and her head throbbed sickeningly. "You could have accomplished my permanent removal by leaving me in Bangkok."

"Did you think I had done with you?" He smiled unpleasantly. "You *have* been more trouble than you're probably worth. You were difficult to find and grossly overpriced, but you'll make it up to me. After all"—his eyes raked her body in its transparent silk—"you've world enough and time to play the whore."

"Don't let this getup go to your head," she said. "These are widow's weeds. I'll kill you if you try rape again!"

"You must apply to some other unfortunate for widowhood. I have no intention of marrying you." He turned to go.

She felt a surge of panic. She could have endured

Prasad better than Harley and the mockery of having longed for him like a child in some empty, ruined dream. Though Prasad would have been vile, his abuse and her hatred would have been impersonal. With Harley . . .

And like that forlorn child, she felt hope seep away.

"Wait." With a note of pleading, she knelt on the bed. "At least have the decency to let Papa know I'm alive. He's never hurt you."

"But you *are* dead, Lysistrata. Upon leaving Rangoon, you entered my world and became dead to your own. Believe it, for in time, it will be kinder if everyone you love believes it, too."

The finality of his words sank into her heart like a stone. Degrading her once had been insufficient; he meant to go on tearing her apart . . . for *what?* Had hatred always lain beneath his desire? Hatred he had now taught her, too?

After he had locked the door and left, she sat frozenly staring through the porthole at the blank, gray sea.

Food arrived but he did not. The stars came out and she watched them alone, afraid, knowing if he came, something in her would die forever. At length, she put on a *longyi*—either purchased for her or belonging to another of his women—from his locker and thrust the black silk through the porthole. The silk unfurled against the red, round glow of the sinking sun, then lay upon the water like a woman against a man. Finally, it sank down, down into oblivion.

Morning came and he had not come, nor did he all the nights and days that the *Rani* sailed west through the Maylay straits into the Andaman Sea. Staying well off the Tennasserim and Burma coasts, she at length passed the mangrove swamps of Baragua Point; there, twilight gleaming on breakers off the Flats forewarned the treacherous shallow entrance of the Irrawaddy River. The *Rani* entered the Irrawaddy by night; then, guarded by three

Remington-armed Karens, was hidden in a swampy channel of the offshoot Thaung du River. Along with the crew, Harley transferred his prisoner to a steam yacht, the *Lady of Shalott.*

As Lysistrata was taken aboard, moonlight revealed deckhands hurriedly carrying buckets below; behind them remained the resinous scent of varnish and new paint. Under a heavy canopy of mangroves over the riverbank, a fishing mesh woven with living creepers was being thrown over the *Rani*'s hull. Open jugs of naphtha were distributed about her decks; not only effective as insect repellent, they provided convenient incendiary grenades when mixed with lamp oil.

Within an hour, the *Lady of Shalott* was steaming toward the Irrawaddy. By breakfast, she entered the Kyunpyatthat River with its lazy morning traffic of dugouts and occasional cargo boats.

Lysistrata was forced to take in the view from Harley's cabin, which despite open-deck ventilators, became oven-hot as noon approached. The glass portholes were bolted shut to prevent her from signaling one of the cargo boats or Irrawaddy Flotilla Company steamers which stopped at crude river landings to take on passengers and mail. At a discreet distance, the *Lady* trailed a steamer upriver as it churned past water buffalo working sweeps of paddy land cut from jungle thicket. Along the shores rambled palm-shaded, tawny villages with small pagodas crumbling into the scrub. Fishing shanties dotted white, blistering sandbanks, their shallows spread with bamboo-strung nets. Dugouts and high-sterned fishing boats drifted drowsily in the heat.

That evening, the cook, Lysistrata's sole visitor on the voyage, brought supper as usual, but with the welcome change of river *hilsa* fish and fresh vegetables. If only the menu had included enough green tea for a bath.

As if in answer to her hope, the *Lady of Shalott*

stopped late the next afternoon to take on wood at a village a safe distance beyond Prome and its British garrison. Adjoining a small creek, the village was unevenly strung along a scalloped bank with the shore sides barricaded by a living wall of thorn and convolvulus. Over the thatched roofs dreamed a grove of tamarind and mango under a waft of toddy palms. Lysistrata was brought on deck in time to see a man who resembled Harley, but for a turban and loose Indian garb, leap to the bank. When the village man who came down to greet the yacht *shikkohed* with great deference to the Indian, she realized Harley had gone native. As Harley bowed with reciprocal respect and began a friendly chat, Lysistrata, in the armed care of an unfriendly, black-trousered Kachin Burmese, was ushered ashore.

Whatever Harley had in mind, Lysistrata was determined to make him regret it. She'd had time to harden on the voyage upriver. If she had to bend, she'd bend: just far enough to lash back in his teeth the first chance she got.

When she came up to them, Harley turned briefly to her and said in English, "This is U Too, headman of this village. You will *shikkoh* to him."

"And if I don't?" she said carelessly. Harley looked half-dressed, the Indian shirt falling open to the waist, the worn breeches cinched so carelessly about his lean middle they seemed in danger of slipping.

With maddening calmness, his gaze slowly glided down her sweat-sheened body. "The Kachin will accidently discharge his pistol into your foot."

She *shikkohed*, Harley offhandedly presented her like a leashed poodle, and U Too beamed. Hearing him compliment her hair to Harley, she rose and thanked him in polite Burmese.

The reward was a widening view of betel-blackened teeth. "It is very fine to meet an educated Engliswoman,'' he said approvingly, as if he had met many disappointing ones. ''Certainly, you have lived in Burma a hundred years.''

As the last was not precisely a question, Harley forestalled its answer by motioning forward a deckhand with a basket of liquors, cigars, and gilt-paper-wrapped sweetmeats Lysistrata recognized from a Fytche Square shop. ''For you and your family, U Too.''

''Ah,'' U Too exclaimed happily, ''this is very handsome of you, *Tuan* Ram Kachwaha. You and Miss Herriott will join me for supper to share these wonderful things, please. We had a fine catch of prawns just this morning and my wife will make *ngapi*. You will come?''

With a smile, Harley patted his shoulder. ''We shall be honored, U Too.''

As they all headed toward U Too's house, Lysistrata murmured ironically in English, ''So you've given him an alias, *Tuan* Ram Kachwaha, but aren't you a little sure of yourself for a kidnapper, telling him my name? Police and telegraphs must be stationed in some of these villages.''

''I am perhaps more Ram Kachwaha than Richard Harley beyond Prome, Lysistrata. Also, these people lie to the police and British as a matter of course. They aren't easily swayed by bounties.''

''You just bribed U Too,'' she observed dryly. ''He looks like a *baboo* who's just gotten a raise in salary.''

''I made a gift to an old friend,'' was the crisp reply. ''An old friend who knows rupees are worthless to a dead man.''

Tuan Ram doesn't bother to hide ruthlessness with charm now, Lysistrata mused. In native dress with those Moroccan boots, he looks as much a Pathan as Masjid, only Masjid is more civilized.

Beyond the pilings of the nearest houses where little girls were playing at mud pies amid the broad-leafed pumpkin vines, she noticed a circle of boys playing *chinlon*. Hands never touching the wicker ball, they deftly juggled it with feet and knees before kicking it to an opponent. Hearing their laughter as one caromed the ball with his bottom, she remembered Harley's teasing playfulness on the Martaban beach. Once he must have been a child like these, or had he? Perhaps he had seen the best way to disarm her was to appear guileless and unthreatening.

Misattributing her absorption in *chinlon* to the open stockade gate beyond it, Harley offered quiet advice. "I wouldn't get too many ideas about bolting while we're here. Tigers and rhino roam beyond that stockade. So do tarantulas and cobras."

"Aren't you neglecting the Bogeyman?" she retorted idly as a colored wooden top spun from under a bush and its naked owner scurried after it.

Declining to answer, Harley ruffled the intent little one's hair. "Moung Phat's getting to be a big boy, U Too." He glanced toward the houses where drop sides on the river allowed one not only to see what the occupants were having for dinner but often their sleeping quarters. Supper smells of roasting pumpkin and banana wafted from the braziers. "Things appear to be going well for you and your people."

"Yes, very well. The fire last year took only three houses." U Too pointed to charred piling remains at the far end of the village, then waved at the water chatties mounted on the surviving roofs. Lashed beside the doors were fire hooks for raking off burning thatch and paddles for beating out blazes. "The fire tools you showed us worked very well." His blackened teeth glinted mischievously. "My uncle's house only burned because he thought it a good show."

Harley laughed as Lysistrata sighed inwardly. U Too halted at the largest house and motioned his guests up the ladder. Lysistrata found the climb awkward in a *longyi*, and negotiating gaping cracks in the split-bamboo floors even more so. The worn mats seemed more suited to sieves than walls, yet feeling the river breeze on her perspiring neck, she appreciated the whole arrangement's shrewd advantage. Where Ma Saw's Rangoon house had a chair, U Too's had a stool; everything else was much the same except for the chipped native crockery and a busy baby boy.

U Too's wife, Ma Lay, seemed highly pleased to receive unexpected guests. When invited to bathe before dinner, Lysistrata accepted with alacrity. Leaving Harley and U Too smoking the new cigars and Ma Lay's eldest daughter to mind the baby, the women headed for the creek. Tactfully, Ma Lay did not comment on the dour Kachin who followed them and squatted on the creek bank. In turn, Lysistrata did not offer an opinion of the village men who lolled in the shade while their women, acting as stevedores, loaded eng wood onto the yacht to supply its boiler.

As she waded fully dressed into the water, Ma Lay carried a bundle and small basket, which she set upon the stern seat of a fishing canoe. Wondering what to do for dry clothes if she bathed in Burmese fashion, Lysistrata hesitated on shore. Having anticipated the problem, Ma Lay waved at the bundle in the fishing boat. "If you wish to wash your clothing, a fresh *tamein* is there."

Lysistrata, her Burmese fairly fluent from native hospital work, grinned with real affection. "Ma Lay, I think we are going to be friends."

Ma Lay's laugh echoed over the glass-green water as she submerged to the neck. "You might do better to be *Tuan* Ram's friend. He has very great *pon.* "

Lysistrata waded into the cool current. "You will find me something of a heretic, Ma Lay. I do not believe any man has the God-given *pon* to order me about."

Ma Lay's head cocked. "Perhaps you do not understand *pon*. What you speak of is *awza*. Our kings often send us men with *awza*. These men puff themselves up and tell us what to do. We agree politely, unless they are too silly, then do as we like. Men with *pon*, like U Too and *Tuan* Ram, do not need to give orders. They do not threaten and plead, yet sometimes we are willing to die for them."

So, Harley has learned to manage everyone he touches. Thoughtfully, Lysistrata breaststroked toward the sunlight-dappled water of midstream. "How do the *tuan* and your husband achieve this *pon*? I assumed every male is thought to be born with it."

Ma Lay joined her. "Every man *is* born with *pon*, but not necessarily enough to make him special. *Tuan* Ram brings us medicine. When the monk who taught our children died, he found us another teacher. Also, our neighbors have only to live near U Too every day to be convinced he is the worthy choice of headman." She grinned wisely as some village females arrived at the water's edge for evening baths. "He would have great *pon* with women, too, if I did not exhaust his potency." Her tongue gave a judicious click. "*Tuan* Ram would be hard to exhaust."

What do you know about it? Lysistrata thought sardonically, then wondered if the Burmese ladies so languidly entering the placid creek ever tested Harley's virility. As if in answer to her curiosity, Harley strolled into view with U Too and two other men. They greeted the women—who appeared delighted to see Harley—particularly when, with a grin, he handed cigars all around. Amid much joking and laughter, he and the other males hunkered down with shells of toddy wine and lit native cheroots on the shore under some mangoes.

Lysistrata's eyes glinted. No wonder he hardly bothers to tie those flimsy drawers up! Sullenly turning her back

on the shore, she dived, intending to swim upstream of
the women tripping daintily into the creek. Without
warning, a huge shadow ballooned in the murky depths
and, before she could react, struck her hard in the side.
Less hurt than panicked, she fought to the surface and
screamed. Harley was nearly to the bank by the time the
other men jumped to their feet and the shrieking women
headed for shore. Ma Lay abruptly ended the drama with
a shout of laughter. "Missy has met with a turtle!"

Belatedly recognizing the huge creature, and realizing
from its quick departure that it was as surprised and
frightened as she, Lysistrata mumbled an embarrassed
admission that she was in no danger. As everyone hooted
and Harley sauntered back to the men, several naked
children swung out on creeper vines into the creek in pursuit of the turtle.

Taking pity on Lysistrata's flushed face, Ma Lay suggested they had been swimming long enough. Perhaps
Missy would like to wash her hair. After leading the way
to the canoe, she produced combs from the basket; then,
giving Lysistrata one, helped comb the tangles from her
hair and apply cleansing paste of aloe. Proud of her own
thick tresses, Ma Lay freely admired the luxuriant gold
of Lysistrata's. With Harley silent in their midst, the men
puffed at their cheroots and commented on the wonder of
Missy's "sunlight" hair as as she twisted it into a high,
sleek knot. When Ma Lay and another woman laughingly
helped her negotiate the intricate, public shift from wet
clothes to a green-and-lilac *tamein*, Lysistrata had to endure another round of male observations on her ivory
skin. Though she felt Harley's black stare as if his hands
were hard on her body, he made no more comment than
the oblivious, hard-shelled leviathan on its solitary path
upriver.

That evening, hors d'oeuvres of pickled ginger and tea
leaves with sesame were served on U Too's porch. As U

Too and Harley amiably conversed with passersby below as readily as with each other, Ma Lay lit kerosene lanterns for dinner. After *ngapi,* mango rice, and fried bananas, Harley and U Too played chess. Lysistrata, Ma Lay, and her daughter played with the baby, tempting him to cross the porch after a rattle made from a creeper pod. Delighted by the dry clatter of the pod seeds, the baby churned forward, plopped on his bottom, and gurgled when Lysistrata surrendered the rattle. Used to being adored like all Burmese children, he showed her all four teeth in a wide grin. With a laugh, she held him up. "Moung Oo, you are a very fine boy." Moung Oo cooed agreement.

"Ha!" An abrupt whack on the thick chess table turned his coo to a startled wail. His father had put Harley's king in check. Undisturbed by the baby's wailing and the danger of his king, Harley eased forward his knight and silently smiled at U Too. With a howl of exasperation, U Too smashed the pieces from the board. As the baby's squawl scaled up an octave and Lysistrata gasped, Ma Lay blandly took the baby and shrugged toward a machete-like sword that hung on the wall. "Do not fear U Too will leap for his *dah,* Missy. All chess games end in this fashion."

So that's why the board's so thick, Lysistrata thought in bemusement.

At length, the closeness of the hut, the smell of spiced cookery and cigar smoke began to affect her. Excusing herself, she wandered out on the porch. The deserted creek was a broad, silver serpent black-banded by trees in the moonlight, the water's lap against the shore easing to a sigh in the current. An owl hooted in a nearby tamarind. Ignoring the Kachin squatting by the door, she descended the ladder and wandered toward the pale shore. The Kachin ambled after. When weary of creekside mango and moonlight that should have been romantic, but were not in her situation, she explored more intently inland toward the deserted *chinlon* clearing. Behind her padded the Kachin. The barricade convolvulus looked like fallen snow under the moon; then a distant flower flamed and Harley walked out of the tamarind shadows. She sighed. "Would you mind putting that out? I've had enough cigar smoke today."

"But apparently not enough exercise." He obligingly snuffed the cigar. "It's a long run to Prome even if you were to get past the barricade." He nodded toward the nearby stockade gate. "After sunset, the gate is guarded."

"Aren't you going to warn me again about all the jungle's long-legged beasties and things that go bump in the night?" she inquired wearily. "I could use a good bedtime story."

He shrugged offhandedly. "U Too's doesn't afford much privacy, but there's always the yacht cabin." He might have been appraising a prostitute.

Flaming for the second time that day, she started to slap him. He caught her wrist. "You will sleep in U Too's women's quarters tonight. Stay there unless you wish to meet that long-legged beastie."

With a muffled cry of rage, she jerked away.

As she disappeared into the darkness, Harley leaned against a tamarind and lit a fresh cigar. Why didn't he bed her? Her damnable pride had cost him millions. Why not break it; exact some return for his losses and blackened name? His lips curved in self-contempt. Because part of him could not stand to touch her for what she had done—and if he did touch her, he might not be able to easily be free of the hold she might weave again with the tricks she'd learned from Lady Mary, that she'd practiced on every male in reach. That she knew from raw instinct. She hated enough now to use those tricks. Remembering Benton Adams's glazed lust turned his stomach. Maybe he had only himself to blame if she'd turned into a vindictive bitch, but he'd be a fool to be drawn into any games before he was dead-certain of winning. Just keeping her made her miserable enough. Sooner or later he'd have her on his own terms. To kill time. Just that. For now, anticipation was sweet revenge enough.

Gazing at the pale curve of the great moon, he thought of Lysistrata's cool, white skin as she wound her *tamein* among the dark women at the creek in twilight. The sleek flow of throat and wet, polished hair. The cling of the *tamein* to her damp, ripe body. The full richness of her mouth in moonlight. The furious vibrance of her eyes. Then his mind roamed farther than he wanted. Imagined the lush nakedness beneath that bit of cloth he could so easily tear away. Her mouth under his. On him. With a low snarl, he flung down the cigar and crushed it under his heel.

At breakfast in the early dawn with U Too's family, Harley and Lysistrata spoke no more to each other than politeness before their hosts demanded. As they prepared to leave, Lysistrata was given a farewell present of the green-and-lilac *tamein*. During the walk to the boat with U Too and Ma Lay, Lysistrata observed a village man flailing a toddy palm with a rare display of energy. Noting her curious look, U Too explained blithely, "He is beating the palm to make her give more sap for toddy."

"Her?"

"Oh, yes. That is a female. This one is a male." He pointed to a nearby stalwart bowed over the bank. "A female will yield more than the male if she is properly beaten."

"Really," was the unenthusiastic reply.

Ma Lay, more sensitive to the animosity between Harley and Lysistrata, added a sage footnote. "One must take care, however. A female improperly beaten is a disappointment. Isn't that right, *Tuan?*''

"He should know," crisply affirmed Lysistrata.

Once aboard with farewells said, Lysistrata was redeposited in the master stateroom for another sweltering stretch of river. After lunch, she was permitted topside as the *Lady* was well into King Mindon's territory. Not seeing Harley on deck, she wondered if he was napping after a night as deserted of sleep as hers. Stretching out in a sling chair under the foredeck's tarpaulined canopy, she found northern Burma was a very different world. While the lush, lower Irrawaddy clung to summer, the upper river lazed under the sun with a trickle of tawny fall through its trees. Soaring, scarlet cotton trees flamed among brick-tinted *dhak,* their silvery trunks feathered by sprigs of bamboo from the dry wood. Distant smoke drifted like a lulling, spicy opiate across the water. Soon, she slept.

She awoke to the alluring scent of roast chicken and tamarind rice; less inviting was Harley's flat gaze as he sat in a deck chair opposite her. A camp table had been laid for dinner between them. The rouged globe of the sun was sinking in a splendid mauve and apricot sky reflected on the eastern plain as if on water. From that mirage rose the thousand ancient, half-ruined temples of Pagan. The *Lady of Shalott* had been moored offshore of the high mudbanks where geese drifted about her snowy sides in reconnoiter of dinner, the cranes and ibis having retreated to the shore to mince in envy. Occasionally, a bird pounced on a frog or took to the air to skim over the river with its silvery, elusive gleams of rising fish.

The Javanese cook, wearing a white tunic, poured French wine from a heavy silver cooler that had been lowered over the side of the yacht. Minnows struck at the cooler's bright sides as it was hauled up; dripping, it was brought to the table. Harley and Lysistrata were silent as they dined; Harley, smoothly handsome in English-tailored evening clothes; Lysistrata in the graceful, delicately colored *tamein*. With relief, she sensed he had not dressed for her benefit, that his preoccupation had nothing to do with her. Their romantic surroundings had an unreal quality of suspension that was not a prelude to seduction. She felt like a participant in some private ceremony she knew nothing about, as if she were in the company of a cultivated Hun capable of kissing her hand before he cut her throat; yet the river's limpid quiet had lulled her into indifference. Dinner done, Harley waived liqueurs and rose from his deck chair. Elegant profile dark against the blaze of sunset, hands in pockets, he inquired absently, "Would you like to see Pagan?"

Lost in her own thoughts, she glanced up at the distant cupolas. "Why not? I could use a walk."

By the time she had gone below for sandals and light stole, Harley had the dinghy lowered. The inevitable Kachin sat in the bow. As Harley impassively handed her into the boat, she could not resist needling, "Can't you keep track of me without an armed duenna?"

He seated her at the bow and unshipped the oars. "Perhaps I'm just too lazy to carry a rifle."

Her eyes narrowed. "Would you really see me shot?"

He considered their nearness to Mandalay. "Yes."

Ignoring her grim silence as they left the boat onshore, he led the way up a narrow, treacherous path to the upper bank. There, they walked along a sandy trail through scattered pagodas in desert barrens of thorn scrub and red flowering cactus. Beyond a tamarind and palm grove reared the great rusty bulk of the Temple of Sala-muni against the vivid sunset. Perhaps a half-mile past Sala-muni were graceful, white Ananda's myriad spires and gold-tipped *ti*.

Harley, like a bored but resigned host, told her how

many smaller temples, most now lumps of weed-grown rubble, dated to Anawrahta, a warrior king whose brilliance and war elephants dominated all Burma in the ninth century. Indian-styled Ananda had been built in the tenth century; after Ananda, Sala-muni, only to be devastated by Kublai Khan. "The Khan kept upper Burma for a few years, then let it drift away. European traders began to scheme over Burma, and for a time a Portuguese bravo named Nicote controlled the lower reaches. In the eighteenth century, the Chinese turned Burma into a battleground over their exiled Ming emperor."

The sun had set, leaving a purple cloak of dusk over the ancient city. They paused while the Kachin lit a kerosene lantern, then walked up the artificial terraces of Ananda. "After acquisition of India," Harley continued, "the British disliked squabbles with Burma along their eastern borders and mistrusted the stability of a country which regularly changed monarchs with bloodbaths that could easily spread to foreigners. So, with bankers' practicality, they sent in an expeditionary force and secured their operations in lower Burma within a year. In 1853, half of Burma was a province of British India. Mindon moved his capital to Mandalay."

As Harley delivered all this in the dispassionate manner of a tour guide, Lysistrata wondered where his interests lay in the colonial dismantling of Burma. If not for the Winchester-bearing Kachin, they might have been honeymooning lovers wandering about in the romantic moonlight of the temple.

Though Ananda showed its great age, its blue-white loveliness was undiminished by time. Each tier of the spires was recessed in terraces into an elongated bell, topped by a gilded *ti* reaching for great diamond, tropic stars in the ink-blue night. Where most temples were solid, a lacework of ornamentation was pierced by doorways and windows. The structure seemed poised above the earth. The surrounding plain was silent, as if time had stopped with only an occasional rustle of leaves in the nearby palms and the distant sigh of the river to sing its passage. One sensed only the movement of constellations, only the breath of the wind. Age that dreamed beyond memory.

Gazing at that lunar plain, Lysistrata, sculpted in moonlight like a pale Gupta figure on the monument, felt Harley's eyes upon her. Seeming to take it for granted she would follow, he turned away and began to stroll the terrace. "Have you noticed this bas relief?" he murmured. "It's quite remarkable."

Remarkable, indeed. Lysistrata's eyes widened as she fully defined the almost life-sized stone figures about the base of the monument. Interspersed with houri-like angels and dancers were exceedingly earthy males and females sexually joined in incredibly imaginative ways. Both shocked and fascinated, Lysistrata saw curve upon curve, breast upon buttock, smile upon smile. Harley paused by a lovely, lascivious figure, and she flinched slightly when he turned.

"This little dancer is my favorite. Exquisite, isn't she?" He touched the small figure's cheek with a graceful hand. His smile seemed soft like a boy's, and she remembered his watching the children and their kites in Dalhousie Gardens.

"Yes," Lysistrata agreed with quiet sincerity, "she is." This dancer was life to him with far less prurience than poetry. And what am I to him? she wondered sadly. Flesh without poetry.

"To touch certain things seems irresistible." Harley stroked the dancer's throat, its shoulder. "She always feels warm . . . even long after the sun has set."

"When did you first discover her?"

"My first trip upriver. I was ten." His mouth slanted whimsically. "She was just the size for a sister."

Sister? Lysistrata thought, uncomfortably following the sensual tracing of his hand over an opulent breast.

He laughed softly. "Father misunderstood. He gave me a *nautch* girl."

"At *ten?*"

He shrugged, his hand now casually resting on the curve of a stone hip. "Children reach puberty early in the East."

"But . . . you didn't . . . ?"

"Why not?" he replied simply.

So much for the innocent boy in him. Abruptly, she turned away.

Harley caught her arm. For a frozen, startled moment, she stood with his fingers warm on her skin, his eyes without innocence. For that moment, she felt naked, clothed only in wind and starlight in the hot, black night of those eyes. Then, his eyes veiled and he dropped her arm. A chill of perspiration pricked beneath her arms and breasts.

"Come, you've not seen the interior." Not seeming to notice the swift intake of her breath, he led the way into a temple passage. Midway down the passage lit by the Kachin's lantern was a chamber where a Buddha towered in the shadows, its gilded gleaming hulk suggesting somnolent, brooding power ominous with invading lantern-light thrown upward across its heavy features.

Still feeling that odd chill, Lysistrata rubbed her arms. "The Bogeyman?" she murmured to Harley.

He had taken a thin cigar from a flat silver case. He lit it from the lantern, his brown hands dark against his snowy shirtfront. "Does he frighten you?" The cigar glowed as he drew in its smoke. "Three more like him are in the other vaults."

The faintly mocking challenge in his voice calmed her. "Why should I be frightened?" She studied the statue's smooth, massive face. "He's only a great block of wood."

"Ah, but if Buddha should walk . . ." His smile was sphinxlike.

She laughed softly. "I can almost see him striding across the plain. How fearful he would be, with footsteps the thunderous echo of thousands."

Harley exhaled a thread of smoke. "You sound disappointed that he hasn't moved."

"I suppose I am. This place, pagan . . . the moonlight, leads one to expect that sort of thing." Anything. Moon-pale breasts under a languid caress, an obsidian glimpse of sin with its promise of delight and destruction . . . Involuntarily, she looked up.

Harley's gaze followed hers to the Buddha's heavy-lidded eyes. "This old fellow has been sitting here since before William the Conqueror. Even Genghis Khan couldn't budge him."

Lysistrata glanced at Harley. The contrast of his sophisticated evening clothes to the faded paintings of the vault was extraordinary, but she suddenly saw his face was indefinably, implacably pagan. Despite his youth, one sensed centuries behind him. She would never think of him as Richard Harley again. "I wonder what sort of man could make Buddha walk," she mused, half to herself. "A man nothing like the Khan or the Conqueror. And nothing like you."

"Then you must await a second Christ," he returned agreeably. "Unfortunately, if the world is not either mortally wounded or dead, it will try to destroy him. And perhaps, he . . . it." He gave her a quizzical smile. "Perhaps more than one Christ will come. You Americans are fond of teamwork."

As they walked back out into the moonlight, she looked about the plain with its silent ruins. "I think the

Buddha-movers will be quiet men. Like this waiting, patient place.''

"You may be right.'' His voice was a mutter, half-indistinguishable because of the cigar between his teeth. "Pagan may not be as dead as it looks.''

"Then you think Burma will outlast the British?''

"Her culture might not. Her men are likely to bend like willows until their roots weaken, but her women . . .''—the cigar took on a jaunty angle—"they may flatten, but they'll be here until the rice paddies dry to dust.''

Ah, yes, the women, she mused. The women you would exquisitely understand. "What is your role in all this?'' she asked as they walked back toward the river.

He watched an owl scout a mouse in the cactus. "Just a bit part. A single entrance.'' The owl dropped. "A single exit.''

Her gaze followed the owl as he flitted into a tamarind grove with his prey. "Owls look oddly English, don't they?''

"Particularly when they make love.''

In spite of herself, she laughed.

That night, after she was long asleep on the *Lady*, Harley came up from his cabin onto the afterdeck. Dressed in Indian white, he handed his black evening cutaway on its wooden hanger to the startled Javanese cook fishing over the stern. "A gift, with my compliments. The chicken was perfect tonight.''

He drifted forward to hunker at the bow. The river's face was silver with moonlight and passing, elusive shapes: stone women who danced about a woman of warm flesh and cold eyes. A Buddha that darkened the sun. Owls: thousands and thousands of them. His own face, blurring into blackness.

Harley's interview with King Mindon at Mandalay was as useless as he thought it would be, and as danger-

ous to arrange. The difficulty was the king's integrity,
which was a frequent pain to anyone who befriended
him. Richard Harley had the misfortune to love him like
a father for he was everything William Harley, Lord
Lyle, was not. William had been vain, selfish, ruthless,
and sometimes rash; Mindon, a monk prior to ascending
the throne, was modest, selfless, gentle, and thoughtful
to the point of inertia. Although the British had expanded
a mere toehold in Rangoon in 1826 into control over half
of Burma, Mindon maintained they could be reasoned
into staying in the south. As a king, he did have several
things in common with William Harley. Once he made a
decision, he stood firm with implacable courage. Unfortunately, his combination of faith in British good intentions and personal honor led him to hamstring any
resistance to British infiltration; this included refusal to
talk secretly with anyone he knew to be anti-British. Harley was obliged to risk his neck just to pay his respects.

Harley made formal application for a royal interview
through Prince Rahtathara, a personal friend.

"I will try to arrange a meeting with His Majesty tomorrow, but I think it wise not to mention your difficulties in Rangoon," advised Rahtathara. "His Majesty
may feel obliged to discuss them with Consul Endicott."

"I'm not likely to leave the Glass Palace without discussion of them," replied Harley. "Endicott is informed
by telegraph about everything that goes on in Rangoon."
He absently fingered the mustache he had begun in
Bangkok. His face dirty, he was garbed in Indian peasant
attire, his head wrapped in a ratty turban.

The prince refilled his friend's teacup. "Just now, the
object is to enter the palace. To get out is something
else."

Alone, Harley entered the glass-and-silver-inlaid doors
of Mindon's royal anteroom. Like much of the palace,

the chamber was a glittering jewel case of gilded teak, glass, and mirrored mosaics that prismed the rich colors of its occupants' attire into a restless kaleidoscope of color. Despite the splendid jonquil brocade tunic of his Rajput ancestors, white jodhpurs, and diamond-and-emerald aigrette turban, Harley blended into the bejeweled crowd outside the royal audience chamber like a brilliant bird in an aviary full of them. The only conspicuous beings were members of the British resident consulate in their gray frock coats. Ironically, they had the meek appearance of doves, although they were among the most predatory hunters in the assemblage. British military in scarlet tunics were less discreet.

Harley, languidly using a fan as a shield from familiar faces, stayed on the opposite side of the room from Consul Endicott; but inevitably, the court chamberlain rapped the floor with his malacca stick and called the name of Ram Kachwaha Harley, Prince of Rajputana.

Consul Endicott's head snapped around as if jerked by a string. Eyes narrowing as Ram Kachwaha Harley came abreast of him, he murmured something to an attaché at his shoulder. Immediately, the attaché left the room.

Upon entering the royal chamber, Ram Kachwaha dropped to hands and knees as his name was repeated to the king. "Rise, my friend," suggested Mindon in his high, slightly singsong priest's voice. "I am aware Western ways are sometimes more comfortable for you." He gestured to a scarlet pillow before the *pyathat*-topped throne. The room was completely mosaicked with mirrors fragmenting the images of the two men: the boldly handsome young Rajput prince and the shaven-headed old man in his simple white robes. As Ram Kachwaha gravely thanked him and seated himself lotus-fashion, the old man's eyes were bright with affection. "We have not had the pleasure of your presence in the Glass Palace for too long, my son. May We hope you have come for Our Birthday Festival?''

"Your Majesty is gracious, but I regret my stay in Mandalay may be cut short. I could not leave until I extended my wishes for Your long life and prosperous reign." The younger man paused. "Also, I seek Your advice concerning a private matter of importance."

"You are to be married?" Mindon's eyes twinkled.

Ram laughed. "It is not so important as that, Your Majesty. Perhaps You will be kind enough to choose a wife for me when I am old enough to appreciate Your wisdom."

The king chuckled. "You need not be old for that, my son; merely apathetic." He waved the guards out. "Now, what is this private matter?"

Aware he had desperately little time, and choosing his words carefully, Ram described the expedition proposed by Bartly.

"I have no objection if the British seek to open a trade route through the Shans so long as they do so peacefully," the king said mildly. "Was there anything else?"

"Sire, if the British open such a route, they will wish to secure it and thereby have an excuse to annex the Shans to lower Burma. They will express official doubt that Your Royal troops are sufficient to the task of protecting the route. Already they are sending military provocateurs into the Shans to encourage rebellion against Your authority. If an expedition is sent into China, as one inevitably will be, and is destroyed as it inevitably will be, their hope of opening trade with China through Burma and plans for the Shans may be temporarily abandoned. At present, it is a valuable distraction. So long as only the hope and not the fact of the trade gate exists, the British will be reluctant to expend men and supplies to seize the Shans, which are often more troublesome than profitable. Without that distraction, they will turn their attention to the riches of Northern Burma and they will be free to do so.''

"What are you suggesting, Ram?" asked the king.

"I have seen to it that the plans for the current expedition will be prolonged, Sire, and eventually come to naught. Unfortunately, the expedition may now be canceled altogether a great deal sooner than I hoped, and I may not be in a position to directly influence the course of another one. I ask only that You do not openly obstruct British passage through the Shans. If You are willing, however, to encourage them to keep focus on China by encouraging future expeditions, You might do much to prolong the integrity of Your realm.''

The old man studied him. "So you feel We are unable to protect Our dominions?"

"Sire," Ram said patiently, "no man can withstand British artillery with Burmese cannon. It is simply a matter of time."

"We are aware of Our military capabilities," the old man said curtly. "I should reproach you for neglecting the intervention of Our lord Buddha," he added more gently, "but then you are not Buddhist and may be forgiven that *particular* negligence. We cannot condone your directing men into a deathtrap. If the British wish to risk expeditions to China, that is their misfortune; however, We will do nothing to promote their delusions.''

"Sire, if—" Ram was cut off by the court chamberlain's reappearance.

"Sire." The man dropped nervously on all fours and parroted hastily, "The British Consul Endicott beseeches Your Majesty's indulgence in requesting an immediate audience. He wishes to present evidence that Prince Kachwaha is criminally liable to his authority for certain heinous instances in Rangoon.'' The chamberlain's head bobbed hastily in Ram's direction. "I most humbly beg

Your pardon, Your Highness. I am merely quoting Mr. Endicott.''

The king addressed the chamberlain's polished bald pate. "Did he specify the nature of the instances?"

"He did not, Your Majesty."

Mindon clapped for guards, who instantly reappeared. "Admit him."

Endicott strode in, an aide at his left shoulder. After a cold look at Ram, he bowed smartly to the royal monk. "Sire, I insist on this man's immediate arrest. He—"

"First"—the king cut him off with a firm gesture—"We must ask that your attaché remove his sword from Our Presence."

"Your Majesty, this man is dangerous!"

The gesture came again, more sharply. "Either the sword or you must leave."

With ill-concealed exasperation, Endicott waved for the attaché to surrender the saber to the court chamberlain, who awkwardly carried out the heavy, unfamiliar weapon.

"Now then, Mr. Endicott," Mindon said mildly.

Sharply, Endicott detailed the murders and smuggling, drug- and slave-dealing offenses his government believed Harley to have committed.

"These accusations are most serious, Mr. Endicott," said the king gravely. "What have you to say to them, Prince Kachwaha?"

"I am innocent, Your Majesty," Ram answered calmly, "of murder and slave-dealing. The smuggling charge is redundant, for I have never taken anything illegally into or out of Your realm. As Mr. Endicott is no doubt aware, the drug trade is not illegal."

"Your Majesty, nothing this scoundrel says can be believed," Endicott protested curtly. "His very presence here is an impudent outrage."

"I have never known His Highness to be untruthful,"

replied the king, "and I have known him since his boy-hood. Certainly, I do not believe him capable of murder. As he says, the other charges do not apply."

Endicott turned red. "Your Majesty, I demand this man be relinquished to my custody to be deported to Rangoon for trial!"

Ram watched, outwardly calm, inwardly taut as a drawn crossbow.

"Mr. Endicott, I must beg your patience. The prince is My guest. He shall leave My presence as freely as he entered it." Mindon smiled at Ram. "Will you be joining Us on Our barge for this afternoon's celebrations, Your Highness?"

"I shall be honored, Sire."

"Good. Prince Rahtathara will see you to Our quarters." He smiled benignly at the infuriated consul. "We hope to see your barge this afternoon, Mr. Endicott. Our celebration would not be complete without it."

At the tacit but clear dismissal, Endicott jerked in a perfunctory bow, and with his attaché, backed from the room.

"Thank you, Sire," Ram said quietly.

"Even if you are a criminal, Ram," said the king with a quizzical smile, "you are at least polite. Our departed representative of the British Crown did not even wish Us a happy birthday."

The royal barge parted chrysanthemum garlands which floated upon the palace's vast artificial lagoon in a blaze of scarlet and gold with the gilded oars of forty scarlet-clad rowers winging over the still surface. Behind it fanned smaller barges receding in magnificence until the plain British barge brought up the rear. Cheering commoners crowded the fringes of the moat. The barges circled the gold-roofed pagodas of the vermilion Glass Palace until its bulk blocked the British boat's view of the royal barge. The king made a small gesture to his oar leader, then murmured to Ram, who sat just below the scarlet-canopied royal dais, "Here you will leave Us. Come soon again to Mandalay, for your presence"—he smiled slightly—"if not your opinions, are always welcome."

"My life is Yours, Sire." Ram turned onto his knees and kissed the dais at Mindon's feet.

"Then keep close hold of it, my son, for Our troubled realm may one day have need of you."

As the barge veered close to the walled bank, Ram leaped ashore. In moments, he had disappeared into the crowd.

For that day and many following, British-trained *gurkhas* fruitlessly watched the roads and combed the Mandalay waterfront for a boat moored above Amarapura.

CHAPTER 8

The Lady and the Tigress

A land of streams! Some like a downward smoke,
Slow dropping veils of thinnest lawn, did go;
And some thro' wavering lights and shadows
broke.
Rolling a slumbrous sheet of foam below.

ALFRED, LORD TENNYSON

Within fifteen minutes after Ram rejoined the *Lady* at
Amarapura, the yacht hauled anchor. Many miles upstream, he debarked with Lysistrata and the two scouts to
go overland east into the mountainous Shans. After bar-
gaining for the use of two elephants from a nearby village, Ram showed Lysistrata how to induce the smaller
creature to kneel so she might mount. When the elephant
presented its leathery trunk as a step stool, she uneasily
studied its sly little eyes, warily placed a foot on the appointed spot, and grabbed at the thicker part. With startling speed the trunk elevated. Making a terrified lunge
for the beast's forehead, she scrambled over its ears. Fortunately a patient creature, it allowed her to clutch whatever she liked. Breathing quickly, she looked down to
see several grinning children a surprising distance below. Among the grins was Ram's tolerant smile. He mo-

tioned her back on the elephant's shoulders, then deftly mounted. With the scouts aboard their elephant, the small expedition lumbered off in the direction of the Shans. Loath to hold onto Ram, Lysistrata balanced like a nervous dragonfly.

The pale sunrise sifted through the haze lying on the plain of Ava, the hills half-shrouded in mist with their summits aglow like a Wen Cheng-ming watercolor. As the sun mounted on the horizon, the elephants lumbered through jade rice fields, then climbed into *indaing* forest where the riders reached parrot-bright autumnal valleys.

Before they had gone a mile through the gathering heat, Lysistrata, tired of trying to keep her balance, wished for breeches so she might sit astride like the men. Ram, in loose-cut Indian cotton and soft boots, looked annoyingly comfortable. The mustache and turban completely altered his appearance; except for his coldly ironic smile, nothing seemed to remain of Richard Harley. When he returned safely from Mandalay, she had felt a dim sense of relief. His crew might have killed her to protect themselves if he had been captured. The scouts, Kanaka and Friedlander, looked capable of dispatching their own grandmothers. The pair were direct opposites; the former huge, brown, and deceptively indolent; the latter small, red, and weasel-wary.

Near midday, they reached a high plateau alive with tiny, fleet deer that darted away through mammoth ferns to send up blurring rainbows of bulbuls and parakeets. Elephant grass mixed with towering catalpa brushed the riders' feet while convolvulus amid flowering bauhinia hung to their shoulders. After a cold lunch in a lichen-velveted grotto by a rocky waterfall they began a winding descent through the jungle.

Gradually, the combination of shade and lowering sun

dropped the temperature to a degree Lysistrata had not encountered in Burma; by sunset, she was chilled. Squatting with a scarf about the shoulders, her bottom too sore to sit, she watched Friedlander build a fire at their campsite. Kanaka hacked down a foot-thick bamboo, sliced a portion through just below two of its joints, then politely requested her to fill the container it formed from the grotto stream. Though inclined to refuse, as Ram had disappeared into the jungle with his gun, she thought better of antagonizing the huge Polynesian. He put the water to boil on the fire, then threw in a few handfuls of rice from one of the modest packs he and Friedlander carried on their elephant. The elephants, with wooden clappers, had been loosed in the jungle to forage for themselves. Hugging the scarf closer, she hoped the scant baggage included blankets.

Shortly, Ram appeared in the deepening gloom with several squirrels. Before long, a smell of crisply browning meat blended with pungent curry.

During the meal, Lysistrata almost forgot the cold, but soon remembered when the fire faded. Noticing her huddling in silent misery by the fading coals, Ram dug into a pack and dropped a rough wool Kachin jacket over her shoulders, then tossed vests to the men. Hair tumbled against the shorn collar, she burrowed gratefully into the thick gray wool with her bare toes tucked under the *longyi*. Drowsily, she watched Friedlander build up the fire for Kanaka to take first watch. Ram gathered leaves for bedding, motioned her to take a pile, then threw her a blanket of the same weave as the jacket. Only briefly wondering if she might be flattened by a sleepwalking elephant, she fell asleep in moments.

While dreaming she was trapped in an igloo of madmen, she awoke to the morning's eerie shriek of gibbons. The clearing was thick with fog, the trees ghostly shadows in the numbing cold. Every muscle screamed as she sat up, bundled to the nose in the blanket. Two woolly lumps snored across the clearing, and Ram, who must have had the final watch, was rebuilding the fire. He glanced up as she shivered. "If you have a call of nature, now would be a good time to answer it."

Grimly gathering the blanket tighter, she headed in the direction of the stream. After relieving herself, she dabbed a hand in the cold water and scrubbed her face. As she was pawing out hair tangles, Ram silently came up behind her. At her startled yelp, he extended a tin cup of hot squirrel broth. "Breakfast," he said briefly. "The rice is on to boil."

"You didn't have to sneak up on me," she said sourly. "I'm not likely to dash back to Mandalay in a pea-soup fog."

"Predators water in the early dawn. Lingering over toilette is unwise." Gun slung over his shoulder, he headed upstream.

To the screech of arriving lemurs, she scurried back toward camp. Rounding a bend in the path, she let out a stifled cry and nearly dropped the blanket. The rear of an elephant was an awesome spectacle at close range. Shrilly trumpeting and tiny tail whipping, the elephant sharply turned. Her elephant. Lysistrata froze. Nothing was sly about the creature's eyes now; they were piggy with irritation. The great ears flapped, then spread. Stiff with fright, she eased off the blanket, held it up like a flimsy wall. There was a long silence. She took a hesitant step backward, only to melt with dread at the elephant's warning blast.

"Don't move, dammit!" came Ram's urgent whisper behind her.

Another blast seemed to shiver the leaves. The blanket withered as the elephant charged. Nearly deafened by the crack of Ram's gun, Lysistrata squeezed her eyes shut, then was yanked off her feet and hurled from the path into the brush. A split second later, Ram's weight landing nearly atop her knocked the breath from her lungs. The ground trembled as the elephant crashed past them, then veered away. She lay rigid under Ram, heard the whistle of his released breath. He did not move.

"Is he gone?" she whispered.

He nodded against her neck.

"Then get off."

His head rose. In a face pale under its tan, his lips took on a crooked curve. "Ah, now that he's gone, you don't want me anymore."

"Will you please . . . I can't breathe!"

Lazily, he propped his weight on his arms on either side of her head. "Do I really take your breath away?"

She weakly pushed at him. "Don't be clever!"

He felt her trembling. Her fear gave him no satisfaction; he had thought it would, although he knew she was more frightened now of the maleness firmly packed against her belly than the elephant.

She glared at him. "For God's sake, *move!* He may come back."

"Not likely," was his dry reply. He eased off her to kneel staring off in the direction of the flattened undergrowth. "I suppose you can't be expected to know better than to walk up on an elephant's rear, but getting that beast back is going to be the devil."

"You *want* it back?"

He gave her a weary look.

She sat up, hugging the blanket, her nerves raw.

He studied her. "What the hell did you think you were doing with that, baiting a bull?"

"You mean the blanket? I was . . . changing my shape."

"You were what?"

"I thought if the elephant didn't know what I was, he might be afraid."

He eyed her quizzically. "While it's true a male of any species might see your real shape as an invitation, he's not likely to forget it in a moment." His head cocked. "Besides, he was a she."

After three hours of hard, temper-trying search, the runaway was retrieved. Unwilling to trust its reaction to Lysistrata, Ram traded mounts with the scouts. "Up," he ordered her curtly. She looked at the elephant, then at the tired, sweaty faces of the men. She went up.

Two days later, due to steepening trails, the elephants were exchanged for shaggy ponies, and Lysistrata was obliged to break in a new set of muscles. As they moved deeper into the Shan Mountains, Friedlander habitually led off as scout while Kanaka brought up the rear. In the high altitude beyond Hsipaw where the jungle already wore the trappings of dying fall, the trees were bare, the undergrowth dry as tinder beneath the ponies' hooves. They lurched and stumbled along trails that grew impossible in spots. Finally, following the men's example, Lysistrata turned athwart her pony to avoid raking her mountainside leg raw. Clutching the pommel and saddle rim, she stared numbly between her toes at treetops thousands of dizzy feet below and felt her heart wing to her throat every time the pony's slipping hooves flung a spatter of gravel into emptiness. Noting Lysistrata's pallor, Friedlander soothed, "You'll only wrestle that nag until tonight. We're turning the ponies in at a mining camp on the Nan-tu River."

"Turning them in for what?" she replied grimly. "Mountain goats?"

He grinned. "No such luck. We'll be using our feet come sunup."

"Oh, bliss."

Despite the dull tone, her excitement was sparked. A mining camp meant civilization and a chance to escape.

Escape was not to be so easy, for when they pitched camp in late afternoon, she was left with Friedlander while Ram and Kanaka went to turn in the ponies. Friedlander misread her restless mood. "You're safe enough with me, lady," he reassured her with a wry grin. "I'd have delivered the nags, only Boss knows I'd hang about for a few drinks and a fight."

She let out a deliberate sigh. "Too bad about the drinks. I could use one myself. It's been a hell of a trip." At his shocked look, she laughed. "Oh, my father lets me have a nip once in a while. He's a great believer in remedial alcohol."

"Ya don't say? He sounds like a sensible sort." He looked thoughtful. "Tell ya what. I've a bottle of rye in my kit. Don't see as the Boss would mind us spikin' the tiffin a bit. It ain't as if we're goin' to get soused."

Needless to say, tiffin was spiked more than a bit. By sunset, the two were mellow. By the time the moon cleared the trees, Friedlander couldn't have distinguished a crumpet from a watermelon. Lysistrata was only slightly better off. She had scant chance to secretly dump her share of the liquor until the scout's sharp eyes began to glaze. At long last, she gave his snoring face a fond pat and lurched off upriver.

Some distance from camp, she stopped by a riverbank mine-tailing to stick her head under the water. At the cold shock, her head jerked out. Coffee. She wanted *hot* coffee. Then sadly she remembered her tin cup was back at camp. A jungleful of coffee, but not a drop to drink. She brightened. The mining camp would have coffee . . . and Ram. Brow puckered in laborious thought, she drifted toward kerosene lamps shining from tin-roofed mud shacks jumbled on the mountainside above the river.

Ram would be in a snit if he saw her snockered; therefore, she would see he didn't. She smiled peacefully. The biggest hut with the most lights would belong to the boss-*wallah* of this ratty establishment. She'd wave every prayer flag in Rangoon if he was English.

He was. His ruddy, startled Yorkshire face told her that. Also the *only* Englishman in the establishment. The North-border Burmese, Indian, and Chinese miners who peered at her through a yellow haze of smoke over the gaming tables told her that. Standing in the open doorway of the hut, she peered back. She saw a lot of scars and cold, wary, narrow eyes. They didn't look nice. Not nicest looking of the lot was Ram, standing with the Englishman by an animal-figured gambling wheel. His cheekbones were the shade of ivory dice, his eyes black as Satan's mind. Defiantly lifting her head, she delicately wove a path between the motley gamblers to the gaping English engineer. "Have I the honor of addressing the gentleman in charge of the mine, sir?" she inquired with dignity.

"Why, yes, madam. I am Charles Lowton."

She gave Ram a cool look, received a grim one, returned attention to Lowton. "I am Miss Lysistrata Herriott. I have been forcibly taken by this gentleman, who is a piss-poor gentleman, from the bosom of my family and friends. I place myself under your protection, sir''—she gave a negligent gesture—"and urge you to shoot this rotter straightaway." She leaned forward confidentially. "Any man who filches women is bound to cheat at cards."

"Mr. Gordon," began the fascinated man, "may I ask what . . . ?"

"My cousin Molly," Ram said easily. " 'Piss-poor' is an American phrase. 'Dead-drunk' is an international one."

"I am not *dead* drunk," retorted Lysistrata. "I'm very

lively indeed. And Molly, your cousin, can go hang.''
She raised a sardonic eyebrow at Lowton. "His name
isn't Gordon. Does he *look* like he has a cousin Molly?''

"I . . . really . . .''

Ram smiled lazily at Lowton's bewildered discomfi-
ture. "Good old Moll. She gets tight every tiffin.'' He
sniffed. "Rye. You've been slumming.''

She smirked. "Your *valet* happened to have some in
his kit. He's really much nicer than you deserve.''

Ram's teeth glinted. "You deserve a good spanking.''

"My backside is sore enough, thanks to you and your
mad elephants and pygmy ponies. I'm not about to tramp
to China!" A finger waggled under his nose. "Here's
where I'm getting off!''

"Here's where you say good night, Molly me girl.''
He hoisted her over his shoulder and she landed a round-
house against his flat behind. He stumbled slightly, then
flashed Lowton a broad grin. "Relatives are lovely,
aren't they? Really lovely.'' He headed for the door.

Hair swinging, Lysistrata yelled, "Put me down! At
least let me play a little Old Maid with these yokels. I'll
take 'em for every cent they've got . . .''

Outside the hut, Ram, with a muttered oath, tossed her
to Kanaka, who waited in the shadows. Five minutes
later, Kanaka dropped her in the river, where her temperature and vocabulary lowered precipitously.

Next morning, the sun rose in a hot, red ball over the
jungle, and ten miles of forced march upriver from the
mining camp, Lysistrata's skull felt as if it contained that
bloodshot sun. She strictly ignored the men. Friedlander,
in disgrace, ignored her. She concentrated on her fingertips, which somewhat blunted her preoccupation with her
swelling, blistered feet and throbbing head. By noon, her
fingertips hurt. Almost hoping Kanaka would heave her
into the river again, she sagged to the ground.

"Camp here," Ram ordered briefly. As the scouts

shouldered out of the packs, he looked down at her unsympathetically. "How's your head, Molly me girl?"

"You don't give a damn, so don't ask."

"But I do give a damn. We're going to do another fourteen miles after lunch. Whether we have to drag you by the heels for that distance is a question of logistics. Part of my job."

"You're enjoying this," she accused.

"No one enjoys doing twenty-four miles in twelve hours, particularly up mountains in near ninety-degree heat."

"Then *why* are you hurrying everybody along like the daft March Hare?"

"Because pretty Alice wandered into Wonderland last night. A Wonderland full of criminal refuse of six countries. Most of those thugs would cut your throat for a *kyat*. The only reason they hesitate is that they don't like to foul their own nest. Trouble obliges them to find another one."

"But Lowton . . . ?"

"Oh, he's straight enough." His mouth curled into a tight smile. "And he's not as dumb as he looks."

Her eyes brightened. "You mean he might . . . ?"

He shook his head. "He doesn't see a newspaper twice in six months, and company dispatches only discuss news that affects profits."

"Still . . ."

"By the time he suspects anything, *if* he suspects anything," Ram stated flatly, "you'll be far out of reach."

Though she hopefully peered over her shoulder for the next two days, she at last had to concede he was right. In those two days, she also realized why he had abandoned the ponies. They encountered specimens of natural and native engineering even mountain goats might have eyed askance.

The mountain slopes grew quickly steep in parallel

tiers until the tortuous trail faded altogether into overgrowth and sheer rock. The flimsy, hemp-strung bridges over canyons severing the mountain walls made her queasy. Though exhausted, she slept poorly at night, thanks to increasingly bitter cold, not to mention roaches and spiders that invariably scuttled through the bedroll. The men did no more than smile at her stifled yelps when she once inadvertently stretched out on an anthill; for the most part, she had stoically borne trek hardships.

They were less amused when she finally, flatly balked at crossing a gorge by hanging with arms and legs from a rope which had only a hoop to encircle the body. "I'm not a blasted monkey!" she protested. "And even a monkey couldn't cross that thing in a skirt!"

"You have a point," mused Ram. "It appears you'll have to take off the skirt, unless you want to double with me."

She envisioned intimately clinging to him, then the prospect of only his strength supporting the two of them across forty feet of rocky gorge. Neither the intimacy nor the risk was appealing. She held out a hand. "Give me your turban."

He cocked an eyebrow. "What for?"

"What do you think?" she snapped. *"Longyis* don't come equipped with pantalettes!"

Fuming, she suffered three male grins as Ram lazily unwound the turban and held it out. She snatched it, then stalked off into the brush. When she returned wearing only brief shirtwaist and loincloth, the grins faded. The overly long legs Lysistrata had been teased about in childhood were no longer a laughing matter. Sadly wasted in an era of prudery, they had been divinely designed for display. When Ram's face hardened and the scouts stared like rapt owls, she firmly fixed attention on the bridge to cover her uneasiness. If they decided to rape her, she could scream herself blue for all the good it would do. "I hope you don't mind if I go first," she suggested with a brash air of confidence. "I prefer the bridge to your ogling."

Ram smiled sardonically. "Go ahead. I don't fancy it myself. The rope may be rotten."

She paled, then numbly went to the wisp of rope. Beneath the few woven strands yawned a seventy-foot gash of jungle-snarled rock. Sweat broke out as she put a hand on the hoop to thread her body through it; the other eased out to grasp the rope beyond. Suddenly, a booted foot slammed down on the hemp; with a startled gasp she jerked back as it vibrated.

"Just checking." Above her, Ram's face was expressionless. "Go feetfirst; it's easier to get a foothold on the far side."

Heart thudding, she did as he directed, then eased out onto the rope with her legs wound around it. It sagged alarmingly; her eyes squeezed shut. Teeth clenched, she went methodically inch by terrifying inch hand over hand, her hair swinging like a pennant with each shift of weight. Near the other side, the rope slanted upward, forcing her to pull against it. At last, thinking her arms would break, she opened her eyes. Earth was only an arm's length below. Gratefully, she unwound and pawed up the rock face to safety on a nearby ledge. Ram came next, the Winchester strung across his shoulder. After making the crossing look annoyingly simple, he pulled himself up beside her with an approving nod. "Not bad. You'll need the practice up ahead."

She tossed her hair back. "There's really nothing to it, is there?"

Eyes ironic, he drew a slow finger through the sweat on the side of her face. "Not much."

It was the first time he had touched her since Pagan, and she felt defenselessly naked as she had then; she jerked back. "Keep your filthy hands off me if you don't want to end up on the rocks!"

His eyes went cold as agate. "Perhaps you'd prefer Friedlander or Kanaka. I can arrange it."

"Anyone but you." Her eyes matched his.

He smiled faintly. "A loose mouth and a tight *yin* are a dangerous combination, Lysistrata." His head lifted slightly. "Kanaka, the lady has a proposition for you."

She whirled to see the big Polynesian clamber up beside them. "I'll jump, damn you!" she hissed at Ram and backed toward the edge.

He made no effort to stop her. "That's up to you. So long as you understand the choices . . ." He beckoned to Kanaka. "Come. This ledge is overcrowded." Ignoring her as if she were a brat in a tantrum, he left her standing awkwardly on the edge.

Caught between relief and fury, she glared after him until Friedlander hopped up on the ledge. With a simian leer, he handed her the *longyi* and motioned her to move on. Defiantly, she donned it before taking a step. Why have him ogle her bottom the rest of the day?

That night, Lysistrata lay sleepless. Ram's intent, dark eyes by the campfire suggested he was less patient than he seemed. Through her lashes, she watched him as he stood guard, the Winchester across his knees. He sat silent, motionless, staring into the jungle darkness as if something secretive moved there only he could see. Her eyes lowered to the fire, watched the blue-violet embers smolder against the belly of the blazing wood, then glanced back to his eyes. Shuttered beneath the black curve of his lashes was a deeper darkness than the night, starred only by reflection of the flame. Then he looked at her, and she had a sensation of cold heat as if he had drawn an icicle down her body. He still had power over her and she hated him for it, yet she felt bitter satisfaction knowing he desired her and hated himself more for that.

Turning her back on him, she curled against the coming cold of the night.

The inclines grew perilous the next day, the trail more rugged. At length, Lysistrata gave up all hope of rescuers following into the Shans. She might have been headed for the dark side of the moon. Raffia bridges appeared more frequently as the small band penetrated deeper into the mountains, and she found her increasing reluctance to cross them difficult to hide. At length they came to a narrow double-plank footbridge strung over a river sixty feet below. Lashed on bamboo poles, the bridge was elevated about twenty-five feet in the air on their bank in order to be near level with the opposite plateau. "I suppose I'm to be guinea pig again," she said with forced carelessness.

"You're the lightest," Ram replied. "You'll make it across if anyone does."

She was startled. "Is that why you've been letting me go first, because it's the safest?"

"No," he replied mockingly, "because you're the most expendable."

Turning quickly away to hide an unexpected thorn of pain, she said with false brightness, "Well, then, I had best get at it. Perhaps I can chew through the ropes before your turn."

But by the time she climbed the rickety bamboo ladder to the tiny suspension platform, the bravado evaporated, leaving her stiff with dread. Ram climbed the ladder. "You *are* afraid, aren't you," he said quietly.

She shook her head and bit a lip.

"There's nothing to be ashamed of. I've seen fear of heights build in a number of people who've used this route. Stay put. I'll take this one."

"Why are you being nice to me so suddenly?" she said tightly.

A faint smile curved his lips. "You may be a pain in the ass, Miss Herriott, but you don't snivel."

"Then perhaps I had better not start now," she replied with a shaky laugh. "A whore is rarely credited with virtue of any sort. Besides, more bridges are ahead, aren't there?"

"This is the last."

"I'd better get it over with, then." She smiled crookedly. "I hope it's not one too many."

It was. Before she had picked her way a quarter of the distance on the flimsy, weather-beaten planks, the worn rope abruptly frayed, unraveling in a spiral whip. Lysistrata clutched as the bridge twisted, then snapped. It shook her loose as a terrier would a mouse. After the first seconds of terror, she felt only bewilderment that the fall took so long. Confusion ended with sickening force as her body slammed into the wall-hard river. Air flattened from her lungs. She had only a brief sensation of water rushing into her nose and mouth before awareness blotted out. The next thing she felt was painful pressure about the ribs. Plucking dazedly at her chest, she felt an arm locked under her breasts.

"Keep still," Ram muttered at her ear, his voice strained because of the river's wicked pull. Rocks along the gorge bit up through the river tumult, preventing him from finding a foothold to reach shore. The current shoved them about and under until Lysistrata lost orientation in its battering gauntlet. Finally finding protected water in the lee of a bend, Ram hauled her coughing and choking from the river's drag. Trying to pull air into their starved lungs, they lay flat and exhausted on the sandy shore.

At length, Ram flopped over, panting, and stared up at the sun's white blaze filtered through big red cotton trees overhanging the bank. From ridges on the terra-cotta rock face shielding the still pool from the river leaned *dyak* streaming with purple wisteria, their blossoms occasionally dropping silently into the water to drift into the current's flow. Ice plant and huge ferns clustered thickly about the shore rocks where they met the shallows. The two people on the beach could only hear their own breathing and lemurs scrabbling in jack trees downriver.

She managed one word. "Thanks."

"Not necessary. Though I'd have let a *fat* whore stay in the river."

For some reason, the image of a plump, painted tart ballooning through the rapids seemed hilarious. Face-down in the grit, she began to laugh and went on laughing until she cried.

At her final choked groan, Ram abruptly raised on his elbow. "Are you hurt?"

"No, no," she mumbled. "At least, I don't think so. I just don't have the wind to sustain hysterics."

"Turn over," he ordered, kneeling over her.

Unthinkingly, she obeyed, then flung her arm up defensively as his hands moved toward her midsection.

"Relax. I'm too tired to rape you," he said with a trace of impatience. He applied firm pressure to her abdomen then shifted to the rib cage. "Take deep breaths."

She obeyed, eyes wary. His inspection stopped just short of her breasts and she let out a breath of relief, only to gasp as he touched the shoulder where the shirtwaist was ripped.

"Hurt?" He sat back on his heels. "I'm not surprised. That scrape will be sore for a while."

"You've a few dents yourself," she observed clinically as she sat up and tentatively examined her shoulder. "Your left cheek looks like it's collected a clout from Gentleman Jim Corbett—he's an American pugilist," she added at his quizzical look. Her attention glumly shifted to the torrent. "How do we get across now?"

"There's a ford farther upstream . . . a good deal farther than I'd planned to go."

She studied his grim face. "Trouble?"

"Perhaps. But don't get your hopes up. It won't be trouble that will cut to your advantage."

She was mulling that over when Friedlander sprouted up in the cotton trees above them. "Thought I might find you here. Kanaka's gone ahead to set up camp at the fork. You coming?"

"In a minute. We're a bit fagged out."

With a knowing grin Lysistrata disliked, Friedlander tossed Ram the Winchester. "Sure. See you in camp." He disappeared.

Lysistrata watched uneasily as Ram stripped off his shirt and boots. Under his darkly tanned skin lay ridged, whipcord muscle that could overpower her with the fluid carelessness that was so much a part of him. He caught sight of her expression. "I need a bath," he explained patiently. "So do you. We're not likely to have privacy for several days."

"I don't call this private," she said coldly, "and I'm not going to bathe with you."

"Yes, you are." He pulled off his turban. "You're beginning to stink, and if the snarls and dirt don't come out of your hair, I'll have to cut it off. I don't intend to do that."

"Perhaps we could take turns," she suggested quickly. As her clothes were already wet, she could undress and dress underwater.

"Ah, but that would mean leaving you on the bank with the gun at some point." He stood and began to unfasten his breeches. Averting her eyes, she heard his soft laugh. "You've seen me before, particularly when I had cholera, Lysistrata."

"I didn't dwell on anatomical details," she parried. Not wanting to remember her terror for him during his illness, her glorious, bitter madness in his arms, she added caustically, " Particularly during the cholera. I was too busy changing your diapers."

He laughed, and wet cloth hit rock. "One might think you were wearing diapers now."

Not deigning to answer, she sulkily wrapped her arms about her knees.

"If you don't get into the water, I shall have to startle you."

Abruptly, she got up and stalked into the water. "There, are you satisfied?" she gritted. Her back turned, she undressed in water up to the neck. In answer, she heard a splash. Whirling, she came nose-to-nose with him, his black hair dripping, a complacent grin on his face. Furiously, she slapped her clothes at his head, but he snatched them with a quick, hard jerk.

"Always impulsive, Lysistrata," he murmured. "Don't you ever consider the consequences of what you do?"

"If I don't, it's a human failing," she retorted. "You're so calculating, you're inhuman. You're as cold as last year's potatoes!"

He smiled slowly. "Am I?" Eyes glittering with mischief, he submerged, his sleek, wiry body blending into the still pool. Scanning the silt-clouded depths, she hastily backed away from the spot where he had been, then gave a sigh of relief as he came up a dozen yards away. Idly as a dolphin, he played in the water while she began to work at her hair. It took some time to work out the mass of dirty snarls and collection of bugs. Out of the corner of her eye, she saw a flash of brown on the tawny bank rocks. A surreptitious peek through her tumbled hair caught a hard, slim line of flank and compact buttock as dark as the well-arranged rest of him. Quickly, her eyes dropped as he turned to sit in yoga-style patience for her to finish bathing. She dawdled as long as possible, then demanded her clothes. Lazily, he tossed them with a sodden plop up the bank to land beside his own. "You're a thoroughgoing bastard," she said.

"Would you prefer them thrown in the river?" His head cocked. "Of course, they might be lost. I don't think my turban will cover all of you."

Very well, my witty lad, she fumed, two can play this game. She swam to shore and, taking a deep breath, rose from the water right under his nose. She looked him in the eye, enjoying the startled, quick hunger there. She flipped her wet hair back, then, her arms lifting, sleeked water from it. His eyes dropped to the thrust of her breasts then to her flat stomach and lower to where the water blended with the gold between her thighs. Feeling it unwise to linger within reach, she strolled as slowly as she dared toward the piles of clothes, then darted for the Winchester a few feet beyond.

Fast as she was, he was quicker. The Winchester brushed her left nipple, then settled with the tip delicately brushing the fluff below her belly. "Believe me, Lysistrata," he murmured, "the last thing I would like to do just now is shoot you, so go quietly to your clothes."

Just below his hand on the trigger, she saw his manhood, poised with the same readiness as the Winchester. Backing away, she angrily kicked his clothes into the river. "Wear your bloody turban!"

To her surprise, he merely slung the Winchester over his shoulder and laughed.

In camp, Ram's reappearance clad only in loincloth and boots aroused fascinated looks, but no comment; Friedlander and Kanaka were considerably less rash than the sullen female who accompanied him. As twilight fell, however, and none of them, even the normally garrulous Friedlander, seemed inclined to talk, Lysistrata's sulky mood altered to curiosity. In the firelight, Friedlander's ferret eyes watched the brush, darting here and there at every rustle, every creak of bamboo. Kanaka's placid bulk shifted often and uneasily. Although, as usual, Ram seemed calm, his head carried high and his body seemed coiled over the Winchester. Friedlander broke the silence. "Do you think he's out there?"

"He followed Lysistrata and me from the river," Ram answered.

"Who?" she demanded, remembering Ram's alert silence on the way to the camp. "Who are you talking about?"

"Tiger, Missy," rumbled Kanaka.

She wished she hadn't asked. "They're afraid of fire, aren't they?"

"Not enough, sometimes," Friedlander said grimly.

"But then, why is it just following us? Why doesn't he attack?"

"I put a bullet in it three years ago," Ram said. "It hasn't forgotten."

"I didn't realize tigers could be so calculating."

"They can," Ram replied, "particularly when they hate." He stood up and eased the Winchester into the crook of his arm. "Keep the fire high, Friedlander. I'll be back in a bit."

Lysistrata was appalled. "You're not going after it at night!"

"If I don't, it'll keep stalking us. That's a good deal more dangerous than the other way around." He smiled down at her white face. "Don't worry. It'll follow me. Get some sleep."

After he disappeared into the darkness, she felt cold, the silence settling around her heart like a pall. She crouched, unthinkingly chewing a thumbnail as she thought of Ram, near-naked and vulnerable, moving through the bamboo. Of the tiger's lethal yellow eyes and shadow-dappled hide as it relentlessly moved after him. Only, there were no shadows for there was no moon. Her head lifted. She could almost scent death as it padded across her mind. Ram should not have gone alone.

Why not let him pay for that mistake, pay for all he had

done to her? Except he rarely made mistakes. He'd left the scouts, his protection, with her. *Why;* if only hate was between them? Her hand clenched. There was more, might always be more . . . until he was dead. Until she was dead and past memory.

"Doesn't one usually use bait to draw a tiger?" she wondered aloud.

"Aye, if you've got any," said Friedlander sourly, "and we haven't."

When he looked up again, she was gone.

Not wanting to draw a bullet rather than the cat, Lysistrata took care to make noise. But she waited until well away from camp to do it. Friedlander and Kanaka were hardly likely to follow. They might not be bright, but they weren't stupid. She was the stupid one, going from one stupidity to another, each greater than the last. She was drawn to Ram like the tiger. With mingled fear, hate, and fascination. Or was the cat a tigress? They couldn't be sure it was not a female, could they? Would a tigress abandon her cubs, her mate, for revenge?

The night jungle was a place of whispers. The wind, the sigh of bamboo, scales moving on bark, a scuffle in leaves; a dry, tiny cry. Starlight was rare, a quick, cool glare on ivory lilies cut by a black fan of swords, on liana serpentined across a lacework of leaves and pendant wisteria. Across the ink-blue sky came a shadow creep of lemur.

Then she sensed rather than saw eyes, low and sulfurous. She stilled, heartbeat filling the silence. The green, rounded eyes sank lower, pupils shrinking into an infinity of death. Her breath stopped.

The stillness gathered itself and unfurled in a sighing rush, then with a yowl of rage and pain, knotted awkwardly as a rifle spat twice. A falling weight stunned the ground. Lysistrata swayed, felt cold again. Fingertips lightly touched her cheek, then her lips, and the darkness swallowed her.

Whimpering, Lysistrata thrashed. For a moment, she seemed to lose consciousness again, then her eyes opened. Dimly seeing a dark figure crouched over her, she started in terror. Ram's hands gently pressed her down. "Why?" he murmured. "Did you want to die?"

"I owed you my life," she breathed dazedly. "I didn't want that kind of debt." Another reason hid in the silence of her soul, but she would not let it whisper in her mind. Tonight she could not let it shriek its end in his blood. Perhaps she would be stronger tomorrow.

Ram recognized the vague note in her voice. Asiatics had different words for it, but like one about to commit a suicide of honor, she had briefly touched eternity. She had taken another irretrievable step from her world into his. He could not let her find only loneliness and strange echoes.

"Tonight of all nights, we are equal." His fingers delicately grazed her cheeks. He moved surely, knowing his way, knowing that yet snared in the thrall of near-death, she was beyond struggle.

As if in a dream, Lysistrata heard his loincloth slip to the ground, felt cold air on her skin when he eased open her clothes. She fought to resist the dream, but it closed about her, rippling away all but dark, shadowy sensation. The rough wool of his jacket parted as his slim warmth covered her. As if to breathe life into her uncertain, wandering spirit, his mouth closed over hers. Supple muscle moved over her bare skin, lulling, subduing her last rebellion into liquid compliance. That phantom mouth sought her breasts, her navel, her vulva until she enfolded him, demanding the first bittersweet surge of his mounting. As sublime beasts they lay, his quickened pulsing within her like the heartbeat of the night. No cry echoed the crescendo, no mark was made upon the earth as two smooth, pale bodies arched, trembled, and stilled.

She was hardly aware when he carried her back to camp and drew her blanket about her.

Ram watched her until she slept. His mind was calm. Tonight in this moonless jungle, he and Lysistrata had been bound beyond flesh. They would mate again, though not soon—for Lysistrata was still mistrustful, hostile. Tonight had been unreal to her. Instinct had asserted itself, but little more than her body had yielded to him. No, even if he starved for the wild sweetness of that body, he would not mate her soon and not out of revenge as he had planned. He would not waste his brief time with her in hate. Yet might not spend it in love, though he would give her an untouchable, unforgettable promise of finding love with another. While he had long ago foreseen his ending, Lysistrata was incomplete. If he had not already damaged her too much, if he could leave her whole, his ending would matter less than the little it once had before she had imbued it with bitter regret. Their Karma was sealed in the death of the tiger; so too would be their parting. With a rueful smile, he studied her weary face. She was tired tonight, but she would fight again at dawn. Karma or no, one could not reliably tame a tigress.

In the morning, as Ram had foreseen, Lysistrata was warier of him than ever. As she huddled by the fire, he dropped his jacket over her. She flinched, glancing up. The night still lingered in her eyes: they held a fear of light, of him, of their bond. She rose, shrugging off the jacket. "I'm not that cold." He could almost read her mind as she strode away.

Under the almost sleepy regard of Ram's eyes, Lysistrata felt her spine prickle from horrible uncertainty. Had their lovemaking been a hallucination or the reality she feared? His scent was on her like a brand, and yet she couldn't, wouldn't . . . only the serene patience of those black eyes disquieted her more than anything.

After breakfast, Friedlander insisted they retrieve the tiger pelt. Ram shrugged. "Why not? It's just off the trail."

When they came in sight of the corpse, however, he turned and stepped quickly in front of Lysistrata, blocking her view. "What is it?" she asked in bewilderment.

"Damn," Friedlander's voice came from ahead, "the baboons have been at it! What a bloody waste."

Lysistrata pushed violently past Ram, then felt as if someone had hit her in the chest. The tigress had been beautiful; enough was left to tell that. Now she was a gutted, mangled mess, and gibbons with bloody faces screeching in the treetops gesticulated with gory humanoid hands. Tears scalding her eyes, she flailed out at Ram. "Damn you! Damn you!" He caught her fists and she sagged against him.

"What's she, crazy?" Friedlander demanded.

"Perhaps she and the tigress had something in common," Ram murmured.

The ascent that day was grueling, and Lysistrata was staggering with fatigue when they came to a village. The first they had encountered since the mining camp, it rose like tiers of thatched bird cages on stilts above a partly burned thorn stockade. The place was utterly silent, without even a pig's squeal to greet the four people who halted in the fringe of jack trees around the clearing. Friedlander dropped into a crouch with rifle ready, and scuttled into the jungle. When he returned, his face was grim. "Just an old Joe is left in the village. The rest of 'em have scattered into the bush."

"You think Boh Chaik?" Kanaka asked.

"Yeah, I think," Friedlander muttered.

"We'd better talk to the old man," Ram said. "Where is he?"

"He's talked too much already. He ain't telling us nothing now," Friedlander said tersely as he led off with Ram and Kanaka on either side of him. Lysistrata, her nerves frayed by weariness and renewed drive to be free of Ram, followed.

The man was dead, and this time Ram was not quick enough to prevent Lysistrata from seeing how he had died. His *dah*-hacked body lay in front of the headman's hut. His head had been spiked on a ladder rail. Gagging, Lysistrata dropped to her knees. While she retched, the men talked matter-of-factly. She snatched at a scarf among the bandits' leavings and wiped harshly at her mouth, then glowered up at Ram. "Where the *hell* are you taking me? What sort of savages live up here that hack old people to bits?"

"Keep your voice down," he ordered curtly. "Boh Chaik is the sort of savage who dislikes loud noises. You saw out there how he reacts to them. He and his bandits hit the village just before noon when the women were preparing meals for the field-workers and all the food supplies were out for the taking."

"Do you think they'll come back?" she asked tensely.

"Quite regularly, but not today. They got what they wanted. Boh Chaik's lazy besides being vicious; that's one reason he's a bandit. He's probably having his men wring chicken necks for supper in Choukchoungyee, the next village ahead." He stood up. "Let's go."

"Not to Choukchoungyee?"

"Boh Chaik doesn't know we're here, but for once we know where he is," Ram explained patiently. "We'll never have a better chance."

"If you don't give a damn about staying alive! He has to have more than two men with him!"

"Probably about a dozen." He grinned mischievously. "But they don't have rifles."

Just before sunset, they reached Choukchoungyee. Smaller than the first village, it had cook fires smoking inside the wrecked palisade. Seven men in grimy finery lolled under the verandahs and on mats as they wolfed rice and *ngapi* from wooden bowls and split coconuts with greasy fingers. One bandit, drunk on jaggery, staggered from a doorway to the raucous jibes of his comrades and, slipping as he missed a handhold, nearly fell down its ladder.

"Where's the Boh, I wonder?" whispered Friedlander to Ram as they crouched in the bush.

"The big hut, probably. Take up positions." Ram waved Friedlander and Kanaka to fences of bamboo screen near the hut in question. "Take care of anybody who heads out the back." They peeled off into the undergrowth. Ram slipped his knife out of the sheath at his waist and eased it over his shoulder to Lysistrata. "Just in case," he murmured. "But don't waste it on a bandit."

Remembering the mutilated old man, she swallowed hard.

Their drunken quarry grabbed a coconut of jaggery from a bandit squatting by a fire and upended it. As it cupped over the bandit's face, Ram took aim with the Winchester. An instant later, the coconut shattered and merged with the mouth the bullet ploughed through. The others leaped up to be caught in a murderous triangle of gunfire. Two bandits darted from huts to jerk in midair and sprawl on the ground. Then from the main hut, a rifle spat. "I thought you said they didn't have guns," Lysistrata protested.

"The Boh seems to have come up in the world."

Kanaka and Friedlander raked the hut, and the gunfire halted. Uneasy silence fell.

Stealthily, the two men moved from hiding and began to prowl under the huts, their eyes raking the floor-slat gaps. Panicky pigs and chickens squealed and squawked, pushing and fluttering against the pen barricades. Friedlander suddenly jerked his head at Kanaka. With a nod, the big man tossed a torch from a nearby fire into the hut. A scramble of bare feet was heard; then a man, screaming and slashing wildly with his machete-like *dah*, bolted from the door. Friedlander shot him in the back. Kanaka was not so lucky. A bandit standing on a mat stabbed his *dah* blade down between floor slats, missing the Polynesian's neck to gouge his shoulder. With a grunt of pain, Kanaka fired upward twice. At a brief shriek, he grinned at Friedlander.

Leaving Lysistrata, Ram eased like a hunting serpent under the main hut. Hearing a wicked hiss overhead, he dodged just in time to evade the slice of a *dah*. He fired, and there was an answering thud. He waved Friedlander to take his place and Kanaka to the rear of the hut, then warily mounted the ladder. As the fabric scrap that had been wound Apache-style about his forehead bobbed on his gun butt above the porch, a bullet whistled through it. At the same moment, Friedlander fired upward and a body crashed through the palmetto wall. When Ram waved the scarf again, nothing happened. Carefully, he peered above the verandah through the door, then crept over the matting.

Nothing stirred inside the hut. Bottle flies were already beginning to buzz about the bodies on the floor. An Enfield rifle lay by the gap in the hut wall the other bandit had torn through. At a slight sound behind him, Ram whirled, gun poised. Lysistrata stood in the doorway, his knife clutched in one white-knuckled hand. "What the hell are you doing here?" he said curtly. "I told you to stay put."

"Having to skewer myself because you're short-handed seemed excessively meek. Besides, I wanted to see the Boh's new gun,'' she replied with a lightness she did not feel. Her gaze roamed to the stray weapon. "Is that . . . ?''

Switching to Burmese, he cut her off. "We missed the boat. Boh Chaik's not here.'' His eyes flicked up meaningfully toward the loft.

"Oh? Too bad,'' she continued steadily. "I suppose he'll keep raiding the district then.''

He waved her toward the shadowed wall where she was less silhouetted by the doorway. "Yes. Pity. Thought we had the slimy bastard. We'll have to check every hut, to be sure.'' Swiftly, he gave her his rifle, then eased a slim tube from his loincloth and motioned her to keep talking.

Lysistrata rattled on in a cold sweat as he quickly slipped out of the window to balance precariously on its frame. His head and shoulders were concealed from view. As she talked, while easing toward the gun on the floor, Ram peered though a crack in the woven palmetto wall, then slipped the tube through a crack just below it. He blew. Inside the hut, the man poised over the ladder to the loft slapped at his neck as if stung, then half-turned to the direction from which it had come. His rifle swung around.

With a muffled scream, Lysistrata staggered back as a body plummeted through the loft hatch to sprawl nearly at her feet. A tiny yellow-feathered dart protruded from his neck; his tongue was already beginning to swell past his lips. Ram swung through the window. "The Boh?'' she asked with a grimace of distaste at the squat bandit.

"Himself.''

The Winchester slung over a shoulder, she eased the bandit's rifle she had recovered around toward Ram's midsection. "And here's his new pretty. Want to see how well it works?''

He toyed with the tube near his lips as if it were a cheroot. ''I prefer this little gimcrack. At close range, it's more accurate than a gun. The poison on the darts causes extreme edema.'' His eyes flickered disinterestedly over Boh Chaik's body. ''That'll split in a while.''

With a faint smile, she handed over the knife and guns. ''I don't suppose you'd trade toys.''

He tossed her the tube. ''Be my guest. It's not loaded.''

Kanaka's bulk filled the doorway. ''Some of the villagers are back. They heard the shots and wanted to know who won.'' He glanced at the body, then at the guns.

Friedlander, who was just behind the Polynesian, also showed a marked interest in the accumulated arsenal. ''They *were* bloody Enfields. Boh Chaik must have got them from those damned—''

''River traders,'' Ram cut in. ''More may be about, so we'd better stay sharp.''

Lysistrata thoughtfully eyed them as they collected the rifles. Something was not quite right. Enfields were English. What if the ''river traders'' were English as well? Ram would not want her to know help was anywhere within miles. Then again, the sort of help that handed guns to a butcher like Boh Chaik was questionable.

She saw to Kanaka's shoulder as Friedlander announced to the villagers that the Boh and his men were dead. A cheer went up, and within twenty minutes the huts were lively again.

That night a celebration was held, and what remained of the village produce and livestock was offered to the rescuers as if no one cared whether he ate a meal again after they left. Grilled *hilsa* in saffron rice, sugared tomatoes, and various curries were finished off with sweets and fruit. Lysistrata unabashedly stuffed herself while several extremely long songs were sung recounting the village history, the wars of Anawrahta, the youth of Buddha, and the events of the day—which were greatly magnified and almost totally inaccurate. Although they ate after the men, women mixed equally with them, particularly after everyone had drunk jaggery for several hours. At length, Lysistrata, sagging upon a mat, went to sleep with a beatific smile.

She woke up without one. Her head felt as if it had been split with a *dah*. The floor was covered with people who had fallen asleep precisely as she had done. Ram was not among them. She threaded through the sleepers to the doorway. Kanaka and Friedlander were sitting under a tamarind cleaning the Enfields. As she strolled toward them, Friedlander nodded toward a battered little pagoda at the fringe of the clearing. "Ram's over there," he announced as if his master's whereabouts were all a woman could be thinking of. She headed toward the pagoda. On edge from too much jaggery and danger, she was in the mood to annoy someone; it might as well be Ram.

Back to the door, he sat with thumbs to midfingers resting on his thighs. Although he must have heard her enter, he remained as still and silent as a carved idol.

"We're lively today," she finally remarked sarcastically. And got no reply. Leaning against the wall, she reviewed the crude, faded frescoes of the Vedas. Several minutes passed. She had never thought of his praying, particularly to an idol Boston would consider primitive and heathen. She began to feel awkward and bored and sullen about her headache. "I suppose you're thanking Buddha for keeping Boh Chaik from filling you full of holes yesterday."

"No," he said briefly. "I'm meditating."

"Like a monk?"

"If I were thinking about God."

"What *are* you thinking about? River traders?"

"Among other things." He looked at her. "Meditation calms the spirit. You might try it sometime."

"I'm more impressed by the sporting way your dart calmed the Boh's spirit. I wonder what he's saying to Buddha about you just now."

"Sit down," he said quietly.

"Have I made the Great Hero of the Peashooter angry?" She plopped carelessly down in front of him.

"Why should you?" he said easily, placing his fingertips on either side of her forehead. Her green eyes becoming wary, she started to protest. "Be silent," he murmured, "and listen." She frowned questioningly. "Listen to the silence, Lysistrata, and think of nothing . . . *nada*. Let it echo . . . *nada* . . ." His fingertips began to lightly move on her temples, around and around. After a time, his thumbs centered along the sides of her nose, then moved firmly upward along the brow bone's lower curve. His hands were soothing, and her eyes closed gratefully. He continued the gentle massage until she began to feel drowsy. His hand eased down to press against the pulse at the base of her skull, released, then pressed again. Her head dropped slightly back against his hand, her hair silk at his wrist. Her breathing came slow and even. As his hand stilled, her eyes slowly opened to find his face very close to hers. She felt nothing, not fear, not sorrow, not longing. They were one, floating in the river again, only without struggle, without boundaries of flesh. She wanted to go on floating forever, into *nada*.

Friedlander pulled her back. "Ready to go?" he questioned cheerily from the opening of the pagoda. "Home's just over the hill."

CHAPTER 9

Khandahoor

When she would think, wher'er she
*   Turned her sight,*
The airy hand confusion wrought,
Wrote 'Mene, mene,' and divided quite
*   The kingdom of her thought.*
                    ALFRED, LORD TENNYSON

Friedlander's "hill" was the steepest mountain they had yet crossed, home a rambling white fortress on a plateau bordering a vast, marsh-fringed lake in the valley below. The crenellated Indian towers that floated above the twilight mist rising from the lake seemed foreign to Burma. Save for a few tiers of rice fields, the valley and surrounding mountains were carpeted with unbroken jungle balked only at the fortress moat. A golden onion dome guarded by slender minarets swelled over a geometric pattern of blue-green reflecting pools and miniature lakes in gardens which threaded among the interior buildings.

"Impressive," Lysistrata observed with grudging admiration, "particularly so in the middle of nowhere. Your handiwork?"

"My father's," Ram replied briefly.

237

"He must have been fond of Indian architecture."

"He built Khandahoor for my mother." His flat tone discouraged more questions.

Papa must have been rich indeed to have constructed a palace, she mused. Many ducal manors must be less elaborate.

Khandahoor was more impressive at close hand, if less welcoming. A huge drawbridge lowered over a wide moat moving with crocodiles. Sharpened teak timbers angled upward like shark's teeth at the wall base. The guards stationed on the massive walls were not Indians as Lysistrata expected, but efficient-looking Kachins and Chinese with wide-shouldered, armadillo-like armor. Khandahoor, she realized glumly, would be as difficult to leave as to enter without Ram's permission.

The interior was marvelously elaborate, with carved screening over windows and lining porticoes and passageways. Blue, black, and gold mosaics patterned white walls and fountained pools, some with artificial islands. Slim, fluted columns supported fretted balconies in a maze of courtyards where mimosa, lemon trees, bougainvillea, and jasmine perfumed the air. It was a paradise, albeit a trifle deserted, if one did not think of the surrounding crocodiles. Lysistrata decided the Rani of Khandahoor must have been quite a woman.

After dismissing Kanaka and Friedlander to their own quarters, Ram led her into the main building. As they crossed cool, tiled floors through rooms lustrous with Oriental rugs, wonderfully carved Indian furniture, hanging brass censers and lamps, she could not help thinking how disreputable the two of them looked, grimed with sweat and blood from insect bites streaking torn, dirty clothes. The impression was heightened when they entered a long chamber fronted by an open, columned courtyard with a pool. A middle-aged Indian woman in a purple and silver sari awaited them. Heavily kohled black eyes in a spare, hawk-nosed face raked them coldly. She bowed. "Welcome, my lord prince."

"Lysistrata, this is Kalisha. She will see you to the *zenana*."

Kalisha's eyes flicked to Lysistrata's bright hair, then she said something in curt, contemptuous Hindi to Ram. Though he replied evenly, she stiffened, then seemed to shrink slightly as if afraid of him. She gestured abruptly to Lysistrata and, with a power ill-suited to a graceful sari, strode from the room. Eager to bathe and sleep in a proper bed, Lysistrata followed with a quick glance at Ram to make certain he did not intend to join her.

The *zenana* was in the eastern wing. At the sight of the two fat guards armed with scimitars outside its door, Lysistrata almost burst into laughter. She was little less amused by the elaborately feminine rooms that surrounded the *zenana*'s communal bath. Though the open rooms were deserted, she wondered how many pairs of curious eyes were applied to peepholes in the closed bedroom doors. After stripping, she descended mauve, terracotta, and gold tile steps into the hexagonal pool. As Lysistrata sank in perfumed water up to the chin, Kalisha sharply clapped her hands to summon a young Burmese girl with soaps, ointments, and soft towels. After the leisurely bath, the Burmese administered a massage with oils, then applied soothing aloe ointment to scratches and insect bites. Kalisha glared so fixedly Lysistrata thought the woman might do well as Medusa.

After dismissing the Burmese, Kalisha showed Lysistrata to a small room prettily decorated with rugs and gauzy draperies, but nearly filled with an oversized bed. The room was virtually windowless, for its carved balcony screen did not open. One had a passable view of the gardens by peering though the fretwork; but at the moment, Lysistrata did not care to view scenery. She only wanted to sleep. Ignoring Kalisha, she flung herself still wrapped in a towel across the bed. She was asleep almost before Kalisha left the room.

She was awakened at mid-morning of the next day when the little Burmese girl, Too, pecked at the door. "Breakfast awaits you by the Chrysanthemum Pool, my lady." Her lashes dipped. "My lord prince awaits you, also."

Lysistrata stretched lazily. Let him wait.

When she appeared at last at the pavilion by the walled, turquoise-mosaicked pool attached to the *zenana* wing, Ram sāt in a cane chair, his crossed feet propped up on an openwork railing. He was bathed and clean-shaven, but despite the splendor of his domain, simply dressed in fresh white cotton. A few remains of breakfast littered his plate. Surveying her green-and-gold sari, he tossed a pomegranate seed into the bougainvillea surrounding the pavilion. "That shade of green is a little harsh for morning, isn't it?"

"I didn't think of pleasing you when I chose it," she replied curtly—the more so because, to some degree, she had meant to impress him.

"You will find there is little to do in Khandahoor but please me," he replied mildly. He waved her to the chair opposite. In front of it was a beautifully painted, barren plate flanked by gold cutlery.

Instead of obeying, she leaned against the nearest pavilion column. "What if I should find that boring? What if I simply tell you to go to hell and please myself."

"Have you ever thought it might be possible to die of boredom, Lysistrata?" Another seed bulleted a leaf. "What have you really done with your life but please yourself? You are perhaps the most bored woman I have ever met."

"What do you know of my life . . . ?"

"More than you might think."

"Oh you must be referring to Masjid's reports! You

must be the bored one, to listen to him rattle month after month about the household of a poor pair of Boston church mice.''

"You were uncomfortable in Boston and also, I think, in its religion," he mused, ignoring the outburst. "To endure the disapproval of a puritanic god as well as that of the community must have tried your patience."

"*You're* trying my patience," she snapped. "I didn't have supper last night. Just where is breakfast?"

"I ate it, I'm afraid," he confessed with a boyish smile. "If I'm kept waiting when I'm hungry, I'm apt to eat everything in sight. It's a bad habit, I know."

"You've a wealth of bad habits," she said. "Among them: promiscuity, adultery, and kidnapping—all due, no doubt, to being doted on by so many people. They must adore you. Kalisha, in particular, seems to hang on your every word. I find your company less thrilling." She plopped down in the empty chair. "Am I to have anything to eat or not?"

"Of course. Lunch will be served around two."

She eyed him balefully. "That's hours away."

"Patience is a gentle art, Lysistrata; one of many you may learn here."

"All, no doubt, to toady up your worship." She burst out laughing. "Eunuchs! My god, they're antiques."

"The eunuchs were purchased by my mother," he replied imperturbably. "She was a traditional woman in many respects."

"She bought them for you? How motherly of your mother."

"She bought them for my father, actually"—his dark eyes looked out over the serene gardens—"in their later years together. The swords are intended to ensure the privacy of the *zenana*. Its women may leave whenever they wish."

"Then why don't they?"

"Because they can never return."

"Are you saying their exalted opinion of your attentions keeps them at your beck and call?"

"In a manner of speaking. Undoubtedly, their opinion of the comforts I provide may be more exalted than of that attention."

Suddenly, his utter lack of interest in what his concubines thought of him, his silent, solitary detachment from all who knew him saddened her. Khandahoor might be beautiful, but it was not of the world. Nor was he of the world, for all his knowledge of it or the charm he applied like layers of polished lacquer to its occupants to both conceal and preserve a curiously intimate distance from them.

"What are you thinking?" he asked softly.

"That I know at last why you brought me here."

He studied her grave face. "Then perhaps you know more than I."

"I was once drawn to you because you were not Boston. You brought me here because I am not Khandahoor."

They were both silent for a moment. "It was unwise, you know," she murmured, "for either you will change or I will change. One of us must destroy the other." Then she shrugged, mistrusting the vulnerability of her mood. "Perhaps eventual indifference will be our salvation."

"One is indifferent either to what one does not know or knows too well." His dark eyes rested on her face. "You are a creature of infinite, sometimes dangerous variety, Lysistrata."

"The same might be said of you."

"Then it appears we are not to be allowed the luxury of indifference."

The monotony as days passed in the *zenana* was stultifying. The three lovely residents, Kim Lee, a Chinese, Too, and a Malagasy black named Rasoherina, whiled away their time in rituals of hairdressing, nail-painting, application of cosmetics, and selection of adornment. Unless Lysistrata wished to swim, eat, or stare at the wall, nothing remained but to turn into a piece of mobile art: all to suit an enigmatic tyrant who could take that art or leave it, literally. So she swam. And swam. And swam. Her hair turned to molten gold, her skin to the deep, tawny shade of a tigress's pelt. Her body slimmed and toned until she was lithe as a cat. And just as restless.

"Being caged agrees with you."

Lysistrata, drowsing in the sun by the pool, started awake to see Ram standing over her. Other than an occasional polite dinner with her, he rarely came to the *zenana*. On those occasions, the lazy, feline look in his eyes always made her uneasily wonder if he might decide to enjoy her as dessert; that look was there now. She affected an uninhibited stretch to hide her tension. "Why do you say that?" she countered.

He studied the long, naked golden curve of her, then grinned. "No circles under the eyes. You often had them in Rangoon."

"Well, my brain is turning into mango pulp. Aren't there any books around this place?"

"Father installed a library in the Peacock Palace. Would you like to choose something from it?"

"You mean if I leave the *zenana*, you'd let me come back?" she mocked, sitting up to shake out her hair and calculate the steps to her sari.

"You've always had the freedom to come and go about the fortress."

With a short sound of exasperation, she rose to slip on the azure sari. "You neglected to mention that. Why am I privileged where the other women are not?"

"They occasionally share my bed."

She turned scarlet. "They pay a high price to be degraded. As I recall, you can be rather crude in that respect."

He toyed with the sari pin which lay on a nearby table. "Have you someone else with whom to compare me?" The lightness of his tone made her wary.

"Didn't you know?" she retorted brightly. "A merman lives in a cave at the bottom of this pool. What he lacks in equipment, he makes up in availability." She held out her hand for the clasp.

Laughing, he ignored her hand and began to deftly fasten the clasp. "Is that a reproach, Lysistrata?"

"If I felt neglected, I would complain to one of the mercenaries," she purred, uncomfortably aware of his sure, cool fingers.

"If one, why not to them all?"

Chilled by the oblique threat, she pulled away. "You can rely on Kalisha to tell you if I stray. She hates me."

"Kalisha once loved my mother. Now she is fond of no one."

"Would your mother have hated me, too?"

"She would have poisoned you."

The library was magnificent. Housed in the Peacock Palace where Lysistrata had first met Kalisha, it held thousands of books from every part of the world. It also contained the only Western art she had seen at Khandahoor. "It was my father's," Ram explained when he saw her studying a Donatello Saint Sebastian. The nude Roman saint was sculpted in bronze as a beautiful, tormented young man pierced by many arrows. Ram might have posed for it. He smiled faintly at her rapt expression. "This particular subject is common to your Christian Renaissance art, chiefly because it allowed artists to portray the nude body without rebuke by the Church."

She lifted an eyebrow. "I gather Muslims are forbidden to portray the human body at all."

"Buddhists and Hindus are less restrained. You will find many examples of religious art in the books on that wall." He nodded to the appropriate sector.

She wandered to the designated shelves and chose a book celebrating the life of Vishnu. It was filled with drawings of erotic dances. She lowered the book. "India seems to enjoy a lively religion."

"Hindus believe in celebrating the body before they leave it. They suggest the act of love is the most glorious earthly expression of the spirit."

"*They* suggest? Which are you, Buddhist or Hindu? You certainly don't seem Christian."

"I leave religion to monks," he said briefly.

Leafing through books, she drifted along the shelves. Finally, she chose Victor Hugo's *Les Miserables*, and *Indiana* by George Sand.

"Why those two?"

She laughed. "Because a scholarly acquaintance once assured me they should be banned in Boston."

He unlocked a mahogany desk, then handed her a small leather book. "Try this one as well. You may find it interesting, particularly on the question of morality."

She stroked the worn leather. "There's no title. What is it?"

"Father's diary."

Lysistrata stayed up the night reading the diary. It was the account of a ruthless, rapacious young subaltern who had climbed to the top of his profession over the dead bodies of men he led to destruction and those he killed in the Sepoy Rebellion in India. He helped to force India and Burma under British rule before his final failure to enter China. He had been fortified by the notion his destiny and Britain's were one and glorious. Khandahoor, built by Sepoy prisoners from the '58 rebellion, was furnished with trappings stolen from the ravaged estates of

India's declining Moghuls. Among the trappings had been Anira, Ram's mother, of whom he spoke with passion and admiration that went beyond love to fetish.

Yet he had kept a harem under Anira's nose, Lysistrata reflected. *I wonder what went on in the mind of a woman capable of murdering her son's mistress, but of supplying her husband guards to support his being unfaithful to her.*

After snuffing the oil lamp at perhaps three o'clock in the morning, Lysistrata slept fitfully, her thoughts unwilling to leave Anira, Rani of Khandahoor. A tiny noise, little more than a suggestion of a change of breeze in the palms outside the window, stirred her to silent alertness. Remembering the cobra loosed in her Rangoon bedroom, she lay still, her eyes closed. After several long moments she sensed soundless movement, a stirring of the air; whatever, whoever was in the room was retreating toward the door. Her eyelids lifted a fraction. In a sliver of moonlight, the window fretwork was blotted out by a veiled, moving figure. Though the head was turned toward her so no detail of face showed, she suspected the intruder was Kalisha. None of the *zenana* women wore veils, none exuded the venom of this creature. She could not have explained why she was sure the visitor meant her ill; perhaps the rigidity of the head in contrast to the swift, fluid stealth of the body gave that impression. She waited, trying to force her breathing to sound natural. The figure stopped, seemed to grow taller. Like a cobra, thought Lysistrata, before it strikes. She steeled herself to ward off an attack. From the complete darkness near the door came a lengthening silence. Lysistrata reared up. The darkness was empty.

Lysistrata strode out of the *zenana* at dawn. One of the eunuchs was asleep; the other made no effort to stop her. She prowled the grounds, then the Peacock Palace's public rooms. In one of these, she met Kalisha.

"What are you doing here?" the woman demanded harshly.

"I'm looking for Ram," Lysistrata lied brightly. "He's here, isn't he?"

Kalisha's lips curled. "He will summon you if he wishes to see you. Do not presume upon his patience."

"Yet you presume to speak for him. He must be very patient, indeed."

"You strut upon his leash, yet he does not even stoop to fondle you." Kalisha smiled maliciously. "Aye, he is patient. He has other bitches to fawn upon him. Why should he trouble with a pallid one with the ill temper of a shrew?"

"It seems I have a choice of shrews," came Ram's quiet voice behind them. "At this early hour, I shall tolerate only one. Kalisha, have breakfast for Lysistrata and myself brought to the Chrysanthemum Pool."

"Well, what do you think of Father?" Ram asked as he folded shredded coconut, curry, and sesame seeds into a flat wafer of bread.

She told him.

"Interesting. Many of your compatriots in Rangoon would think him heroic."

"Now that I've met your noble father *ex libris*, I'm curious about your mother. What sort of woman was she?"

"Father found her more difficult to win than most things."

"That covers a great deal. I should say he stole more than he won."

He smiled crookedly. "He did not have to steal her. She wanted him even more than he wanted her."

She frowned slightly. "Then . . . more lust than love was between them?"

"Why do you say that?"

"Something about the tone of your father's writing . . ." She looked up. "Ram, why did you give me that diary?"

"I told you. I wanted to know what you'd think of it."

"I believe you wanted to know what I think of what's happening to Burma . . . and to you."

"Nothing's happening to me, for a while, anyway." He waved at the guarded towers.

"One day the British will come even to the gates of Khandahoor. That poor old man in Mandalay won't stop them."

"He can't stop them, not with cannon Louis Fourteenth could have bested. So he goes on trying to believe they're civilized." His lips curled with the first touch of anger Lysistrata had seen in him for weeks. "They're all, all honorable men, the British, but they'll never take Khandahoor. I'll be damned if I hand it over to a bunch of box-*wallahs*."

She was startled by the naked contempt on his face as he looked out over the pool. "Am I one of them? The box-*wallahs?*" she asked quietly.

He looked at her oddly. "Box-*wallahs* are bourgeois merchants like Bettenheim. Only, most of them eventually take up their booty and go home. The Bettenheims stay and breed more Bettenheims. They are usually forced to begin with a woman who has little choice of a husband." He sipped at his cocoa. "In finding you, Bettenheim was more fortunate than most."

"And more determined," she said thoughtfully. "He wasn't the sort of man to cool his heels at afternoon tea parties. That made me take him more seriously than the others."

"You considered marriage to him?" he asked abruptly.

She lifted an eyebrow. "I'm surprised Masjid didn't tell you." She picked up her own cocoa and looked at him over the cup rim. "Yes, I considered it. It would have been practical. Father and I would have been secure for the rest of our lives. When you've never known security, it can mean a great deal. Bettenheim came to tea on twenty-two separate afternoons. That was unwise of him. By the time he proposed on the twenty-third, I had listened to enough rain and jingoism to last a lifetime. He made quite a scene.'' She laughed wryly. ''You were right. Perhaps I am too easily bored. And if I were less impetuous, I might be mistress of several plantations now instead of a not-quite mistress of your royal . . . *nada-ness.*''

''Yes, you could let him breed his dynasty on you.'' His voice had a curious tightness. ''I wonder if all his plantations would be worth that.''

Eyes narrowing at the rebuke, she taunted lightly, ''Perhaps. I might even enjoy him as a lover. He has a strong body and a certain brutal appeal. At worst, he could be no more ruthless than you. Perhaps I should reconsider marrying him if I return to Rangoon.''

''He would not ask for your hand now,'' Ram said curtly. ''He would simply take you to bed.''

''Then I must begin to study the *nayaka* erotica from your library''—she gave him a feline smile—''so he will want to keep me there.''

His smile took on a similar curve. ''Do you really think you can learn how to fly from just looking at pictures, little bird?''

Lysistrata now rarely did more than take meals and spend nights in the *zenana*. Every morning after breakfast and a swim, she roamed the huge fortress. One morning she encountered a peculiar group on the field by the guard barracks. Dressed in Chinese black tunics and breeches, Ram and several guards stood immobile like ballet dancers in plié second. Easing into an arbor, she waited to see what they would do. They appeared to be as paralyzed as stone Phinias and his warriors. She tried the stance herself, but within minutes her muscles shrieked.

Nearly two hours went by. Finally, the men came to life in one serpentine movement followed by a strangely beautiful, perfectly synchronized dance she was to learn was not a dance but a *kata* of *kung fu*, a deadly concentration upon an unseen opponent. No wonder Ram danced well; his body was completely graceful, completely disciplined. When matched in mock combat, he was adder quick and just as dangerous. In weeks that followed, she discovered his bare hands and feet could shatter stone.

Ram, along with his mercenaries, had several unpleasant skills. Leaning from a galloping horse, he could unerringly bull's-eye an arrow at a hundred yards; his accuracy with the Winchester was as precise. With hook and cord, he could scale a sheer wall in seconds and crop flower buds by hurling a small metal star. That he knew his practice was observed she did not doubt, yet she continued to watch him with the preoccupation of trapped prey for its captor.

When not absorbed by *kung fu*, she delved in the library. After making a selection, she curled up in some secluded spot, preferably the Phoenix Pavilion, a small bungalow on the far end of the fortress from the Peacock Palace. The Phoenix, its stucco partly cloaked with cyclamen, was perched by a hyacinth-covered lake with an island. There she took an armful of Hindu literature one afternoon.

Out of idle curiosity about Ram's Hindu namesake, she scanned the *Ramayana*. Part of the epic poem dealt with the exile of the princely hero, Rama, and his attempts to reclaim his kingdom and his beloved consort, Sita, from the demon King Ravana. Rama appeared to be more faithful to his mate than Ram would ever be, she thought dryly as she tossed the book aside.

The *Abisarika Nayaka* was a poem about a married

woman's affair. So wild was the heroine's desire, she literally tore off her clothes and trod on serpents to reach her lover. Their union was as intense as the wild scream of peacocks and sullen storms which had preluded it. Melodramatic, Lysistrata judged uncomfortably. The *Nayaka* joined the *Ramayana*.

The *Kama Sutra* was a sometimes clinical, sometimes ludicrous manual for lovemaking. Perfectly suitable for unscrupulous lechers, she decided, though many of the positions were fascinating, if startling. She had always thought lovemaking was a rather forthright, if often stealthy procedure. The drawings skillfully suggested the curve and resilience of flesh, the languor and intensity of the lovers. She began to feel unaccountably restless and irritable.

The sun on water glinted with mirror brightness into her eyes. Perhaps this once, an afternoon nap might break the routine; otherwise, she would spend the rest of the day nursing a headache.

The *zenana* was deserted, its residents dozing in their quarters in the mid-afternoon hours—or so Lysistrata thought until she entered her room and heard low voices and laughter from the adjoining balcony. One of the voices was male. Instantly curious, Lysistrata laid the books on the bed and crept to the cutwork partition. Ram and the Chinese, Kim, lay naked on a cushioned mat, their bodies lightly intertwined. They were carrying on a playful conversation in Chinese, for Ram laughed when Kim murmured something in his ear with a wicked roll of her eyes. With a lazy stretch, he shook his head. Eyes twinkling impudently, Kim slid down his body until her long hair covered his groin. Her head lowered and lingered until Lysistrata realized suddenly what Kim must be doing. Her fingers pressed hard against the screen, she saw Ram's eyes close, the hard muscles of his belly contract in a tremor of pleasure. As the sunlight through the screen dappled their shadowed bodies, his hands moved lightly over Kim's hair, then tightened and pressed the sides of her head. His slim body grew rhythmically taut as if in some silent torment, then relaxed, only to react more intensely than before. Lysistrata's attention had been so drawn by the curve of his belly where Kim's hair met his loins, she did not immediately notice his head had twisted toward her. His eyes, half-lidded and drugged with desire, had fixed on the screen. She froze. His lips parted in a gasp as his hands gripped the concubine's shoulders, his muscles cording. By the time his eyes opened again to meet Kim's triumphant ones, Lysistrata was gone from the balcony. Shaken and burning with a shaming excitement, she fled the *zenana*.

Ram found Lysistrata reading in the library. Although she offhandedly returned his greeting, she could hardly bear to look at him. He was fully clothed from boots to turban, but she could not stop envisioning the maleness defined by those tight breeches. His *lingham* enveloped by a woman's soft mouth, imbued with mysterious shadowy decadence.

"How's the *nayaka* coming?" he asked quietly, and she flinched. He knew. He had to know.

"I really can't get into it," she managed to say lightly. "George Sand's *Indiana* is much more interesting. He's rather clever, don't you think?"

He smiled oddly. "How did you find Sand's attitude toward love?"

"Oh . . . he seems to be . . . impartial . . . at times."

"Impartial." The smile grew odder. "Yes, that describes Sand rather well."

She felt limp with relief. "I thought you might agree."

"I wouldn't think of not agreeing," he said obliquely.

Now that dangerous waters seemed left behind, Lysistrata quickly decided to change tacks. She eased out of the chair and walked out onto the upper terrace overlooking the central courtyard. "I was wondering," she blurted, "that is, would you mind if I moved out of the *zenana*."

His head cocked. "Where would you like to move?"

"To the Phoenix Bungalow. I'm not used to living closely with anyone but my father. I prefer to be alone."

"Of course. Kalisha will have the servants prepare it for you."

She was surprised at how easy it was. Almost too easy. He must want her out of the way so he could visit the *zenana* without tripping over a naive, truculent nag. Perhaps he had decided she was no longer worth pursuit. Why not, when experienced beauties were willing to perform any sexual service he wished? "Thank you," she murmured, "but I should like to go there tonight before anyone touches it and clean it myself tomorrow. Then perhaps it will seem more like my own home." She was unaware the last words had trickled out like those of a deserted waif.

"Don't forget to take George Sand with you," he said softly.

Though the first night in the Phoenix Bungalow was long, Lysistrata knew it would have been far longer in the *zenana*. With new ears, she would have listened to every creak and sigh in the place. Of course Ram must have either frequented the *zenana* after she was asleep at night, or the women had gone to him. Perhaps all three of them at once. Unable to stop thinking about it, she restlessly turned on the great, deep cushion of a bed. Finally, she slept and dreamed, which was worse, for Ram appeared as a many-armed, animist god who danced lasciviously before her in a jungle pagoda. Naked goddesses embraced him, kissing and caressing phallus of stone. Then she was entwined in his arms, which first lured her until he relentlessly forced her downward. Feeling blood gush from her loins, she shrieked with terror. Then awoke sitting rigidly upright, hands clamped to her face. The linen sheets under her thighs were soaked—but not with blood—and she hugged herself in humiliation. Minutes later, hearing the whisper of an opening shuttered door, she stiffened. A tall, lean figure was silhouetted in a widening wedge of moonlight. "Ram?" she croaked.

"I heard you cry out," he said quietly. "Don't worry, you're safe. No one ever comes here."

"Except you," she managed to retort feebly.

"My quarters are in the grove on the other side of the lake."

Her throat went drier than before. "I thought . . . I thought you—"

"I've never stayed in the Peacock Palace. Like you, I prefer solitude." He leaned against the doorjamb. "Or did you leave the *zenana* out of fear?"

She rallied scattered defenses. "If you were going to use rape, you would have tried it long ago."

"Perhaps I just haven't made up my mind yet." His head rested against the jamb. "Or perhaps I'm too lazy. I don't usually have to resort to rape."

"Well, if you think I'll ever roll over for Your Indolence," she retorted, "you're going to wait until you have a long, gray beard."

"If the British come to Khandahoor, I shall not likely get that old. So, it seems if you will not come to me, I must come to you." She stiffened as he straightened and walked toward the bed. Bars of blue moonlight from the louvered window curved across his wet nakedness. With a slow flick of his wrist, he tugged at the bed's white woolen blanket and let it fall to the floor. For a long moment, he stared at her body in the moonlight. "You were not made to lie alone. When you are ready, I will teach you that."

"Men are so insufferably vain," she hissed. "They think a woman cannot exist without them. That she hasn't a brain, much less a will. I don't need a man, and most definitely, I don't need you!" She snatched out the knife he had given her from under the pillow. "Now, get out of here!"

"I will go for now," he said quietly, "but soon you will discover some things cannot be fulfilled in the mind and some can be stronger than will. The mind can lead to traps and temptations. To think often of the thing one most fears is to surrender to it." He lightly tossed the blanket on the bed. "You may hide a little longer, but do not rely too much on my patience. When I have been a while from 'civilization,' I am apt to revert to the ways of my ancestors."

Moments later, only moonlight remained where he had been, and Lysistrata might have thought him a dream if not for the cold glimmer of steel in her hand.

For the next few days, Lysistrata threw herself into making the Phoenix Bungalow comfortable. Whatever simple furnishings she requested were brought, including a bright yellow hammock for the verandah that extended to the rock garden at the edge of the lake. Mosquito netting hung in a tentlike canopy over the huge pillow-like bed; white cotton curtains loosely drifted at the arched windows. White cushions with violet and chocolate silk pillows made a divan and chaise which were casually comfortable on a rattan rug. At night, brass lamps softly lit the white plaster walls, and by day the gardens and lake outside were reflected in a glass-mosaicked mirror near the bed. Surveying the room, she was almost sorry to have refused Ram's offer of a lovely, life-size carving of the Chinese goddess Kuan Yin, which would have been perfect by the door. She might be merely gilding a new cage, but she wanted to make perfectly clear whose cage it was.

Now nothing remained but to transfer more books from the library so she would not have to encounter Ram there. She had declined his every dinner invitation, and intended to continue doing so. All meals were brought to the Phoenix Bungalow by a servant.

Ready to relax, she headed for the hammock with some fruit juice and Sand's neglected *Indiana*. After less than an hour, she realized *Indiana* was a woman's protest against social conventions which chained her to a marital life she could not abide. No wonder Frank Wyatt had smugly denounced the book. It was a plea for common sense and humanity for women . . . by a woman. This copy had belonged to Ram's mother, whose scrawled, cryptic notes in the margins included a sympathetic reference to the female author who had been forced to employ a male name in order to be published. So Ram *had* seen her watch him make love to Kim, seen her voyeuristically join an intimacy she had no right to share. He knew she had lied, all the way through her ridiculous babbling about Sand in the library. No wonder he felt her capitulation was only a matter of time. She snapped the book closed. Watching him fornicate did not mean she wanted him . . . or did it?

Another inconsistency nagged her. Had Anira, who had read *Indiana* so intently, bought a pair of harem guards for her husband out of duty? Or as a private joke? Could the eunuchs' lack of manhood reflect a wish to emasculate William Harley for being unfaithful? Other than Ram and Kalisha, few people at Khandahoor might recall much about a woman who lived in the seclusion of *purdah*. Strangely enough, the only Indian in the place besides Kalisha was an ancient gardener she had often greeted as he puttered about the grounds. Ram seemed to maintain few ties with his mother's race.

* * *

"Greetings, Pandit Singh." Lysistrata stooped by the old gardener and handed him a marigold plantling as he groped for a basket containing marigolds and fuchsias. "Your chrysanthemums and marigolds by my back terrace are lovely. Thank you for taking so much care with them."

He nodded vigorously, highly pleased. "If they survive the monsoons, they will bloom all year. Chrysanthemums and marigolds are sacred to Buddha, so they bring good fortune."

"What was the Rani Anira's favorite flower?"

"She had no great love for flowers."

"But these lovely gardens were designed for her, weren't they? I had no idea her husband had such exquisite taste."

"Lord Harley only cared for architecture. I designed the gardens."

"You!" She was startled. "Pandit Singh, you're a genius!"

He laughed without humor. "A man can be very clever when his life depends on it."

She frowned. "I don't understand."

His beady eyes fixed her like a mongoose's. "I am the last of the convicts who built Khandahoor. The others are in the moat."

Mechanically, she reached for another seedling, her mind jerking, recoiling from the vision of screaming, hopeless men being eaten alive by crocodiles. "I see . . ." She looked at him sharply. "But I don't see. The architecture is as spectacular as the gardens. Why should Harley . . . ?"

"The Rani could change gardens; she could not alter stone so easily, though had she lived I think she would eventually have done so. She was rarely satisfied by anything; all had to be perfect, and at the end, simply different.''

Sagging onto the walk, Lysistrata murmured, "Lord Harley must have been a monster."

The old man shrugged. "Lord Harley might have sent us back to Madras for execution, had it been less troublesome. He considered a firing squad, but the Rani persuaded him to be economical by using the moat. She watched, smiling, from the ramparts. It was the last time she came out of *purdah.*"

Lysistrata felt ill. She could not listen to another word. Yet she must. "Pandit Singh, could you put in some fuchsias by the Phoenix Lake tomorrow afternoon?"

He looked startled by the cool change of subject, then his eyes narrowed in understanding. "As you please, Missy."

She spent that night and the next morning reading Anira's notes in *Indiana.* The more she read, the more difficult it was to reconcile the sensitive, passionate Anira who cried out for human justice with the Rani who enjoyed mass murder.

When Pandit Singh arrived with the plants at the rock garden, he was less garrulous that afternoon than the day before; also, wary. "Perhaps I was wrong to speak ill of the Rani," he began nervously.

"Why? Did you lie?"

"No, no, but . . ."

"I will tell Prince Ram nothing. I am a prisoner here as much as you."

He blinked, then became suspicious. "If you seek a way out, I do not know one or I would have used it long ago. Besides, Missy, outside lies only endless jungle, warring Shan tribesmen . . . and worse."

"I know." She smiled ruefully. "I am only exploring

my cage, Pandit Singh. Also, I have been reading about the Rani; she fascinates me.''

''You are fortunate she is dead. She was said to be the daughter of Naga the Cobra God. She hated her own people, but hated *feringhis* more''—with an oddly malicious smile, he set down the plants—''particularly *feringhi* women.''

''She married a *feringhi*,'' Lysistrata retorted.

He spat on the sunny rocks. ''The Sahib never married her.'' The smile came again. ''He built Khandahoor for her, but he never married her. She was a princess, yet made herself a *feringhi*'s whore, unfit for even the company of untouchables. The *feringhis* would not have her either. That is why she demanded Khandahoor to rule.''

Lysistrata stared at the golden mass of flowers that spilled down the stones. Pandit Singh's tale explained a great deal about Anira's disillusionment, but still not enough. ''You said yesterday that the Sepoy execution was the last time the Rani came out of *purdah*. Had she previously imitated the freedom of Western women?''

''She was shameless,'' he said bitterly. ''She did not even wear a veil. She was very beautiful and knew the prisoners lusted after her despite their contempt. That amused her—'' He stiffened, staring fearfully beyond Lysistrata's shoulder.

She turned to see Ram astride a creamy Arabian stallion and leading a matching mare. His face was cold. ''You have work at the Peacock Palace, Singh,'' he said curtly. ''Hereafter, you will consult me before making changes at Phoenix.''

With a hasty bow, the old man fled, forgetting his seedlings.

Ram held out the mare's reins to Lysistrata. ''This is Soleil's sister, Parvati. Come.'' It was an order, not an invitation. When she had mounted, he said sharply, ''Do not encourage that old man. He hacked white women like you to bits in the 'fifty-eight rebellion.''

"But that was years ago and he's partly senile," she protested. "He's afraid of you. Surely he's harmless now.''

"The senile sometimes forget fear when their minds return to the past. If Singh decides you are part of his past, he may try to permanently consign you to it."

He spurred his horse, leaving her to follow across the flat green turf. To her surprise, he halted at the fortress drawbridge to order it lowered. With hooves rattling on the bridge boards, the two riders left the fortress.

Ram led the way along a narrow path hacked across the densely jungled plateau until they came to its edge overlooking the lake. Beyond the marsh-bound shoreline, tiny boats skimmed like water spiders across the surface. "The villagers live there." He pointed to huts on stilts over the lake. "Some of them never go ashore. They're fishermen, but also grow crops directly on the water." He indicated huge, woven sheets of palm blanketed with marsh mud which grew neat rows of vegetables.

"The lake people provide part of our food supply; some we grow in the jungle on a rice plantation that flanks two sides of Khandahoor. The workers live in huts nearby."

"It all looks so peaceful. Don't the Shans ever raid?''

"They did steadily before Khandahoor's walls went up. That's why the moat and the stake abatis were put in first." He gazed over the treetops. "Father and I dug that moat with the Sepoys. On some nights the jungle seemed to breathe with Shans. We only had a few mercenaries then, so we didn't have many rifles. We wore pistols while we worked." He grinned faintly. "Every time I dozed off, I never knew whether I was going to get a Shan *dah* or an Indian *kris* in the ribs.''

"So you didn't grow up at Khandahoor," she said thoughtfully. "You must have been what, fifteen, when it was begun?"

"Fourteen. I spent most of my boyhood in India, and altogether less than a year here."

"Then you must feel India rather than Burma is home."

"You lived many years in Boston. Do you feel a particular attachment for it?"

She smiled ironically. "Where is home, then?"

"As you said once," he replied, "I am a prince of *nada.*"

Or perhaps Hades, her mind murmured, looking for his Persephone.

CHAPTER 10

The Hunt

> *And there shall be for thee*
> *All soft delight,*
> *That shadowy thought*
> *Can win.*
>
> JOHN KEATS

The heat of the dry season began to build, and with it, Lysistrata's tension. At night, the bungalow was watched, but not by Ram because once when she suspiciously called out, the bougainvillea near the lake rustled as if someone had quickly left. Kalisha kept *purdah* and Ram would not have bothered to hide. Possibly, his warning about Pandit Singh had been merited. Although the old man now took care to avoid her, he sometimes wore a furtive leer. He must think her as shameless as the dead Rani. Ram also left her alone, seeming to realize her mind was shut against him; yet as he had predicted, she often thought of him as the nights became sultry. Memories of Hindu erotica both fascinated and mocked her. On some nights, her body felt as if it were ripening like a pomegranate until the confinement of flesh seemed unbearable.

After one such restless night, when threads of dawn

mist still lay on the lake, she wandered naked to the shore. As she swam through the mist and twining hyacinths, her hair hung sleek, body grew languid. Idly, she threaded hyacinths through her hair and about her limbs until their clinging verdance made her body seem part of the water and green, primal life that filled it. She turned onto her back and, floating in the slow current, touched herself: her breasts, her vulva as Ram had done on the night of the tiger. Exquisite sensations that trembled on the edge of mystery intrigued, frightened her.

Leaving the water, she threw herself down on the bright, sandy beach and, eyes closed, let the early sun dry the moisture on her skin. Again, as if the last of her will had been bewitched away in the lake, her fingertips roamed, brushed, probed. Found a silky wetness, a fragile, delicious ripeness. Grains of wet, clinging sand pricked the skin as her hand caressed, then lifted her breasts as she offered herself to desire. Offered herself to Ram, whose wet-lashed dark eyes burned into hers as they dazedly opened. Startled, she went wide-eyed with fear. He was naked, still dripping from his dawn swim. Adam, with the fruit of the forbidden still on his lips, might have once looked so at Eve, with his loins aflame and his soul heedless of perdition. When she scrambled up and ran, a low, triumphant laugh echoed over the sun-streaked water.

A brief twilight fell as did a light rain; Lysistrata's eyes raked its hazy screen as she paced the bungalow verandah. Arms hugged to herself, she listened to birds call, monkeys chatter. Listened. For tonight Ram would take her. He would play no more games. He had cleverly loosed her leash each time she strained at it to give her an illusion of freedom, yet all the while played upon her mind. Tempted. Taunted. What a subtle, devious seducer he was! And how ruthlessly he could humiliate her.

That horrible night aboard the *Rani* in Rangoon had left weals too livid to forget. Tonight the tether would pull tight, and she could not bear the thought of his dominion. She was trapped . . . unless she killed him. Then she would probably be butchered by his mercenaries. Once those terrible realities settled into her marrow, she felt a certain resignation, a dull calm.

When the birds ceased calling and huddled away from the rain, Lysistrata strapped on the knife sheath. Her wool jacket, dark *pasoh*, and leather boots would not show by the slender crescent moon skirting the swollen clouds. She stole through dripping jack trees that edged the lake; beyond the palm grove on the far side was a glimmer of white lacquer screen, shiny with rain. She crept toward the small building. The screen was propped outward from its window to admit the rain-cooled breeze. Beyond the screen, the room was dark. She eased around the verandah. The place was empty. He must have already gone to the Phoenix Bungalow.

Rather than chance on encountering Ram returning, she stripped, then slipped into the lake. A fading patter of raindrops pelted the night-chilled water as she swam through pale hyacinth blooms to the island. Except for its steep banks, the island was thicketed with palms and mangroves, the bamboo and magnolias allowed to go wild. Underfoot the ground was slippery with mud and rotting leaves.

Shivering, Lysistrata peered through the bamboo at the Phoenix Bungalow. The verandah overhang cast the place in shadow, for no light had been left burning. As the moon passed behind a cloud, the creak of the swinging front door came over the water. Then the slight ripple of a body entering water. Heart pounding, she retreated into the thicket to seek an ambush point. Minutes later, she heard a drip of water in the island shallows as she crawled along a low, twisted mangrove boll that hung over the single path across the island. There she crouched, ready to drop as Ram crossed the island.

Misty, humid heat was rising now the rain had stopped, and she trembled less with cold than tension. Her wet hair felt heavy on her back and her thighs ached from the strain of keeping balance as time drew on. As the birds and cicadas were still silent, Ram had not left the island. He must be circling to look for her. Knife clamped between her teeth as she dropped from the tree, she went to all fours, senses alert.

The moon was out again. To find the origin of his trail in the muck, she headed toward the spot where she had heard him come ashore. Moon-glistened mud oozed between toes as her footprints mingled with his; they skirted the island for a short distance, then cut inward across a glade. After that, they led to a bamboo thicket which he could not have penetrated in silence. She crouched warily, her stomach knotting as she heard a rustle in the bamboo. It came again, more loudly. She skirted the glade toward the bamboo to avoid being caught in the open moonlight, then heard the cough of a tiger. A shape burst from the bamboo. She nearly screamed in panic, then saw it was a rabbit as it shot across the glade into the palms.

Relief instantly faded with horrible realization. The rabbit had been startled by what it had thought to be a tiger. And no tigers prowled inside Khandahoor. Only a man who must have circled behind her from the bamboo where she had been lured. Almost sick with fear, she shrank away from the bamboo into the deeper part of the forest. Her only chance was to use the trees as delaying barriers, ambush points. Ancient and gnarled against sloping palms and heavy magnolias, black mangroves writhed across the misty earth. Trying to pick up his trail, she made a stalk, moving a few feet, then crouching, tautly alert. With moonlight along the long line of her back and flank, she moved deeper into the wood, then froze as the tiger's cough sounded just in front of her. Her hand slippery on the knife haft, she retreated in mounting panic, started as her hip grazed mangrove. Whirling, she came face-to-face with Ram, naked as herself. Leaning indolently against the tree, he murmured, "Now you know what it is to lie alone."

His belly sucked in just as her blade slashed past it to meet the mangrove's unyielding bulk. Desperately, she dragged at the buried blade. His hand clamped on her wrist as she tried to twist away, clawing and kicking, but her foot slipped on the wet leaves and she went down. Before she could roll away, Ram was on her, his lean body pressing her into the muddy leaves. One knee thrust between her thighs as he pinned her wrists. In numb, silent terror she bucked against him, trying to throw him off. With his hunter's patience, he waited until her struggles weakened; then silently, surely, he began to take possession of her.

As his lips brushed beneath her ear, Lysistrata's head twisted away, inadvertently exposing her throat, then she went taut as his teeth sank gently into the arched flesh just above its hollow. His mouth grazed her breasts, moving over their swells to explore her armpits with his tongue, then to the peaks that brushed the hollow of his shoulder. Shivering, she hated him, hated the skill that had begun to madden her, hated the slick, hard feel of his rain-wet body sliding over hers. The hard threat of his sex against her belly. His teeth sank into her nipple and she moaned, her thighs weakening as he forced them apart. His mouth moved over her parted lips, moved on them, tongue probing, luring. Drugging her. Then she felt his belly contract as he poised. Felt the urgent, irrevocable thrust of his flesh into hers, the terrible fullness of him. He began to move, animal taut, animal hard, his mouth taking her, his maleness thrusting her down, down into the warm, primal mud that sucked against her body until she opened to the heat of him, that white-hot spear searing, branding her until she cried out from the death, the life of him lost forever inside her.

After a time he led her to the lake. Unless she wanted to drown, the swim to his bungalow offered no chance of escape. He carried her to bed, where he gave her no time to regain sanity as he mesmerized her with his body, the erotic incantations he murmured against her flesh until it dreamed only of yielding to whatever he willed. When the sun's light flickered over the pillows, she lay languid with sleep and sex, his body partly entangling her. Her lashes brushing his damply curling hair, her eyes opened, focused vaguely on splinters of sunlight, then widened in awareness of abject surrender. Abruptly, she tried to wrench away from him, but his hand clamped on her shoulder, his arm hard across her breasts. "So restless, *cara?*" he murmured sleepily. "Am I neglecting you?"

His light mockery infuriated her. "Let me go," she said through gritted teeth. "I can't bear the smug sight of you."

With a peaceful smile, he glanced down at his manhood. "I apologize. It does look rather pleased, doesn't it?"

When she fruitlessly tried to knee him, he lazily rolled over on her, pinned the offending leg and nuzzled her neck. "You're practiced enough at rape," she hissed. "It must be your only alternative to buying a bed partner."

"But I only had to rape you a little," he teased, "and of course, I will pay if you prefer."

"I prefer to be left alone!" she nearly screeched.

He laughed. "After last night, even you do not believe that lie. Why not admit you enjoy what I do to you?"

"Go to hell," she muttered sullenly.

"Admit it, Lysistrata." His tongue traced her earlobe,

then teased her nape when her head snapped away. Securing her hips with one long leg, he began to caress her breasts until she squirmed, her eyes losing some of their mutiny as he teased sensitive peaks. She gasped as his thumbnail raked down her belly, just grazing the cleft of the mons. Firmly, he pressed her onto her side. His thigh pinning her hips, he delicately slipped his finger into her, teasing, tantalizing until her breath caught. Liquid warmth welled between her thighs, her body instinctively moved to aid his exploration. But as his finger withdrew to ease farther back, she went rigid. "No, don't!" But his finger was already inside her, gently, gently deeper, then pressing firmly inward more quickly as his sex teased her swelling vulva. An explosion of sensation made her clutch at the bed with a muted cry. Before she relaxed, he penetrated her in a deft, deep thrust that made her contract in another intense spasm. Alternating strokes made her shudder over and over, until at last, sensing her peak approaching, he drove into her with such intensity that she screamed against the pillow. Dimly she felt his grip tighten on her shoulder and heard a muffled sound in his throat.

He turned her to him and, stroking the drops of moisture from her brow, kissed her lips, then whispered against them, "Tell me the lie again, Lysistrata."

I can't. I can't give in to him, her rational mind repeated dully. If I do, he'll use me, then leave me to rot away in the *zenana* when he's done. Her hands clamped to the pillow, she forced a cold murmur. "No, I'll tell you the truth. You think you're the first man who's had me? Didn't you notice how easy it was on the *Rani?* Or did you think your new 'virgin' was so eager for you, her maidenhead miraculously parted like the sea for Moses?"

Confusion, then anger filled his eyes. Also quick, harsh pain she did not expect, did not believe. As if he had lain with a scorpion, Ram jerked away and left the bungalow. Moments later, his body knifed into the lake.

By nightfall, she learned he was gone from Khandahoor. After Shans, with his eyes like death, Pandit Singh told her gleefully. With Kanaka and Friedlander riding after him. They would be gone for days, perhaps weeks. Perhaps forever.

And with sick shame in her soul, she was not glad.

The days crawled by, slow as centipedes in the mounting heat, with only the rattle of palms and racket of birds and monkeys to stir the heavy air. The moon grew full, waned, and slipped behind the curve of the earth. Lysistrata came to hate the moonless nights; the loneliness; the black, watching silence. She sensed eyes like those of mean, stubborn pigs through a fence, never coming closer than the bougainvillea. They could belong to anyone: one of the mercenaries, Pandit Singh, even Kalisha. She did not quite dare take the knife and find out, for Ram had demonstrated her limits.

Lest her mind play more games, she diverted it with histories of Burma and India. She learned the Rajputs had been the fiercest warriors in Northern India. After the failure of the Sepoy revolt against the British, most Rajput rulers had been either deposed or killed, their estates confiscated—probably Ram's maternal family's estates along with them. Anira had more than one reason to resent her British lover, a pillager of that district.

Oddly, now that Ram was gone, she felt free to wear the lovely saris and jewelry allotted to her upon entering the *zenana*. Each afternoon, she dressed as if expecting a lover, not because she did, but because she no longer felt at odds with her femininity. Ram was unscrupulous, but he had proved she *was* a woman, warm, resilient and desirable even to a man of his experience. So much so that he had gone to inordinate time and trouble not only to have her, but to give pleasure.

Frank Wyatt had pursued her, but so furtively and with such a sense of sin, he had made her nearly as ashamed as he. He had entered the Herriott home as a distant relative and friend, and even after he began to court her in private, he pretended only platonic interest to Dr. Herriott and everyone else. That should have been warning enough, she bitterly realized later, but he had explained himself as too shy, his emotions too delicate to reveal his love to the world. He had been believable because he *was* shy, and poetic and sensitive. Afterward, she would have described him as cowardly, maudlin, and morbidly preoccupied with himself.

Capitulation had been understandable. She had been vulnerable to his seeming sympathy, romanticism, and learning. Too, he was as poor, lonely, and frustrated as she. Smooth-featured, with soft brown hair falling over a pale brow, he appeared to be the Galahad of any maiden's dreams. He pleaded for love, and love had been easy to give. She agreed to a secret engagement, for Frank had not yet enough money from teaching to take a wife. Still, through months of his pressing for consummation of their "sweet union of souls," as he put it, she resisted.

Then, one night when Dr. Herriott was away, Frank had brought a pistol to the house and threatened suicide if she cared so little for him. Frightened, she yielded. Then found, after being thrust down onto a scratchy horsehair couch, that his delicacy did not extend to physical love. He tore open her bodice and pawed her with the harsh, feverish haste of a madman. Then, taking only time to work open his breeches and push up her skirt, he rammed himself into her unprepared body to relieve his lust in a few painful seconds. He buttoned himself, apologized profusely, and ran out the door.

When he returned only a few hours later to beg, then

demand accommodation, she was revolted by his insensitivity and refused. He called her a whore, unfit to be a wife and mother. Within the month, he married a plain but well-dowered spinster from Salem to whom he had also been "secretly engaged."

While she did not become pregnant, her mind and heart were poisoned. Only once since had a man drawn her. Ram. Who never asked for anything. He had taken it. With all the patience, skill, and unashamed virility Frank lacked. And therein lay the seductive danger of learning to crave the sheer sensation of loveless fornication. Ram could make that possibility all too easy if he ever came back. If he still wanted her.

When the moon rounded with the Prince of Khandahoor still gone, Lysistrata felt increasing, unaccustomed anxiety. What if Ram never returned and she was left for life in this jungle-bound prison? What if he was dead? The last thought had haunted her for weeks now. He might have gone hunting the men who distributed guns at his door. The feudal Shan *sawbas* would dislike having their supply of bright new rifles cut off, particularly by a man they hated for carving a personal kingdom out of their hereditary domain. And as Pandit Singh had said, they were formidable enemies, never wholly controlled by the Burmese monarchy or anyone else. Why would Ram go to stop their arms now, after doing nothing about them for months except remain at Khandahoor? With her.

At length, she knew she was more afraid for him than of him.

Hammock swinging lightly, Lysistrata stared at the verandah ceiling, a book unopened in one lax hand. Ram must have been waiting for reconnaissance by Friedlander and Kanaka, logic argued; it was like him to be perfectly sure of himself before he acted. Surely, other than a slap to his vanity, a woman's lack of virginity could not matter so much. He had once said he preferred married women.

Then, swiftly nearing hoofbeats startled her from reverie. At the sight of Ram riding toward the bungalow, she ran with unthinking relief to meet him. He dismounted, his body and loincloth covered with sweat and dirt. In a grimy turban with knife sheath strung across his blood-streaked shoulder and rifle in its saddle scabbard, he resembled a swarthy Shan bandit. Even his stance was different: he strode tensely, as if pacing toward a cage door. Only the eyes were Ram's, and looking into them, she saw why he had gone when he did. To keep from killing her.

Without breaking stride, he scooped her up in his arms and headed for the bungalow. Inside he dumped her on the bed and jerked off his loincloth. Then he knelt, his thighs arching her body as he ripped the silk of the copper sari from it. Swearing something in Hindi when she made no resistance, he roughly knifed himself into her, heedless of her muffled cry. Blood from his shoulder seeped down his arm as his fingers dug into her flesh, then his need obliterated the pain and took her with him to the edge of *nada*. Only the maddened torture in his eyes remained. Her own eyes filled with tears as she caught his head between her hands. "Don't . . . don't let me hurt you so," she whispered. "I might come to believe you care for me." His eyes darkened as if he were a wounded animal facing a death blow that would end both torment and mortality. With a strangled sound, he buried his face in her neck. His long body shuddered, then went limp.

After a time, she touched his shoulder with a soft command. "Come. That dirt will infect your wound." Unresisting, he let her lead him to the lake, then stood mutely, hip-deep in the shallows, his head drooping with fatigue while she bathed him. But when she would have taken his hand and returned to the bungalow to clean his wound, he turned and dove into the darker, deeper water. Moments later, his head broke surface just off the far shore, the mist distorting his rising, solitary form as if he were a wraith. Then he was gone and she was alone.

Days passed without his return. Uncertain of his mood, she did not seek him out until anxiety became unbearable. One morning as the dawn mists still feathered the lake, she swam to the opposite shore. Upon finding Ram's bungalow deserted, she uneasily returned to the lake. She had only taken a few steps into the shallows when Ram soundlessly emerged from the water mist. For a long moment, they looked at each other, then she said quietly, "I waited for you."

A glimmer of sadness seemed to pass through his eyes. "Lysistrata, I will never love you."

She paled, then silently turned away toward deeper water. Lightly catching her shoulders, he murmured into her bright hair, "Take from me what you will. I will be your merprince forever bound to dwell in a cave beneath this lake. One day you will remember our time together as no more than a dream." He turned her to him. "Do not ask more, Lysistrata, for it is not mine to give."

"Then let me go, Ram. I want the real world, not a dream of what could be."

"You may leave when I am dead," he said quietly.

"What have I done that you should so hate me?" she whispered.

"I do not hate you."

"That night aboard the *Rani* when you—Was that not hatred?"

"If it was, then have you not repaid me for it in kind?"

She shook her head, bewildered. "I don't understand."

Briefly, he described where the Bartly investigation had led, the false murder charges, his ruin.

"But . . . what has that to do with me?" Then her eyes widened in dawning comprehension. "You think I set Lord Bartly on you?"

"Did you not?" he retorted curtly. "If I had not done as I did, you would soon have met another Lop Ear and a far less pleasant end to your Samaritanism. If I had not done as I did, you would have tempted us both into ruin."

"So that's why you . . ." she breathed. "You meant to frighten me back into my own world."

"What does it matter? You had reason to hate me, but you must admit an inordinate price was exacted for your pride."

She laughed mirthlessly. "I had not gone from the *Rani* more than a few minutes before I was abducted. I thought it was you."

After a silence, he said slowly, "Then I did you a great wrong in buying you out of revenge in Tennasserim."

"*Now* will you send me back to Rangoon?"

He laughed softly. "I did not buy you only for revenge. Still"—he tipped her chin up—"I did not bring you here only to conquer my lust, though each time I vanquish it, it seems to be reborn like Hydra. Perhaps one day you will understand the reason and not think too badly of your merprince." He stroked her hair. "Stay a little with him and let him give you what happiness he can . . . for he will always answer when you call and he is made to please you."

Gently, he guided her hand to his groin. When she would have drawn away, he kissed her, his lips warm, knowing, until shyly her fingers explored him. He pressed her back onto the water's surface, then with her hands on his shoulders, swam with her to the honeyed shadows of the island's sloping, cyclamen-carpeted bank. There he drew her with him and stroked the silk of her as if she were a sunning cat. As she stretched languor-ously under his hand, he began to caress her inner thighs, persuading them to part for him. He took her with his mouth, teasing, tantalizing, probing—until with a soft cry, she arched against him.

Drawing her into the water, he lifted, then lowered her upon himself, moving her upon his sex until she wound about him. Then he took her beyond longing, beyond the dream, beyond hope of forgetfulness. Long after they were both spent, he held her still enfolded about him like a lovely petal furled about its potent, hidden center.

During the long, warm weeks and nights of that early spring, Ram and Lysistrata explored all the ways of love with a sensitive intensity that left its mark on them with the delicate indelibility of a tattoo. Still, Ram remained almost as much a mystery as ever. Sometimes, after nights when he had made love to her most exquisitely, he stayed away for days. She learned to accept his moods with a silent patience Dr. Herriott would not have imagined she possessed. She knew the time would come when Ram would hurt her beyond bearing. That knowledge made her more beautiful with a translucent sadness beneath the fragile armor that melted only when he made love to her. Then she was naked to him in soul as in body and could not hide herself. It did not seem to matter, for Ram—so perceptive of all else—was blind in this.

As if preparing her for their time of separation, he taught her something of the languages he knew and perfected her Burmese. He taught her to meditate, to leave her body, to leave Khandahoor, yet somehow he was always part of the place she went to; and at times when their bodies joined, she felt her soul was lost within him.

Time passed in a tranquil stream with only a single ripple of disturbance. One night while Ram lay with his head upon her breast, he idly drew patterns upon her stomach with a forefinger.

"What are you thinking?" she asked softly, toying with the hair on his nape.

"I was wondering what man would have you next."

His unexpected cruelty made her stiffen in startled pain, then she forced herself to relax. "Does it matter? After all, you do not love me."

His fingers continued to repeat patterns. "But I am vain and inquisitive. Who was the first man? Bettenheim . . . Harry?"

Then she realized he was tracing interlocking initials: C. B., H. A. She jerked away. "How many lovers have you had since that *nautch* girl?"

"I never bothered to count," he replied lazily, "did you?"

"Whores rarely bother to count. Some of them don't even know how—they just know how to be used and despised and humiliated. But never, *ever* loved." The words wrenched out. "Go ahead, why not just put a pillow over my head and have me? Or am I too dirty? Maybe all those *other* men left me with a disease!" Shaking, she curled away, into herself. When he touched her shoulder, she knotted more tightly. "You needn't worry. I haven't been long in the profession." Then she told him about Frank, and when she was done, uncurled and with eyes blind with tears, opened her legs. "There, you see? Use me all you like. It doesn't matter."

Ram drew her tightly to him. "Where is he now, this Frank? Safe in Boston?" At the harsh coldness of his voice, he felt her tremble and caught her head against his neck. "The fool is fortunate to be in another hemisphere; yet the greater luck is mine, for if he were more than dung under your feet, you might never have come to Burma." He stroked her hair. "Does he still matter to you?"

"Matter?" Her voice came stifled against his shoulder. "I haven't thought of him since—"

"Since I continued where he left off." They lay silent.

"I cannot fight you anymore, Ram," she whispered dully at last. "And I cannot stop you from doing whatever you want to me. I cannot stop you from hurting me. Why do men take so much pleasure from destruction? Does it make your manhood any harder to use a woman rather than care for her?"

"Do you know the ancient *romans* French for 'lily,' Lysistrata? It's *lys,* which symbolizes purity. Your name sounds like the plucking of lute strings or falling water. One only has to say it slowly, each note clear, separate and lovely. *Lys:* the lily of pure passion; *ist:* pride; *strata:* the steadfast. Yet this remarkable symphony that might be a masterpiece is out of tune, each note warring with the other. The impulse to draw out the real loveliness of your music is irresistible, but as I begin to hear its promise fulfilled, I think of the composition as mine. That it has never been and never can be, tempts me to destroy what I cannot keep, so that at least the memory will be mine." He kissed her hair. "Do you understand what I'm trying to say, Lysistrata?"

"How do you know the music you imagine is what it ought to be?" she replied softly. "In the end, only I can decide the composition."

"True, if you remember music is also shaped by the one who hears it. Still, you are right." He tipped her chin up. "I have been presumptuous. Thanks to an autocratic ancestry, I am accustomed to suiting myself. Will you forgive me?"

"You've taught me my body is expendable; for that I forgive you," she said gravely. "But you've also tried to rape my mind. Whatever your intentions, I'm not sure I forgive that." She sat up. "I would like to be alone tonight. Will you please go?"

"No." He pulled her back down.

"Why not?" she protested weakly as his mouth poised over hers. "I thought you'd—"

"Understand? I do. That's why I'm staying."

But even Ram's seductive persuasion could not stop her from wondering what he would do if seriously thwarted. He recognized no authority but his own. He admitted inheriting his parents' ruthlessness, but how much?

CHAPTER 11

The Maniac

But in dark corners of her palace stood
*   Uncertain shapes . . .*
White-eyed phantasms weeping tears of blood
*   And horrible nightmares,*
And hollow shades enclosing hearts of flame
                    ALFRED, LORD TENNYSON

"Pandit Singh, where was Prince Ram the day the Sepoys were killed?" Almost certain he watched the bungalow at night, Lysistrata had not wanted to approach the old gardener; she was more certain when he leered up confidently.

"Why not ask him? Or do you not have leisure for pillow talk?"

"As much leisure as you for nightly strolls in my garden," she replied coolly. "Perhaps I should mention them in pillow talk. His Highness would amply reward your interest in my nocturnal habits."

The old man went white. "You are mistaken! It is a lie . . ." Ducking his head, he fumbled among his plants.

She might have weakened if not for open guilt in his

eyes. "I am not in a mood to quibble over semantics. Answer my question. Where was he?"

"On the rampart," harshly answered the old man, "beside his witch-mother." The sly, rheumy eyes slitted over a skull-like grin. "He enjoyed the Sepoys' screams. Do you hear? He watched them being torn to bits! And some had befriended him, though he was dirt under their feet!"

"I don't believe you!" she cried. "You're a vile, lying old wretch!"

"Do you see Indians other than that evil crone, Kalisha, and myself here now?" he retorted. "He could have brought more from Rangoon. We are far more efficient than the lazy pigs of Burmese. He hates us as much as his mother ever did!"

She snatched at a possible reason. "Why not? Wasn't he in India during the rebellion? Didn't you slaughter half-castes along with the whites?"

He grunted. "The Rani took him to the Hindu Kush. If she had not, his infidel hide would have been flayed at her city gate."

"Then you are no less monstrous than you accuse Ram of being!"

"If so, does that lessen his guilt?" His cackle followed as she abruptly turned and left.

Yet, the old man's amusement was brief. Two days later, Lysistrata found him dead in the rock garden near the bungalow. He had no gardening tools, so she could only guess he had been surprised during one of his nightly surveillances, for he had been stabbed several times in the back. He lay on his side; after turning him over, she almost retched. He had been hacked about face and groin as if by a maniac.

Her mind quailed. Ram? He was due back from a routine sortie beyond the plantations this morning. Had he returned the night before and, on his way to the Phoenix Bungalow, come upon the gardener? She remembered the old man's fearful face when Ram had warned him not to go near the bungalow without his permission. Under his cool veneer, Ram's emotions ran deep; whatever Pygmalion cloak he might put on it, he was jealous. If he had found Pandit Singh spying, his first reaction might have been extreme. The old man had no chance to defend himself: one of the wounds in his back would have been instantly fatal, and an untouched knife showed under his sash that had been pulled askew. She could imagine Ram killing the man, but not mutilating him so sadistically. Yet, if one of the mercenaries had found Pandit Singh, he would have either taken him for Ram's judgment or slit his throat. The sexual orientation of the wounds and possible effort to destroy the face or eyes—for one of them had been put out—all pointed to someone who wanted to punish the old man for his voyeurism. Only Ram could care that much.

Slowly, hoping to find it empty, she walked to his bungalow. In the garden's dappled sunlight, she found him in meditation. Though aware of her presence, he did not speak. She studied his handsome, tranquil profile. The cleft chin could be his brigand father's, but the predatory curve to the nose came from a line of Rajput warrior-despots. A man like this did not have to stab another man, particularly an old one, in the back; yet he had not troubled to warn the bandit, Boh Chaik, before killing him with merciless subtlety. A sunning cobra suggested little danger until it struck.

How little she knew about Ram. He never turned away from personal questions, yet somehow never answered many of them. Even then, had he lied? One puzzle led to another like the turns in the maze where he had first kissed her. Was it all as simple as lust, or had each with some perverse longing sought his inevitable destruction in the other?

Ram's dark head turned. He waited for her to speak, seeming to know she was troubled, for she never came uninvited to his quarters. "Pandit Singh is dead," she said simply.

His face was expressionless. "He was old."

"He did not die of age, Ram." She described finding the gardener.

A fleeting frown marked his brow as she spoke, but no puzzlement. "Don't worry. I'll have him taken away."

"Is that all you have to say?"

His eyes held a trace of impatience. "Do you expect me to be sorry? He was himself a murderer."

"Still, whoever killed him is walking around Khandahoor at this moment. Who do you suppose it is?"

"Are you afraid of being bludgeoned in bed?" A hard, mocking smile curved his lips.

"Have I reason to be afraid?"

"Perhaps, but I will try to see it does not happen."

"Thank you. I hope it will not be too much of a strain on your omnipotence." Feeling cold despite the heat, she returned to the Phoenix Bungalow.

That night as a full moon rose, Lysistrata stood watching the garden, Pandit Singh's creation and memorial. She had disliked him, despised him, yet the beauty he had conceived suggested poetry in him and she mourned its loss. Could she, in the same way, love a murderer? Was it possible to love only part of a man and hate the rest? To touch his fine lacquer surface, but forget the flawed, common base beneath? To solve a maze of complex patterns that fascinated yet defied comprehension?

A subtle noise behind her made her start. She whirled, then recognized Ram, though his face was still in the shadow of an overhanging mimosa.

"I'm sorry I startled you," he murmured.

Involuntarily, she rubbed prickling gooseflesh on an arm. "You're quiet when you want to be, aren't you? Even tigers aren't always aware you're stalking them."

"If they were, I would be the one hunted. I prefer it the other way around."

"Yes. I remember."

He came to her. "You were frightened a moment ago. You still are." His hands glided down her arms. "You're trembling."

"Ram, Pandit Singh's body"—she could hardly manage to say it—"was *hacked.*"

"And perhaps now the butcher has come to call on you"—he lifted her chin—"perhaps to come into your bed."

She closed her eyes, wondering if he had a knife. "Ram . . . don't—"

"No," he whispered. "No. Believe me, not like that." His fingertips slipped up her arms to caress her throat. "I wonder how you would make love to a murderer."

"Ram, stop torturing me!" She tried to pull away.

His fingers clamped. "Why should I? I don't like what you're thinking. Shall we see how hard a murderer's cock is? Shall we see if a woman gets any softer for a killer?"

He picked her up, took her into the bungalow, and threw her on the bed. Slowly, he took off his clothes with a soft command, "Undress."

"No." Numbly, she shook her head. "Please."

"That's a pretty sari. I should hate to ruin it." He walked toward the bed.

She shrank away. "Ram, I *want* to believe you."

"Then you want to make love to me. The sari, Lysistrata."

Desperately, she hurled a pillow at him and flung herself toward the door. The scarlet sari ripped away, then Ram's arm locked about her waist. She dragged at his arm, trying to wrench away, then gasped as his free hand closed over her breast, his thumb torturing the nipple. Her fingernails dug into his hand to draw a muffled sound of pain, but still he caressed her until she whimpered, drawn inexorably from pain to pleasure. Her head fell back against his shoulder, her hands covering his, then pressing them, guiding them. She heard a soft, harsh laugh, felt his hand lock in her hair and twist her around to crush her against the hard length of him. His mouth covered hers brutally, hurtfully, plundering with a savage certainty until dizzied, needful, she fought him in her own way, arms locked about his neck, mouth tempting, taunting him. With a strangled groan, he pushed her down on the bed, his body locked against hers. His fingers demanded entrance until he found warm honey, teased it into the tighter entry.

Rolling her over, he slipped between her thighs, then felt her stiffen as he slowly pushed inward. Sobbing, she flailed at the bed, but as he moved rhythmically deeper, the cries grew breathless. She writhed, taking him until sweat sheened his skin. He felt her shiver, then thrust against him, mate him. Until he craved her beyond sanity. His muscles knotting, a primeval howl rose from his bowels.

Listening to Ram's ragged breathing, Lysistrata felt a Pyrrhic sense of victory: in conquering her, he had defeated himself as well. In abject surrender, she knew, now and forever, she did not care how he came to her, so long as he came. And he *would* come, like a hunting hound after a bitch he could never get enough of. Now, like Frank, he had begun to treat her like a contemptible slut. Perhaps both of them were right. Ram lay beside her. When he touched her mouth, his fingers came away with a faint trace of blood. "The going rate is ten *kyat* in Rangoon," she muttered. "Just leave it on the dresser."

"I'm sorry," he said softly. "I'm not wearing pockets just now. I suppose I'll just have to wash dishes or something."

Turning on her side, she began tiredly, "Ram, I—"; then choked in terror as a maniac face appeared over his shoulder. Warned by her stunned look, he rolled atop her and carried her with him off the bed. As he crouched over her, they saw a knife flash in the moonlight. A gecko on the mirror split scarlet. The mad creature dabbled curiously in the blood, then with a hideously girlish giggle, smeared its face. Prattling in a mixture of Hindi and English, it scuttled into the garden. But not before Lysistrata had seen a shadow of Ram in that bloody, obscenely distorted face. "Anira!" she whispered in horror.

A sharp dig of Ram's fingers warned silence. He slipped to the door and scanned the garden. Wrapping on his loincloth, he murmured, "Bar the windows and door behind me. I'll be back as soon as I can." Then he was gone.

Ram saw Anira run across the garden, run like a wild gibbon who had stolen a laundry line. In white, flapping shift, hair a black, demonic halo, she gibbered in fear and fury as she scurried for the fortress wall. He sprinted after her, but she reached the wall before him. Adroitly lifting herself into a tree, she swiftly scrambled up branches that brushed the wall, then swung onto the parapet. With panicky shouts, the startled guards raked their crossbows into position. Ram's cry topped theirs. "Don't fire! Hold your fire!"

Leaping about, Anira squealed and gibbered; then perceiving she was surrounded by fear, giggled and, with one hand clawed and the other slashing with the knife, lunged at the guards. Her palm jabbed by a feinted arrow tip, she shrieked, then retreated, nursing her hand. Ram swung into the tree, and as he mounted, Anira, hurling abuse at the guards, settled midway between them. Ram sprang onto the wall, then sharply signaled the guards not to move. Anira, not recognizing him in the shadows, calmed somewhat at the guards' absence of aggression and gradually grew preoccupied with the blood on her hands and shift. Stroking herself, humming tunelessly, she squatted on the parapet. She began to comb knife and fingers through the heavy, knotted mass of her hair, a shrunken, warrior profile still recalling an eerie, terrible beauty against the moon's pale shield.

Ram silently eased forward. "My royal lady," he crooned, "may I comb your hair? Ebony silk of India's keeping, black tears of her weeping, sorrow's lingering sigh . . ." She glared at him warily, hovering on the edge of another frenzy. Then, head cocked, she was distracted by his low monotone as he inched nearer. "Night's hair," he whispered, "star-jeweled for your diadem. For you, a winding spell of dreams."

Black, glittering eyes watched as he slowly extended his hand. "Give me the comb, my lady, and all the Nile, the Ganges cataract and streams of Babylon shall flow through your heart to ease its woe . . ."

Perhaps his voice was too much like a lover's; perhaps the moonlight drew too many memories from his face. The knife clattered at his feet. In a split second, all that remained in Anira's place was that knife and empty darkness, its silence broken only by a splash, then a tear of white in the water below, a writhing churn of leviathans.

Ram returned to the Phoenix Bungalow, his face rigid. He sat heavily on the bed, poured wine from a decanter, and started to swallow, then slowly set it down. He leaned his head against the wall.

"What happened?" Lysistrata asked softly. "Did you find her?"

"I found her." Dully, he told how Anira had died. "She must have thought I was Father or one of the dead Sepoys."

"Ram, not . . . oh, Ram, I'm sorry."

"The dead have had their revenge after all." His mouth twisted. "She would have appreciated the justice of it, only she hadn't a shred of sanity left."

"How long was she like . . . tonight?"

"I scarcely remember her any other way," he said bitterly, "if you care to niggle about degrees. Over the years, she grew increasingly violent. I assume you've been told Father never married her. I had to confine her after his death eight years ago when she strangled a maid with a necklace. All because she thought the girl had flirted with me." He stared into the wine. "By that time, she often confused me with Father."

"She must have loved him terribly."

"Terribly. That describes it well. She was as passionate and terrible in love as in hate, and in the end, saw no difference between them."

"You say she was confined. Where?"

"She was kept in her own suite in the west wing of the Peacock Palace. That's one of the reasons I never stayed there. You couldn't have heard it in the *zenana*, but she had a tendency to howl at night." He sounded detached, remote. "It was a prison of her own choosing. I doubt if she would have left even if she could. She had retired voluntarily to *purdah* there with only Kalisha for contact with the outside world for several years."

"Then how do you suppose she got out after so long?"

"I went to her quarters today after I examined Pandit Singh's body. She was there, sedated with enough opium to keep her quiet for several hours. She must have returned there after roaming the grounds last night." He went on thoughtfully, "Perhaps 'roam' is the wrong word. Either she came directly here or someone would have seen her. The only reason she would do that, would be to find you. Offhandedly, I should say Kalisha goaded her about my neglecting her for a Yankee mistress."

"But why should she attack Pandit Singh? Why mutilate him?"

"She probably thought Singh was me," he said with a lack of emotion Lysistrata found appalling and dreadfully sad.

"It seems so easy for you to accept," she said quietly, "but so difficult for me. I read her notes in *Indiana*. She seemed to be such a different person than the one you describe. Your father built Khandahoor as a tribute to her, didn't he? Surely that must have eased her pride a little?"

"You forget, my mother was a Rajput princess and a despot. While Khandahoor may be remarkable, she regarded it as her due, just as she considered the lives and deaths of those in her domain hers to dictate. Being a woman, she was often more subtle about those dictates than male rulers.

"Had the British never come to India and Father with them, she might have been a great and highly enlightened ruler. As she was stronger and more intelligent than her two brothers, they would either have assassinated her or she them. When my father arrived on the scene, they were making plans to marry her to some dying wreck. *Suttee* would have solved their problem within a year."

"How did she and your father meet?"

"He was a frequent diplomatic courier to the court after the appointment of the new British resident governor of the district. Once he glimpsed Mother, he made certain one thing led to another. They were both ingenious and charming; no one suspected him, even after she and Kalisha disappeared from the palace.

"Until she showed up at Jaipur three years later with

me and a story of rape. Given a choice between her and his commission . . .'' Ram shrugged. ''Few believed her. Ordinarily, we would have been strangled, but Uncle Sanga had already assassinated Uncle Gulab. She promised Sanga help in consolidating his power; then, aware he would kill her once he had fulfilled that aim, stirred up enough minor factionalism to keep him unsure. She might have succeeded indefinitely, but it was unlikely: he was far from stupid. She dared not kill him. He was her only protection against assassins and ignominy, for after her liaison with Father, she would not have been allowed to rule.

''After the failure of the Sepoy rebellion, we were relatively safe as the British looked for any excuse, including assassination, to confiscate estates. At Sanga's natural death, they would have seized Jaipur anyway for they decreed royal estates could only be passed to direct male heirs and Sanga's only son died of typhus.

''Father had tried for years to persuade her to return to him, but not until Sanga became partially paralyzed after an apoplexy did she bargain for Khandahoor.

''When the construction ended, so did the relationship. I never knew precisely why, for I had been sent to school in Bombay at Father's demand. Mother agreed, as no possible life existed for me as a Hindu. Also, she knew I could never hold Khandahoor unless I made a place among the British who by then had overrun lower Burma. I assume she expected Father to make Khandahoor his first residence; when he did not, she became cold to him. After his British wife in Mandalay died mysteriously a few months later, Father never returned to Khandahoor. He was killed in a Naga ambush in the Arakans. Quite possibly, Mother arranged both deaths for by then she had contacts among traders with the Nagas.'' He gazed at moonlit nothing. ''She may have decided upon his murder in a fit of madness, for she had become more frequently prone to violent tempers she could not later remember. At any rate, she retired into mourning. Eventually, she became as you saw her to-night.''

As his head lifted, he noticed the taut look upon Lysistrata's face. ''Don't worry,'' he said coldly, ''her madness was not hereditary. If I have given you a bastard, it will likely be a healthy one.'' Flinging himself from the bed, he left her alone . . .

To think. She had not really thought of what having Ram's child might mean and was thinking far less of its mental condition when he had become angry. To her, a child was to love and protect, bastard or no, and her father would feel no different. The Burmese were not fastidious about bloodlines. To hell with the British.

And to hell with Ram if his father's treatment of his mother had taught him nothing. For she had seen not only Ram's shadow in Anira but her own. Ram had made her his whore as his father had done Anira, with as much ruthless calculation as desire; even a kingdom like Khandahoor remained only William Harley's payment for use of Anira's body. Ram had taken her and paid nothing. Anira must have been even more frustrated and trapped than she when William Harley rode into her life. Not only was he exciting and virile, he meant escape from *purdah* and a disgusting marriage. How disillusioned she must have been to be disabused of all hope of marriage and hidden away again so her selfish lover could pursue his own life without embarrassment of being linked with an ''inferior.'' Had William denied Anira love and shared no more than his bed as Ram had with her? With pensive, brooding eyes, Lysistrata stared out at the moorlight-dappled shadows. Except for that first night, Ram came to *her* bed; his own remained private as a monk's. All the while he took her heart, her pride, her freedom, even tampered with her mind. Had William Harley tried to change Anira to suit his British tastes? No wonder she had come to hate him, even her love for him. Anira, not Kalisha, had stolen into her room in the *zenana*. A decade after William's death, Anira had come in search of his new, flame-haired mistress. No wonder she had twisted, twisted . . .

Ram was right. Anira's insanity was not hereditary: the seed was nurtured. Possibly angered by her own refusal to be reshaped, Ram had become cruel, well aware of how he could hurt her most. If she gave in, either he would grow bored or she would wither with self-contempt. She might go mad and murderous as Anira.

Hugging herself, she curled up on the bed. Could Ram be possibly trying to drive *her* mad as revenge against European whites who had shunned him and his mother? The parallels between her and Anira occurred too frequently, particularly after Ram kidnapped her, to be incidental. Had he been drawn in the beginning because she shared certain characteristics with Anira? Was he now trying to destroy the "white" in her? Or what seemed "black" to him: her impetuousness, temper, and hostility to her own world. Probably she would never know. She either had to get out of Khandahoor or let Ram tear her heart and mind to shreds. And there was only one way out. Kalisha, who hated her enough to want her dead. Where Anira had failed, the jungle would quite probably succeed.

"Ha!" Kalisha laughed shortly, pale face swathed with mourning veils as she sat stiffly in the dead Rani's favorite chair. "You are not quite so stupid as I thought. I wondered how long you would take to discover the truth. Or is he already tired of you?"

"Perhaps *I* am bored, Kalisha. I am not used to living in virtual *purdah.*" Lysistrata strolled the former Rani's magnificent rooms. The priceless rugs smelled faintly of excrement. The gilded walls and wonderful tapestries were gashed and scratched as if the place had caged a troop of monkeys. Not a mirror remained unshattered. Lysistrata shrugged with seeming carelessness. "The truth about Ram seems to vary a great deal. What is *your* version, not that it matters?"

The woman laughed malevolently. "So you do not know, for if you did, you would not be so blithe. Because of you, my mistress is dead. So, shall I let the jungle take you happy, or with the knowledge your half-caste lover hates you and all your kind as he hated his father. We saw to it, Anira and I; and what we did not teach him, the English school did with slurs and cruelty. He suffered as the English made his mother suffer in Bombay after his birth. No woman will ever make him forget he is a *feringhi* bastard. He took you as his father did Anira to avenge her honor and the honor he has never known. Help you escape? Why not? You are less than refuse now."

As if anxious to be rid of Lysistrata's stench, Kalisha coffee-stained her skin and placed her among a group of kitchen servants departing for their nearby village in less than an hour. When Lysistrata joined them in the kitchen courtyard, they stole looks at her native dress and scarf-hidden hair; at her green eyes, startlingly bright in her stained face, even under a paddy hat. Fearful of Kalisha, they hurriedly averted their eyes as she waved them to crowd around Lysistrata, then curtly motioned toward the fortress gate.

Stooped to hide her height, Lysistrata swung a basket onto a shoulder. In the midst of the servants she shuffled along, her head ducking as they approached the gate with its pacing, scaled warriors. Her heart began to thud in her ears as the Chinese in charge of the drawbridge squatted down to look them over. God, she wondered, was he taking a head count? Rising, he nodded to another guard to loose the drawbridge winch. Slowly, the bridge cranked down. The instant it settled, the nervous servants began to hurry across. Fearing they would draw suspicion, Lysistrata slowed, forcing them to hold back. Also, for usually cheerful natives they were too silent. She muttered a joke in Burmese, then laughed. Fortunately, one of the women was quick-witted enough to pick up the cue. She cackled loudly, nudging a neighbor to join in, then handed betel around and began a conversation that limped but was better than nothing.

The chief guard who had been staring down at them suddenly yelled something. Lysistrata nearly choked on the betel she had gingerly put in her mouth. A man nudged her in the ribs. "He says hurry, you turtledung!" At that and the face she made at the taste of betel, everybody grinned, then hauled her along by the elbows until out of sight of the bowmen.

Once on the jungle path to their village, the group sobered. For Lysistrata to go alone into the Shan wilds was madness, they warned, but no one was reckless enough to advise return to Khandahoor. After gravely thanking them for their assistance, she headed into the jungle. She took only the knife and a bundle of food Kalisha ironically had provided; the woman wanted her dead, not easily retrievable. Painfully, she wondered if Ram would bother to look for her. If he did, it would be only out of possessiveness or, if Kalisha was right, the urge to torment her further. Her head lifted. She would be hell to find.

CHAPTER 12

The Long Run

I am half sick of shadows—
ALFRED, LORD TENNYSON

Exasperated, Kanaka squatted on a rock above the river and wiped his arm across his sweating forehead. "If she got this far, *Tuan*, she has crossed lower down. All she must do is descend the southwest mountain steps and follow the river to fords. Very simple."

"And very predictable."

"Then how come we haven't found her?"

"Every now and then she's dodging upstream over the rocks where tracking's nearly impossible." Leaning his tired body against a tree, Ram peered up at the waning light. "Cutting all the bridges behind her is damned effective, too."

Kanaka eyed Ram's face, knife-sharp with alertness and tension the big man had never seen in him. Women. Why did the ones who were the most trouble always seem to get their hooks deepest into a man? This damned Lysistrata Herriott had run too far with the line. The old Ram Kachwaha might have cut her loose with a shrug, but this new Ram? The hooks were showing blood in this one. Kanaka scratched his bottom. "Been nearly two weeks. She's got to sleep, lose time."

"That's why I sent Friedlander ahead. From now on, we'll go in shifts, alternating one man ahead, two to follow four hours behind."

Kanaka grinned approvingly. "Wear her out; she'll make a mistake."

Ram did not reply; in the jungle, mistakes were invariably deadly.

Lysistrata uneasily shifted in a tree crook. On a moonless night she felt relatively safe from human pursuit, but was unable to sleep soundly for fear of falling out of an aerial bed—and when on the ground, was afraid of falling prey to a prowling animal. For the last two days she had been miserably cold and hot in alternating rounds, sometimes shaking uncontrollably. Spending a night by the river had been foolish: its mists had given her a nagging chill. Mosquitoes, too, were a nuisance, for seeming to sense the coming monsoons, they whined and bit mercilessly.

If only she could sleep a few hours. Yesterday, Friedlander had nearly stumbled over her hidden in a ravine for a few minutes' rest. Ram was efficient. He allowed her no time to set snares for food now, or to eat more than a few mouthfuls of rations before sleep. In a day or two the moon would appear; then they would follow even at night.

Her head sagged against the tree, then snapped upright as a water drop licked her cheek. Another fat drop fell, then more, until the sky loosed a downpour. By morning, the rain had not stopped. The monsoons had begun, the river to flood the lowland. Soaked to the skin, she shook with cold until her teeth rattled. Uneasily, she watched the murky light darken with promise of heavier rain. Rain would not stop Ram: he would use it. Still shivering, she awkwardly descended to the ground, only to slip in a sea of mud and wrench an ankle. Swearing steadily, she tightly bound the ankle with a strip from the tattered *longyi*. Not realizing the lowlands could inundate for nearly a mile beyond the banks in minutes, she hobbled with a makeshift cane parallel to the river. When a flood did hit two hours later, she was fortunate to be near a slight rise. For twenty minutes, she struggled free of waist-deep water to gain high ground—only to meet a more lethal result of its rise.

Precariously perched on a mudfall scattered with ripped tree limbs and flood debris, Friedlander gave a bird call, his signal for having spotted prey. In a few moments, Ram was down the mudfall at his side. "She's just ahead." Friedlander gave him the binoculars. "See, tracks come out of the dip. Looks like she's dragging a foot."

Ram studied the erratic trail across the sheet of mud spiked with denuded trees and leaf-snarled underbrush. "Skirt around that far hill rim and head her off toward the river."

Hearing the nearby bird call, Lysistrata headed for a banyan; she had learned too much of the jungle to believe birds called in the rain. Unfortunately, the tree had another, irritable occupant. Weakly laboring into the lower limbs, she felt a painful stab in her wrist while reaching for a handhold. Startled, she looked up into the fangs of a yellow-banded snake reared back for a second strike. With a muffled cry, she flung backward to fall heavily on the marshy ground. For a moment, she lay paralyzed with terror: with few exceptions, snakes in Indonesia were poisonous.

Stifling the urge to panic, she crawled into the undergrowth. After gashing the fang marks with her knife to let it bleed, she lay still on her side, willing her racing heart to slow its pump of venom into the bloodstream. Most bites were quickly fatal, some horribly so. She sucked at the wrist. Then heard a faint suck of mud releasing something. Her grip tightened on the knife; then as a hand came down hard on her shoulder, she stabbed swiftly toward her heart. The hand chopped with a numbing blow and jerked her over on her back. She gazed up into Ram's incredulous, furious face.

His eyes flicked to the gashed fang marks. Swiftly ripping another strip from the *longyi,* he knotted a tourniquet about her upper arm. "What was it?" he snapped as he bent to suck hard at the wound.

"Just a pretty . . . bit of string. Only it had teeth."

Her grim whimsy drew a black look. "What did it look like, you smug bitch!"

"A little . . . like you around the eyes just now—You hurt!"

"I'd like to wring your damned neck!" He spat, then noticed Friedlander. "Look for a snake around here."

A few minutes later, a *dah*-beheaded reptile dropped from the banyan. "Poisonous," briefly commented the descending scout.

With a faint smile, Lysistrata closed her eyes and Ram grimly kept sucking. Friedlander studied her color, stooped and felt her forehead. "She's got more than snakebite trouble, boss."

"If she dies of this, then we won't have to worry about that, will we?" snarled Ram.

"Guess not."

After some time, Friedlander pried one of her eyelids back. "She's out, but she ain't dead."

Ram swiftly scooped her up. "Let's get out of this mudhole and make camp."

Not once during the long, arduous trek back to Khandahoor did Lysistrata regain full consciousness. Racked by malarial fever and pain from an increasingly swollen hand, she tossed deliriously on a crude litter.

Even when back at Phoenix, she was too weakened by the jungle ordeal and too apathetic to make progress toward recovery. Only for brief periods did pain jab her into awareness of Ram's taut face and his anger when she let the gruel he offered trickle from her lips. "You have quite a temper . . . under that frozen exterior, don't you?" she murmured once. "You're like a spoiled child yelling about . . . a broken doll he never cared for."

"I may have to take off the doll's arm," he said tightly. "You're not strong enough to survive that. If you don't eat, I'm going to put a tube down your gullet."

"Just get a new doll," she said drowsily. "A British one, this time . . . like you've always wanted. Why not kidnap Evelyn? I'll bet she has room . . . for a lot of pins. You can pull them out, then stick them in again . . . until she runs out of skin. Like me. I'm just holes . . . you can see right through. To *nada*."

"You enjoy feeling sorry for yourself, don't you?" he said curtly. "You always have. It lets you feel whatever unpleasant things happen to you are never in any way your fault. I warned you to stop stirring up trouble in Rangoon. I warned you to stay away from me. Why the hell didn't you?"

Eyes dark with drugs, she laughed faintly. "You're wrong. I'm not sorry for any of it, even you . . . particularly . . . you. They wouldn't let me have any life in Boston, so I took it in Rangoon. Now I can do . . . what I damned well please with it."

He kept his word about the tube, but each time he tried to feed her, she stubbornly forced him to use it. Sometime later, she felt him cut her and heard a distant, opium-dulled cry of pain that was swallowed in the greater pain of having the wound repeatedly drained and soaked in a burning poultice. Irrevocably, she began to heal—until trying to die became pointless.

"You ought to shave," she weakly teased Ram late one night when finally able to focus on his haggard features. "You look years older." When he came to the bungalow the next morning, she was a little surprised he had taken the suggestion. With a smooth face, his customary cool politeness returned. She shook her head. "I still prefer you mad enough to spit tacks."

His eyes darkened. "Even now, after these months together, you think I am not just an ordinary man?"

Her smile held a touch of wistfulness. "How would I know? You may be the merprince that haunts the lake. I wonder if anyone knows who you are. You've withdrawn into yourself until you might as well live beneath a pool of water. All you give away are reflections, distortions. You touch no one." When he made no answer, she added gravely, "Some ways of living are worse than dying. Khandahoor is only a gravestone now; do as you please, but I won't crawl under it. I won't take my shape from your shadows. I'll run again . . . and again, even if I have to do it over the backs of those crocodiles. Lock me up if you like, but you'll never keep me that way alive."

"Another ghost to haunt Khandahoor," he murmured. With a restlessness that seemed alien to him, he began to wander the room. "Would it help if I said you mean more to me than Khandahoor . . . even my life?"

"I think this place matters to you very little, and life sometimes even less. So you do not place me in exclusive company."

"I never realized how completely you hated it here," he said slowly. "I thought for a time at least, you didn't mind too much."

Her lips curved sadly. "I can never be happy with you. You've taken more and more from me that you'll never return and I cannot retrieve. Those last days, each time you bedded me became a humiliation.''

Pausing at a window, he stared out at the rain-wet brilliance of the garden; then as if in afterthought, said tonelessly, ''Then you must return to Rangoon, of course.''

Lysistrata thought she might have misheard him. ''It is this simple then. Now I may leave?''

''Simple? Yes. You've contracted malaria. You cannot remain here. You should leave the East altogether.''

''That far.'' She felt a strange, detached loss, as if departure were already accomplished. The hidden, stark pain of it waited, she knew, to follow across the years, even to death. Memories would be everywhere. In the fragrance of unfamiliar flowers, a silvery fall of rain, the silent moon. In every lost and lonely face she saw. In her own face. Short of death, how far did one go to escape the forces that decreed this man's alienation and that of so many others? To escape her own heart leaden with a love that should never have been. The defenses that had melted, then hardened again into a dragging weight of agony.

''I'll take Kanaka and Friedlander tomorrow to scout the route to Lashio. A Scots missionary is based there. He will see that you reach Rangoon safely.''

An alarm went off in her mind. ''And once he contacts Lord Bartly, the army might come sniffing around Khandahoor.''

''Don't overestimate your importance. Sending a punitive expedition in here would be expensive, unprofitable . . . and terminal.''

''Not if you've given them other reasons to root you out. Haven't the British been sending agitators to stir up rebellion among the Shan tribes and furnish them guns?''

For a flicker of an instant, he looked startled, then his eyes narrowed. ''What makes you think that?''

"Because 'river traders' don't circulate new, British army-issue rifles without access to them. The British don't want anyone, particularly a renegade, closing the door to the China Trade for them." She pushed higher on the pillows. "That's why you didn't draw attention to your presence here when we came. Not because you were afraid of being hunted for murder; they probably wouldn't make a concerted effort to destroy you just because of a criminal record. But if you killed Shans and British agitators to discourage rebellion, why then, you'd be a nasty thorn in their ambitions." She regarded him squarely. "I'm not going to Lashio. I'm going to Mandalay to the king, with a tale of your having nobly rescued me from slavery. Perhaps if I'm noisy enough, the British will be too publicly embarrassed to attack you."

He smiled ruefully. "These past months seem to have taught you nothing. Noisiness is what sent you to Bangkok. Next time, your silence will be ensured. Besides, they would not believe you."

"Why not?"

"One look at you will tell them I did not keep you all this time to darn my loincloth."

"That look will also tell them I am ill, too much so to travel until recently. And you need not have found me in Bangkok. You could have bought me from one of Chang's people, say two months ago, during negotiations over Bartly's Yünnan expedition. They might think you're still on their side, that you merely killed the agitators for endangering Khandahoor. It would be to their interest to welcome you back to the fold and see negotiations with Chang are not jeopardized by public knowledge of his sanctioning purchases of white women. I would please everyone by discreetly going back to America." She watched his eyes. "It might work."

His smile turned grim as he leaned against the fretted window screen. "You were on the Bartly verandah quite some time the night of the ball, weren't you? That's a neat little notion you've got, except for two things. Sir Anthony tried to push through the expedition three months ago. Charles Endicott, its leader, was killed in an ambush a few miles past the Chinese border. Also you forget Prasad was at the auction. He recognized me and sure as hell won't forget you.''

"If he visits Bangkok less voluntarily than before and goes on the block, what he remembers won't matter,'' she replied sweetly. "And as for the expedition, perhaps if Lord Bartly had not been so eager to ruin you in Rangoon, it might have succeeded. And still might . . . if he makes amends.''

"You are more like Mother than I thought,'' he murmured ironically.

"Because I'm a trifle unscrupulous?'' She laughed softly. "Whatever my merprince is, he is far better than that slug, Prasad. Prasad would say anything to revenge his lost expedition money. But I think he was privately relieved to have lost me.''

"He does not know you as I do, but then he is easily intimidated.''

"I thought we had done with insults,'' she said quietly.

"It is no insult to say I do not willingly let you go.'' His eyes, dark as the rain-swept lake, held hers. "Remember that when you tell yourself we did not touch.'' He eased off the screen. "When the monsoons are done, you will go to Lashio.''

"But . . .''

"My game with the British is nearly done, Lysistrata. Whatever you do can only muddy the ending. I do not have as many regrets as you might think, for I played the game longer than I liked and it was not a game I could win. Your merprince only appears to you in the guise of a young man; in reality, he is a dark, wrinkled, ancient thing you would shrink from." And as he had once disappeared on her horse in the rain of Rangoon, he left her to the veil of the monsoon.

Within a month, the rain ceased and Ram left with Kanaka and Friedlander to scout the route to Lashio. After his departure, Lysistrata let the waiting sadness creep to her side where it stayed a faithful, sole companion. Until Kalisha paid a visit. "Well, he is gone," the woman mocked, derisively glancing at the medicines on the brass bedside table. "Would you like to try to escape again?"

"That will be unnecessary," Lysistrata replied indifferently. "He is sending me home."

Kalisha's face twisted in rage. "That weakling fool! If he had not meddled with the Shans, we would not be expecting the British army any day! And now, to coddle a *feringhi* bitch who throws his manhood in his face!"

"Perhaps he is so fond of me he does not always think as you would like, Kalisha."

"Do not flatter yourself. He has always been weak." Kalisha paced about the room, examining everything with a miser's preoccupation. "Even when he was little, Anira despised him for it. She would strike him and curse him, but he had no pride. He could always persuade her to repent in moments of weakness. She tried to teach him to love nothing, even her, for as a *feringhi*'s bastard he could rely on no one. To test him, she ordered him to shoot his dog, then had to kill the cur herself."

Kalisha settled like a dark cloud on the divan nearest the bed. Idly, her long-nailed fingers toyed with a pair of tiny gold figures of Rama and the demon king Ravana, which were on the low table in front of her. "Later, he pleaded to return from the *feringhi* school and only stayed because she willed it. *Then*"—her eyes glittered with disgust as her talons coiled about Rama's image— "when his father executed those filthy Sepoys who would have cut his throat, he had to be ordered to watch. I saw *tears* in his eyes!'' She tossed the figurine back on the table. ''He left for Rangoon next day and only returned to Khandahoor twice after that; it was as well, for his mother could no longer bear the sight of him.'' She grimaced. ''William Harley may have been a *feringhi,* but at least he was strong. Ram, pah!'' She spat. ''He has water for blood!''

Oh, Ram. Forgive me, thought Lysistrata in growing anguish at Kalisha's words and the terrible realization they brought. Even I turned away from you. Come home. Only come home to me and I will never deny you again. I will bring you a blaze of sunlight that will burn away the stars. I will love you beyond your dreaming. I will set you free.

Aloud, she said softly, ''Ram is more of a fighter than you know, Kalisha, for if he were not, his spirit would either have been broken long ago or he would have become a monster. Anira was eaten away by hatred of herself and everyone around her. All because she became a devotee of Kali the destroyer, instead of Kali the lifegiver. I think you deserve much of the credit for that. I wonder how many times over the years your hate gave form to hers, that you helped to twist her. What a sense of triumph it must have given you to punish her for turning from the ways of her ancestors, from *your* way. You sacrificed everything to be near her, yet do not mourn her, whatever your pretense. You wear a vulture's disguise, Kalisha, beloved of Kali, and still you hover over her son. Was it Anira who killed Harley, I wonder, or was it you? Did you have to shoot *her* dog, Kalisha, because even after all your training, she would not?''

Kalisha's teeth gleamed like a wolverine's as she rose with a gesture of careless dismissal. ''For all her intelligence, I was far cleverer than Anira. I brought her to trust no one but me. I would have persuaded her to kill her be-

trothed husband in Ladakh and we might have ruled in
the old dotard's place, but she went after William Harley
like a stupid, fawning bitch.'' Kalisha's coal-black eyes
glittered. ''Anira robbed me of what I had labored for for
years. For her, I did not marry, bear children. But she
had no thought for me. Only for William Harley. When I
saw he might become weak enough to marry her, I told
him she had other lovers, so he proposed instead to that
whey-faced rich *sahiba*. Why should Anira have what I
had not, and her a dog's whore?''

Kalisha's long nails fanned over her gaunt face as she
stared through the window at the distant Peacock Palace.
''She ran back to India to hide and grieve under her
brother's thumb. When the rebellion broke out, fear of
Ram and herself being murdered began to work on her
mind. With his *feringhi* face, he was nothing but a re-
minder of her shame and Harley, but she was more afraid
for him than for herself. So she sent him north.'' She
shrugged. ''Sanga would not have dared kill her after the
rebellion, but she still feared another Sepoy uprising.
When he became ill, I realized we must leave or be made
zenana drudges after his death, so I allowed the letters of
Harley, who was unhappy with his wife, to get through to
her. She would have gone back for nothing, but I persuaded her to demand Khandahoor. To suggest she be rid
of the Sepoy laborers was even easier, for she mistrusted
them.''

With a smile of chilling confidence, she strolled toward the bed. ''Then I had Harley's wife killed, so he
would believe Anira responsible. Even he could not
stomach bedding a murderess. He left, and to see he
could never change his mind and demand Khandahoor's
return, I arranged for Nagas to ambush him in the
Arakans.''

Her smile took on a cobra's menace as she looked
down at Lysistrata. ''Unfortunately, a madwoman is an

unreliable weapon, so I have yet to finish with Ram; but that too will be accomplished. Khandahoor will be mine to rule as I have done in effect these past many years. I should have had Ladakh, but this is better for I do not have to share it.''

"Aren't you a bit premature?" Lysistrata replied coolly. "And aren't you forgetting the British? Ram knows you loosed Anira, and he's fairly sure you did the same with me. He's hardly fond of you, so the kindest treatment you can expect is to be sent back to India.''

"Ram and his British brothers will have little to say about what I do in future,'' was the complacent reply.

Lysistrata's eyes narrowed. "What are you planning? You must have something immediate in mind.''

"You will know all in time." With a rustle of black, the woman turned to leave. "Patience. What can you do but wait? And wonder?''

"Indeed, I wonder if anyone so sure as you of skill in treachery will not inevitably overreach.''

Kalisha laughed over a shoulder. "Console yourself with that thin hope if you like. William Harley was ever an optimist, too.''

CHAPTER 13

The Conflagration

. . . deathful-grinning mouths of the fortress, flames
The blood-red blossom . . .

ALFRED, LORD TENNYSON

Lysistrata, too weak to leave bed, was left to brood. She could blame no one, no force of bigotry other than her own suspicion for her desertion of Ram. He had said it. Self-pity had been her armor, that paper defense he had always been able to brush aside so easily. In these months at Khandahoor, he had tried to make her stronger than a creation of paper and paste. She had bandaged her hurts over the years with flimsy, makeshift repairs, but never let them heal with new, vibrant flesh—which required patience and more pain than she had been willing to face. He had made her face life and the future, face him . . . and a future without him. In her he had heard not only the dry, brittle crackle of paper but the store of music written upon it. Made her hear it too: a loveliness she had not dared imagine and knew would not exist again outside his arms. Much of that music he seemed to have improvised, guiding her variations so easily that she was unaware she had metamorphosed into the symphony he promised and that she was now hearing . . . alone. If Kalisha had her way, perhaps finally and forever alone.

Whatever Kalisha planned would occur before Ram returned to Khandahoor, for she would never have revealed so much if not certain her invalided adversary would have no chance to warn him. Lysistrata considered the Chinese and Kachins patrolling the walls. Had Kalisha bribed them to turn against Ram? She'd had sufficient opportunity, but at a high risk due to her vulnerable position. Also, Ram must have been certain of the mercenaries' reliability to leave them in control of the fortress for long periods. Kalisha had probably set an ambush for him as she had for Harley. As Kalisha had mockingly suggested, Lysistrata could only wait in a torment of uncertainty.

Quang Ho swallowed a yawn. To express openly the boredom of guarding a fortress as secure as Khandahoor was to invite the captain of the guard, Chou Shih, to insert bamboo splinters under his little toenails to insure alertness. Still, the duty was not too bad. Three four-hour watches a day along with martial drills had everyone on their toes. Good pay and frequent rotation leaves in Shunning kept them well satisfied, but once in a while he felt a nostalgia for lively days with his former warlord, the solid, satisfying sound of his sword sinking into an opponent. Almost eagerly, his ears pricked as a voice hailed from the darkness across the moat. "Hey, open up! We've got two carts of foodstuffs you ordered from Bhamo."

"Hey, yourself! I'm in charge of the drawbridge, not the kitchen! And you've arrived at a crazy hour. You'll just have to wait until light." He grinned. "Otherwise you may fall into our moat; it's full of crocodiles!"

"Let them in, Quang," said a harsh, familiar voice behind him, "unless you want only rice for breakfast. We're out of everything." Kalisha shouted over the parapet. "You took your time getting here! I should half your price!"

"Don't do that, beautiful lady! We've traveled day and night. We had to shoot one of our oxen due to snakebite!"

"Don't give me excuses!" Her head jerked toward the drawbridge winch. "Well, hurry up, Quang. I'll go down to meet them."

He summoned a guard. "Wo Sam, go with her to check the carts."

As Quang and another guard heaved at a wheel, the great bridge ponderously creaked downward. In a few moments, a heavily laden cart was heard rumbling across the bridge. Apparently waiting to make sure the first one did not end up in the moat, the second cart waited until the first nearly reached the rising portcullis before it started. As the first cart pulled directly under the portcullis and unexpectedly halted, the second stopped on its end of the drawbridge. "Hey, come on," Quang yelled. "We haven't got all night. Wo Sam, see what the fools' trouble is!"

Wo Sam trotted forward to the portcullis cart. The oxen were on their knees, blood puddled around them. Seeing no driver, he warily climbed up on the cart, his sword drawn. After a prod at the wagon contents, he swore. "The wagon's full of rocks!" he yelled. "Get the bridge—" A scarlet bullet hole in his neck choked him off. A pistol disappearing into the folds of her sari, Kalisha vanished into the shadows of the massive wall. The watch guards lowered their crossbows to the parapet bow slits as Quang and his helper jerked at the winch and portcullis crank; the drawbridge, weighted by the rock-filled cart at the far end, would not budge. The portcullis jammed into the cart, keeping itself pried open like a fanged but useless mouth. Quang sounded the alarm, crying for reinforcements as a yelling, motley horde emerged from the jungle and charged across the drawbridge. No reinforcements came. On pallets below in the guardroom, all lay dead from the poisoned evening meal Kalisha had sent them. The twelve men on the ramparts, hopelessly outnumbered, died quickly in a whirling, slashing melee that lasted only minutes. Khandahoor fell.

Except for one man who did not eat meat, poisoned or otherwise. As the sun rose over the mist-sheeted jungle, Lysistrata awakened to a subtle stench from the moat. Though she had slight appetite, any interest in breakfast was completely quelled by the unaccustomed odor. Uneasy, she turned over to look out of the door; Captain Chou Shih was squatting on her porch. His presence was startling, for he had never come into her garden, much less to the bungalow; but as he did not move to enter, and aware he was unlikely to rape a bundle of bones, she curiously watched him. To have her guarded was pointless; his only errand would be either word from Ram or her murder. "Chou Shih," she called softly, "why are you here?"

His head lifted slightly, but he did not turn. "Thanks to Lady Kalisha, Khandahoor has fallen, my lady, to pirates of the lower Sittang. Now, they pillage, but soon they will come even to this obscure place. My lord Ram bade me to watch over you." He paused. "I will kill you with little pain if you wish. If they find you alive, it will not be pleasant."

"I have a knife, Chou Shih," she replied calmly. "Surely one of them should pay for my favors with a slice of his hide. Would you kill yourself rather than fight?"

He chuckled. "I see now why my lord prefers you. I am honored to have so fierce a tigress at my back."

"And I, to have so gallant a defender. We will hunt together well."

"And quickly." He rose to his feet. "Six of them are passing under the mimosas."

Lysistrata felt relief more than fear. Sittang pirates were mortal enemies of the Shans and the Sittang River was far from Lashio, which meant Ram probably had not been waylaid . . . unless Kalisha had lied to the Shans about their chances of regaining Khandahoor and sent them after him. As she did not know that and was now unlikely ever to learn Ram's fate, she nurtured hope of his safety like a talisman.

Sword poised, Chou Shih took position just inside the door. He allowed the first man through, then sliced quickly through the second just behind the first. The first man whirled to meet a backslash to the throat. The next pirate through the door hacked at Chou Shih's back only to be run through by an underarm stab.

Lysistrata tightly clutched her knife. At this rate, the phenomenal Chou might kill them all!

A pistol shot punctured that thought. Chou Shih, his hand spasmodically clawing at the spreading red splotch on his back, went down on one knee. A *dah* hacked down on his neck with a splinter of bone. He collapsed in a pool of blood. The turbaned Kachin who had wielded the *dah* turned toward the white-faced Lysistrata, then with a grimace, nudged his nearest companion, a squat, muscular Karen. "So this is what that bitch vulture promised us! We should have gone to the *zenana* with the rest."

"Skinny and dog-sick! We ought to throttle that old bag of wind."

The third pirate, a thin, mustachioed mongrel, became impatient. "Kill this bag of bones, then, and let's get to the women while they still have some juice left."

As the squat one readily raised a pistol, Lysistrata tensed. But just when he started to squeeze the trigger, the Kachin knocked the gun aside. "We'd better let Moung Tet have a look at her first. Kachwaha wouldn't have had her guarded for nothing." He waved at the squat one, who grunted and advanced on the bed. Under the sheet, Lysistrata readied the knife. As he leaned over her to pull her up, she buried the blade in his belly and rammed up toward the diaphragm. With a shriek, he fell clutching at his belly across the bed. She made a grab for the pistol, but his weight and her weakness only allowed her fingers to brush the gun barrel before the Kachin wrenched it away. He dragged the dying bandit along with the blood-soaked sheet to the floor. "Stupid oaf. Your brains always were in your gut." He impersonally leveled the gun at Lysistrata. "Give me the knife or I'll shoot you in the hand. Don't worry about rape; you see how it is."

"Why not just kill me and get it over with?" Lysistrata said flatly, trying not to look at the gory body tangled in the sheet.

"Ransom. If Kachwaha doesn't pay up, you get your wish." He watched her eyes. "Use that knife on yourself, and we throw you in the moat with the guard. How's Kachwaha to know you're not alive when he's told to pay?"

It was a poor chance, but better than none. Lysistrata handed over the knife. The Kachin, whose name was San, and his thin companion slung bamboo with a sheet to make a litter, than carted her off to be inspected by Moung Tet.

Tet, with several of his men, was up to his neck in the *zenana* pool. They had all been at the wine stores, but Tet's bright little eyes sharply surveyed Lysistrata as he listened to San's brief account of her status and dispatchment of his chunky confederate. "Get her a couple of pillows, Moung San." When they were brought and

Lysistrata propped into a reasonable position, he grinned at her. "How's your Burmese?"

"Better than yours."

He laughed. "Yes, yes. Prince Kachwaha polished it personally, I hear. He has gone to needless trouble. You are not the sort of pillow girl he would want now. Even my men do not want you."

"Fortunately," she replied dryly, as if impervious to the sounds behind the closed doors of the concubines.

"Do not smile too soon. There are not enough women to keep us happy." He tapped his chest. "I have had all three already. The little one is likely to die, I think," he added, watching her face. "Ah, so you are sorry for your lord's other women. You must be very sure of your place with him—"

"She is nothing but offal," snarled a familiar voice. "Kill her! I command it!" The figure who swept into the *zenana* wore the former Rani's finest raiment. The effect of shimmering gold and rubies was stunning even on Kalisha. She stamped a foot. "Boh Myin agreed you were to touch nothing at Khandahoor. You were paid in plenty and I do not tolerate thieves in my army."

Tet smile lazily. "We are merely enjoying ourselves. After all, we did a bit of work this morning."

"Bah! What did you do but catch the ripe fruit I dropped to you?" Her eyes raked them in disgust. "I care nothing for the women, but you will see to it your men return every last *mohur*, Moung Tet."

His smile did not waver. "I take my orders from Boh Myin, old woman. Take your grievances to him."

She turned white with rage. "Boh Myin is on the Sittang. You will do as I say!"

"Mind your nagging tongue," he advised equably, "if you wish to keep it."

Lysistrata could not resist. "A lifetime for this, Kalisha? Did you think they would allow you to keep so much as a rupee?"

Kalisha leveled a long, venomous stare. "I thought of *everything*. What is mine *will* be mine!" In a flash of gold, she was gone.

Tet's idle interest returned to Lysistrata. "She wants you dead, so you must be still valuable to Kachwaha." He absently cleaned out his ear with his forefinger. "Women's minds are simple enough to read if one does not look at the pages."

"Prince Kachwaha is not simpleminded. You would be wise to take your booty and go."

"He is on the wrong side of his defenses now. Without a friend inside these walls, what can he do but bay outside his own window?" He cackled. "Will you help him? Will—" Suddenly, his complacency vanished; he waved sharply to San. "Finish that Indian witch before she causes trouble."

Shortly, San returned out of breath with anger and exertion. "The bitch has fired the Rani's quarters and the drawbridge! More fires are beginning on the floor below this!"

Tet leaped from the pool. "All of you, get those fires doused! And find the crone before she burns this place about our ears!"

San kicked open the closed *zenana* doors. "Out, out, if you don't want your peckers fried off!"

In the melee, Lysistrata was forgotten. The *zenana* emptied in seconds with the faint smell of smoke already drifting through the air. Kim, the Chinese; then Rasoherina, the Malagasy, stumbled naked and lead-eyed from their rooms. "Run!" Lysistrata cried urgently. "Kalisha has fired the place. You can still get out if you hurry! Take Ma Too with you."

The Malagasy took to her heels. Kim checked the Burmese sprawled on her bed, then limped painfully to Ly-

sistrata's side and sagged to sit forlornly on the floor.
"She is dead and I cannot walk. We are done."

Lysistrata's mouth tightened in exasperation. Kim was
so coddled in the *zenana* that she lacked the nerve even
to save her life. The smoke was thickening, becoming
acrid. "Crawl, then, you twit!" Lysistrata snapped.
"Don't just sit here like a useless toy!"

"*You* take on a dozen animals like those greasy bandits
and see how you feel!" the girl cried defensively. "You
wouldn't even make one man happy, no matter how kind
he was!"

I had to have more than kindness from that man, Lysistrata wanted to say, but the girl did have a point about
satisfying an even dozen. She sighed, knowing Kim
would not budge. "Get into the pool then." To put off
the inevitable. She rolled into the water, then almost too
weak to surface, fought a moment of panic. Finally, she
managed to grasp the edge and ease to the steps to lie submerged up to her nose. Kim, coughing and ducking to escape burning cinders sifting through the air, huddled in a
smoke-filled corner. At length, they could scarcely see
each other through the gray pall; breathing was agony.
Flames began to lick painted water lilies and gilt on the
walls. I wonder which will collapse first, Lysistrata wondered hopelessly, this pool through the blazing floor or
the ceiling into the pool. We'll probably suffocate before
we ever know.

Running feet sounded, then without warning, a hand
jerked hard at her hair, dragging her out painfully up the
pool steps. Her scalp feeling as if it were being detached
from her skull, she tore at the hand and heard a yell of
pain.

"Keep that up and you boil, you bitch!" San warned
roughly.

Faint with relief, she made no further protest as he
ripped off a sari strip, doused it in the pool, then hauled

her up over his shoulder. "Wait," she gasped. "What about Kim?"

"Belly-up on the bottom. And Kalisha's roasted on her own spit. Now shut up and keep this over your face." He handed her the dripping wad of silk. His turban wrapped wetly about his own face, he took off at a quick dogtrot, and as they dodged through a nightmare of flames, she feebly caught at her swinging hair to keep it from incinerating. The main stairs rattled out the little breath she had until drowning in peace like Kim seemed a mercy.

Abruptly, they entered light and life-giving air of the main courtyard, though scant air remained clear enough to breathe: the whole of Khandahoor was aflame. The golden domes budded through huge, sooty flowers of smoke; the delicate stems of the columned arcades were burned through and toppling; the roofs' ornamental tiles cracking away from scorched plaster which fell to shatter on pavement scattered with blazing debris. The library wing of the Peacock Palace was an inferno, and sick at heart, Lysistrata saw its priceless art and literature engulfed by sheets of flame. The gardens seemed to writhe in searing heat, the very air to twist in death throes. As they neared the fortress walls, San stumbled through more debris. The wooden guardwalks on the ramparts were collapsing, their heavy support beams dropping from the walls. The drawbridge was cindering into the moat. San, easing her down by the portcullis, looked at the hissing remnant of bridge collapsed on the far riverbank where a seething mass of crocodiles had fled the fall of burning timbers. "Shit," he observed succinctly.

Tet waved from the jungle where the rest of the impatient pirate band waited, uneasily eyeing the wandering gap-jawed leviathans. "Come on! We'll shoot a path for you through the muggers!"

"Right," muttered San. He turned to Lysistrata. "I'll

heave a log into the water to float over on. But first we need bait.'' He left, then reappeared shortly with poisoned meat scraps from the guardroom bundled into his turban. He kicked loose a charred timber into the moat, caught her up, and jumped in.

Lysistrata was to remember that moat crossing in nightmares the rest of her life. The smoke reflected a sheen of flame on black water that held blacker shapes of waiting man-eaters which made the far shore move. ''In case I don't have another chance,'' she muttered to the Kachin, ''thank you. This is the second time you've kept me alive.''

He kept kicking, pushing the log along. ''I'm greedy, not a lunatic. This was Tet's idea.'' He craned to see the approaching shore through the smoke. *''Shoot,* you sons-of-bitches!'' he yelled. ''I'm kicking bottom *now!''*

Shots rang out; the mass ahead began to thrash and flail. Not waiting for the uproar to die down and more crocodiles to move into the opening gap, San reared up in the shallows, heaved Lysistrata over his shoulder again. It was a nightmare, the huge reptiles roaring and thrashing in rage and pain, San trying to run, the sticky mud and water around his knees slowing them to what seemed a crawl. A quarter of the way through, he slung meat to left and right, and Lysistrata heard the sickening crunch of huge jaws. She *was* sick, and heard him curse again as he pelted through mud and slippery carcasses of cannibalized crocodiles. Then he gained the banks and ran like hell.

Suddenly, he slid and collapsed with her landing atop him. Stiff with terror, she waited for the first mauling teeth. Then blinked as Tet's face grinned down at them. ''Better get up! We might have trouble telling you muddy beasts from the crocs and shoot you.''

''Huh!'' angrily panted San. ''You took time enough to shoot before, damn you!''

"No need to waste ammunition!" Tet amiably slapped him on the shoulder. "But don't worry. The woman will pay for the bullets many times over."

Lysistrata's head weakly lifted. "Not that I'm arguing, mind you, but just how do you figure that?"

"What does your father do?" he asked briskly.

"He's a doctor," she replied faintly, "in Rangoon. Why?"

Tet rubbed his hands together. "Good, good. Very simple." He held up a finger for her bemused regard. "Papa will pay and Ram Kachwaha will pay to get you back." His eyes twinkled mischievously. "Of course, my master, Boh Myin, cannot please them both, but that will not matter"—he held up a third finger—"for Kachwaha will also follow us. His capture will mean a third ransom . . ." His face lit as if a new idea had dawned. "And his head." He held up a fourth finger.

CHAPTER 14

Buddha's Skull

Wherefore wilt thou rush on death?
MATTHEW ARNOLD

"We've word of your daughter, doctor." Sir Anthony Bartly turned from a wall map as Dr. Herriott was ushered into his office by Harry Armistead. Bartly nodded to Harry, then introduced the two other officers in the room. "We propose to take immediate action to recover her, this time with military assistance." He pointed to a sharp bend in the lower reaches of the Sittang as Herriott swiftly joined him. "She's here in Buddha's Skull, the stronghold of Boh Myin. He and his pirates have ravaged the Sittang and Tennasserim coast for the past several years." He looked sympathetically at Herriott's tense face. "She's alive but in a bad way from malaria. We'll have to leave immediately."

Herriott stared at the remote point on the map. "How do you know all this?"

"Boh Myin sent a ransom message." Bartly's mouth tightened. "Impudent of him, but then he either isn't aware or doesn't care that we know his location." He tapped the river bend. "Below Buddha's Skull, trees and spiked stakes have been sunk for the last two miles of river that only Boh Myin and his captains know how to navigate. Also, except for the first hundred miles or so, most of the river is impassable by anything but village craft. Artillery would have to be dismantled and taken upriver by canoe. Any effort to attack him must be pressed overland for the last few miles through heavy jungle muck, which would be hell on men and worse for artillery. He has some reason to be complacent."

"Are you proposing a military maneuver because I have no money to pay him?" Herriott asked harshly.

Bartly smiled faintly. "Indeed not, sir. The time has come to clear Burma's rivers of their more dangerous refuse. Rivers are her only roads until others can be built. The Salween is also infested with pirates. In this case, Lysistrata is not the only reason we will begin with the Sittang. Khandahoor, the fortress of Richard Harley, or Ram Kachwaha if you will, is farther north. Not only is he wanted for his crimes in Rangoon, but for the recent murders of two British officers in the Shans and attacks on friendly natives. He is also probably in league with Boh Myin." He shifted the pointer to a large lake. "After recovering your daughter, the expedition will continue to Khandahoor." He paused. "The officers in question have agreed the considerable bounty on both men's heads should go to you as reparation."

Herriott's head angrily snapped around. "I only want my daughter, sir."

"Dr. Herriott," Bartly said more quietly, "you will need passage home to America. You, of course, realize Lysistrata cannot remain in this climate."

"And you, sir, of course, realize that if Boh Myin refuses to surrender Lysistrata and you pulverize his fortress with artillery, she will hardly be faced with that difficulty!"

Harry quickly intervened. "If I may propose another

possibility, gentlemen, perhaps the bounty could be paid to Boh Myin as ransom . . . in gold coin." He smiled pleasantly. "After the Boh hands over Lysistrata, we could recover the coin when we blow him up."

By murky light of dusk, Friedlander scanned the surrounding jungle, lushly green and dripping from last night's rain into heavy mud and rotting vegetation. Undisturbed monkeys and birds carried on a shrill exchange that echoed across the brown eddies of the nearby rock-strewn river. The palisaded fort on the slight rise above the water shielded all but an occasional murmur from the guards on watch about its parapets. Pagodas of an abandoned monastery within the fort spindled above its walls. Crumbling into the jungle beyond the fort were more pagodas long left to snakes and scuttling insects. Friedlander shivered slightly in the river damp. "Where is he?"

The Naga addressed jabbed a forefinger upward without interrupting his vigil over the mist-shrouded hulk of Buddha's Skull, Boh Myin's lair on the Sittang.

With a muttered oath, Friedlander began to shimmy up the tall cotton tree indicated to Ram's lofty perch. At length, he scrambled into a precarious crook that was level with Ram's dangling foot. "Say, there," he whispered, "I'm beginning to eye the bloody lady monkeys. Let's have a bit of civilization after this."

"Anywhere you like," Ram murmured pleasantly. "What did you find out?"

"The Naga we sent in says she's in the big pagoda." Friedlander pointed to a squat, crumbling stone tower which prodded above the mist that obscured most of the other pagodas enclosed inside the thirty-foot-high palisade of stone and teak. "That's his nibs' quarters and the magazine as well. It's crammed with cutthroats wary as palmrats. There's a particularly alert, nasty type guarding your lady. Seems they're expecting not only you, but the British. Remember that Karen that came scampering into the fort an hour ᵤgo? Well, he had news for Boh Myin's fat ear alone, and I hear the pig's face attached to it is a bit on the gray side just now.''

Ram thoughtfully fingered his new mustache. "I sent Kanaka downriver when the Karen entered the Boh's pagoda. He ought to be back shortly.'' His fingers stilled. ''How is Lysistrata?''

Friedlander shook his head. ''Not good. Barely conscious; shakes. It's a long way from Khandahoor. That girl's made of iron, but even iron rusts in the jungle.'' He cocked his head. ''Why not let the limeys be the white knights and us just get the hell out of here? You were going to hand her over to them anyway.''

''Because if they demand his surrender, Boh Myin may peevishly cut her throat.'' A slight frown creased his brow. ''Even if Dr. Herriott had enough money to ransom a pet parrot, the British would rather have her dead than alive. She'd make a nice, manageable martyr and a convenient excuse to move more military into this area—'' He broke off, noticing Kanaka waving from the ground. Lithe as an acrobat, he maneuvered out of the tree crook and swiftly downward, leaving Friedlander to follow.

Friedlander arrived on the ground in time to hear part of Kanaka's quick report. ''. . . anchored the pylons. A British-officered Sepoy regiment is headed overland. They're hauling a howitzer with them. With any luck, they'll be sitting in front of the gate by tomorrow dawn.''

Seeing the fort gate swing open and shadows emit from it into the jungle gloom, Friedlander tugged at Ram's sleeve. ''Look, boss. That's too many men for reconnaissance.''

Ram nodded. ''They'll try to pick off that artillery unit while it's dragging through the muck. Friedlander, take five Nagas and see to them . . . quietly. Collect souvenirs for the Boh.'' Friedlander touched his forehead and was gone.

Less than forty-five minutes later, Friedlander and his tiny band were back. ''The lot's laid out like Sunday dinner, boss. The lads even had time to retrieve their darts.''

''Good work. Here's your next assignment. Pick off the watches on the Boh's war canoes moored below the bend, then fire the canoes . . .''

''But the guards'll see—''

''I want him to know he has no retreat, no boats, not even the chance of melting into a jungle full of Nagas.''

Friedlander looked askance at their twelve Nagas. ''Full, hey?''

''He'll believe what I tell him when his patrol doesn't return and he finds samples of them on his doorstep.''

''You tell him? *You're* going in there?'' Friedlander mottled red. ''He'll have you tacked to the gate, he will, to catch the first British shell in your teeth!''

''Then you had better listen to me now,'' Ram calmly advised, ''because dawn may find me with a mouthful of lead. Hang about with the Nagas in case Boh Myin tries to send out another patrol. When the British get that howitzer set up, fade. The yacht is yours and Kanaka's. Pay off the Nagas, then get out of Burma. You two have been with me too long not to be recognized.''

Kanaka touched his arm. ''Wait, boss. Let us help. We might be able to get you in and out of there.''

''Not with Lysistrata. If she could walk, perhaps. This way . . .'' He shook his head.

''This way, boss,'' Friedlander said angrily, ''*you* got no chance! No woman's worth it!''

''Boh Myin also destroyed Khandahoor,'' Ram replied lightly.

''You thought Khandahoor was a shitpile,'' was the disgusted retort.

* * *

Boh Myin's nervous irritability was equal to Friedlander's. As he brooded—a massive hulk of muscle capped by a shrewd, porcine face—the others squatting about the pagoda waited uneasily for his silence to break. Boh Myin's normal garrulous benevolence was a shield that could shift in an instant from sunny selfishness to murderous resolution. He ruled by superior battle tactics, brute strength, and an absolute ruthlessness that gave him an aura of profound evil and indestructibility. In actuality, nothing was profound about him: he was singlemindedly greedy. His appetites for food and women fell in with bottomless craving for satiety. While not a natural sadist, he was a natural despot. If not intelligent, he was sly and unpredictable, not in the end he sought, but in the ways he achieved it. Tet was his mimicking shadow, subtle and envious. As reward for overambition and loss of the riches of Khandahoor, Tet lost a hand. Resulting gangrene lost him his life.

San, the thin, hook-nosed Kachin, was more subtle than Tet, with a cold intelligence that dwarfed the slyness of Boh Myin. He alone of the bandits in the pagoda sat calmly as if he knew exactly what the future held for him.

Lysistrata, lying on a corner pallet, was aware the silence in the dingy pagoda after so many days of hivelike activity boded ill, but she had acquired more than a little of Ram's fatalism. As time passed with no word of ransom payment from either Rangoon or Ram, she accepted abandonment and its inevitable conclusion. At first, Boh Myin took mischievous pleasure in keeping her near, but as she was rarely able or willing to banter with him, her wasted appearance and diminishing promise of profit began to depress him; thus, the shift to the far corner. Now, she was not only a deficit, but a liability. The presence of British cannon did not imply the opposition's willingness to dicker over the hostage's health. More than once, Boh Myin's sullen, pig-eyed glare shifted to her. At length, she murmured wryly to San, "I believe the tedium of guarding me is to be shortly relieved."

He smiled faintly. "There is still hope. If the British gun is destroyed, you may yet live to look as you do quite naturally."

"Like a creaky crone?" She laughed. "Moung San, you make even death seem tolerable." Then added softly, "I won't make a fuss when the time comes . . . unless, of course, Boh Myin decides to make a nasty mess of me." She hesitated. "Could you persuade him to let you do it quickly?"

"Yes," he answered simply.

"Thank you." Her eyes closed. "In your way, you've been more than a friend." Death, you are my last, chaste lover.

He laughed softly. "Yes, I will play the shade of him who is not here, for if he had come, he would have most certainly died. While your arms may be warm, the embrace of Death is bitter cold. Do not think ill of him for turning from such a choice."

"My arms were never warm, Moung San. They clung in passion, locked out in hate, but never were they tender. I reproach him for nothing."

"Yet you love him," he replied dispassionately.

"Was it love to do as I did?" she whispered. "Now it is too late to love and you are a shade twice welcome to give form to what is lost and what is to come."

San watched the firelight flicker high and torches mold disjointed light about the restlessly prowling shapes of the man-mongrels encircling it. All seemed to be phantoms except himself, even this girl who would soon die. Only at the brief moment when his knife found her heart would he allow her to be important to him. In that single consummate act and her absolute surrender to it, he would both possess and release her. And the man she loved would be as far from both of them as if he had never existed. Then he would forget her. Her courage he would remember.

Then, serenely, he knew he was not to have his moment. He smiled ruefully at the dark, bearded Pathan whose black eyes regarded him with the sleepy intensity of a panther. The gray-clad Pathan, having entered unnoticed among the preoccupied bandits, now lounged just behind Boh Myin's left ear. San studied the Boh's jowled, brutal face and squat bulk, then the slim Pathan's spare, predatory features. Aware a nearby exit was available if need arose, he eased against the wall to wait. Firelight playing on faded paintings of Shiva and his avatars about the mildewed stone walls seemed to add to the eerie tranquillity. Stacked below the paintings were wooden crates of ammunition and explosives; also, ironically, Enfield rifles pilfered from Shans upriver.

He felt the girl stir, then grope for the calabash of water by her head. Perversity made him take the gourd and, lifting her head, hold it to her lips. Deliberately blocking the Pathan's view with his shoulder, he sensed rather than saw the man's knife unsheath, poise in anticipation of the slightest movement toward his own weapon. Lysistrata, her gaze flickering upward, saw something in San's face: subtle tension, amusement. "If I should kiss you, I wonder whether your true love would leave me breath to enjoy it," he whispered. Her eyes widened, then involuntarily started to look past his shoulder. "Do not gawk. His remaining time on earth is short enough. Whatever happens, keep silent. The less Boh Myin thinks of you, the better."

Obediently, she lay back on the pallet. Only after San resumed his place against the wall did she surreptitiously scan the dim room. After a brief look at the Pathan, she closed her eyes, the dark coals of his answering glance still burning her inner lids. She lay tense with ecstatic relief and horror. Ram cared enough to come for her. And to die for the coming. She had heard enough since leaving Khandahoor to know Ram and Boh Myin were old enemies. Myin wanted Ram's head almost more than he wanted his gold.

Those thoughts were cut off as a palisade guard burst through the door. "The canoes, Boh Myin! They have set fire to the canoes!"

For a man of his size, Boh Myin rose quickly to his feet as a flurry of consternation went round the room. "Shut up! You're not a flock of chickens! The British can't do much without their gun and our boys have destroyed it by now. Besides, if we have to we can always take to the jungle."

"The British can, your boys haven't, and you can't," murmured a soft voice at his ear. "I fear you are in for a disappointing evening, Boh Myin." At the chillingly familiar voice, Myin started to whirl, hand going for his *dah* when a needle-prick in the ribs warned him not to be precipitate. "Your men are beginning to stare at me most impolitely, Boh. I suggest you ask them to be seated. Their lack of manners may make me uncomfortable." At the Boh's abrupt signal, his sullen men reluctantly eased down like a nest of coiled adders. "Ah, I feel much better," Ram commented amiably. "Don't you?"

"Much," agreed Boh Myin just as equably. "Only your assurance of my disappointment this evening troubles me a bit."

"Yes, anticipation is not always pleasurable, is it? You have waited an unduly long time for your men to return with news of the gun. It is no longer necessary to wait. The answers to all your questions have been at your gate this past hour."

Boh Myin curtly nodded to a man near the pagoda's main door. He went out to shortly return, white-faced, with a pair of oozing, scarlet-glossed sacks. From one of them he drew a puffy, severed head and held it up before his chief. Choking, Lysistrata turned her face to the wall. Silence, more ominous than their earlier unease, fell over the men.

"Empty the sacks," roughly ordered Boh Myin.

"Shall I save him the trouble?" Ram interjected lightly. "There are twenty heads . . . and the gun is still moving this way. Who of you will go now to try to stop it?"

Boh Myin scowled. "You did this?"

"As I will do to anyone who leaves this fort without my permission. My Nagas are extremely reliable, particularly at night."

Boh Myin laughed. "You are in an untenable position, Ram Kachwaha, and bright enough to know it. I can force the permission from you. If you kill me, Moung San there will kill the girl. Even if you resist torture for an inconvenient time, I still have the girl. Will you see the skin peeled from her body a strip at a time?"

"No," admitted Ram, "but then you would get no money for her."

Boh Myin's eyes narrowed. "How much will you pay?"

"Not so much as I might have, had your men been less impetuous in Khandahoor. Also, as you know, I no longer hold property in Rangoon. I can call off the Nagas and either offer you the *Rani* or money from the sale of her. She's worth a hundred times the price of your canoes."

Boh Myin sat back. "That's not enough. You probably burned them to begin with."

"Have you other offers? Better something than nothing. While we quibble, that British howitzer is lumbering your way."

"*Our* way," corrected Boh Myin with a slow smile. "They want to hang you even more than they do me."

His smile widened to show a gold fang. "You know what I'd like."

"Sorry, if you want my head to top off those sacks, you'll have to take it." Ram smiled back. "Suppose I throw in my services if it comes to a fight with the British. Now that you've grabbed the girl, they probably think I'm in with you, anyway. If you lose, you at least will have the satisfaction of knowing I'll die with you; if you win, I'll take you to the *Rani.*" He paused. "Only, the girl must be released to the British before a shot is fired."

"You don't want her?" Boh Myin asked suspiciously.

"I don't want the British to have an excuse to come after me again," Ram replied flatly. "She'll keep them satisfied, for a while at any rate."

Lysistrata listened to his answer with a cold sickness in her heart. So he did not care; he was simply being careful as usual. If she died at Buddha's Skull, the British would hound him indefinitely. He had said if she once saw him clearly, she would shrink away as if from some living horror. And yet . . . she could not turn from him no matter what face he showed. He held her soul to cherish or rend, to keep close or let perish.

A guard stole into the pagoda to squat before Boh Myin. "The British have sent an emissary, *Tuan.* They wish to parley."

Boh Myin straightened. "Is the gun already in place? How can that be?"

"No, *Tuan.* The emissary is alone but for two foot soldiers and a guide."

Boh Myin sat back. "Admit him."

A few minutes later, Harry Armistead entered the pagoda. He instantly noted Lysistrata and her condition, then his eyes hardened when he saw Ram in Pathan gear among the pirate captains. He strode before the Boh, made a ceremonious bow. "Greetings, honorable Boh

Myin, on behalf of Her Royal Majesty, Victoria, Queen of England. I am Leftenant Harold Armistead of Her Majesty's Guards. I have been sent to negotiate the return of Miss Lysistrata Herriott.''

"Negotiate, Leftenant?" Boh Myin purred. "I do not recall mentioning a howitzer as part of the price for Miss Herriott."

Harry looked sheepish. "I admit my superiors had no intention of acknowledging your demand when the expedition originated; however . . . the gun suffered damage in transit through the jungle. Therefore"—he slowed as if galled by the words—"we are obliged to meet your price."

With a soft laugh, Boh Myin turned to the impassive Pathan beside him. "You see, my friend, you have overestimated my need of your help." He looked sharply at Harry. "The gold, Leftenant? Where is it?"

Harry waved his two men forward. Between them they carried a small chest which they lowered by Harry's feet and opened; inside was a fat pile of gold coins. Myin waved them to bring it closer. He dug deep into the chest, drew out a coin and bit it. His metallic tooth gleamed in a broad smile as he scanned Victoria's embossed portrait, then looked again at Harry. "I admire your plump queen. Round women are often generous." He nodded toward Lysistrata's corner. "Take her, take her"; then added mischievously, "only do not blame me if she does not reach Rangoon. She was in very poor condition when I acquired her from Ram Kachwaha."

"I am sure you have done everything possible, sir, to guard the lady's health," Harry said icily. "Ram Kachwaha is also renowned for his kindness to women. I hope one day I may amply repay you both for your generosity." He nodded to his men, who went swiftly to retrieve Lysistrata.

She gave San a whimsical smile. "May all your *nats* be little ones."

He laughed softly. "And yours, lady. Never fear, I shall always appear in your crocodile dreams."

As the bearers carried the litter past the Boh, she lifted a hand for them to pause. "I have one request, Boh Myin. May Prince Kachwaha escort me to the gate?"

He shrugged. "Why not? My bowmen will ensure your trustworthiness."

Harry looked sharply at Lysistrata, then at Ram, who lazily rose to join them. As they reached a point several yards from the pagoda, the Englishman began angrily, "What the devil . . . ?"

"Be quiet, Harry," Lysistrata murmured. "I thank you with all my heart for saving me, but for the moment, just be quiet."

He stared at her, then his lips clamped together in wounded silence.

"Ram," she said softly, "what will Boh Myin do with you now?"

"Trade me for the *Rani*," he replied matter-of-factly.

"He'll kill you once he has it."

"He'll try."

The broad-beamed stockade gate loomed ahead. "You've thrust your head in his jaws for nothing." Her eyes were stinging with tears. "I'm sorry."

"For what? Being alive?" An almost gay smile teased his lips. "I'm not." He studied the moon's calm lambence above the treetops. "Marry her, Harry. She's a nice girl."

"I intend to," Harry snapped to Lysistrata's surprise, "but I damned well want to know what's going on here."

"I'm not quite sure myself, Harry," Lysistrata intervened unsteadily, "but I'll marry whom I please, thank you both very much. My future isn't precisely the issue at the moment." She looked back at Ram. "Don't die for me. I can bear anything but that."

"Boh Myin and I have several bones to pick," he replied easily. "You're only one of them." With the gate shadowing them, he held out his hand. "Good-bye."

Her chest seemed to constrict until her heart felt bloodless. She clasped his hand as if her fingers might shatter. "Good-bye."

Ram started to turn away, then glanced back at the Englishman. "Was the gold your idea?"

"Yes."

Ram smiled enigmatically. "I thought so." As the gate closed behind them, the last Lysistrata saw of him was a slim, ghostly gray figure strolling back toward the pagoda.

"He's lying, Harry," she whispered. "They're going to kill him and he knows it."

"He probably prefers the Boh's *dah* to a British rope, which is what he'll get if he's still in that hyena den at sunrise," replied Harry unfeelingly.

"What do you mean?" she asked tautly.

In no mood to tolerate ill-placed sympathy, he was curt. "You'll see."

While walking back to the Boh's pagoda, Ram watched the moon as if he could follow its movement. He could remember many women by moonlight; Lysistrata would be startled to know how many, although the last had been Anira, for whom he was only a delusion. His most powerful memories of Lysistrata came from velvet silences, from nights without a moon.

She was safe now, his tigress. That vital wisp of sinew and skin and bone with the burning, beautiful eyes. Could the jade flames of those eyes light that coming darkness that might flow deeper than death? If so . . .

He made a brief, ironic salaam to the moon, then

reentered the pagoda where a ring of dark, feral faces waited, relaxed now they felt the danger over, eager for murderous entertainment.

"Sit down, Ram Kachwaha," Boh Myin said heartily. "Have a bit of jaggery to celebrate my good fortune."

"I have never much liked jaggery," Ram replied lightly, "and perhaps you should wait until the British depart to celebrate."

"Their gun's wrecked. You heard what the officer said." Boh Myin wiped liquor from his mouth with his arm.

"I heard."

"He paid in gold. Why should he lie?" Boh Myin demanded. "I have everything I want," he grinned maliciously, "and I have you."

"Correction. If that gun is intact, the British now have everything *they* want. Including the gold, unless you propose to shoot it at them. None of us is going anywhere until they say so . . . or I say so."

"Bah. Your Nagas can shoot at their toes. Do you think I am stupid? That gun is mired two miles from here with a cracked axle. They are squealing like pigs in the river mud. Did you suppose I wouldn't keep an eye on them?" He lazed in his chair. "I'm not so sure you're much good as an ally, Ram. I cannot trust you, I do not like you, and you owe me more than a single ship as payment for your life, my eight canoes, and twenty men. Besides, I can always locate the *Rani* myself. I have not seen you fight in some time. How do I know you're worth having anymore?"

"Try me."

"Yes. Yes, I will." As Ram eased off his vest, Boh Myin summoned forward a squat Chinese with a pair of long, single-bladed knives in his belt. "This fellow is quite good with the knives. Suppose you match him." He motioned another pirate to hand Ram a pair of like weapons. "Mind, I will be most annoyed if you kill him"—he chuckled—"but merely grieved if he kills you."

Adroitly poising the knives on his forefingers, Ram tested their balance, then with a wrist-flick, sent them spinning to settle with his thumbs hooked around the butts, blades nestled points-up along his inner forearms as he critically checked their length. Crossing his wrists, the Chinese swiftly slid his knives from his belt, extended them like twin scorpion stings. Ram's knives remained chastely reversed. Grinning pirates nudged one another: this mongrel did not even know enough about knives to utilize their range. He was all flash, nothing else. The Chinese appeared less complacent, and San's eyes gleamed with amusement. The Chinese was right to be uncertain; he must have recognized Kachwaha's mantis technique, rarely seen beyond the China border.

"These knives are mediocre, Boh Myin," observed Ram. "Suppose your man and I trade one to make sure I don't slice him up by accident."

Boh Myin roared with delight, particularly at the Chinese's sour face. "By all means, trade all you like."

The Chinese swiftly loosed a knife at Ram's head. Ram seemed to blur into rotation at the waist, then deftly between forefinger and third, plucked the knife from the air behind his back as his own weapon spun toward the Chinese's belly. With a startled hiss, the man leaped aside, sucking belly to backbone. The knife glanced off stone to land in the dirt. The Chinese hastily scraped it up, warded off Ram's advance with a thrust at his belly. At the same instant, Ram's knife butt slammed into the Chinese's inner wrist nerve, numbing the hand. In the next moment, his arm slid past the man's body, the tucked knife slashing the brachial artery under the armpit, its return stroke severing the top of the deltoid at the dacoit's shoulder, then ripping down the top of his forearm to the wrist. The Chinese stared mutely at his dangling, forever-useless arm and the blood that poured down deadened fingers to form a puddle at his feet.

First to collect his stunned wits, the pirate who had provided Ram's knives scurried to wrap a dirty tourniquet about the wounded man's arm. Disgustedly, the Boh waved the Chinese from the tiny arena. He eyed Ram's patient smile. "Lest you grow bored, Your Highness," he said grimly, "I must provide an element of diversion. Tok."

From a shadowy corner at the rear of the pagoda rose a figure. It seemed to rise for some time until its ducked, blocklike head appeared to buttress the ceiling. Its owner, Tok, was Malay with a generous strain of Samoan. Heavy-browed, heavy-lidded, he stood over seven feet tall with a paunch that equaled a huge, barrel chest. At a nod from the Boh, he picked up a war hammer and lumbered forward through hastily parting brethren.

"To assure your amusement, friend Ram," purred the Boh, "suppose you surrender your weapons, I should like to observe your clever wits pitted against Tok's hammer . . . though I greatly fear those wits will be shortly dashed about these walls."

Silently, Ram handed over his weapons, then careful as a cat on a fence, turned to face his Goliath, who eyed him with sleepy tolerance. Presuming his prey to be rooted by fear, Tok casually swung the hammer down at Ram's head as if splitting kindling. Ram sidestepped, openhanded the giant's meaty jowl with an insulting crack. Tok went livid with anger and embarrassment. The war hammer whirled into a stinging blur above his scarlet, scowling face. Ram swiftly ducked, then dropped to one hand, his legs slashing at Tok's knees. Deprived of his footing and propelled by the hammer, the startled Malay went over backward, slamming against cringing spectators, then skidded on his face through their midst, bowling them over like tenpins. The Boh howled with laughter. "Well done, you fox whelp! That'll wake the great sloth up!"

Nose bloodied, Tok surged back from the crowd as if shot from a catapult, right into Ram's rigid fingertips which stabbed into the precise spot a Chinese doctor would call the lung meridian. Staggering, Tok tried to catch his breath, then dropped, helplessly hacking as if in the throes of asthma. The Boh frowned at the curled, thrashing Malay. "What have you done to him?"

"Nothing permanent."

Tok writhed in another paroxysm of coughing as his brother bandits stared in bemused, ghoulish fascination. San eased to his feet and with an ironic glance at Ram, strolled over to the helpless man. His fingers jabbed the same spot in the giant's shoulder Ram's had struck. Tok gasped, breathed, gaped up at San as if he were a faith healer, then heaved himself as far as he could get from the devil who could incapacitate him at a single touch.

As San resumed his place, the Boh's fingers irritably drummed a chair arm. "You would have done as well to kill him, Kachwaha. Now you've left me with a great, useless chicken to feed." The drumming abruptly stopped. "No more games. Let us have the *lathi* from your own wretched country. You high-and-mighty Rahtors think *lathi* is only fit for peasants? Well, here's a peasant for you." He waved forward a small loinclothed Hindu. In one hand was loosely held a simple staff. Middle-aged, chest slightly concaved from childhood rickets, the Indian glanced quietly at Ram, then contemplatively at the wall paintings beyond him. "You, Ram Kachwaha, will take the rope dart," ordered the Boh. Ram was handed a dart linked to a coiled cord.

The pair, silent as monks, squared off. And boredom for everyone and frustration for Ram finally became fact. As often as Ram threw his retrievable dart, the Hindu foiled it with the *lathi,* his crude stick. The wizened creature might have been meditating, so tranquil was he. The failure of his own attacks on Ram seemed to discourage him not at all. With deadly patience, he began to wear Ram down. The restless pirates rooted around for cheroots and toddy. Halfhearted wagers were made. Only the Boh and San retained dogged interest in the match. Then suddenly, Ram simply, deliberately dropped his weapon. Instantly, the *lathi* swung at his neck. Stepping under the lethal arc into his opponent, Ram grabbed the stick and, using it as a fulcrum, hurled the small man across the arena. At the moment the Hindu struck ground, the *lathi* butt connected sharply with his temple. The Hindu's body might remain on earth, but henceforward, his mind would be with his gods. "Out with him!" spat the Boh.

Narrow-eyed, the Boh pitted Ram against two more men. Ram concentrated carefully, for his reactions were dulling with fatigue. Though he incapacitated his opponents, rendering them useless against the British, he did not escape unscathed: his body was covered with cuts and bruises, his cheekbone laid open, and an arm gashed from shoulder nearly to elbow. The cotton he wore was blotched with blood, sweat, and dirt. It was a matter of time before one of his adversaries got lucky, because Boh Myin seemed determined to make him fight until he dropped. How long Myin would allow his men to be damaged was a moot point.

At length, as he stood panting over the last pirate he had sent sprawling at Myin's feet, the Boh sighed with genuine regret. "Truly, you are all you have ever been, Ram. It is a pity we could not have been friends and a pity, too, to match a Saluki against mongrels. Unfortunately, I must have your head, but it is not for one of these dolts to take it. Offal as they are," he scowled disgustedly at the sullen crew, "I am obliged to put up with them for the moment." A rueful eyebrow lifted. "You can see how it is."

Ram touched his forehead. "I am at your service."

Boh Myin issued a summons. "Moung San."

Ram looked into San's lethal eyes impassively staring at him over a crossbow. A crossbow could tear through an elephant's hide at just under three hundred yards. "Rest easy," Boh Myin advised amiably. "He, at least, is a good marksman."

As the bow cocked, Ram's head lifted, his spine stiffening in anticipation. At that moment, a blast knocked him flat. Covering his head against a shower of rubble, he gave a soft laugh as he listened to the shrieks. When the dust settled, he lifted his head with a grin at Boh Myin, who huddled against his gilded chair. "Your British seem to have repaired their howitzer."

"*Our* British!" Myin snarled. "Perhaps you may redeem your head yet." He lurched to his feet, shouting orders to men scrambling for weapons and rushing out of the pagoda. San was already gone.

"What would you like me to do?" Ram asked lazily, leaning against a stack of magazine boxes.

"Do what you like," Myin snapped, shoveling shells into his pockets. "Only, I expect twenty British heads for yours." He ran out of the pagoda as another blast rocked it.

Ram eyed the magazine.

Five minutes later, with an ear-splitting explosion, the magazine disintegrated, bodies scattering through the air. Boh Myin, atop the palisade, gave a bowman a shove. "That was no fucking shell! Get that half-breed bastard! I don't care if it's only pieces, I want him!"

A shell hit the next section of teak wall; it splintered and toppled, crushing pirates it did not spear. Boh Myin scrambled away as his adjoining segment began to list. He swung down a fallen beam to the ground to see a squad of British-led troops running from the jungle toward the gap. "Halt them," he howled at sniper bowmen in the overhanging dak and cotton trees. In answer, the nearest one screeched and fell, a bullet in his back. That, judging from the direction of the shot, had been no more British-originated than the magazine explosion. Another bowman pitched from his perch. "You fucker, Kachwaha! I'll kill you myself!" Boh Myin yelled.

The bowman sent after Ram appeared briefly from behind a tiny pagoda at the fort fringe to fire at a spot under a log. An instant later, the bowman dropped, a splash of blood at his chest. Boh Myin darted from cover to cover until he reached the log, his *dah* raised. The shelter was vacant with a streak of blood against bark. Outside the palisade, he heard the British gun roar.

His teeth bared in a mirthless grin. Warily following the blood spoor, he reached a nest of pagodas hazed with acrid smoke from the exploded magazine. He began to crawl through the overgrown elephant grass, then halted where the blood stopped. Guessing Ram had paused to bind his telltale wound, Boh Myin extended the *dah* at arm's length and wriggled the grass. A shot sang against the blade tip, almost numbing his arm. He eased to the side and moved in the direction of the shot. When he reached a point ten feet farther, he wriggled the grass again. Another shot sang and he winced. When the third ploy brought only silence, he began to resent being forced to blindly crawl on his belly while Ram moved and shot at will. Where's that damned San when he's needed? he thought irritably.

He snaked along a crumbled pagoda's offside, cautiously lifted his head to see a gray-clad figure just out of range limp back toward the fighting. He pelted after him. Ram disappeared inside a pagoda. Spotting San trotting toward him across the compound, Boh Myin signaled him to the pagoda. Moments later, they were at its doors.

Flattening against the wall, he called cajolingly, "Come, Ram, you are not showing the proper spirit. You can only die once. Besides, we are two clever fellows. If we put our heads together, we can get out of this. We need each other. You, to escape the fort; I, to get through your Nagas." He waited. "Eh, what do you say?"

"Why not?" was the soft reply. "Come in and we'll discuss it."

Boh Myin hesitated only a moment. "Of course, but things are looking bad. We haven't much time." He kicked his gun into the pagoda. "Just to show my good faith." He waved his *dah* in front of the door to see if Ram would fire. "Mind if I keep this?"

"Whatever you like."

Boh Myin eased into the aperture to see Ram leaning against the wall to keep the weight off his wounded leg. His pistol dangled loosely. When San moved, bow cocked, into the opposite doorway at Ram's back, Boh Myin's *dah* thrust into his *pasoh*. "Can you travel on that leg?"

"After you."

With a shrug, Boh Myin turned to leave. He heard a slight movement, then the expected hum, *thunk* of a released arrow; but unexpectedly in his own back. He was dead before recognizing his bewilderment.

Ram stared up at San from the dirt floor where he had dropped with pistol poised to fire, expecting a man at his back.

"Well," San said amiably, "does that pay my passage out of here?"

"The Nagas left at the first shell," Ram replied ironically.

San touched his forelock, then trotted off.

When Ram left the pagoda, he saw why San had not lingered to waste words. The British were pouring through the main gate and breaches in the palisade. The melee was a moving thicket of hacking blades and jabbing bayonets sparked by gunfire. Skirting the mob and heading for the nearest breach, he fired quickly and accurately at intervening pirates, once strategically toppling one into a British corporal who leveled a pistol at him. He hurled the empty gun into the face of a second Britisher, then flattened him with a hand chop to the neck.

He turned just as a pirate's knuckles grazed his jaw. Seeing another pirate come at him as he parried another blow, Ram caught the first man in a headlock and, using him as a brace, leapt up and put a head-scissors on the second attacker. Rotating in midair, he crashed both men's heads into the stone debris from the magazine. Only to have a Kachin pirate come at him. Cautiously, they circled each other. Ram, backing, stumbled over a *dah*-hacked body. As the pirate shot in a throw-kick, Ram grabbed; but with a backflip, the man slammed a heel-kick to Ram's jaw and hurtled him over the dead body.

As Ram staggered to his feet, the pirate aimed a round-house kick to the temple only to be met with a swift kick. With a quick "tiger climbing mountain" maneuver, Ram drove a sharp fist to his opponent's bladder, hooked a leg behind his knee to take him to the ground in a centrifugal throw. The pirate airborne, Ram's fist connected with his jaw in a lightning uppercut, then a chop to the throat. As the pirate was about to hit the ground, Ram's leg shot over the body, heel connecting with the jaw to break his neck.

Ram dragged himself up by a water jug among the pirates' food supplies scattered about some *gharry* carts. Pirates swarmed the spot like bees with stinging *dahs*, and he drew his own weapon. Hampered by a wounded leg, even his swordplay was no match for jabs that sought him from all directions. At length, a hack to his head sent him stumbling back against a pile of ripped rice sacks. He went down, grabbed a shield from a fallen pirate to protect his head, then heard a crunch as a war ax descended. When it withdrew for another crack at the damaged shield, he hurled the shield like a skipping stone over water. With a screech, the pirate went down, his kneecaps shattered, to be overrun by his comrades. Half-blinded by blood, Ram gasped at rending pain as a barbed spear drove deep into his chest. He involuntarily caught at the shaft as, with a growl of triumph, a pirate wrenched at it to make another thrust. Impatiently, the bandit snatched for his *dah;* as the *dah* raised, a British sword split his rib cage to the spine. Harry kicked the bandit away in mid-shriek. British fire mowed down the rest of the swarm at the supply pile.

By now most remaining combatants were British; Harry shoved away a subaltern eager to finish Ram. "Back off!" he yelled. "This man's my prisoner!"

Glancing down, he saw Ram's white-lipped, futile effort to pull out the spear. "Stop that, dammit! Do you want to carve up what's left? Let me . . ." He eased Ram onto his side and eyed the protruding speartip in his back. "Hold on, this is going to hurt like hell." With a strangled sound, Ram went rigid as Harry sharply thrust the spear through to the haft. Harry broke the shaft, threw away the barbed head, and helped Ram over again.

His face beaded with perspiration, eyes black with pain, Ram gazed up at the Englishman. "You're not . . . doing me a favor, Harry. I'd rather go . . . this way than on the end of a rope."

"The favor's to Lysistrata," Harry said coldly. "I want her to see you as the lying scum you are, not some kind of mysterious, glamorous tin god. After this, we're square. All I owe you is escort to the gallows." He jerked out the haft, hardening himself against Ram's brief, stifled cry before he went limp. Harry, feeling oddly ashamed, ripped Ram's bloody shirt into strips to bandage the bleeding spear wound. As the last bandit was subdued, he knotted the bandage. He looked down at the still face. "You're still a nervy scoundrel, damn you."

He carried Ram toward a row of litters the field surgeon and his adjutants were spreading on the ground for British wounded. "Not here," the doctor said curtly. "With them." He waved toward a wheeled bamboo cage of prisoners.

"He won't make Rangoon in that," Harry protested. "At least keep him separate until he has a chance."

The doctor eyed the scarlet-stained bandage on Ram's slim brown torso. "He's already done the way he's pumping blood."

"Look," Harry argued, hardly knowing why, "Sir Anthony Bartly wants this man alive to face trial for crimes in Rangoon. This is Richard Harley, the white-slave trader and murderer." His voice lowered. "He's made Sir Anthony look a fool and cost him a lot of money."

"Oh. Well, if that's how it is, I'll have a look at him when I've finished the critical cases. But get shackles on him"—the doctor jabbed a finger—"or I won't be responsible."

As the howitzer's first shell screamed into the fort, Lysistrata had buried her face into the cot. Refusing to listen to any defense of Ram, Harry had packed her away in a hastily pitched tent behind British lines. He seemed angrier with her than Ram, and now she understood his suggestion that Ram might be lucky if Boh Myin killed him outright. When the second shell whistled its eerie song, she struggled from the pallet to the tent flap, but could only see a rising pall of smoke above the jungle. The magazine went up in a blast that toppled trees. As they plummeted downward, she sank to the earth, spirit weighted by the leaden knowledge that Ram would meet his fate in the same terrible solitude to which he had been exiled all his life. A savage hand seemed to clamp her chest, crushing all breath and hope. After the battle, an ensign found her senseless nearly twenty yards from the tent.

CHAPTER 15

Garotte

Be near me when my faith is dry
ALFRED, LORD TENNYSON

Lysistrata awoke in Harry's cabin aboard the *North Star*, the steam launch that had ferried the British expedition up the lower Sittang. Mercifully, she had been oblivious when shifted to one of the canoes used to transport the howitzer parts. In a long thread, the canoes had worked back downriver through the treacherous snags and cataracts of the Sittang to the *North Star*, waiting seventy-five miles above Moulein. Harry sat reading in a desk chair, his feet braced against the humming cabin wall. "Damn you," she whispered. "Damn you all."

He looked up, frowning. "Would you rather Boh Myin had cut your throat?"

"Yes," she replied fervently. "God, yes."

"We haven't seen eye-to-eye on many things," he snapped, "but I never thought you were a complete fool until now."

"You British are the fools, Harry. You've been hounding an innocent man." She laughed bitterly. "Didn't you come up here because of Sir Anthony's

345

wounded pocketbook and white man's jealousy? Marry me, God, how *noble* of you.'' She began to shake with illness and emotion. "I'd sooner marry a *viper!*'' Her voice cracked. "He gave you your life and you've murdered him . . . murdered him!''

Harry slammed down the book. "He's the murderer, Lysistrata. I wasn't sure in Rangoon, but I was sure when I saw you. Are you so besotted with him you can even forgive his *selling* you to Myin?''

"He had nothing to do with any killings in Rangoon,'' she retorted. "He didn't abduct me and he didn't sell me to Myin. If it weren't for Ram, I'd be the property of Sir Anthony's pet, Gopal Prasad.''

Harry's eyes narrowed. "Prasad took you?''

"No, but he had no scruples about buying me.'' Briefly, she told him about the abduction and Bangkok auction. "Ram only took me to Khandahoor because he thought I'd set Sir Anthony on him.''

"And why would you do that?''

"Because I *am* the fool you think me. Because I was angry and threatened him when he wanted nothing to do with me.''

"And I suppose he had nothing to do with you all those months at Khandahoor?''

"He didn't touch me.''

"You're lying.''

"What you believe doesn't matter now,'' she replied tiredly.

"It will matter to Ram, if he lives to come to trial.''

Instantly, her defiant manner collapsed. "He's alive?'' She tried to lift her head from the pillow.

"He's with the wounded on the barge behind us.'' Seeing relief flood her eyes, he added flatly, "He took a spear in the chest. It's unlikely he'll make Rangoon.''

"Can you . . . will you help him at all?'' Her eyes were pleading now.

"I'll see he's not mistreated until he reaches prison."

"Harry, he isn't what you think. You must believe me."

"Can you prove anything you say, Lysistrata? All you know is what he told you . . . and he's an accomplished liar."

"Harry, he had more reason to kill me than anyone, but he didn't. And why should he pay a small fortune to buy me if he had stolen me in the first place? Prasad can bear witness to the slave auction if you can make him admit being there. Ram was going to take me to the mission at Lashio when Myin's men burned Khandahoor and took me."

"What about the British officers he killed in the Shans?"

"This is his country far more than yours, Harry, and you're stealing it. Will you hang him for defending his home?"

"I might not, but Sir Anthony is less sentimental." He leaned back in the chair. "Why was Ram with Boh Myin?"

"He offered him the *Rani* to let me go." She stared at the bulkhead. "Why, I don't know. I do know Boh Myin wanted him dead. He was committing suicide to put himself at Myin's mercy. You British weren't expected to come up with the ransom money. Boh Myin was on the verge of killing me; so whatever Ram's motives, he did try to save my life at the risk of his own."

When Harry said nothing, she put a weary hand over her eyes. "Why do I waste my breath? You British are going to use Ram now as you always have, only this time as a scapegoat. I'll wager no one has asked who *else* might profit from his ruin, just as no one has inquired too pointedly about the persons who wanted me to disappear." She gazed at him sharply. "Well? How did Papa's investigation fare until Ram was so conveniently thrust into the public eye as a catchall?"

Bluntly, Harry described how Sein and the other women had been found.

Lysistrata laughed shortly. "You, of all people, should know Ram better than that. Sein helped save his life from the cholera. He does not ill repay people for favors, as you may recall, and he is hardly so unsubtle a killer. I have seen him kill."

Harry unwillingly listened to her voice, dull with increasing exhaustion of dogged argument. Her early demand naggingly echoed in his mind. "Why do *you* want him dead? Your white man's jealousy?" He could ill imagine any man refusing what Lysistrata admitted offering to Ram. Indifference had not led Ram to keep her at Khandahoor so long, for each day added to his guilt in the eyes of the British authorities.

Harry pictured Lysistrata yielding to that long, brown knowledgeable body. If he knew Ram better than most, he knew too Lysistrata's bright passion, her tempestuousness and disdain of convention. What would all those traits be like in bed? He had not really thought of Lysistrata sexually, not when he had offhandedly courted her in Rangoon, not even when he had begun to idealize her as the maiden to be rescued and honor vindicated. Lysistrata now forced him to think of her as a woman: a bold, sensual woman who considered vindication for her desires ludicrous.

After Lysistrata fell into exhausted, distracted slumber, Harry went back to the flat barge towed by the *North Star*. Ram, the least favored among the wounded British, had drawn a spot under the canvas awning that caught the most slanting sun. His hair was perspiration-soaked, his parched lips gasping for air in the sweltering heat of the bare, baked deck. His wrist and leg irons, the latter with a bar pin between them, had been stapled to the planking. Harry dipped a handkerchief in the river, roughly laid it across Ram's brow, then snapped to an orderly smoking in the bow. "Water here. Be quick about it."

Ironic amusement overlay the pain in Ram's dark eyes. "You're like Lysistrata, Harry," he croaked. "You don't know when to let go."

"You think I wouldn't like to?" Harry retorted. He turned to the orderly who sulkily brought a water bucket. "If I find this prisoner neglected again, I'll have you up on charges. Now, fetch the surgeon around; these bandages are blood-soaked." The orderly scurried off.

Harry hunkered down to hold a water gourd to Ram's lips.

"No, thanks."

"Don't be an ass. I need some answers from you, and for Lysistrata's sake, I'm going to have them."

"Nothing I can say will help her."

"Damn you, have you any idea of the hell they'll put her through when she gets to Rangoon? Haven't you done enough to her? Or don't you care?"

As if pain were mounting, Ram closed his eyes. *"You* care, Harry. She's your concern now."

Harry's eyes narrowed. "Why should I take on your baggage? You bedded her; you look after her. I gather she didn't exactly fight." He laughed sardonically at Ram's cold stare. "I owed you a life; that's paid. When we get to Rangoon, I'm handing you to Sir Anthony and collecting a promotion. Your tart can join your nigger ass on the gallows." He shrugged as Ram, composure splintering and eyes deadly, jerked violently against the chain. "She just might, you know, if someone were to suggest murderous collusion between you."

He strolled away toward the stern to loiter until the harried surgeon grudgingly checked Ram's wound and changed his bandages. Ram lay still for some time after the surgeon left. Then he tried to reach the gourd of water. In seconds, Harry was at his side, holding the

water to his lips. Ram started to dash it away with mana-
cled hands, then relaxed with a short sigh. "I didn't realize you had so much fox in you, Harry."

By the end of the week, the *North Star* reached Rangoon. Lysistrata was sent home to her relieved father,
Ram to prison. Harry was little more informed about the
Rangoon murders than before, although Ram had been
cooperative in his restrained fashion. He revealed so little
about his business dealings Harry suspected most were
interlocked with criminal elements. Far from idle at
Khandahoor, Ram had made a private investigation of
the murders; now, he reviewed its few resulting leads
with minute care before passing them to Harry. He might
trust Harry with his life, but not others' lives. The exasperated Englishman soon saw the Oriental strain in Ram
went deeper than his native dress. To Ram, life was life,
but business was business.

Too, while both Ram's and Lysistrata's conditions improved with care on the journey to Rangoon, Ram was
only strong enough to talk for brief periods. Although he
had various enemies, he suspected a drug competitor
would have made the most profit from the murders. Boh
Myin himself was a drug-runner who had benefited by
Ram's removal; so had many others. But Myin had not
boasted of such a victory, and usually pursued more direct measures to increase his income; therefore, Ram
considered someone else had planned the affair. "Follow
the profits, Harry," he advised on the barge, "but be
careful. I had two men killed making inquiries. Before he
was knifed, one came up with the name of Garotte. After
my elimination, this Garotte began to consolidate control
over the opium entering the city. The price is climbing
out of reach for medical use."

"Have you anyone I can use in the city?" Harry
asked.

"Only Naswral, my former body servant. Unfortunately, Wa Sing has gone to Kowloon because of his association with me in the Yünnan fiasco. He had more contacts than I with dealers."

Harry doubted that, but was even more dubious about the skills of the soiled-looking doctor in charge of the hospital in the civil prison outside Rangoon where he delivered Ram with the pirates. With the other prisoners, Ram was stripped and tossed a loincloth; but as he was yet untried, his head was not shaved. Two surly prisoners were ordered to support him until his turn came to be shoved into the smithy where irons were bolted on his ankles and a numbered tag was run onto a metal band riveted about his neck. After being shackled, the pirates shambled across the sunbaked prison work yard to their ward, a big, iron-roofed teak-barred cage circuited by North Indian guards. Ram's destination was almost as grim.

The hospital was a leaky, open-sided shed set up along a prison wall. Only a single attendant besides the doctor cared for the few patients lying on rickety cots, and drugs were pathetically limited. Sanitation was nonexistent; disease more common than injury. Food was rice gruel laced with half-rotted vegetables; the single well in the work yard was polluted.

"Sorry about this," Harry apologized as Ram was chained to a cot. He watched the stolid Punjabi guard head out to the yard for another prisoner. "I'll do what I can for you with Bartly, though he'll likely turn a tin ear. Certainly I can see you get better food than prison slop."

"Don't bother about food, Harry," Ram replied with his wry half-smile. "I'm in no shape to defend it. Just collect your promotion and watch your back."

"You might keep that last bit of advice in mind for yourself." Harry eyed the sullen hospital prisoners who stared at them without blinking; some were malingerers, some wasted wrecks.

Ram's eyes still held patient amusement. "A less than fond cousin once gave me a scorpion to play with when I was yet scarcely able to walk. Mistrusting its looks, I smashed it with a wooden ball. My reaction was no more than instinctive, but one that experience has not dulled." The amusement faded. "Now you must learn to play with scorpions; Bartly the least of them."

"Any suggestions?"

"If you don't lead him beyond his reach, he'll be predictable. Tease him too much and he'll sting."

"And this so-called Garotte?"

"If I knew, Harry, I wouldn't be here."

"Well, good-bye . . . ," Harry said reluctantly. "Good luck."

"Yes. To you, too."

The Englishman hesitated. "Do you want me to keep seeing after Lysistrata?"

Ram gave him a whimsical smile. "No, but you will anyway, won't you?"

After Harry left, Ram lay staring up at the rusty tin roof with its corroded pinpricks of sunlight. It appeared he might have time to learn to hate Harry after all. A stupid waste. Harry was a good man: a good man who could have a life with Lysistrata, touch her, love her, take her. He felt himself going stiff, hands and jaw rigored. Like a corpse. Already . . . yet not soon enough. He could will away his breath, his life: his Chinese masters had taught him that. To will away all thoughts of a woman should be simplicity itself, only he had become less than simple; he had become stupid about Harry, even more selfishly stupid about Lysistrata. Such longing for an earthly creature would never take him to Nirvana. Never-ending Hell, if it exists, awaits thee, fool, in the flaming shape of a woman.

* * *

Harry quickly found Ram correct about Bartly. Hoping to transfer Ram to a British military hospital, he reported to Sir Anthony at Government House to find him elated about the Sittang expedition's success. Harry *had* been put in for promotion, news that found him indifferent. Bartly did not notice. He had taken to wearing scarlet 73rd regimentals from his India days much as a boy fired with enthusiasm over directing mock battles with lead soldiers. He seemed to forget he had merely plunged pins in a map and supervised ordnance. Briskly, he paced under a portrait of India's master manager, Lord Dalhousie. "We will set the trial a week from today and finish this thing cleanly. Lysistrata Herriott and her father will be immediately leaving Burma, I presume?"

"I believe they will await the outcome of the trial," Harry said slowly.

Sir Anthony shook his head. "If the girl has a shred of sense, she'll get clear of this mess as soon as possible."

"You're probably right, sir; however, things may look even messier if Harley appears in court after a stay in Rangoon Prison hospital." He described the hospital conditions.

Bartly waved the suggestion aside. "The man has chosen his side. If he prefers to be with the natives, let him."

"Have you ever thought Harley might have been, ah, 'set up,' sir?"

"Why do you say that, Lieutenant?" Sir Anthony inquired sharply.

"That girl being found in his bed seemed a trifle blatant to me, sir, if not the act of a madman. Harley seems sane enough."

"You forget, Harley is a half-caste, Leftenant," Sir Anthony said coldly. "His breed is noted for emotionalism and cruelty. I don't find it strange at all that he might dispatch an inconsequential whore, particularly if he thought she would not be found until he was safely gone.''

Although Bartly's frame of reference when he spoke of Sein was questionable, Harry thought better of asking who considered Sein to be inconsequential: Ram or Bartly.

In two days, Harry located the scar-faced Naswral who was, as Ram suggested, hiding on a deserted plantation a few miles north of Rangoon. Masjid was recalled into the Herriott household to provide bodyguard service and ease the burdens of Lysistrata's convalescence. Through Dr. Lighter, Harry obtained a barrister for Ram's defense. After that, he only succeeded in nearly getting himself axed.

Appearance altered by beard stubble, a patched eye, and weatherworn, merchant-seaman's gear, he mangled his speech into a Cheapside whine to comb the harbor dives. At first unsure of his accent, he kept his mouth shut, ears open while appearing to be a drunkard. Not until he reached a mean little brothel on Blackwater Street did he hear a breath about Garotte from a Siamese prostitute addicted to opium. She was taken with his looks which—downplayed though they were—compared brilliantly with her usual customers; too brilliantly, for when he next came to call, the Javanese madame gave him a false smile and claimed the girl was ill. More likely she was in the harbor with her drug-muddled chatter stilled, thought Harry. The partitions between the prostitutes' ratty rooms were screens; quiet as he had tried to keep their conversation, the girl had been careless. Garotte, she had drowsily told him, was indeed the new king of opium. ''Greedy pig,'' she grumbled thickly. ''He's brought the poppy price up to forty *kyat*. I don't make that in a week!''

"Yet you seem to have a good supply," Harry observed, stretched beside her on a mat. "You must have secret lovers who are slaves to your beauty," he added teasingly.

She gave him a coy grin. "Are you jealous, English? Bring me fifty *kyat* next time you visit and I will put you before them all."

"Tell me how to buy opium from Garotte and I'll give you a hundred *kyat* and devoted attention every day until my next ship, little orchid. I crave the poppy more than whiskey these days."

With a laugh, she caught his stubbled chin in one hand. "What about women, pretty sailor? Your stalk doesn't seem wilted!" Drug-glazed eyes peered into his unpatched clear one. "And you don't look like you have the poppy need."

"I've been at sea. When my supply ran out, I was in hell for a while." He played with her fingers. "You wouldn't want to see me suffer again, would you?"

"You think my heart is soft because I am a whore, sailor boy?" she jibed. "You think my head is soft? Garotte would have me strangled with my own hair if I sent you to his peddlers."

"Maybe you could buy it for me." Harry's voice held a deliberate note of desperation. He could follow her if she agreed.

"All right, sailor. Maybe is better to die young. We will not be pretty soon, you and me. The sea for you is like too many lovers for me; it will make you old and tired." She turned away onto her side. "Don't forget the hundred *kyat* tomorrow."

He did not forget, but he wondered as the madame turned him back into the street if Orchid had remembered. Had any recollection of why she had been strangled with her own hair.

He became more intent on finding Garotte, more aggressive in drinking with bar thugs. One night after leaving a murky Portuguese bar on the waterfront, he was less wary than he might have been. If he had not stumbled over a discarded liquor bottle in the alley adjoining the bar, he would not have outlived Orchid more than a few days. As he lurched over the bottle, a hissing sting at his ear and solid thunk snapped him upright to see a gleaming hatchet quivering in the bar's corner beam. With a muffled oath, he dived flat-out for the rubbled ground to roll behind the corner's shield. Yanking out his gun, he warily peered into the alley. A shadow shrank back into the gloom at the alley's end. "Hey, you!" Harry called softly. "I just want opium. Why all the fuss?" He got no answer; minutes later when he warily circled behind the would-be assassin, it was clear he would get none. The alley shadows were now only shadows.

Aside from the Orchid incident, he assumed his accent might have given him away. "It may sound like a stew to an Englishman or a colonial," declared Dr. Lighter after hearing a sample of Harry's deckhand imitation in his office, "but fair enough to pass an Eastern ear." He studied the young Englishman's grubby disguise. "Your own mother wouldn't recognize her dapper boy in that getup. Looks like you've several possibilities besides Orchid's crew. If you weren't overheard by a limey in somebody's pay or attacked by a random thief, I'd wonder if your untouchable fellow with the scarred face might be working the other side of the fence."

With a sigh, Harry shoved up the eye patch. "Well, someone's taking a chop at me confirms Ram isn't as guilty as Sir Anthony thinks, especially if Naswral knows more than he's telling about Sein's murder." He glumly scratched his moth-eaten beard. "Still, a week isn't enough to build a defense; and getting a trial postponement out of Sir Anthony is harder than dragging a ferret from a rat hole.''

''Aye, he likely wants a quick trial to keep questions from being stirred up. More than one of his cronies may have a finger in this pie. Bartly's honest enough, I think, but in his position, he has to be practical. Some of the nabobs in these parts have a deal of influence in Whitehall. They can slide his commissionership out from under him and sail him back to England on the next steamer if he embarrasses them.''

Lighter looked thoughtfully at Harry for a long moment. ''I haven't said anything until now because it's not likely to get you anything, but Anne O'Shaunessy, one of the girls Harley's supposed to have taken for slaving, is here at Queen Anne's. She wasn't lucid at first, but she's come around in the last few months. Her former mistress, Evelyn Chilton, after a single visit when Anne first arrived, has neither offered to come again nor provided money for her care. I've let her work for her keep as a maid. She's mute, of course, and listens only to what she pleases; one subject she does *not* listen to is what happened on Harley's ship.'' He ferreted for a cheap cigar in his battered humidor, then offered one to Harry, who wisely declined. Lighter lit the cigar, then poked it at the Englishman. ''Much as I'd like to help, Harley's as good as hanged in my book; Anne O'Shaunessy's mind needn't be destroyed with him. If you try to put her on the stand, I'll testify she's batty and her testimony will be thrown out of court. If you want to talk to her privately, fine.''

Her pretty Irish face as cold as stone when she was summoned to Lighter's office, Anne O'Shaunessy reacted to Harry's questions with no more interest than in a recitation of the alphabet. When he continued to press, she picked up mop and scrub bucket and left him talking to the air.

Discouraged, Harry called on the barrister that Dr. Lighter's solicitor had engaged, Barnett Leacock. The portly, benign little man informed him they had achieved a tiny victory in gaining another week's postponement of the trial. The judge in question had agreed a week was insufficient to prepare a defense. In every other area, however, they lost. The judge refused to try Ram separately from the bandits with whom he was captured, although Leacock stressed Ram's case was singular. Also, Gopal Prasad refused all requests to discuss his part in the case. The lawyer spread his hands. "Unless Lysistrata Herriott is willing to expose herself to more scandal, I have no evidence that warrants issuance of a subpoena to Prasad."

Harry smiled wryly. "You need not fear Miss Herriott will spare herself on that point or any other in the matter."

Leacock's shrewd blue eyes glinted. "Is she in love with Ram Harley?"

"No less than he with her, though he's as likely to let her know it as the moon showing itself at noon."

"Um. Wise of him. That may also explain one of the reasons he refuses to take the stand . . ." The barrister leaned forward. "If you have any influence with her, you must absolutely convince her not to show affection for him in any way if her testimony is to be credible. Also, she must tell the exact truth on the stand; one slip, and whatever is said will be disbelieved. But no matter what, she must remember the jury will easier stomach a half-caste having killed her than having had carnal knowledge of her."

"If you'll pardon my curiosity, may I ask, sir, why you sought out this case when no other English barrister would willingly touch it?"

"I was a friend of Ram's father."

"I see."

Leacock smiled sadly. "No, Leftenant, you don't see at all, and will not until you have lived and loved where you should not."

Lysistrata, as Harry predicted, was entirely ready to affirm the sordid details of the auction in court. "If the British accomplish nothing else for their colonies," she observed, "they may end the slave trade."

From the bedroom chaise, she gravely looked at Dr. Herriott. "I must do something else unpleasant, Papa: see Prasad."

He frowned. "He's a dangerous man, isn't he?"

"I'm afraid so, but even more dangerous if we don't force him from under his rock now. If we let him stay there until the trial, he may testify for the prosecution."

"Shall I try to bring him here?" asked Harry.

She smiled oddly. "Not here, Harry, and not you." She took Ma Saw's hand. "Ma Saw, will you take a message to Prasad?"

When she dictated the message, both Dr. Herriott and Harry began to bellow in unison. "Absolutely not!" Herriott yelled. "I won't have it!"

"Papa, Prasad must feel safe."

"Safe?" Harry protested. "The Golden Dragon may be safe enough for him, but you? Besides, that message sounds like an invitation to an assignation!"

"Does it?" she murmured innocently.

Herriott knew that tone too well. "Lysistrata, you aren't well enough to . . ."

She looked at him, and his protest dwindled into a sigh. For the past week, he had watched her tormented distraction. Ram Kachwaha Harley was perhaps the last man on earth he would have wanted her to love, but the choice was not his and it was made.

* * *

Little to Lysistrata's surprise, Prasad agreed to the Golden Dragon on the following night. Lysistrata's carriage halted in the alley behind the Dragon an hour ahead of time. Harry, in his sailor garb, drifted into the place while—in veils and dark-colored saris—Lysistrata and Ma Saw waited in the carriage with pistols. At the appointment hour, with Ma Saw's assistance, Lysistrata dismounted the carriage and entered the Golden Dragon. The crowded opium den was murky with yellowish smoke. Grimy walls lined with crude tiers of pallets surrounded a few tables laid out with various drug apparatuses. Lysistrata selected one set for *chandoo* near the bunk where a curled-up Harry mumbled with convincing incoherence. She paid the proprietor for opium, some of which she and Saw roasted into balls on stylets over live charcoal at their table. They pushed the balls into pipes, then pretended to smoke.

Prasad was late, so much so that his tardiness was an insult. He entered, a supercilious smile curving his petulant mouth. He scanned the room, first idly, then with growing irritation as the American woman he expected to grovel for his silence appeared not to have come. Then he noted an unusually tall Indian woman seated beneath a low-burning gaslight. Her black sari was richly encrusted with silver, her dark-eyed, veiled companion in similar but less elaborate costume. He advanced to the table circuitously, unsure whether an armed body servant might be nearby who would reprove an approach by a stranger. If the tall woman was Lysistrata Herriott, he meant to be sure she was not accompanied by someone even less friendly. As he neared the table, he heard an amused murmur in Hindi. "You remind me of a crab, Gopal Prasad, sidling up to a tidbit he is not sure smells bad enough to be safe." The tall woman's head turned, and above a filmy veil, gray-green eyes the shade of a river mist impassively surveyed him. "We can retire to another room if you are mistrustful. Or my friend and I can simply leave."

Squaring his shoulders importantly, he strolled up to her. "As *you* requested the meeting, Miss Herriot, I assumed you would be loath to terminate it at your expense."

"I suggested a meeting to serve our mutual advantage; however, if you reject possible profit to yourself, that decision will be far more to your cost than mine."

He lifted an incredulous, mocking brow. "I do not see it that way."

Lysistrata laughed. "I confess I am surprised at your lack of vision: you seemed more intelligent and shall I say"—her lashes lowered demurely—"forceful, on the occasion of our meeting in Bangkok." Trying not to choke on the potent smoke, she drew a languid puff on the *chandoo* while he eyed her warily. "Please, Mr. Prasad, if you do not wish to sit down, you should leave before someone takes notice of your speaking to me."

He frowned. "I beg your pardon. You would be the one compromised."

"My dear Mr. Prasad, do you presume Ram Harley is the only Indian in Rangoon who could be ruined for indiscreetly associating with a Caucasian woman?"

Knowing now where she was headed, he sat down with an angry, feral gleam of teeth. "You will say nothing, not of tonight and not of Bangkok, unless you wish your family name to be dragged in filth."

"My father and I have shaken off more filth than you can shed, Mr. Prasad. I think you are less accustomed to humiliation."

"You think I will keep silent for fear of you?" he sneered. "I am respected. You and your renegade lover are reviled throughout the city. Who will believe anything you say?"

"Come, Prasad, you should know a whore's word will carry farther than a prince's if the court is British, the whore white . . . and the prince"—she shrugged—"not." She roasted more opium and offered him the *chandoo.* "Besides, I do not ask your silence. I merely suggest you tell the truth. In turn, I will refrain from going into detail about your part in the auction." He eyed the *chandoo* as if it contained poison. "I might even paint you as defender of a helpless woman you did not recognize until Ram Harley's lawyer summoned you to testify for the defense." She smiled. "Wouldn't you like to be a hero?"

He fingered the *chandoo,* his thick lips curving with unpleasant insinuation. "What would I gain from you?"

"Nothing. I won't pretend an eagerness to share your bed now any more than I did in Bangkok." She paused. "But Ram Harley is in a position to pay you well."

Prasad laughed derisively. "He is ruined, Khandahoor burnt. Everyone knows it. Do you take me for a fool?"

"Do you take Harley for one? Why would a man like him place all his eggs in one basket?" She smiled languidly. "If you will pardon the Western expression."

He took a tentative puff from the *chandoo,* his eyes bright with pricked greed and suspicion. "Why are you going to trouble for Harley? Unless you were his willing paramour?"

"Paramour." Her eyes twinkled with amusement. "What an endearingly old-fashioned word, Prasad. You *are* gallant, after all. So many others have used less delicate terms to describe what they believe to be my relationship to Harley." She toyed with her veil. "I will not bore you with a description of that relationship, for you may hear it soon enough in court. Suffice it to say, I owe him a debt that I hope to repay. Also, by diminishing his so-called guilt in the matter, I reduce my own embarrassment."

"And if I do not choose to cooperate?"

She shrugged. "You will have your day of fleeting but unprofitable revenge in court . . . and I will have mine, after which you will have to leave Rangoon with accompanying reports of mishandling your office to your lord in Kashmir."

Frowning, he puffed thoughtfully on the *chandoo*, then his eyes slid to Saw. "She is discreet?"

"Completely."

"I wish to be paid in advance."

Lysistrata shook her head. "A percentage only, to show good faith."

"How much in total?"

"Say, a thousand pounds," she suggested, calm in the knowledge he would never see more than a pittance of that.

He set the *chandoo* pipe down and played with a stylet. "Five thousand."

"No. Your testimony is a convenience, not a necessity."

He flicked the stylet aside. "Very well. Have you the money with you?"

"That would be silly of me in this district, wouldn't it? Mr. Leacock, Harley's barrister, will pay you after privately hearing your testimony."

Prasad sighed so profoundly the effect might have been lugubrious if not for the weasel alertness of his eyes. "I see I am to be disappointed once more, Miss Herriott." He rose. "That is fortune. I shall await Mr. Leacock's pleasure."

Encouraged by his agreeable mood, Lysistrata risked a probe. "Mr. Prasad, Ram Harley will also pay well to learn who made him appear a murderer."

Quick fear flickered in his eyes as he almost recoiled. "I know nothing of that," he muttered, already hurrying out of the place.

With a scorpion's stare, Ma Saw watched the door close and pronounced her only comment of the evening. "He knows all."

"And if he is so afraid, he will never testify openly for Ram," Lysistrata said tiredly. "He must hope to gain only the advance payment."

"Perhaps," was the terse reply. "And perhaps he only came to hear your plans and put you from your guard."

"Yes, I have thought of that. An unpleasant notion, it is, too." Lysistrata's fingers drummed on the table. "Are you a fair shot, Ma Saw?"

Ma Saw cast a derisive glance toward the door. "For that, yes."

Lysistrata rose. "Not for him. Prasad is too sly for 'that.' " She adjusted the sari. "Let us hope Harry is no laggard."

The alley remained deserted, but the women had no more than settled in the carriage when the far door was jerked open; Naswral appeared in its dim block of coach light. "I must speak with you, Miss Herriott," he said urgently in better English than she had suspected he knew.

"Of course, what is it?"

"Not here." His gaze raked the alley. "Too dangerous. I will meet you where the *Rani* used to be moored."

"Very well."

The next instant, he was gone. Ma Saw caught up the reins. "I do not like that man. The scar gives him one face too many."

Ram lay still on his cot. The pinpoints of silver light in the tin roof seemed larger tonight. Within his immediate range of vision were 183 of them. If he turned his head, the angle blurred the holes together; trying to make them tally was maddening, so he had not counted more than once beyond the ones just over his head. Focusing on the holes diverted him from other, pointless thoughts. Like his imaginings of Lysistrata with Harry. That they would not come together while he lived was scant comfort. The inevitability was there; it wormed into his brain until he could almost see them making love.

Take Harry's place and touch her. Even now he felt the whisper of her hair across his mouth. In spite of himself, his head lifted. Only to be sharply wrenched back by a choking noose. No dream, it jerked tight as he tore at it. His eyelids flew open; in place of Lysistrata's face was a grinning skull. A steel garrote was biting into his throat, an explosion in his brain deafening him with a silent scream beyond sound, "She's mine!"

Mist idled over the water lapping against the raw, new wharf of *Rani*'s long-vacant berth. Lysistrata leaned against a piling. She felt weak from lingering illness, from dull anticipation of the horror approaching Ram, from defeat. She had tried not to think of him in prison, yet her mind and heart had been shackled to him, for they shared the chains of the same injustice, the same desperation. If he loves me, might I better bear this? Or is the torture the more exquisite? If he loves me not, shall I mourn the more to have twice lost him? The harbor damp seemed to mold the glittering sari veil against her lips, her eyes, obscuring all sense of human shape until she felt unreal as any wandering spirit. Yet she was not alone. Watching the mist was like watching a drift of ghosts, among them the sails of the lovely *Rani*. She saw again Ram's dark, wet profile as he swam silently through the lake mist of Khandahoor. Anira's insane mask, distorted and murderous. Now, reflected in the water, another face with a scar that parted it from jaw to brow. She turned to see Naswral.

He shifted restlessly. "Where is your maid?"

"Was she not in the carriage?" No one approaching the area could miss seeing *her*. If Naswral meant well—and Harry had suggested he might not—he would have had no reason to investigate the carriage.

He missed the implication. "I did not see her." Then added, "This is not a safe place for a woman alone."

"Then why did you suggest it?" she replied in Hindi.

Surprised, increasingly wary, he eyed her. "It is assuredly private. You meddle with more danger than you know, Miss Herriott. Some wish your silence."

"I was told that repeatedly before the last time I disappeared. Who proposes I evaporate again?"

He scanned the wharf. "Are you not concerned for your maid, Miss Herriott?"

"She is attending to a private matter," Lysistrata murmured. "Need I elaborate?"

Unexpectedly, he flushed. "I am sorry. I merely wondered—"

"Where she was. I am wondering what you have to say."

He hesitated, then began, "You must stay away from Gopal Prasad and desist from speaking in the British court. No good can come of it. Prince Ram Kachwaha is to hang. It is agreed by the British, and those . . . of less obvious power in Rangoon."

"Those less obvious ones, who are they?"

"I dare not know. I have only heard what is said in the evil places of the city."

"Such innocence, my friend," she purred, "for one who looks so knowledgeable. What are you afraid of? That those who hire you will discover you are unreliable?"

"I . . . do not understand."

She threw back the sari veil. "How long have you been informing on Ram . . . to those obscure ones? How long will you prattle here before you dare linger no longer waiting for Ma Saw and attempt the errand Gopal Prasad gave you?''

He stiffened, then a mirthless smile distorted the scar like a second glance. ''You are clever, Miss Herriott, but still as rash as when you came to Ram Kachwaha's house during the cholera. This time, you will not be found when you disappear; but do not worry, I *will* find your maid.''

''Others know I met with Prasad tonight. He will be instantly suspected.''

''I would not hire to that fat toad,'' Naswral sneered. ''He has become dispensable. It is only fitting that he entangle himself in one of his greedy schemes.''

Playing on his indignant pride, Lysistrata laughed softly. ''So you intend Prasad to be blamed for my death. You are the clever one . . . but then you did not think of this scheme, did you?''

Piqued, he frowned. ''That does not matter. I will execute it.''

''What if Prasad does not keep silent when the authorities question him?''

Scarface grinned. ''He will find it difficult to speak with a garrote about his neck.''

''As Sein found it difficult to speak with a mouthful of tamarinds. A unique touch.'' She eyed him as if with new respect. ''Your work, too?''

He laughed. ''Behind those smiling whore's lips, the bitch had naught but a sour tongue. Yes, I killed her, with pleasure.''

''But Ram, who took you in, why betray him?''

He spat contemptuously. ''He has no pride, that *feringhi*'s cur. He is lower than I, yet expects me to be his servant. Kali curse him, the British will soon give him the dog's death he deserves.''

She felt sick. ''The ones who ruined Ram, do they hate him as much as you?''

He laughed mockingly. "You should know."

As she stared in puzzlement, he drew his knife, a slim *kris*. His taunting smile faded to a thin, curved line.

"Wait," she murmured, "if you will forgive a woman's endless curiosity, the women on the *Star of Calcutta,* were they also your doing?"

Perhaps she did not show enough fear; perhaps Naswral sensed he had already said too much, for he was done with talking. "Enough! Prepare the way for your mongrel lover, harlot." The knife glinted in a swift movement, then froze; Naswral saw a pistol muzzle glint under the filmy black of the sari.

"Even a harlot cannot miss at this range," Lysistrata warned. "You have been clumsy tonight. Are you so afraid of failing your errand that you cannot think clearly?" The pistol lifted slightly. "Tell me who sent you and you may go. If you leave the city tonight, you will shortly have nothing to fear."

"You lie!"

"Try me. You have nothing to lose and much to gain."

Shaking his head, he backed toward the wharf godowns. "You dare not kill me. You need me alive."

"Why? For a public confession you dare not make?" Her voice lifted. "It is already public. I have witnesses at hand, you see."

The leather baggage flap swiftly unfurled at the rear of the carriage. Harry swung his legs out, pistol in hand. "Besides," she added as Harry advanced, "I need only put a bullet in your knee to keep you conveniently close."

Desperation twisted the assassin's face. He whirled and flung himself toward Harry, knocking him down as Harry's pistol discharged into the dirt. Afraid to fire for fear of hitting Harry, Lysistrata tried to find an opening as they scuffled with flailing fists and rolled in a dark blur

against the wharf planks. Then, with his knife haft,
Naswral clouted Harry across the head. Stunned, Harry
fumbled at the Untouchable's throat. The knife reversed,
drove down. A shot rang out. With a cry of pain,
Naswral caught at his arm, wrenched away from Harry,
and jumped into the harbor. As Lysistrata hurried toward
Harry's sprawled body, Ma Saw ran to the wharf edge,
pistol nosing after the fleeing murderer. Lysistrata, seeing Harry merely dazed, helped him sit up. "Damn," he
muttered, "my skull feels like a smashed coconut."

Ma Saw, reluctantly realizing Naswral was out of
reach, returned to them. She looked down at Lysistrata's
drawn face. "I am sorry. I could not see well enough to
stop his escape without killing him."

"No," Lysistrata agreed dully, "you could not and I
could not. He gambled on that." Naswral was more useful alive than dead, but to allow him the opportunity to
murder again was a hideous responsibility. Ram, too,
might pay dearly for their evasion of justice.

That payment began the next day. When Harry's efforts to aid a felon guilty of killing his fellow officers
came to the notice of his colonel, he was grilled, then
given duties to usurp his time until the trial. He could no
longer hope for advancement in the army. All because of
a man he hardly knew and scarcely trusted. Yet he only
felt relief. How long would he have gone on, he wondered, with a career already tarnished by his country's
greed? Indefinitely, perhaps.

He was galled by his inability to help Ram. He realized
far better than Lysistrata that Ram had been doomed
since the failure of the China Expedition. Once his reliability had become suspect, it was a short step to becoming dangerous to British interests. Now they would
exterminate him as coldly as an irritating mosquito. Even
if Naswral were convicted of the murders, Ram would

still hang for killing the British agitators in the Shans. Of that, he was guilty, and for that he would die.

Then, in conversation with Leacock, he found even the formality of a trial to be uncertain. Ram's condition was deteriorating due to the foul prison conditions. If the trial were more than two days away, he would not be fit to take the stand.

Despite orders, Harry went immediately to the prison. As the heavy gates of its high, stone walls swung open, two shackled Burmans with digging tools preceded a pair of Kachins stumbling in their irons and sweating under a bamboo pole that sagged under the weight of a shrouded body. With rifle prods, Sikh warders herded them into the jungle. "Which prisoner?" Harry quickly asked a warder.

"Number twelve." The man flushed slightly. "I do not remember all the number, sir. There have been very many dead these last few days."

"Epidemic?"

"Riot, *sahib*, sir."

After another hard look at the burial detail, Harry headed for the warden's quarters. The warden, at accounts in his office, was calling out a supply inventory as a Chinese trustee convict shuttled through an abacus at a writing desk. "Sorry to interrupt, Warden," Harry told him as he was ushered into the office. "I met a burial party at the gate. Not Ram Harley's, surely?"

The warden, a gray-haired man with muttonchop whiskers and break-veined face, flipped through some papers until he found a list. His thumb slid down it. "No. Not this morning." He looked up. "But it might have been. We had a bit of trouble Tuesday night."

"A riot, one of the warders told me."

"Yes, well, I wouldn't say it was all of that." The warden tossed the list on the desk. "More of a minor brawl. One of those pirate fellows you brought us went into the hospital with a festered leg sore from his irons. Witnesses in the hospital ward say Harley tried to kill him. Harley claims it was the other way around; that the pirate crept up on him as he was sleeping and tried to strangle him with his identification collar. Whichever way it was, Harley must have gone berserk. The pirate has a cracked breastbone, collarbone and jaw, and a damaged windpipe. Harley has only a cut neck, though nearly every stitch your surgeon put in him was wrecked when he went at the pirate.''

"I very much doubt if Harley was the instigator in this, Warden. Boh Myin's crew hate his guts. I'll warrant your witnesses were pirates?''

"About half.''

"And the others hate Indians because they feel the guards give them preferment, eh?''

"Possibly.'' As if bored, the warden dropped into his chair. "It doesn't much matter who began it. Disruptions aren't tolerated here. Both Harley and the pirate did a turn in the box to discourage future incidents.''

"The box? You don't mean—'' Harry's head snapped toward the window facing the dusty work yard and the cramped tin boxes that forced any man put into them to crouch and fried his mind to incoherence. "You put wounded men in *those?*''

"Only for twelve hours. Less than that would have been mistaken by the prisoners for weakness.''

Harry's temper nearly fired to the explosion point. "May I remind you, sir, these men are not proven criminals?''

"If they were, Leftenant,'' replied the warden calmly, "they would likely be dead. Twenty-four to forty-eight hours is the usual penalty for fighting.''

Harry let out his breath with a hiss of exasperation. "May I see Harley?''

"Of course." The warden rose and waved to the door. "Only, you will find him uncommunicative."

"I daresay," Harry snapped. Spinning on his heel, he left the warden and impassive secretary to their lists and clicking abacus.

The tattered canvas awning which stretched out to shade the hospital added to its gloom. After the bright sun, Harry squinted in the half-dark as he went down the row of cots with their sweating, nearly immobile occupants and faintly rattling chains. Ram had been moved to the far end; the first man in the line, Harry assumed, was the pirate who had tried to kill him. He winced, thinking of Ram's fate had he been put unconscious into the prison cage with the Boh's men from Buddha's Skull. When Harry came to the end cot, he assumed at first he had made a mistake, that no man could be so changed in a fortnight. This bearded, bandaged skeleton was not Ram; yet, when the skeleton opened black, appraising eyes, he saw it was Ram. "Good God, man," he muttered, "Leacock never told me half of this."

Cracked, blistered lips curved ironically. "He's a good lawyer. Lighter did well by you."

"I'll have Lighter over by noon to look at you," Harry said tersely. "If he's not free, then Herriott."

"You sound angry, Leftenant," Ram rasped. "Haven't you learned life in the Orient is cheap? The British innovation has been to make death efficient. That box out there can do in a few comparatively kind hours what starvation and disease take years to accomplish."

"Damn you," Harry said vehemently. "You and your damn *que será, será!* Aren't *you* angry!"

Ram thought of the swinish incompetent who ran the hospital, who dispensed platitudes and privately peddled medical supplies in Rangoon. Of friendless, godless, hopeless men who twisted in chains, and of trustee orderlies who stole their rations. Of a prisoner stifled in his sleep who was found at dawn with tattoos picked of their decorative bits of gold. Of dreaming of a throttling hangrope and finding the nightmare reality, the hating face of death gaping down as he clawed at a steel ring slicing into his throat. Of feeling his chest tear, and listening to howls for his blood as he forced the steel away and smashed a wild blow into the nightmare. Of being forced into an oven in a white glare of heat under a brazen sky. Of craving water until his skull seemed to shrivel and exploding pain in his chest made him retch emptily. Of being ravished by a green-eyed woman of flame, of writhing under her searing touch as she lifted him beyond hideous ecstasy to agony. He had bitten blood, yet had not shrieked, had not whispered the secret of his exalted damnation, his beguiling hell. He thought of all the horrors he would not share. The hate he would not dilute. Pity Harry who did not know a monster when he saw it, but took it to his bosom.

"Anger would be a fatal luxury in my position, Harry."

The young Englishman sighed, then pulled up a camp stool. "I suppose you're right. I'm sorry. I'll try to keep my head."

"Have you found any evidence?"

"None that'll do much good in court"— Harry smiled wryly—"but enough to convince me you're no monster."

Ram's answering smile was oblique. "Then keep Lighter and Herriott away."

"What?"

"The hang-rope is a trifle crude. I prefer to expire . . . naturally."

Harry's eyes flicked to the gouged, blood-dried groove on Ram's throat. "I can see where you might . . . but I can't just let you die of neglect. I wouldn't do it to a dog."

"No, you wouldn't," Ram said softly. "You've a heart of mush, Leftenant."

"You think me weak?" Harry inquired stiffly.

"I would the world were porridge from pole to pole." Ram held up a hand. "Now get out of here before you're court-martialed."

Harry gripped his hand tightly. "They can only shoot me. My taste in executions is less particular than yours. See you in Sessions."

Lysistrata sat immobile, watching a wagtail building a nest from the bedroom window. How sure the bird seemed that tomorrow would see the nest done and a need for it; that the fragile bower would stand whatever human or natural elements might bring against it. She felt as naive and transient as that nest, that she was blindly performing a useless function in the face of certain destruction. Yet, as if driven by the same instinct that governed the bird, she would continue to seek justice as long as Ram was alive.

As long . . . Weeks? Days. The British were in a hurry for their hanging. She had not needed Leacock's insistence to realize she must not go near Ram, yet all her soul strained to be with him. Restlessly, desperately, she pondered. Was there nothing else to do, no one else to help him? Then she thought of a slim, unpleasant possibility.

"Help Ram Harley? Miss Herriott, your tasteless effrontery never ceases to amaze me. I am still in mourning for my husband." Evelyn Chilton's mauve-gray widow's weeds admirably suited her, and the pose of righteous indignation struck in her drawing room would have impressed a Drury Lane theater audience.

Lysistrata coolly surveyed her. "I had not noticed. You must be vastly relieved." She sat down on the sofa as if intending to take root. "I gather his demise followed hard on the heels of Ram's exile."

"I was more fond of Nigel than you may think, and Ram Harley caused his death," Evelyn said coldly. "In the strain of pursuing the investigation of Harley, my husband suffered a fatal hemorrhage."

"What had General Chilton to do with a civil matter?"

Evelyn's eyes narrowed. "Ram Harley's crimes are not limited to civil ones."

"They were at the time your husband died, if indeed Ram perpetrated them at all." Lysistrata paused. "Unless they intend to blame him for the failure of the Yünnan Expedition?"

Evelyn gazed at her speculatively. "Ram told you of his part in that?"

Lysistrata sidestepped the compromising answer that promised questions by Lord Anthony if Evelyn saw fit to relay it to him. "Hardly. Ram would never be so indiscreet, but some of the gentlemen who called on me last spring were more confiding. The expedition was never a secret among the most prominent Rangoon merchants. If it failed, they can hardly lay the cause at Ram's feet. It was a reckless, hazardous, unlikely venture. And rather a complex failure to delegate to a man of your husband's capabilities and discernment. Did Lord Anthony assign him to sort through the heap of difficulties surrounding the venture to discover its point of collapse?"

"As a matter of fact, it was Nigel's idea. He didn't like being taken in."

"What made him think he was?" Lysistrata reviewed the expensively furnished room. She had been there to a dinner and piano recital before the cholera epidemic. Several antiques and a French tapestry had been newly acquired. The general did not seem to have lost a great deal.

"For one thing, Ram invested nothing in the venture."

"Did he ever pretend he would?"

Evelyn slowly walked about the room. "A message he was to have sent to the warlord Yin Chang in Yünnan was never delivered."

Lysistrata laughed. "Anything could have happened to such a message between Rangoon and China. Besides, how can Sir Anthony be certain it didn't reach its destination—simply to be ignored or regarded with hostility? This is all rather thin. Surely they have something else?"

Evelyn smiled faintly. "Very little. Ram is too clever."

"You must admit he is too much so to leave a murdered woman in his own bed."

"So you think someone is out to destroy him," Evelyn mused. "I begin to see your point."

Bleakness entered Lysistrata's voice. "In such a climate of hostility, Ram will most certainly be hanged if Lord Anthony cannot be persuaded to review the evidence. He won't listen to me now, but he might listen to you." Her voice steadied. "Ram *is* innocent."

"Possibly, but Sir Anthony does not gladly take advice from women."

"He takes it from his wife. Surely Lady Mary owes you some favor."

Evelyn smiled. "Possibly." She dropped to the sofa next to Lysistrata and carelessly crossed her legs. "This is beginning to intrigue me. Besides furthering the dubious cause of justice and attracting undue embarrassment, tell me, just what advantage do I gain from aiding the most unpopular man in Rangoon?"

"You gain Ram," Lysistrata said briefly, "for however long the arrangement mutually suits the two of you. After the trial, I shall return to America."

"I fear my romantic interest in Ram Harley has

waned, Miss Herriott,'' Evelyn returned with a calm smile. "However, I do owe him a service or two." Her fingers formed a pyramid. "Very well, I will do what I can, but I promise nothing, you understand. Also, you should know Sir Oliver Triton, the barrister for the prosecution, has asked me to testify for the Crown. Perhaps, in the meantime I ought to call on my maid, Anne O'Shaunessy, and try to persuade her to recollect some clue—Has the poor girl been able to recall anything so far?"

Lysistrata shook her head. "Dr. Lighter says she wants no part of remembering the past. You might do as well to call on Claus Bettenheim . . . delicately."

Evelyn's head slowly turned. "Claus? Whatever for?"

"He is involved in the drug trade. He may know the identity of Garotte, who is now rumored to control the opium trade in Rangoon. Perhaps he is himself Garotte."

Evelyn smiled faintly. "Stolid Claus?" She shrugged. "Very well. I shall have a talk with him."

Lysistrata hesitated. Evelyn was being remarkably cooperative. Was it because she still feared potential blackmail from her affair with Ram? She decided to give the woman the benefit of a doubt. "Thank you. I admit I didn't expect you to be so generous. I fear I have greatly underestimated you."

"Yes, you have," Evelyn replied coolly, "but I shall be delighted to forgive you once you are on the ship for America."

That night, Lysistrata received a note. "Anne remembers nothing. Claus knows nothing. Sir Anthony is reviewing the evidence."

CHAPTER 16

Monkeys and Parrots

> *Tho' many a light shall darken, and*
> *many shall weep*
> *For those that are crush'd in the*
> *clash of jarring claims,*
> *Yet God's just wrath shall be*
> *wreak'd on a giant liar . . .*
> ALFRED, LORD TENNYSON

Lysistrata was unsurprised at Evelyn Chilton's news of Anne and elated about Bartly, but suspicious of Bettenheim's oblivion. If he was as powerful as Ram suggested, he would have heard of Garotte, but how could he be induced to admit it? Without leverage, she could not maneuver him like Prasad—not that blackmailing Prasad had done any good, for he was on his coward's way back to India. Yet . . . perhaps she did have leverage; the thought of using it was revolting and might give Bettenheim the advantage, but with Ram in the shadow of the hang-rope . . .

Finally she decided. No one must guess her intention, least of all Harry and her father; not even Ma Saw, who had become more than a housekeeper to John Herriott during the past year. Despite their discretion, Lysistrata had perceived tiny clues: their similar thinking and private smiles, the doctor's fresh lapel flowers each day, and Ma Saw's abandonment of gay earrings for a modest pair of pearls. Once Lysistrata might have been shocked, not only at a liaison between middle-aged people of such disparate backgrounds, but because it ran against expectation. Young, delectable Sein was an obvious target for the passions of an older man—she was understandable; Ma Saw's charms were less evident. Now, Herriott's affection for Ma Saw's loyalty, kindheartedness, and practical intelligence appeared completely natural. The strong physical appeal of Ma Saw's vivacity and earthy wit would outlast Sein's shallow beauty; sadly, had already outlasted it.

And if Claus Bettenheim was Garotte, her own life might be as short as Sein's.

Sure his loyalty lay with Ram rather than Dr. Herriott, Lysistrata asked Masjid to deliver a message to Bettenheim. After hearing it, he made no comment, but performed the task. Now I know why Ram employs him, she thought: silence *is* golden.

Masjid returned late that afternoon. "I presented the message to Mr. Bettenheim at his plantation, Missy. Only one servant saw me."

Understanding, she nodded. "What is his reply?"

"He has agreed."

"Good," she lied. "Now I must beg, borrow, or steal a dress."

"We have nearly a week to manage that, Missy."

"We, Masjid? And why a week? I suggested this evening to Mr. Bettenheim."

"There is no need to attempt more alone in this venture than you must. I will procure a suitable gown. As for the rest"—he paused—"Mr. Bettenheim regrets this evening is inconvenient. Thursday next will be free."

"Free!" She snorted. "Thursday will be three days

into the trial! He's trying to make me squirm by shoving me farther into a corner.''

"Dealing with Mr. Bettenheim is never pleasant.''

She bit her lip. "I don't trust him. If he has some of his box-*wallah* friends with him on Thursday, and then appears for the prosecution, he could accuse me of trying to influence a witness.'' She began to pace. "He could prove it and wreck Ram's case at a blow.''

"Perhaps his lust will not brook company,'' mildly suggested the Indian.

"Once, perhaps; not now. He hates Ram more than he fancies me.'' She paused. "What if . . . Masjid, tell him I accept Thursday. At nine. That hour will leave him sure of my willingness to accommodate him.''

Masjid's head cocked with a small smile. "You do not plan to keep that assignation; am I right?''

"You are right. I shall arrive early: several evenings early. Just which one you may help me decide by persuading a member of his kitchen staff to tell you what night our troll will dine alone.''

"I excel at such persuasion, Missy.'' The big Muslim smiled benignly.

Sandwiched between Harry and her father, Lysistrata stared blankly at the black-robed backs of Leacock and John Markham, the barrister appointed by the Law Society for the bandits' defense. Overhead was the plaintive creak of *punkahs* plied by white-jacketed Burmese boys. Lethargically, they tugged cords tied to their big toes as they gazed with droop-lidded curiosity at the restless, tight-packed crowd in Rangoon Sessions court. Smaller fans of every shape, color, and size spasmodically fluttered or sluggishly batted, according to the boredom and sex of the owner. Brass Netherlander chandeliers hung over sere teak benches on an uncarpeted floor. The walls, half-sheathed in teak, were light gray with crack-trailed, yellowed moisture stains. On the east side, louvered windows were shuttered against the morning sun, making the large room more airlessly appropriate to stoic, jowled Queen Victoria's portrait over the justice's bench. As if to defy Her Brittanic Majesty, garish parrots in the courthouse lawn palms saucily screeched at somber humans who, mopping their brows, silently cursed the heat for which they were ill adapted and dressed.

With perspiration coursing down her spine, Lysistrata glanced up at the icy, patrician Bartlys. Evelyn, modish in dove silk, sat beside them in an upper tier that surrounded the room. Just below the Bartlys were the prosecution barristers, Sir Oliver Triton and his assistant, Andrew Guess. Lysistrata fixed attention on her foolish, fingerless, mesh gloves. Demure in mud-colored serge, Leacock had chosen to make her appear a step from the dead. She was to play a part; the trick was not to behave like one of the cynical parrots who mocked this murderous farce.

Where was Ram? Why hadn't the prisoners been brought in yet? Her thumbnail plucked at the mesh across her palm until waiting another humid second seemed unbearable.

A side door opened; she stiffened as sandaled and unshod feet shuffled on the bare floorboards. Careful to appear only casually interested, she quickly scanned the prisoners, who were parted into two lines by rifle-wielding Punjabis and sent into the prisoners' box. Some had to be brusquely helped into place. Uniformly swarthy, dirty, and skimpily clad, they returned the spectators' stares with the sullen hostility of caged animals; like caged animals, they had the capacity for making the ones uncaged feel both fortunate and insignificant. Bewildered, alarmed at not finding Ram, Lysistrata scrutinized each man more carefully; when she recognized him, both Harry's and Dr. Herriott's hands crushed down on hers as she started. If she had not once seen him wasted by cholera, she would never have known the white-faced, skinny, bearded creature with black eyes roweled into bruised, hollow sockets. He looked at no one, his once trim, black head set high with a stiffness as unnatural to him as the vermin and filth that covered his unkempt hair and raggedly clad body. For an instant, the memory of him urbane and aristocratic needled her mind.

I brought him to this, she thought hollowly behind her rigid mask of detachment. They must drag his pride in the dirt before they kill him, to reassure themselves he's something less than human from the gutter. How can he not hate them? Hate *me* for being part of them?

Ram knew where she was. He felt her urgency, the near-wild pain in her. Be still, his mind murmured to her, you did not bring me to this so much as you imagine. Now you must think clearly and let go cleanly. Do not be afraid of them. Do not fear me.

Lysistrata felt silence brush her mind, a stillness almost as if it were willed from outside her. Ram had once led her to this kind of stillness. Then taught her to find her own way. She must find it now, whatever its terrible path.

That path began quickly to take shape. After the jury was selected, she dismissed them in a fatalistic glance. Box-*wallahs*. They might be open-minded about murder, but never piracy that preyed on their purses.

"Silence!" In the wake of the clerk's abrupt command, only a last-minute ruffle of papers at the bewigged barristers' bench broke the hush.

Then, the entire court rose as in a startling blaze of scarlet, the Honorable Lord Justice Winston Parke-Allis, with the curls of a Queen Anne wig flowing like a ram's charge, strode briskly from his chambers into the courtroom. He dropped into the high-back chair behind the Queen's Bench on the dais with an air of finality. "Good morning, gentlemen." He nodded amiably to the court, then to the barristers. "Will you approach the bench?"

Briefly they discussed the probable length of the trial, and the barristers returned to their places. After the jury was sworn in, the counsel for the prosecution outlined the Crown's case. The charges were piracy, kidnapping, and murder. Richard Harley, also known as Ram Kachwaha, was included by association with the pirates at the time of the raid—his alleged crimes glossed over and buried under theirs. When the charges of sedition and murder of the two British officers were not mentioned, Lysistrata felt a spark of hope that the prosecution's case against Ram might be weaker than Leacock imagined. But Ram's eyes reflected no encouragement and that spark faded as quickly as it had quickened. Crimes against the military did not come under civil jurisdiction. The army was waiting its turn. Even if Leacock managed to snatch Ram from Sir Anthony's jaws, the army would never let him go.

The first witnesses called for the prosecution were representatives of English nationals and Sittang villagers who presented affidavits of evidence supporting the charges against the pirates. As each one was called, Leacock rose after Markham's cross-examination to ask if the witness was prepared to positively identify his client as a pirate. If the witness was tempted to do so—as Ram was now indistinguishable from the Boh's men—Leacock briskly pummeled his testimony until the witness had to admit he did not absolutely remember.

At length, late in the afternoon after the luncheon recess, Lysistrata's turn came. As hers was the clinching prosecution testimony with the most recent concrete evidence of piracy and abduction for ransom, the prosecution—aware she might later testify for Harley's-defense—steered clear of Harley's part when questioning her. Though her emotions were on tight rein, she gave no sign of her inward turmoil. Calmly, briefly, she gave the salient facts pertaining to the abduction by Boh Myin, then faced Leacock.

Leacock thumbed a fold of his robe as he studied Lysistrata, less to gauge her control than to give the jury a moment to feel her importance as a witness. "Miss Herriott," he began at length, "do you recognize the defendant, Richard Harley, among the prisoners?" She indicated Ram who gazed impassively at her. "Was Richard Harley in any way responsible for or a participant in your abduction by Boh Myin?"

"He was not. He and Boh Myin were mortal enemies of years' standing." She described the destruction of Khandahoor. When she came to the part about everyone's being killed except her and the Malagasy, the jury's ears strained.

Feeling Triton's frown behind his back, Leacock went on. "When did Harley arrive at Boh Myin's camp?"

"Just before Leftenant Harold Armistead came to state the British offer for my return."

"Was he alone?"

"Yes. Except for a number of Nagas he had placed about the fort to prevent the pirates from escaping."

"Did he speak openly with Boh Myin?"

"Yes."

"What was the conversation between them?"

She told them, concluding with Ram's offer of the *Rani* for her release.

Leaving the jury to digest that, Leacock nodded satisfaction. "No further questions at this time."

Triton took his place. "Miss Herriott, did you at any time see your abductors in Rangoon?"

"No."

"Then you cannot be sure they are not Harley's hirelings. Did you actually see any Nagas about Buddha's Skull?"

"No, but . . ."

He swept on. "Did Richard Harley mention any cause previous to the destruction of Khandahoor for enmity between Boh Myin and himself?"

"Mr. Harley did not take me into his confidence."

"Yet you say Boh Myin thought your abduction would bring Harley to the rescue. That suggests more than common intimacy between you and Harley, does it not?" It was time, he decided, she was warned to watch her tongue.

"I believe Mr. Harley would risk his life for any woman under his protection." She eyed him flatly. "As a gentleman, he is not a niggler."

"So you considered yourself under his protection," Triton shot back, a trifle nettled. "May I ask why and to what extent?"

"He rescued me from slavery and kept me alive for nearly a year when I might have been several times killed. To me, that is a considerable extent."

Triton decided his track of questioning had better shift, lest Harley shortly appear the knight-errant. "Isn't it possible, Miss Herriot, that Harley's antagonism toward Boh Myin was as recent as the raid on Khandahoor because his ally in crime had turned on him?"

Leacock shot up. "Objection, my lord. My learned colleague is calling upon the witness to draw a conclusion."

Justice Parke-Allis nodded. "Mr. Leacock has a point. The jury will disregard that last question."

They wouldn't, of course, so Triton was satisfied. "No further questions at this time, my lord."

Leacock rose as if suddenly remembering something. "I beg the Court's indulgence, but I should like to direct a few additional questions to Miss Herriott. Miss Herriott, did you see evidence that Mr. Harley's Nagas were present and hostile to Boh Myin?"

"Yes. When Boh Myin expressed doubt as to whether

Mr. Harley had employed Nagas to cut off his escape, Mr. Harley directed him to send a man to the fortress gate. He returned with two sacks containing twenty heads.'' She continued through audible gasps and hasty exits of several spectators. ''They belonged to men the Boh had sent out to ambush the fieldpiece the British were moving to the fort. Boh Myin also attributed the burning of his war canoes to Mr. Harley.''

Triton sourly regarded her. Not having expected an invalid prisoner to have seen activity outside the fort, he had thought himself secure in that area. Leacock had jumped the opportunity to make an important point in Harley's favor.

''In regard to your knowledge of past animosity between Boh Myin and Richard Harley, did the Boh ever specify a long-standing reason why he hated Mr. Harley?''

''He did.''

''And that was . . . ?''

Ram's lips curved a hair's breadth when she looked coolly at Triton. ''Mr. Harley's friendship for the British.''

The British commandant who had directed the raid on Buddha's Skull was questioned the next morning. When asked for evidence of Nagas, he had seen nothing for the gruesome sacks had blown up with the magazine. He had seen smoke from the burning war canoes, later their charred remains, but had no idea how they were fired.

''Could the magazine explosion have been caused by a British shell rather than Richard Harley's efforts?'' inquired Triton.

''Possibly.''

''Did you observe Harley's behavior during the battle?''

"Only at the last. He was attempting to escape the fort."

"Did he make any effort to aid your men?"

"On the contrary, he struck a sergeant, Sergeant Mules, with his rifle butt."

"Thank you, Colonel Crew." Triton gave Leacock a triumphant look. "Your witness, sir."

Leacock strode forward. "Colonel Crew, you have stated you saw Richard Harley strike a sergeant during the fray. Did the sergeant attack him first?"

"Sergeant Mules attempted the first blow, yes." The colonel leaned forward. "But Harley was dressed much like Boh Myin's crew and clearly trying to get out of the fort."

"Would you say Richard Harley resembles the other defendants in that he looks like a native at this moment?"

Crew coldly glanced at Ram's gaunt face. "I would."

"Under the circumstances you have described, you would hardly pause to question his hostile intentions in a battle, would you?"

"Not after seeing him strike one of my men, no."

"And if you had not seen him do so?" Leacock pressed. "How would you have reacted?"

Crew became a trifle impatient. "It was no time or place to split hairs. I thought we had established that."

"Yes," Leacock mused, "it would seem we have, haven't we? Richard Harley may have simply defended himself against soldiers, *any* soldiers inclined to attack him without splitting hairs over his innocence." He toyed with his fee bag. "Is the sergeant dead?"

"No."

"Severely wounded?"

"He suffered a concussion."

"How soon did he return to duty?"

"Three days after the raid."

"Then the concussion was slight, wouldn't you say?"

Triton popped up. "Objection. Mr. Leacock is leading the witness. Colonel Crew is not a doctor."

"My lord," Leacock countered, "Colonel Crew is a professional soldier obliged to judge the fitness of his men for duty with or without the benefit of medical advice. I propose he is qualified to express a reliable judgment in this instance."

"Mr. Leacock, this court is not equipped to estimate Colonel Crew's lay knowledge of medicine," Parke-Allis stated. "Objection sustained."

"Then, by the court's leave, my lord, I should like to rephrase the question. Colonel Crew, was Sergeant Mules given the chief medical officer's leave to return to duty?"

"He was."

"Then according to professional medical opinion, Sergeant Mules's injury was slight?"

Crew's arms wearily folded across his chest. "It was."

"Had Richard Harley the time and opportunity to kill Sergeant Mules?"

"He had the time." Crew smiled ironically. "He may not have had the cartridges."

"Still, you did not at any time see him fire his rifle at a British soldier, did you?"

"I did not."

"Did he engage any of the Boh's men?"

"I personally saw no such instance."

"No further questions of this witness, my lord."

When Guess, Triton's assistant, produced several British soldiers with similar testimonies, Leacock boiled them down to the admission that Harley had not fired at them and had done equal damage to pirates who blocked his path to freedom. "I suggest to the court"—Leacock's forefinger leveled at Ram—"Richard Harley found himself in certain danger of losing his life to British troops unable . . . or unwilling to 'split hairs,'

as Colonel Crew put it, over his innocence." He gestured
to the grim band surrounding Ram. "And even more certainly, he was threatened by Boh Myin's pirates, whose
entrapment and defeat he had helped assure. I suggest
Richard Harley had good reason to escape both factions,
for he was perilously caught in the middle of their quarrel." Leaving the pirates' scowls at his client as an un-
derscore, he resumed his seat.

"I should like to call Leftenant Harold Armistead to
the stand." After Harry was sworn in, Triton began.
"Did you see the sack of pirate heads Miss Herriott so
colorfully described in Boh Myin's stronghold?"

"Yes."

"Did you know them to be the work of these Nagas no
one who was present at the fort and now in this court
ever saw?"

"No. At the time, I assumed the Boh had ordered several of his men executed for some reason."

"At the time . . . Has anything occurred since to
make you now believe otherwise?"

"Both Harley and Miss Herriott told me Harley had
the pirates killed. I believe them."

"Why do you believe them?"

"Myin must have had a watch on the river and he had
to know we were bringing up a howitzer to destroy the
fort. He had time to run, yet he didn't. It seems possible
he was prevented by the Nagas, who, I might add, are
never seen by anyone unless they wish to be."

"But you admit, sir, that aside from Harley and Miss
Herriott's testimony, all this is sheerest supposition?"

"Yes."

"So we are back, as *always*, to relying solely on what
Harley and Miss Herriott say happened in the fort." He
looked skeptically at the pair. "Harley is on trial for his
life, and Miss Herriott spent nearly a year with him under
circumstances which still leave a good deal to be ex-

plained.'' He turned back to Harry. "Have you personal reasons, Leftenant, that might lead you to believe Miss Herriott and the defendant?''

Harry looked at Triton squarely. "I do, sir. Richard Harley once saved my life at dire risk of his own. And I have had sufficient acquaintance with Miss Herriott to know she ill tolerates anything less than truth and justice." He smiled. "Mr. Leacock can fill the court with witnesses who will testify to that.''

Triton gave him a tolerant glance. "Isn't it possible that by saving your life, Harley might have seen an opportunity to profit by your gratitude at some future date?''

"I suppose so.''

"You have known Miss Herriott for some time, you say. In fact, you squired her to several events last year, did you not?''

"I did.''

"Were you then, or are you now in love with her?'' Triton asked sharply.

"Objection!'' Leacock bounced up. "This is irrelevent and harassment.''

"My lord, I wish to show this witness's testimony is grievously biased.''

His eyes oddly gentle, Ram seemed to settle into his chains as the barristers argued. Finally, Parke-Allis ended the matter. "Objection overruled.''

Harry gravely regarded Lysistrata, who met his gaze with sadness tinged with some bewilderment. "I am and was then, I think, though I was unaware of it.''

"No further questions.'' Triton gave the jury and spectators a conspiratorial smile. "We all are aware of the reliable judgment of a man in love.''

Leacock let the laughter die down completely before he addressed the witness. "Leftenant, have you any facts to refute my learned colleague's estimation of your testimony?''

''I do, sir. Love does not necessarily make a man blind. May I point out to Sir Oliver and the court that it was a pirate spear I pulled from Richard Harley's chest.''

Beneath his genial air of amusement and anticipation of victory as the court closed for the day, Triton knew the case was going badly as far as Harley was concerned. Leacock's unperturbed, sleepily benevolent expression confirmed his fears. Next morning, if he did not request an audience with Justice Parke-Allis and press for a separate trial for Harley on the Rangoon kidnap and murder charges, Harley would be automatically absolved of them along with everything else if found ''not guilty,'' and the jury would have to acquit him so, for Triton could not hammer at Lysistrata's testimony without endangering the rest of the prosecution case. He could almost hear Leacock's summation. Given her testimony, Harley could not be proven guilty beyond reasonable doubt. If Sir Anthony wanted Harley, he would have to see his can of worms opened in a new trial.

That evening, Triton held conference with Sir Anthony, who reluctantly concluded the Rangoon murders had been too publicized to be shuffled off. The worms must have their day to crawl about in the sunlight.

Next morning in the Lord Justice's chambers, Leacock, hoping Sir Anthony would back off, fought to keep the trial moving. At length, Justice Parke-Allis made his decision. The trial would continue. Triton was at leisure to explore the charges he had largely ignored, but he warned him not to try the court's patience.

So Triton was stuck with the thorny problem of Lysistrata. The only way to get to Harley was to bring her testimony in his behalf severely into question. Finally, assuming sufficient testimony had been given by witnesses other than Lysistrata to hang Myin's pirates, he decided to go for broke.

After looking at Ram's taut, skeletal face day after day, Lysistrata was even more determined than Triton. When she arrived home after the trial that day, a shocking fuchsia dress was spread in a fan of silk and crystal beading on her bed; on the skirt lay dove silk slippers, opal jewelry, and a filigree fan. Under the pillow was a note: "Tonight." Herriott and Ma Saw, their own nerves raw from the trial and badgering journalists, were understanding when she pleaded a headache and retired early. She very nearly developed a headache from trying to hook the florid dress: its willowy former owner was similar in height but had the curves of a pencil. Lysistrata's bosom looked as if it might explode from its scant confinement; her hips split the seams. Only the waist was comfortable; as Bettenheim was unlikely to invite her to dinner, it would probably be the only part of her untourniqueted by the evening's end.

She debated changing to native dress, then decided against it. Ram had once mentioned Claus was replete with *bibee* mistresses. In that respect, Masjid, despite his efficiency, had made a Muslim's natural mistake in the wardrobe. He had provided a *bibee*'s underwear; in other words, none. As Boston underthings were not cut for the vivid dress, the clinging silk would leave nothing to the imagination of a two-year-old male, much less Bettenheim. With a sigh, she sat on the bed to put on the slippers. Breath compressed until she turned scarlet; stitches popped like tiny champagne corks. Less yielding than the stitches, the small shoes were unwearable. She pawed her own worn kid slippers from under the armoire with a chair leg and put them on.

The jewelry was magnificent: the earrings large opal studs tasseled with diamonds, the pendant throat as large and seductively designed as la Chilton's once envied

baroque pearl. An opal and diamond bracelet circled her
wrist. As a final touch, she pinned a jeweled ostrich
plume in her upswept hair. Ma Saw would have devised a
more dazzling coiffure, but Bettenheim was unlikely to
notice. If his conversation was not leveled at her décolle-
tage, she would be much surprised. She peered through
the fan filigree. Forget the dress and try to look like . . .
she searched for a word. Limp lily. He'd never believe
it; besides, he detested watercress. Vulnerable, even
desperate—Yes; she would not even have to act. She
picked up the reticule to carry evidence if she could get at
Bettenheim's desk; papers would never stuff down this
bodice!

As she debated whether to take off the shoes to sneak
out of the house, a soft whistle sounded outside a window. She went onto the verandah to cautiously look
down. Masjid stood below. He pointed up at a roof
beam. Hanging from it on a pulley rope was an apparatus
like a child's swing. When she stared at him as if he were
demented, he urgently indicated Herriott was reading in
the drawing room and Ma Saw busy in the kitchen; there
was no way to get past them undetected. Swallowing,
she grabbed the swing. After all, she had crossed Shan
gorges with less support . . . and landed in the river.
Moments later, with a horrified gasp, she plummeted
downward.

Masjid, embarrassed as he helped her from the swing,
muttered a tactful apology as to the amount of silencing
oil on the pulley. He had not remembered American
ladies were heavier than tiny Indian ones. As they stole
away from the house, he was even more upset at her refusal of escort to Bettenheim's. "Masjid, while Mr.
Bettenheim may not have European friends in attendance
tonight, he will have servants able to describe me in court
if this interview goes awry. Tampering with a witness
will be ill taken. If they identify you as well, matters will

be worse. I have American citizenship, my womanhood, and Mr. Bettenheim's lecherous reputation for some protection. You, on the other hand, are a stalwart Muslim male. If called to the stand, you cannot languish and bat your eyes at the jury. You can merely look affronted and lie. Being affronted will be insufficient refutation, and lying against your religion.''

"Missy, lying to *feringhis* does not count and Bettenheim is a determined man.''

"If you are saying I may be raped, I *have* been raped; and for all practical purposes, am little the worse for wear." At his shocked expression, she patted his shoulder. "If Bettenheim kills me, we may be sure he is linked with Garotte and you may tell the Sikh police so when you advise them where to find my remains.''

He glared. "This is not amusing, Missy!''

Though giddy with tension, she sobered for his sake. "No, Masjid, you are quite right—but you do see the point about your not being seen?''

Grudgingly, he growled assent. "Come, the victoria is by the rear gate. You can drive it?''

"Of course," she fibbed, having driven nothing larger than Harry's dogcart.

With a dubious grunt, he took her to the carriage, handed her up, and closed the curtains. The result was sweltering privacy. He handed in a hand-drawn map. "Bettenheim's toddy palm plantation north of the city. Use the Prome Road out of town." A derringer slapped into her hand. "If you must use the gun, use it quickly. The reticule will help to muffle the sound." He handed her extra cartridges. "The derringer's range is very short—only a few feet—and it has a hair trigger, so handle it gently.''

She slipped the gun and cartridges into the reticule, then gravely looked down at him. "Thank you, Masjid. You've been a good friend.''

"You may not believe so after this night." He handed her the reins. *"Inshallah."*

When the victoria lurched forward with a jolt, he sighed, but bit his tongue.

The stifling ride to Bettenheim's plantation was long; before she reached Rangoon's outskirts, Lysistrata's wrists and arms felt the unaccustomed strain of driving a pair of lively nags. Her gloveless hands soon blistered. Despite the heat, she could not risk opening the carriage curtains for fear of being remembered by coolies and *gharry-wallahs* who strayed the roads. La Chilton, who sometimes drove her victoria alone, was evidently not so flimsy as she looked.

Idly, Lysistrata wondered if the lusty Bettenheim had ever been one of Evelyn's lovers. She very much doubted if Ram had been the brunette's first clandestine bedmate. Evelyn was capable of wriggling out of widow's weeds and into a lover's arms before the last clod of earth dumped on poor, silly Nigel's grave. As the victoria rattled along the rutted, dusty road past water- and moon-glossed paddies, she wondered if Nigel had stumbled upon anything when prying into the *Star of Calcutta* murders; even if he had, he might not have guessed it. But what if Evelyn had? What if Bettenheim *was* her lover and she'd told him? What if the maid, Anne O'Shaunessy, had overheard more than she ought? That might explain Anne's being included with the murder victims. It didn't explain why Evelyn would persuade Sir Anthony to review trial evidence that might backfire on Bettenheim and herself. Unless . . . She thoughtfully clucked to the horses. *Unless* Evelyn somehow wanted to get Bettenheim into trouble. Why, then, claim Bettenheim knew nothing of Garotte? She eased the victoria over as an ox-driven *gharry* lumbered by. Puzzle pieces danced through her mind, but no matter how they were put together, did not quite fit. The idea of collusion between Bettenheim and Evelyn was tempting, but sheerest speculation; less, it was wishful thinking.

And no amount of wishful thinking would put Ram in Bettenheim's place tonight. They were so different: Ram with his clean, spare quickness and beautiful, lucid mind; Bettenheim with his heavy, brutal bluntness and narrow bigotry. God, how could she endure Bettenheim after Ram, choose death after life? Strange, that she'd once accused Ram of existing only for death. How wrong she had been. He had endured and taught her how to do so, despite impossible odds. Tonight, those lessons would be sorely tested.

Rare lights among scattered villages, then the lights of Bettenheim's plantation glimmered across tree-banded paddy water. The bungalow and outbuildings were half buried in palm-topped black groves of mango and jack. Pale under a low-hanging moon, the diked road arrowed through the paddies and groves to the bungalow's front door. Only a light crunch of pebbles under the carriage wheels carried over the water with its rasping crickets and full-throated frogs, but Lysistrata took care to tether the carriage out of earshot of the buildings. Besides a verandah gaslight, only lights in the kitchen at the rear of the bungalow and a few servants' quarters burned. No servants were about; only the soft sound of a flute came from the bungalow under its few spindly palms. Reticule clutched in one clammy hand, battered slippers in the other, Lysistrata mounted the verandah steps. The boards squeaked underfoot, then the front door smacked open with an ear-shattering crack and her hand nearly drove into the reticule for the derringer.

"All right, you filthy, sneaking . . ." Bettenheim shoved the black bore of a Martini-Henry at her face. The gun lowered a fraction. "Who the hell . . . ?" Abruptly, a laugh barked as he recognized her in the dim light. "You're a trifle early, Miss Herriott. I'm hardly dressed for the occasion." Clad in unbuttoned native jacket, loose-fitting breeches cut off at the knee, and pattens on bare feet, he seemed amused by her survey of the welter of fur on his thick, barreled chest and belly.

With a tempting curve to her lips, Lysistrata hung a slipper on his gun barrel. "We shall have no need of formalities, this evening, Claus. I have never had champagne drunk from my slipper; it is a notion I often entertained these last months at dreary Khandahoor, particularly when I thought of you."

He looked at her sardonically. "So the wog prince gave you a dull time, did he?"

"Certainly he was not much given to champagne," was the dry reply. "I have rarely seen a man more monkish." Her lower lip protruded sulkily. "If you're going to be equally boring, you may give my slipper back."

Mockingly, he surveyed the clinging gown, then lifted the slipper from the gun barrel with his little finger. "Forgive me, Miss Herriott. Do come in." He stood aside and, with exaggerated courtesy, held open the door.

With the sway of hip that had fascinated the auction in Bangkok, she sauntered into the bungalow. The flute, which had briefly ceased when Bettenheim had charged the door, tootled on as if the musician were accustomed to violent interruptions. Without asking permission, she followed the sound through the empty drawing room to the rear of the house. With an amused look and the Henry crooked through his elbow, Bettenheim followed.

The bungalow was smaller than the one where the previous year's bird-shooting had taken place, but solidly furnished with a few heavy Chinese and German pieces upholstered with ornate brocades. Aside from a sepia photograph of a stiffly posed Prussian artillery company which featured Bettenheim in a tight, high-collared tunic, no personal pictures hung on the walls. Guns were mounted everywhere along with dusty heads of deer and boar, two tigers, and a mammoth rhino that looked as if it might collapse the wall. Feeling as if she were in a mausoleum, she murmured admiringly, "You appear to be a crack shot, Claus; in fact, adept at everything." Her voice lowered, design transparent; it did not matter if he believed her, only that he feel he had the upper hand. "I should have paid your advice more heed last spring had I not been such a ninny."

"Oh? And are you wiser now?"

"Perhaps not," she said softly, "but sadder. . . . I have learned to my rue that you were right, right about everything." She turned to suddenly face him in the narrow corridor outside the flautist's door—so suddenly, he nearly stumbled into her. She lightly rested a hand on his bare chest, then quickly drew away as if unsure of her boldness. "I . . . I came here as much as anything because I wanted to tell you . . . how deeply I regret rejecting your proposal."

"I see," he drawled, "and now you hope I might like to resume negotiations in that respect."

She turned her back on him and opened the door. The bedroom held a worn divan, an ornate bed with gaudy cushions, and a tarnished brass hookah on a low table. "No," she replied, surveying the two dusky girls who gazed back incuriously. Both were naked, under fourteen, and heavily drugged. One had a cut on her upper lip that turned into a bruise that stretched to her ear; the other had swollen lash weals from shoulders to knees. The flautist, an old man in turban and *pasoh*, glanced up, continued his monotonous playing. "No, Claus," Lysistrata said huskily, "I suggest no such thing." She gave him an appraising look. "I do, however, have a proposition that might interest you."

"And what might that be?" He tossed the shoe onto the table.

She dropped the mate beside it. "Send them away."

He shrugged, then after replacing the Henry in its rack, clapped his hands. Followed by the old man, the girls drifted from the room. Bettenheim closed the door and leaned his bulk against it.

Trying to look only normally uncertain, Lysistrata put distance between herself and Bettenheim with a nervous laugh. "Indeed, I see I did not realize the depth of my naïveté. Was it you who beat those girls?"

"Wogs need a firm hand"—his thick lips curved—"like horses and mean-tempered women."

"I see," she answered shakily, inwardly feeling more mean-tempered than he could imagine. "Perhaps our failing to marry is just as well. I would not have made the most tractable of wives."

He studied the quick rise and fall of her bosom, the wide eyes. "Oh, we would have come to terms, I think." His head cocked. "You said you had a proposition?"

"I—" She hesitated, hands fluttering.

"You've changed your mind?"

Her eyes flicked toward the bed, then his heavy, mocking face. "No," she gulped. "No . . . I haven't." She began to pace the room as if it were a cage, yet shied from the rattan-screened windows as if not quite willing to escape. "I suppose you think . . . everyone thinks I'm rather a soiled dove now."

"I do not think of birds at all except for hunting. As for everyone else . . ."

Now was the time to appear less limp and more of a challenge. "I'm not," she said vehemently. "I'm as virtuous as when I left Rangoon."

He laughed.

"It's true," she snapped. "Harley bought me at auction before . . . well, you know. And *he* was the perfect gentleman! I think he's too much in awe of European women to lay a finger on one!"

"You seem so disappointed," he jibed, "I might half believe you if I were not well aware Harley is not in awe of women of any tint."

"Well, whatever his usual habits, he didn't touch me."

Musingly, he regarded her petulant face. "And the Boh's men?"

"I was rattling with malaria."

"Very well"—he smiled—"you are virtuous."

"Don't look at me like that, you . . . !"

"Ah, this is the fiery Lysistrata Herriott I remember. Are you no longer frightened of me?"

She took a deep breath as if to calm her temper. "I didn't come here to quarrel, Claus. I want to be . . . friends."

"Friends?"

"Very well. More than that." She moved toward him, her walk taking on a seductive swing. "What does it matter if I'm still a virgin when no one believes it? I reap the blame, but enjoy none of the pleasure." Pausing a breath from him, she looked up, her green eyes defiantly tempting. "I intend to have the pleasure and more to make up for my losses." Her finger traced his stubbled jowl. "I can excite you more than those children can," she murmured. "Or a woman, say, like Evelyn Chilton." He looked startled, dubious, then smug. There's one answer, she thought triumphantly. "You've only to teach me what you want, Claus; as I've wanted you. Not those mealymouthed fops in Rangoon." Her finger moved to his brutal lips. "You cannot imagine what I've thought of doing to you."

His hands closed hard on her shoulders, his mouth grinding wetly as his tongue stabbed into her mouth. Feeling as if she would retch, she pressed against him. Cupping her hips, he thrust obscenely against her until she pushed away. "Claus, please. You're making me faint."

"So much for your virginal imagination," he rasped, mockery now modified by lust. He reached for her again and she backed.

"Wait. I must have more than tonight, Claus. I want to start fresh."

His eyes narrowed. "You expect money?"

"Only passage to Australia for Father." She smiled alluringly. "I want to stay with you."

"How do I know you're worth it?" His thick fingers beckoned. "Come here."

Instead of moving, she unpinned her hair and shook its brilliance about her pale shoulders. The ostrich pin stayed in her hand, plumes wafting across her slim thighs. "I'm worth more. If Harley hangs, the remains of my reputation hang with him. Staying in Rangoon would be impossible, even as your mistress. I've no intention of ending in a dirty brothel."

He stared at her bronze-gold hair against her white shoulders; then his eyes moved over her magnificent breasts to the taunting plumes. "What do you want me to do about it?"

"Simply suggest to Sir Anthony that someone other than Harley might have staged the *Star of Calcutta* murders." She shrugged as if the name had just come to mind. "That mysterious Garotte, for instance."

The daze of lust left his eyes, which turned coldly speculative. "I don't know that."

"You know Harley didn't kill those women," she said bluntly, hoping for some spark of anger, guilt, even murder in those pale eyes. "He isn't that stupid, that crude." There was anger. She probed harder, reversing tactics to gauge the effect. "It took someone clever, like this Garotte. Someone subtle, powerful . . . who moves in Rangoon's underworld like some phantom dragon."

The anger remained, nothing else. "Perhaps you should try to seduce Garotte if you think he has the answer to those killings."

Her eyes flashed. "I'd give myself to the devil to blow the prosecution's case sky-high! You have underworld connections; Harley said you did. Whatever you know, I'll buy."

"Just to whitewash the scandal?" He shook his bullet head. "You'd have already left Burma if you only wanted to get clear. That miser Lighter would have come up with ship's passage for you and your father just to be rid of the smell of you. You stayed too long at the fair for the prestige of his hospital not to be tainted as well." He grabbed her wrist. "You stayed. You also rutted with a dirty, half-breed wog. You think I'll bargain for a slut to save poaching scum like Kachwaha?" His meaty hand hooked her bodice and ripped. She gouged his face with the jeweled pin, and he howled as his jowl split scarlet. If she had wanted murder in his eye, she had it now. That intent saved her life.

As his hands closed about her throat, driving her down, a shot cracked through the wet matting screen at her back and raked his neck. His head jerked up, then he dropped atop her, carrying them both to the floor. Still not sure of what had happened, she lay stunned under his leaden weight. Leaving her exposed to the marksman, he rolled under the bed as a second shot from the opposite window smashed the oil lamp, snuffing the light. Hearing Bettenheim go for the Martini-Henry, Lysistrata scrambled up, snatched the reticule, then ran like a rabbit through the house.

Gunfire sounded behind the building, then again as she crossed the moonlit lawn to the copse where she had left the victoria. Just in front of her bare, flying feet, a shot fountained the dusty expanse fringing the lawn. Oh God, my shoes, she thought in near hysteria; I've left my shoes like an idiot Cinderella! Now Bettenheim has absolute proof I've been here! She whipped loose the tether, lunged into the victoria, and gave the startled horses, already frightened by gunfire, a nasty crack of the whip. The horses bolted down the paddy road. By the time they raced past the plantation's border marker, they were pursued in fact: racing hoofbeats pounded after them. Lysistrata let them have their heads and prayed one of them wouldn't break a leg in a rodent hole. On the other hand, to break her own useless neck might be just as well. She was nearly allowed that luxury as the carriage swerved off the road into a palm grove. The traces rattled and the carriage swayed alarmingly, ricocheting off palms and bouncing off scrub roots.

Suddenly, a huge shadow loomed out of the moonlight and hurtled into the carriage. Seeing the shape of a turban about a dark head, she screamed and slammed her arm across the man's head and shoulder as he dragged the reins from her hands. Yelling a curse, he hauled the horses in by brute force as she flailed. "Missy, stop it! By Allah, it is I, Masjid!"

With a gasp, she sagged against him. "Masjid. Oh, thank God. I thought you were—"

"Naswral?" He grimaced. "That one is now being pursued across the paddies by the irate Mr. Bettenheim. Do you hear those dogs?" In the distance receded a high, excited howl of a hunting pack.

"You mean . . . ?" She dazedly shook her head. "I don't understand. What happened back there? Who was shooting at whom?" Her eyes cut sidelong at him with a sudden glint. "What are you doing here?"

"You will learn all, Missy; only have patience. We dare not linger here." Swiftly, he dismounted the carriage, unhitched the horses. From under the carriage baggage flap he drew an extra bridle and a voluminous black sari. He tossed her the sari, then his knife. "Quickly, split your dress for riding and put the sari on over it.'' In less than a minute, he had a carriage mount bridled, with her aboard it. He leaped upon his own horse, the extra animal in tow. ''Come!'' He led her deep into the grove, cut at a canter along a wide bund across a shimmering rice field, then into black jungle beyond. ''As they are after that filth, Naswral, we are safe now, I think,'' he said, slowing the pace to a trot. ''It does not matter if they find the victoria.''

Impatiently, she pushed back the sari veil as they threaded through the tangle onto a crooked path. ''Now can you tell me what's going on?''

''Indeed. My role is simple. With all respect, I apologize, but my lord Ram's orders supersede yours. I followed you and kept watch through Bettenheim's window lest you need assistance. When he seized you, I was about to leap into the room and soothe his temper.'' He tapped the gun butt on his hip, then looked thoughtful. ''At that moment, a pistol fired through the opposite window. Lest it fire again, I shot out the gaslight, then rushed around the corner. The assassin was already headed for a pineapple field at the rear of the house. As I pursued him, he turned to fire and I saw Naswral's evil mark in the moonlight. His shot missed; so I fear, did mine. When I heard Bettenheim shoot at you, I turned from the chase; fortunately for me. Had Bettenheim decided to pursue Naswral rather than you, I should very likely have been caught in their crossfire.''

''And you said this was simple,'' she sighed. ''How do you suppose Naswral knew I was coming to the plantation tonight?''

''A paid tongue may wag two ways, Missy, but by sunrise it will be silenced. Naswral will not chance being traced.''

''Bettenheim probably thinks we tried to murder him,'' she observed glumly.

"Probably."

"That's not the worst, Masjid. Now he has positive proof I was there. I left my shoes. I practically made him a present of them."

"Just so, Missy." He smiled benignly. " A present."

CHAPTER 17

The Verdict

But often in the din of strife,
There rises an unspeakable desire
After the knowledge of our buried life,
A thirst to spend our fire and restless force
In tracking out our true, original course
MATTHEW ARNOLD

"Sastri Potaswamy." The jury, hopeful that final addresses would begin that day, squirmed wearily as the meek clerk crept to the stand. In moments, as he haltingly described the gory discovery of the dead and mutilated women aboard the *Star of Calcutta*, they sat alert and appalled. The following testimonies of the port authority and police commissioner filled in ghastly details, which Triton milked to the dregs.

Leacock asked only a few questions of the commissioner in order to ascertain that the killer seemed methodical rather than mad and the crew dumbfounded at seeing the victims' remains debarked. He was particular about Sein's condition. "Her death wounds were basically similar to the *Star of Calcutta* women, the stroke in the throat penetrating from left to right. Does that suggest the killer was right-handed?"

"It is quite likely."

"And the degree of physical abuse?"

"Aside from their starvation, Miss Sein was far more bruised than the other victims and suffered several broken teeth from a blow which preceded her mouth being forced full of tamarinds. Blood and hair were found only under her nails."

"Hair color?"

"Black."

What was Leacock up to? Lysistrata uneasily wondered as she watched the jury scrutinize Ram. Why was he fitting Ram's physical characteristics neatly into Naswral's role? While Naswral might be clumsy, he was hard as hell to drag into court for an accounting. Her fingers began to drum against her reticule.

Shortly, they began to drum faster. Lysistrata, though unsurprised to see Claus Bettenheim appear as the next witness for the prosecution, was infuriated by his testimony. Fortunately, the court—still somewhat sympathetic to Ram after Lysistrata's and Harry's accounts —was only a few degrees less irritated. While Claus was adroit, under Leacock's needling he became blatantly hostile and so crudely bigoted even those who patronized the natives with contempt were uneasily impatient with him. His diatribe, which Triton, sensing the court's mood, tried to stem, was filled with so many innuendoes and rumors about Ram's alleged criminal ties that Leacock bounced up at every third minute with an objection and the judge reprimanded both Claus and Triton with the warning that Claus should be fined for contempt and removed from court if he continued in such a manner. Through it all, Ram showed no more reaction than a deaf man. Still, Claus managed to do considerable damage to his defense. The jury might be charged to forget hearsay slander against him until Justice Parke-Allis turned blue, but they would not forget. While Claus, like Prasad, did not dare bear personal witness about the slave trade, he brought out Ram's connection with the merchant Wa Sing, who was a known slaver, and claimed he had himself seen the *Rani* debark slave cargo in Tennasserim and load slaves in Madagascar. He mentioned Harley's association with several brothel owners in Rangoon, Singapore, Djakarta, and other ports throughout the Indian Ocean, Andaman and South China seas.

A string of dockhands, seamen, and "eyewitnesses" followed. Under Leacock's grilling, they proved to be either Claus Bettenheim's employees or suspiciously vague about their livings. Claus's credibility sagged, particularly when Leacock suggested a great many merchants and less respectable sorts stood to profit by Ram's ruin. He cited high inflation of drug prices since Ram's competition had been eliminated. When Leacock returned to his place, Lysistrata whispered, "I think, sir, while Claus may have helped to ruin Ram, he has handled this too badly to be Garotte."

"I agree," murmured the barrister.

At length, the prosecution's case for slave-trading foundered because no "respectable" citizen could afford to be too knowledgeable about Harley's criminal activities without bringing himself under scrutiny of the law.

Bettenheim, mottled purple with anger, sharply beckoned Triton to his side. As they whispered together, Lysistrata sighed, "And now comes the tale of Cinderella."

She was accurate. Bettenheim had saved his surest gun.

"Mr. Bettenheim," began Triton, "are you acquainted with Miss Lysistrata Herriott?"

"Intimately," sneered Bettenheim.

"How . . . intimately?"

"I was her frequent companion last spring. You might say I was her lover."

Lysistrata's eyes narrowed to icy slits as Ram straightened a fraction, his face like a death's-head.

"Have you seen her recently?"

"Last night. She came to my toddy plantation after bribing a servant to make certain I was alone. She was dressed like a whore and made me a whore's offer to lie to the commissioner about her latest wog bedmate, Kachwaha."

"Objection!" Leacock snapped as Ram's hands knotted in their chains.

"Sustained!"

"When I refused"—Bettenheim stubbornly plowed on, jabbing a finger at his ripped face—"she gave me this, then had another wog try to shoot me." He recounted the murder attempt. "She took off in the dark, and I and my *shikkars* chased the wog until sunup. No good. When we got back to the bungalow, we found old Ko Phan, one of my manservants, split ear to ear. Likely he was the—"

"Objection," Leacock cut in wearily. "Sheer supposition."

"Sustained."

"Well, I have something to say that isn't supposition!" snapped Bettenheim. "Miss Herriott left her calling card last night. Sir Oliver . . ."

The barrister nodded to his assistant, who soberly produced a pair of slippers. "Mr. Bettenheim, are these the slippers you say belong to Miss Herriott?" After Bettenheim described finding them, Triton turned to the bench. "I ask the court's permission to admit these shoes as evidence of the defense having attempted to tamper with a witness for the prosecution."

Parke-Allis studied the little defense barrister's calm face. "Mr. Leacock?"

"I assure the court neither I nor Mr. Markham have countenanced any effort to alter Mr. Bettenheim's testimony outside this courtroom," replied Leacock as he rose to his feet. "I have no questions of Mr. Bettenheim at this moment; however, with the court's permission, I should like to recall Miss Herriott to the stand."

Sir Oliver made a mock-gracious bow. "My lord justice, I defer to my learned colleague."

Sir Oliver resettled, Lysistrata advanced to the stand, her face as serenely innocent as Leacock's. She dared not look at Ram. "Miss Herriott"—Leacock twiddled with his fee bag—"are you aware of the seriousness of tampering with a trial witness?"

"As a lay person, yes. I really have no idea of the exact penalty involved."

"Did you visit Mr. Bettenheim last evening with any intention of persuading him to testify in Mr. Harley's favor?"

"I did not. Not only was I unaware Mr. Bettenheim was to appear for the prosecution until he was called in that capacity into the dock this morning, I knew he would not speak in behalf of any person of color, however certain he might be of that person's innocence." Lysistrata's voice held the ring of truth. She never *had* expected Bettenheim to help Harley, only that he might be startled into revealing some clue either of guilt for himself or someone else.

"Have you ever attempted to harm Mr. Bettenheim in any way?"

"Certainly not."

"What of that scratch Mr. Bettenheim purports you gave him?"

"Possibly Mr. Bettenheim was pressing his attentions upon a reluctant lady?"

"Objection!"

"Miss Herriott, was Mr. Bettenheim ever, as he claims, your lover?"

"Never," she replied coolly. "As many reputable

gentlemen of the city can affirm, we were never alone together except on one occasion.''

"And that was?"

"For twenty minutes in the drawing room of my home last July while I refused his proposal of marriage.''

Bettenheim, flushed with irritation over having his rejection made public, glared like one of his sullen trophy boars.

Leacock turned her over to Triton. The prosecution was direct. "Miss Herriott, did you or did you not go unchaperoned to visit Mr. Bettenheim last night?''

"I did not." Masjid had been a very proper chaperon.

He paced like an impatient hunter. "Have you a fuchsia silk gown set with crystals in your wardrobe?''

"I own no such dress.''

Abruptly changing tacks, he turned on her. "Did you not wear such a dress in an effort to seduce Mr. Bettenheim?''

"The notion of having carnal knowledge of Mr. Bettenheim is as revolting to me as his person.''

"Did you know one Ko Phan in Mr. Bettenheim's employ?''

"To my knowledge, I have never seen the man.''

"He plays flute, you lying trollop," snarled Bettenheim as Lysistrata's eyes widened, realizing why the flautist had been so unruffled at her appearance.

Parke-Allis banged the gavel. "Ten pounds, Mr. Bettenheim! Be silent!''

Triton sauntered to the prosecution desk, and with a forefinger hooked one of the slippers that reposed thereon. Extending it with a cat-that-ate-the-canary smile, he strolled back to the dock and held it in front of Lysistrata's nose. "Would this slipper be yours, Miss Herriott?''

"It would not.''

"Would you care to try it on?''

She stared him in the eye. "If you like. Would *you* care to do the honors?"

He smirked. "Delighted."

She descended the stand, daintily lifted her skirts slightly, and held out the appropriate foot. Triton unlaced the black boot with a flourish, then thrust on the slipper. She winced. *He* winced. His proposed evidence was two sizes too small. "They do not fit," blandly observed Parke-Allis.

"Ah, no, my lord," replied the kneeling Triton with an awkward smile, "they do not appear to . . ."

"That's impossible!" yelled Bettenheim, jumping up. "She left them in my room . . . she left—" Confused realization dawned in his mind even as Parke-Allis waved abruptly to a pair of burly Sikhs who hustled him from the courtroom. As Bettenheim passed the docket, Ram gave him a bone-tight smile.

Lysistrata had an idea Bettenheim still didn't have it quite right, thanks to Masjid. It had occurred to him she had deliberately left him slippers of a wrong size to wreck his account of her visit. It probably had not occurred to him the slipper she had hooked onto his gun on his dimly lit verandah was not one of the pair found in his room. Devious Masjid had known the dove silk slippers he had originally given Lysistrata would not fit, had indeed intended them to mislead any court inquiry. Tucking them in his sash, he had taken them to Bettenheim's. Observing her barefoot in Bettenheim's room and guessing she had forgotten her own kid shoes when fleeing the bungalow, he had quickly returned to the deserted bedroom when Bettenheim's attention focused on Naswral, retrieved her shoes, and left the silk ones.

Serenely, Lysistrata regarded Bettenheim's empurpled face, then the dove silk slipper half-wedged on her slim, stockinged foot. "Do you mind, Sir Oliver? It does pinch frightfully."

* * *

Trial proceedings done for the day, Triton stalked into his offices, threw his gold-headed cane into its Delft stand. Nicking the rim, it bounced out and clattered to the floor. With an exasperated snort, he dropped heavily into his desk chair. On the morocco-trimmed desk blotter rested a scrawled note. "Throw the two wog wenches into the dock! They *saw* the bitch! Bettenheim."

And the court would see them, thought Triton in disgust: a pair of barely pubescent, dull-eyed creatures, their so-called father, the third witness, murdered—however one looked at it—for betraying his master. Even if everything happened as Bettenheim claimed, the old man had obviously hoped Bettenheim would have his brains blown out. Those girls would join the ranks of Bettenheim's other "reliable" witnesses Leacock had picked to pieces in court. Triton firmly crushed the note into a hard ball and hurled it toward the Delft stand. It centered, spun, and dropped neatly.

Evelyn Chilton was first witness the next morning, and the prosecution climbed onto solid ground though she gave Triton no more information than he demanded. She stressed that Ram's association with her husband and her had been on pleasant terms. When Triton, seeming to sense she was not saying all she might, continued to prod, she repeated, "As I said, sir, I know nothing of Mr. Harley's business affairs. In my presence, he was always a perfect gentleman and completely charming."

"Isn't it true that your maid, Miss Anne O'Shaunessy, also found him charming . . . and possibly less than a gentleman?"

"Objection!"

"Sustained."

"Let me phrase the question more directly. Mrs.

Chilton, did you ever observe Mr. Harley flirting with Miss O'Shaunessy?''

Evelyn hesitated. "Indirectly, perhaps."

"Mrs. Chilton, did you or did you not state to your husband and the Bartlys when Anne O'Shaunessy disappeared that she had had a flirtation with Harley?''

"I simply remarked that he seemed interested in Miss O'Shaunessy."

"Interested," Triton repeated succinctly. "Did you not also remark that Harley knew three of the five women kidnapped?''

Evelyn made a nervous gesture. "I . . . was merely thinking out loud at the time. One is inclined to speculate, no matter how foolishly, upon scandal or crime—"

"Yet your speculation, in this case, proved to be accurate. Sein, the Burmese girl found in Harley's bed, was one of his several mistresses, according to the deposition of his houseman. Your maid was, at the very least, acquainted with him. And"—he looked pointedly at Lysistrata—"we must not forget Miss Herriott.

"Would you say, Mrs. Chilton"—he smiled disarmingly—"as a disinterested party, that Harley is a man attractive to women?''

"Objection," put in Leacock. "I fail to see what Mr. Harley's physical appeal has to do with the case."

"With the court's permission, my lord," Triton countered, "I wish to show Harley to be capable of persuading, even luring women to behave indiscreetly, to put themselves at his mercy."

"You speak as if he were some sort of monster!" Evelyn protested.

"Exactly."

Justice Parke-Allis glanced at Evelyn. "The witness will refrain from unsolicited remarks. And this line of questioning, Sir Oliver, can only lead to supposition. Objection sustained. The jury will ignore remarks concerning Mr. Harley's charm,'' he added dryly.

Lysistrata's nails bit into her palms. For someone attempting to help Ram, Evelyn had managed to undermine his cause.

Leacock gave her hand a quick, consoling pat. "We've had a touch of luck," he murmured. "Mr. Harley's former houseboy was scheduled by the prosecution for the dock this morning. He has disappeared— whether prudently of his own accord or with our friend Naswral's assistance, I do not know. In any case, he cannot now describe your attending Harley during the cholera, which could only have done our case ill.''

No, she thought, now he cannot describe me. And he cannot describe Evelyn. Could she have bribed him to leave the city? Lysistrata glanced up as Evelyn resumed her seat. Evelyn's eyes met hers, read their speculative expression. Her lips curved in a small smile, whether of apology or mockery, Lysistrata could not tell.

As the days crawled by, Ram, increasingly gaunt and pale, seemed oblivious to the proceedings. His eyes were black, blank wells; his only, rare reaction sardonic amusement. As if he were already dead, Lysistrata thought anxiously. For God's sake, how long can this go on?

At last the turn of the defense came to present its own witnesses. Doctors Lighter and Herriott testified to the invaluable medical-supply service Ram had rendered to Rangoon at far less than the remuneration he might have demanded and, in some circumstances, for nothing. Lighter also mentioned his saving of Harry's life at dire cost to himself. He produced hospital inventory lists which proved that ships of Ram's which had been "seen" with slave cargo in certain ports had actually been elsewhere—and had returned with drugs which either could not have been obtained in those ports or returned in the time span which had elapsed after setting sail from Rangoon. Triton was too wise to prod the prickly Lighter, but he sharply questioned Dr. Herriott about his daughter's acquaintance with Harley prior to her abduction. "Was Mr. Harley a frequent guest in your home?"

"He came to the house only four times, three of them connected with hospital affairs, once to escort my daughter and me to a *pwe.*"

"Did he ever call on your daughter in your absence?"

"Never."

"Are you certain?"

"My daughter would have mentioned it if he had. She knew I welcomed his visits."

"Did she . . . welcome his visits?"

"No. At the time, she avoided potential suitors of any kind."

"Yet she became for a brief period popular in society with a large following of gentlemen callers."

"Mr. Harley was not among them."

"Were they ever alone together?"

Dr. Herriott looked at him coldly. "To my knowledge, only once and with my permission."

"Will you describe the circumstances, doctor?"

Briefly, Herriott described the island excursion.

Triton smiled skeptically. "You are a trusting man, sir. Did you continue to trust Harley after your daughter's disappearance?"

"No," Herriott answered slowly. Eyes troubled, he looked at Ram as if willing him to supply Triton proof. Ram's face offered only pity.

"Why not?"

"I was ready to clutch at any clue to her whereabouts. Everyone was pointing to Harley, but—"

"Now you believe him innocent. Why?"

"My daughter explained—"

"She explained . . . and the court knows you are a trusting parent."

Though Leacock salvaged what he could, Lysistrata knew Triton's way was now open to her. She was not wrong. Dr. Herriott had scarcely descended the dock when Triton clarioned her recall. After she was settled on the stand, he began, "Miss Herriott, while you were in Harley's keeping, did he confine you in any way?"

Lysistrata appeared affronted. "I could have left Khandahoor at any time." Had she only realized it earlier, Kalisha would have seen to that.

"Through miles of almost impenetrable jungle?"

"Mr. Harley offered to be my escort."

"He and some of his mercenaries."

"I assume so."

"How many men did he employ?"

"Very few, considering the size of Khandahoor," she replied evasively, aware of his direction.

"But how many exactly?"

"I never counted, exactly."

"Would you say more than ten?"

"I suppose," she drawled maddeningly.

"Twenty?"

"Perhaps."

Exasperated, he went for his point. "Was Khandahoor an armed fortress?"

"It maintained guards. The Shan tribesmen were a constant menace."

"And the British—weren't they a menace to Mr. Harley as well?"

She smiled benignly. "There are no British in the Shans, Sir Oliver. Everyone knows that."

Angry, he said sharply, "If free to return home, why did you remain with Harley in Khandahoor for so many months with no word to your father?"

"To return to Rangoon was unsafe. Those who wished me ill might have intercepted any message to my father."

"Those who wished you ill?" He smiled tolerantly as if she were a foolish child. "Who might they be, Miss Herriott?"

"If you really care to hear it, Sir Oliver," she said coolly, "the list includes several of your most prominent clients."

Startled, he hastily withdrew. "This is all irrelevant without evidence. I assume you have none?"

"At the moment, I do not," she conceded.

Fiddling with the cord of his fee bag, he studied her a long moment like a plump cat deciding how many claws to use on a mouse that has teased him overlong. "How would you describe life at Khandahoor, Miss Herriott?"

"As rather boring, unless one enjoys Vedic meditation."

"And to relieve the monotony, did Harley and you conduct an affair?"

"Objection!"

"I must establish the reliability of this witness, my lord. If she is lying out of a lecherous attachment to Harley, her entire testimony in his behalf is suspect."

"You will answer the question, Miss Herriott."

"My virtue is as intact as it was when Mr. Harley and I met at the Government House ball last February. As many of the ladies and gentlemen who attended that ball will agree, I was hardly equipped to be a *femme fatale.*"

"Your appearance is not in question. Were you still virginal when you met Mr. Harley?"

"Objection!"

"Overruled," Justice Parke-Allis said reluctantly. "Sir Oliver, you had better make your point." His voice grew soft. "You must answer the question, Miss Herriott."

Ram sat like a white stone.

Lysistrata had planned to lie. A lie would serve so easily. She would not martyr Ram for a principle. Yet, if she lied, she made Ram and herself part of the greater lie of bigotry and enlarged a cruel, bloody monster. "I was not a virgin," she answered dryly, unable to look at her father. Her throat was tight, her head drumming.

With an inward sigh, Leacock pleated his brief.

"Did you have an affair with Harley?"

"He did not seduce me. He wanted nothing . . . no intimacy with me. He avoided—"

"Avoided you?"

"Yes." She heard the croak, as if from a distance. What lay ahead meant the end for Ram. They would hate him more for being desired by one of their women, one they had once elevated to their adulation, than if Ram had been the initiator.

"You pursued him?"

"No."

"So, you 'avoided' one another." He turned to the jury. "I believe the reason is self-evident." He circled. "Did you avoid each other at Khandahoor?"

"Yes." She stared at him hopelessly, defiantly.

"Yet, you still bedded him, didn't you?"

"Yes," she whispered. A buzz of whispers filled the room.

"You have evaded the court's inquiries to the point of falsehood, Miss Herriott. Perhaps you have reason besides lust. What did you share besides Harley's lecherous bed? His questionably gained wealth, perhaps? Did you care that his hands might be those of a murderer when he fondled you? You did know of his alleged crimes, didn't you? Perhaps you were even his accomplice."

"Objection! Counsel is hounding the witness. She is not on trial!" The court was in an uproar, the Justice's gavel barking for silence. Then, in nervous waves, silence dropped, impelled by an uneven howl from a wild-

eyed figure in dirty rags who shook with weakness and
fury.

"God damn you all to hell! Leave her be! I'm the one
you're yapping to hang. It's easier scavenging after
women, isn't it? Put me on the stand, you filthy hyenas;
I'll give you the offal you want!"

Triton would have jumped at the chance, for Ram was
out of control, the incarnation of a lunatic capable of killing not only the victims in this case but anyone in reach.
Hoping to calm him, Leacock urgently called for a recess, which Justice Parke-Allis instantly granted. The
court was cleared.

With his face rigid, Leacock came out of private conference with Ram. After a brief, muttered argument with
Dr. Lighter, he went to his bench. The doctor left the
court. Lysistrata, rigid next to Dr. Herriott who stared
fixedly at some point on the judge's dais, whispered urgently to Leacock, "What is Ram doing! He refused to
testify before; he must be silent now!"

Leacock shook his head.

When his name was called, Ram stumbled toward the
docket. He curtly shrugged off a guard's rough assistance
from the prisoners' box, but finding the few steps up into
the docket unmanageable, allowed himself to be aided by
the Chinese court clerk. Dark eyes dilated, he gazed distantly at the crowd as if he either did not remember where
he was or did not care.

After Harley was sworn in upon the Vedas, Leacock
went directly to the dais. "My lord, before we begin, I
must protest Mr. Harley is ill from his wounds and in no
condition to testify at this time. I beg the court's leave to
recess these proceedings until he is better able to defend
himself."

"My lord," Triton interrupted swiftly, "the defendant
has withstood the strain of the trial these many days as
has the jury, who have the right to return to home and

family without undue delay. If Mr. Harley is in his right
mind as he appears to be despite his previous outburst,
surely it is more just to him and his illness and to the jury to complete the trial without delay. A few simple
questions of the defendant will serve to ascertain whether
he is capable.''

"The court agrees with prosecution, Mr. Leacock.
Please address your client.''

Leacock gave Ram every chance to vindicate himself,
but Ram, like a hunting dog on a chase, pursued the death
sentence. He claimed no noble motives in business affairs, no chivalry with Lysistrata: only opportunism, casual lust, and contemptuous hostility to the British. Even
his denials of the murders seemed like confessions; as if
had he chosen to kill, he considered it his right, a rajah's
right. His voice was clipped, tight, with odd spaces between the words, but no one could doubt his mind was
clear; its precision shone like a diamond with hard,
unnerving clarity. Only at the end of Leacock's examina-
tion did the spaces between Ram's phrases lengthen, his
eyes grow more intent on a harsh glint of sunlight off the
brass ball of one of the chandeliers.

When the prosecution's turn came, Triton nearly
leaped from his bench. Minutely he raked through all the
coals of the Buddha's Skull debacle, deliberately ex-
hausting Ram mentally and physically until he leaned
perceptibly against the docket rail. Then Triton began on
Lysistrata. "Did you abduct Miss Herriott from Rangoon?''

"No, I abducted her from Bangkok.''

Triton blinked. He had not expected so flat an answer.
"Forcibly?''

Ram shrugged. "I believed she compromised my
standing with the British commissioner.''

"Why would she do that?''

"She feared my advances.''

Lysistrata jerked against her father's restraining hand. "That isn't true! He never—"

"Silence in the court!" The gavel thundered.

Herriott jerked Lysistrata down with a muttered hiss, "Be quiet unless you want to follow him to the gallows!"

"Did you continue to press your attentions upon Miss Herriott in Khandahoor?"

"I raped her."

Triton's eyebrows lifted a fraction, then lowered dubiously. "Then why has she gone to such lengths to protect you these last days in court?"

"She is a scrupulous woman," Ram said negligently, "who believes in repayment of debts. She believes I preserved her life a time or two in traversing the hazards of the jungle."

"And did you save her?"

Ram shrugged wearily. "She's fetching enough, and as she observed, Khandahoor is damned boring."

A ripple of shocked disapproval went about the room. Lysistrata, bleak in a tiny well of silence, felt like an isolated, falling pebble with the murmur of Ram's gray monotone a world away.

"Why then, if she was of only transitory interest, did you offer your last possession, a ship of considerable worth, to Boh Myin for her release?"

"She was too sick to bother with any longer, so I had decided to send her home . . ." Ram's concentration wandered. "When Myin intercepted my plan, I had to get her back . . ." He swayed slightly against the docket. "Had to . . ." His voice slurred, then he abruptly stiffened upright.

"Why, Mr. Harley? Why did you have to get her back?"

"Why?" Ram vaguely stared at him, then wearily shook his head. "British," he mumbled. "Had to get British off my back."

Justice Parke-Allis summoned the bailiff. "A chair for Mr. Harley." He looked at Triton. "Finish this quickly, if you please, sir."

After the chair was brought, Triton went on sarcastically, "If weary of Miss Herriott, Mr. Harley, why did you make such an impassioned protest earlier on her behalf?"

Ram's faint smile had a twist of rakish impudence. "I never said I was weary of her."

"Answer the question, Mr. Harley."

"What was it?"

With a sigh, Triton repeated it.

"She's better than you," Ram muttered. "All of you."

"What do you mean by that, sir?" Triton snapped.

"You ought to be in trees . . . flinging coconuts," Ram impersonally informed the chandelier.

Triton reddened. "Sir, do you mean to insult—"

"You shit . . . on everything you touch." In the squawk that followed, Ram's tongue clicked softly. "Hail, Britannia . . . ta, ta, ta, ta, tah, tah."

Leacock protested over the clamor, "My lord, my client is out of his head. Delirious . . . the strain . . ."

The gavel rapped and silence eventually fell. "I agree the defendant's behavior is irresponsibly reckless, Mr. Leacock," Justice Parke-Allis said sternly. "He will be silent or reap the consequences." In the deeper silence that followed and Leacock's ironic look, the justice felt belatedly foolish. What possible consequences could intimidate determined gallows bait?

At Triton's ready agreement, Ram was dismissed from the docket. This time, he made no protest as the Sikh bailiffs took him under the arms and hauled him back to his place.

"I presume Mr. Harley is your last witness, Mr. Leacock?" Justice Parke-Allis said grimly.

Leacock rose. "As a matter of fact, he is not, my lord."

Parke-Allis sighed.

"I should like to call Miss Anne O'Shaunessy, my lord."

Heads turned, Evelyn Chilton's most swiftly, as her former servant entered on Dr. Lighter's arm. Uncertain, wary of the strange faces, Anne O'Shaunessy shrank closer to the doctor as they moved down the aisle. Upon request of Justice Parke-Allis, Lighter seated her with the Herriotts, then stepped into the docket to affirm her fitness to testify. "Miss O'Shaunessy underwent an understandable period of withdrawal after her ordeal but is now demonstrably sane. I should judge her completely competent under any circumstances." At Parke-Allis's nod, he led Anne to the docket where she futilely clung to his hand in mute appeal as he left her with a smile of reassurance that made him feel like a traitor.

Leacock, taking his place, spoke gently. "Miss O'Shaunessy, you have met me as a friend of Dr. Lighter's and he has explained to you why you are wanted here. A man's life depends upon your willingness to give evidence as to his innocence or guilt in the matter of the crime against you and the four women he is accused of murdering." He firmly went on, "Until now, you have been too distraught to describe that ordeal, but the time has come to bring it forth and force the one who so terribly mutilated you to answer for his crime." He paused. "Did you recognize the person who brutalized you?"

Her mouth worked nervously, her eyes turned furtive.

"Are you acquainted with Mr. Richard Harley?"

She frowned slightly, then looked wary again.

"Miss O'Shaunessy, do you wish to see your attacker go free, perhaps, and most probably to kill again?"

The girl's eyes sparked angry disgust.

"Do you wish to see Richard Harley hang?"

She appeared briefly puzzled, then disinterested.

"Ah, so you are not in love with him?"

A bluntly negative sound emerged.

"Do you recognize him among the prisoners?"

She scanned the block, then shook her head.

"Will the prisoner stand?"

When Ram did not move, a guard shoved a hand under his armpit to thrust him up. Ram hung from the guard's beefy support as if his weight had grown too heavy to keep upright.

Anne gazed at him in startled puzzlement. "Do you know him now, Miss O'Shaunessy?"

She nodded slowly.

"Is he the man who mutilated you?"

She shook her head; then, as if daydreaming, drew a jagged line across her face.

"A scarred man. Would he have been scarred like Richard Harley's Hindu servant Naswral?"

Violently, she shook her head, face working with frustrated effort to communicate.

Leacock frowned slightly. "Then it was not Naswral?"

She nodded energetically, then waved her hand at Ram as if to dismiss him.

Leacock looked puzzled. "Are you trying to say it *was* Naswral, but that he was not acting for Mr. Harley?"

Relieved he understood, she nodded vigorously.

"Whom was he acting for, Miss O'Shaunessy?"

Anne studied the faces in the courtroom, row on row, then stopped. Her eyes fixed in recognition, then vitriolic hatred. Heads turned to follow her gaze to a chicly clad woman in white whose face suffused with a dark flush of fury. "She's lying," Evelyn Chilton snapped coldly. "The ungrateful creature is lying . . . or mad! How can this court permit a demented person to be placed on the witness stand—"

"Silence in the court!" Parke-Allis barked. "Another such outburst, madam, and I shall hold you in contempt. Continue, Mr. Leacock."

"Then, Miss O'Shaunessy, do you mean to say Naswral was not only in Mr. Harley's employ, but"—he gestured to the woman in white—"that of your mistress, Mrs. Evelyn Chilton?"

Anne made gestures suggesting drug use, prostitution, and money collection, then made a sweeping motion to indicate the city. She cupped a hand by an ear to indicate overhearing and seeing too much.

A furious gasp issued from Evelyn, and Justice Parke-Allis held up a restraining hand. After watching Anne gesticulate for a few moments more, he advised, "Mr. Leacock, the court must ask the witness to write her testimony in detail. Miming leaves too much to conjecture and may easily be misconstrued."

Evelyn sat white-lipped, watching her former maid scribble marks made awkward by furious haste. At length, Leacock handed the affidavit to Judge Parke-Allis who read, then reread it in lengthening silence. As he handed it to the court clerk, Triton put up a weak protest. "My lord, this is highly irregular . . . ."

Parke-Allis ignored him. "This document will be entered as evidence. The clerk will read it aloud to the court."

"Miss Evie has a finger in many pies, I tell you," the clerk related tonelessly. "She pretends to be a man called Garotte. Nobody who deals with her sees her face; even that monster, Scarface Naswral, who murders people she asks him to. I always followed her to their secret meeting-place and listened close so Naswral don't murder me. But I never heard her say, 'Murder poor Anne.' Poor Anne. Miss Evie said a lot of other things. Like she must get more money from the Golden Dragon. The pipemaster was cheating her. He had to pay up or

wouldn't be pipemaster long when the poppy price went
up . . .''

The affidavit continued as a profile of a cold, calculating mind that had engineered a network of drugs,
prostitution, and murder not only in Rangoon, but in
Moulmein. Harley had served as a profitable distraction
and scapegoat.

The courtroom crowd, shocked and awed, stared at
Evelyn. Aware of their incredulity that a woman who had
moved smoothly through their midst could be so accomplished a criminal, Evelyn stared back with a tiny, hard
smile of cold defiance and contempt. "The envious
bitch is lying," she stated flatly, and strolled from the
courtroom. When a bailiff moved to stop her, Parke-Allis
waved him back to his place.

Herriott convulsively clasped his daughter's hand.
"It's over," he muttered. "Thank God! That Medusa will
be tried within the month."

Her hand lay slack in his. "Do you know," she murmured, "as much as I loathe Evelyn Chilton, I feel as if I
were her sister."

After hearing Triton's stoic summation gleefully de-
molished by Leacock's following broadside, the jury retired. Ram was declared innocent with indecorous
rapidity, so much so that he was unshackled from the
other prisoners and escorted through the excited, milling
crowd before Lysistrata could reach the prisoners' box.
Still in an uncertainty of disbelief, she worriedly clutched
Herriott's sleeve. "Papa, we must find him! He can
hardly keep his feet."

"Don't worry," said Harry, who with Lighter was just
behind them. "I'll run him down. After all, he can't
move too fast."

But the quarry proved nowhere to be seen; by the time
Harry located two subalterns to assist the search, Ram,

ejected from the courthouse, had disappeared in the labyrinth of surrounding streets.

"Go home, Lysistrata," Harry ordered over the babble of journalists and departing crowd at the courthouse gate. "You're exhausted. When I find him, I'll bring Ram there . . . with your permission, Dr. Herriott."

At Herriott's brief nod, Harry, followed by the two subalterns, pushed through the throng, then took to his heels.

Lighter, beside the Herriotts, grew impatient with the prodding, yammering newspapermen. Abruptly, he laid about briskly with his cane. "Enough, you infernal, noisy hounds!" Shielding heads and clumsy cameras, the men backed, less intimidated by the irate Irishman than by the huge, scowling Scots intern who moved into the breach.

"Come a wee bit closer," invited the Scot, waggling a finger, "and I'll crack yer heads together like a lot of farm eggs!" He shepherded the Herriotts into a sheltering alcove and planted his massive bulk in front of them. Lighter went for their carriage.

While the frustrated reporters hopped and danced beyond the Scot's reach, Lysistrata looked up into Herriott's face. "Papa, I'm sorry. I would have given anything not to shame you."

He smiled faintly. "In teaching you to doubt the easy road, I fear you've learned to shun it. Do you feel shame, girl?"

"Not of Ram. And not for him."

"And of Frank Wyatt?" His eyes were grave.

She started. "You knew about Frank?"

"I guessed." Watching the gesticulations of the reporters, he shoved his hands into his pockets. "A long time ago. I just didn't want to deal with more wretchedness I couldn't undo." He looked at her directly. "I didn't come to the East to escape just memories and failures, but weakness. I told myself I didn't want to see you broken by Wyatt, but I was the one breaking, not you." He smiled with wry pride. "I think you're strong enough to bear anything, even losing Ram Harley."

"I couldn't have borne seeing him hang, Papa," she whispered. She looked at the gaping, gossiping crowd beyond the newspapermen. "Do you hate us very much?"

He looked startled. "You? Never!" Then his hands dug deeper into his pockets. "But him? Yes . . . I think I may. I envy him his courage. I envy him a woman of your courage and the youth to have a future with her. I hate him for turning his back on it all. For courting death as if she were his only love, not some rotted whore he could find in any gutter. I saw enough of his kind in the war."

Lysistrata paled at his vehemence. "Papa, please . . ."

He sighed. "Still, Harley thrust his neck in a noose for you, and while that's nothing to his sort, he let people he despises spit on his pride as well. Pride: that's what runs in his veins instead of blood. For that I'll stand by him, however the crap flies."

Her arm tensely linked his. "If Harry finds him."

During the last hours of the trial, Ram heard only a low, annoying drone of arguing voices. He saw less. Ruddy haze fogged his eyes; at its center burned a sun whose light bored into his brain, removing coherent thought to leave only dull, throbbing pain. Frustration at his helplessness, cold anger at his captors, gnawing regret for Lysistrata he had shut away by leaving his body through meditation, but that damaged body had betrayed him, inexorably dragged him back day by day until he was aware, as a man staked on a desert is aware, of ceaseless torment and hatred. He did not remember what he said last to Triton, something about monkeys. Fanged monkeys who raked and clutched, gibbering madly as he tried to drive them away from Lysistrata but found his arms too heavy to lift; his head too heavy.

Then suddenly, the manacles and irons snapped open. He was hauled to his feet, given a heavy slap between the shoulder blades that nearly sent him to his knees. He was prodded through a press of bodies with curious, indifferent eyes. Then they were shut away behind the courtroom door. He was led through a dim hall, thrust from the rear courtyard door into blinding sunlight.

Involuntarily, his arm went up to protect his eyes, and he peered at the trembling silhouette of his hand against the white glare. His head and tongue felt swollen; he wanted water. Sweat coursed his body, dripped to the dust. The sun's glare was intensified by blank, white faces of blocky buildings, their silence deafening after incessant sound as he aimlessly stumbled down the dirt street. Succor was nowhere. Lysistrata was nowhere. His luring, lovely mirage had faded. One street linked to another, then another, each more narrow, more menial, more deserted until, with an abrupt jar, his knees bit sharp stones through frayed cotton, slid on a slime of refuse and mud which oozed through his splayed fingers. He sat limply against a crumbling plaster wall. Feeling the heat more than pain now, he studied the wet mud on his hands, then the dank water pooled in their prints, and more muted footmarks of the denizens of that obscure part of the city. Water. A murky mirror, it trisected a dimly familiar face. Not Lysistrata's. Wearily, he put out a hand to wave the face aside, lost anchorage against the wall, and sagged into the mud. Into warm, wet blackness.

Naswral glanced quickly toward the sun-glared slit of the alley entrance, then drew his knife. "It is a pity I cannot rely on you to drown, but one tongue not properly si-

lenced wagged today. That mistake I will not make
again.'' He jerked Ram's muddy head up.

"Don't move a muscle, damn you," a sharp voice
spat. "Just let that knife drop."

The knife split the mire, but Naswral whirled on his
knee, his hand diving for the revolver in his sash.

From the yellow glare, Harry fired.

The subalterns sauntered after him to view the dead
man splayed in the mud. "I suppose you should have
mentioned, sir," one observed, "that you had an Adams
revolver aimed at his skull."

As Harry knelt to ease Ram onto his back, the subaltern squinted. "Looks like this sod's come to the end of
his road, too."

The young officer crouched opposite flipped open
Ram's shirt and wrinkled his nose at the sickening odor
from the wound. "No bloody wonder. What do we do
with him, Leftenant?"

"You carry him."

The junior officer's eyes dropped to his spotless uniform, then back to the inert mud- and garbage-streaked
Ram. "Sir?"

Harry smiled grimly. "At least until I locate a *gharry.*"

"Couldn't we wait here until you—" the subaltern began.

"You just displayed an excellent sense of smell, sir,"
Harry snapped. "Did it suggest anything about delay?"

CHAPTER 18

A Question of Starch

Look in my face; my name is Might-have-been . . .
DANTE GABRIEL ROSSETTI

"You knew, didn't you?" Lysistrata hotly accused Dr. Herriott and Leacock as she paced outside Herriott's bedroom door. "You saw Ram in that filthy prison just two days ago! His critical condition must have been obvious. Those private murmurings between you in court . . . *why* didn't you tell me? I had a right to know!"

"Your testimony might not have been handled to Ram's advantage if you had known, Lysistrata," Leacock replied simply. "He thought it best, and your father and I concurred you should be spared additional stress."

While recognizing the cold logic of the barrister's argument, Lysistrata was even more infuriated by their male presumption and collaboration. She was also almost hysterically distraught after being forbidden Ram's sickroom, where Herriott and Lighter had been working on him into the waning afternoon. Eyes glittering with tears, she turned on Herriott. "So this is what you meant this morning when you said I might lose Ram. Not to a military tribunal, not to whatever godforsaken place he might

next have chosen for exile." Her hands twisted at the
peignoir sash. "You meant he was going to *die* of infection and neglect and a prison quack's stupidity! You
could have given him medical help! I'll never forgive
you . . . never!"

Seeing Herriott pale, Leacock intervened. "Your father had little to say in the matter, Lysistrata. Ram knew
he was becoming dangerously ill. He refused medical
treatment from Dr. Herriott and Dr. Lighter during the
trial though they urged it on him. While determined to
see you clear of this affair, he did not wish to be forced to
endure a military trial if cleared in civil court." He
puffed on the pipe, eyes mild and unflinching. "He cannot now survive a tribunal, you know. They have absolute proof he killed those officers."

Her hands went to her ears. "Stop it! You're not talking to a child. I've been bullied enough!" She swung on
Herriott. "I'm going to be with Ram, Papa. If there's
only a last scrap of time with him, I'm taking that scrap!"

The door abruptly opened; an arm shot out, locked her
elbow, and jerked her inward. "*Anything* to stop this caterwauling! God knows some black part of you must be
Irish!" The door slammed.

Whatever hot rebuttal Lysistrata might have directed toward the intrepid Lighter died on her lips when she saw
Ram's wasted form thrashing deliriously on sweat-soaked
sheets. A heavy compress was bound to his chest. His eyes
were glazed, lips moving erratically in Hindi. He tore at the
sheets, then at the compress, and Lighter moved swiftly to
drag his hands away. As Lighter held him down, Ram
strained against his hands. "Water," he croaked. Lysistrata
quickly held a draught from the pitcher to his lips.

"No," Lighter said sharply. "He's likely to choke
and hemorrhage. I've had to resuture most of his surgery.
Just moisten his lips and face."

Avidly, Ram sucked at the soaked cloth. Oblivious to

Lysistrata, he was intent only on water. The moment the cloth moved away, he began to beg again, eyes glassy above dark, gouged circles. Despite sharper mingled odors of carbolic and chloroform, a pestilent stink of mortification hung in the air.

At that familiar, deadly smell, terror gripped Lysistrata even before Lighter spoke. "Well," he said flatly, "you see how it is. If the trial had been shorter by even a day, he might have had a chance."

She gazed downward into the dark emptiness of Ram's eyes. She remembered that seductive oblivion from her own illness in Khandahoor. *Nada.* That distant, caressing dream of death. As much as infection, she feared that terrible detachment, particularly in Ram. Long familiar with the dangers and delights of *nada*, he had ruthlessly dragged her from it when her snakebite wound had gone foul. But what drugs had he used? Her memory flailed. Opium. Crude poultices and herbal potions. "Are you willing to experiment, Dr. Lighter?" she asked urgently.

He considered the desperation in her voice. "That depends. What do you have in mind?"

She told him.

He looked dubious, then shrugged. "I don't suppose a dose of witch-doctoring will make him more miserable than he is."

Lighter was shortly to regret his agreement. After Ma Saw returned with ingredients for a remedy from a *sayah* she insisted was the best in Rangoon, a combination of them was given Ram. The wounded man convulsed. "Something's wrong." Lysistrata distractedly ran her fingers through her hair. "I don't remember a reaction like this."

"We've probably either misjudged proportions or left

out something.'' Lighter grimaced. ''We'll just have to call in the *sayah* himself for consultation.''

Though the *sayah* arrived to cheerfully share his expertise and concoct even more bizarre remedies, Ram was ravaged by fever hour on hour until his ravings ebbed to a dry, futile croak. They shattered a forty-pound block of ice from Harry's club, then packed it around Ram's burning body. The *sayah* shook his head at such barbarous handling of a sick man, but with typical Burmese tolerance, forbore to express his opinion of it aloud. Ma Saw and San-hla hurried to Shwe Dagon to burn prayer papers, then returned with neighboring servants to bang kitchen pots and drive away malevolent *nats*. When one crew was exhausted and deafened, another crew relieved it. The Chinese among them brought fresh joss papers for luck to hang in all the doors and windows until the house had an incongruously festive air.

Lysistrata viewed the joss papers with mute horror. They rustled like dying whispers of longing by night; by day, they uttered dry echoes of unalterable regret. Like skeletons they rattled until she went through the days in silent despair. Remote from her so often, Ram was now unreachable though he lay beneath her hand. For three days, the clamor meant to banish the *nats* cleaved her mind until she had the look of a cornered animal. How could she tell the beaters their racket had the throb and cry of unbearable pain? At length, she sat immobile by Ram's bed, waiting for all sound to cease. In the doorway, Dr. Herriott stood watching her face until midnight, then mixed powder into a cup of warm beer. ''Drink this.'' When she did not respond, he held it to her lips. Like a doll, she drank. All sound mercifully ceased.

Of all the concoctions attempted, Dr. Herriott never knew what actually worked, but by morning, Ram's fever broke. At noon, the doctor woke Lysistrata. Her eyes still dazed from sleep and strain, she rolled over to gaze vaguely up at him when he told her. "Thank God," she whispered. Ram had become too weak to sustain another assault on his system. That they hadn't killed him was a wonder. She had fallen into drugged sleep with a last vision of his spent, white face and body, eerily still after so many hours of ebbing struggle. At first sight of Herriott bending over her, she had been sure he had come to say Ram was dead.

She slept again, heavily, dreamlessly, until Leacock arrived that evening. After meeting Ma Saw with Ram, she descended the stair to join the gentlemen for dinner. Upon entering the hall, she heard Lighter on the way out of the house. "You tell her," he barked. "I can't dawdle. I have a hospital to run!"

She joined Leacock and Herriott at the front door just in time to see Lighter yell impatiently to his dozing driver and jump into his *gharry*. "Tell me what?" she inquired, doubting she wanted to know.

"Mr. Leacock has brought bad news," Herriott said gravely. "Anne O'Shaunessy is dead, undoubtedly murdered; Evelyn Chilton has disappeared."

"Oh, no! Poor Anne! What happened?"

"Bizarrely enough," said Leacock, "she was found drowned in a scrub bucket at the hospital. She had been cleaning a hall which wasn't often used. Someone must have come up behind her."

"But Evelyn surely couldn't be strong enough, even if she did hate Anne's vitals."

"Who knows? All we do know is that Evelyn's gone and the only person willing to give evidence against her is dead." He squinted against the sun. "If Mrs. Chilton is Garotte, she could not have realized Anne knew so much or she would have killed her long ago. As she may have done her husband when he learned more than he ought. Several papers were missing from his reports on the *Star of Calcutta* murders. Anne must have been included with the other murdered women only as a general precaution: a wise one from Mrs. Chilton's viewpoint for Anne must have intended blackmail.'' He filled his pipe and sat against the verandah balustrade to light it.

"As for Bettenheim, I believe he was merely Mrs. Chilton's dupe, as were many others too intent on their own greed and ambition to comprehend the extent of hers. She and Bettenheim may have been lovers, but I very much doubt if she confided in him, given his bludgeon-like mentality.''

"I must say, you don't look particularly upset about her eluding justice, Lysistrata,'' he remarked quizzically.

"I don't think she's eluded it. To Evelyn, being celebrated was everything. Now, she must sink into oblivion. She may rule over a host of foul dens like the Golden Dragon, but never again can she cover herself with jewels to enter a ballroom. She cannot risk public recognition.'' Lysistrata smiled sardonically from grim experience. "Once you're ruined in English society, you're ruined.''

"That sounds like a twinge of sympathy for her,'' Herriott quipped dryly.

"We're both pariahs, only Evelyn overcame the social system for a time because she used it. I was beaten from the beginning because I butted heads with it. Evelyn is a horror, but I respect her courage and intelligence, perhaps because I've learned to respect the law of the jungle. In that, I'm like Ram now.'' Sitting in a high-backed plantation chair, she crossed her legs. "Jungle survivors wear camouflage to wait their chance; they never trust in luck.'' Abruptly, she changed the subject. "I hope you will join us for dinner, Mr. Leacock.''

"Thank you, no,'' he replied. "Like Dr. Lighter, I must return to my customary duties; however, I did not come merely to bear my usual quota of ill tidings, but for-

tunate news as well. Harry Armistead sends his greetings
and regrets he will be unable to call until certain of his affairs are cleared up. He also sends a tidbit of information.'' The barrister's lips curved in an arcane smile. ''As
you said in court, Miss Herriott, there are no British in
the Shans.''

''I don't understand what you're implying,'' she replied, puzzled.

''Harry was called into his commandant's office this
morning and given strict orders not to ever discuss with
anyone Ram Harley's anti-British actions in the Shan
mountains.'' His pipe gestured delicately. ''Officially,
the British respect King Mindon's sovereignty. If the
military tries Ram, Sir Anthony must publicly admit,
rather sooner than he would like, that his government is
fomenting rebellion against that sovereignty. Mud-ball-
ing the royal back, so to speak.''

Lysistrata sagged against the chair. ''You mean . . .
you don't mean . . . ?''

''Ram's free,'' Leacock said smugly. ''They hate his
guts but can't do a damned thing to him.''

''Officially,'' Dr. Herriott added succinctly.

Leacock sobered. ''Yes. The sooner he's out of reach,
the better.''

But Ram's healing could not be hurried. Cooled by a
palmetto fan in Dr. Herriott's room, he slept with more
restlessness as days passed and his drugged stupor less-
ened. When he was awake, he and Lysistrata had little to
say to each other, as if a barrier had dropped between
them. Steeling herself for the harsh parting to come, only
once when he was asleep did she touch his face. And
Ram? Was he relieved to be soon free of her and all the ill
fortune she had brought him? While he could not be
blamed, his polite indifference tore at her soul. Best he be
gone soon, for many reasons.

One of which did not escape her father.

On a late morning when she was hacking at a stubborn root in the vegetable garden behind the house, she was swept by dizziness. Just as it engulfed her, Herriott's strong hands hauled her up. As he helped her to the verandah, she muttered dazedly, "Where were you? I didn't see you . . ."

He thrust her a trifle ungently into a chair. "Don't you think it stupid to root around under the midday sun? Or are you trying to be rid of more than weeds?"

Startled by his anger and uneasy at the choice of words, she wiped at damp hair under an ill-tied bandanna. "I lost track of the time."

"I haven't. About four months now, isn't it?"

She took a long breath. "I didn't think it showed so much."

"It doesn't. It's the retching in the chamber pot that I've been unable to miss hearing through the wall every morning." His mouth tightened. "Does Harley know?"

"No." Tautly, she watched him. "Are you going to tell him?"

"Not if you don't want me to."

She stared into the shimmering heat of the garden with its lazily cruising insects. "I don't."

He started to say something, then closed his mouth on it and went inside the house.

A week later, Dr. Herriott sensed a certain tenseness in Ram while redressing his wounds. His condition much improved, the younger man sat propped up by bed pillows. "Am I hurting you?" Herriott asked briefly as he snipped through the heavy bandages.

"On the contrary," Ram answered wryly, "you're remarkably gentle for a man who must wish me well hanged."

"Shot, Mr. Harley," Herriott said laconically. "I do

not consider you worthless enough to hang.'' He eased off the bandage.

Ram laughed softly. ''Thank you, sir.'' At Herriott's discouraging shrug, he gave him a quizzical look. ''May I ask, sir, if you have a pistol at hand?''

''Why?'' demanded the doctor as he swabbed the wound with alcohol.

Ram sucked in his breath at the disinfectant's sting. ''Because I am about to make a proposal you may wish to answer with considerable finality.''

After Herriott heard what Ram had to say as fresh bandages were tightly bound in place, he went to a desk and opened the drawer. Ram stiffened, then relaxed as Herriott turned with a liquor flask. ''You've got starch; you practically squeak with it.'' He took a swig from the flask, then held it out. ''Starch gives me hives.''

A trifle uncertain, Ram accepted the flask. As whiskey blazed down his gullet, he heard Herriott observe further, ''You don't fold; you don't bend. Your collar's so tight, it's only fit to wear in a coffin.'' He took back the flask. ''You're a bloody proper English gentleman, you are.''

Ram eyed him as he swigged. ''I take it you reject my proposal.''

The flask rammed back at his face. ''Not until we discuss it over a bottle.'' Herriott rang for Ma Saw.

''I'm even less amusing when I drink, sir,'' Ram warned coolly.

''If I wanted to be amused, I'd invite Triton to join us,'' Herriott bit back. ''We are about to dilute some starch.''

''That may take some time, sir.''

''Then we'll make it grain alcohol.''

''How could you, Papa?'' Lysistrata jerked the bedroom windows open wide to air the liquor fumes. She glared at the inert Ram slumped over in a mound of pillows. "You could have killed him!"

Eyes glassy, Herriott looked owlish. "You don't appreciate scientifrick exper . . . experimentation, girl. See" —he pointed gleefully— "he *does* bend in the middle."

Lysistrata could get nothing more from Herriott about the episode and knew better than to pry at Ram's oyster, had she been minded to, which she had not. Anchored in a convalescent chaise, he could not avoid her; but she avoided him for she was in panic lest he detect her dread of his departure. One morning while reading under the banyan, she had to face the problem, for it was walking toward her with the help of a polished malacca cane.

"If the mountain will not come to Mahomet . . ." Ram touched his cane to his forehead in a light salute. He was clean-shaven, bandit mustache gone, hair neatly trimmed though a trifle longer than he had been wont to wear it in Rangoon.

She recognized the French suit of cream silk, its jacket flung over his shoulder. "I see the *Rani* has entered port. Have you come to say good-bye?" She prayed she did not sound as wooden as her tongue felt.

He studied her pale cheeks against curls burnished gold under the banyan's shifting play of light. The pastel blue and violet flowered muslin was becoming, but tepid after the lush saris she had worn in Khandahoor. She looked very American. "Actually, I have come to propose."

Her mouth went dry, wits blank. "Why?" came a blunt, defensive croak. "Papa didn't . . ."

He smiled wryly. "Your father disapproves of me, so you need not fear this is his idea." Seeming to brace himself, he forged on as if he had memorized his lines. "I have compromised your reputation and future beyond repair. While the name of a half-caste is scant advantage, it at least offers some respectability and protection. I no longer have my former income, but I can keep you comfortably." She felt her face tighten, and as if he wished he had not begun, Ram looked away, the cane sharply tapping against a boot. "If you prefer a separate residence, I shall see you established wherever you like."

She felt as if she had touched an open door only to have it sever her hand as it slammed. "You mean after the ceremony, we need not see each other at all?" she said distantly.

"If you choose," he replied tightly, his own manner hardening at her frigid tone.

"I choose to reject your proposal, sir, considerate of my welfare as it may be."

He paled, then bowed abruptly. "Good-bye, then, Miss Herriott. I wish you every good fortune." The next moment, she was looking at his back.

A short time later, Dr. Herriott tapped Lysistrata's shoulder. Slowly, as if lost in concentration, she looked up from the book. "Harley has gone. He seemed in a great hurry." When she said nothing, he asked sharply, "Did you quarrel?"

"Ram rarely permits himself the luxury of a quarrel," she replied tonelessly. "He offered marriage."

At her bleak brevity, Herriott's head came up slightly. "Oh?"

"He was quite noble."

Letting out his breath, Herriott hit his palm to his forehead. "I ought to have known he'd botch it. He squeaked when he should have bent."

"What are you talking about?"

He waved a disgusted hand and dropped onto a dilapidated bench. "So you refused him?"

"Of course." She carefully laid the book in her lap. "You ought to be pleased. After all, you dislike him."

"I never said I didn't like him," Herriott growled. "He could charm every crocodile out of the Nile."

Uncertain of his attitude, she leaned forward to touch his sleeve. "Papa, we haven't discussed the future, but I will shortly become an embarrassing burden to you. It might be better if I went away . . . perhaps to a Dutch colony."

Herriott turned scarlet. "You're not satisfied with insulting your child's father; you insult his grandfather as well!" He leaped up. "What do you take Harley for? What do you take *me* for!"

"You're men who answer for what you believe to be your obligations; I do not happen to be one of them. I know Ram must have asked your permission to propose; you shouldn't have encouraged him." Her voice became unsteady. "What happened between Ram and me was not rape, Papa, though he made it plain he was not in love with me and never could be. The day on that beach Triton was so curious about in court—Ram could have had me even then if he had been willing to dishonor you. Ram honors his responsibilities, no matter how unpleasant. That's the only reason he offered marriage. He doesn't love me." Her eyes filled with tears. "I won't trap you and I won't trap him!"

He scoffed impatiently. "You talk about responsibility, then you'd better think about your baby. *His* baby. *My* baby. You've got us to consider beside yourself. Ram has a right to know he has a child and a say in what happens to him. If you had little consideration for me before, you've none now. I won't be cheated! Not again. My wife and sons were taken from me, my life's work, my country. Now you speak of disappearing like some melodramatic tragedienne and taking my last hope and accomplishment with you!" He shook a fist. "I won't have it!"

Lysistrata was taken aback. She had never seen him in such a violent temper, much less one directed at her.

"Papa," she began weakly, "Ram and I can never be happy together. Even a child—"

"Twaddle! Where's your spunk!" Hunkering down, he seized her hands. "You love the man. If he had died, I think your mind would have gone with him. Are you going to stop fighting for him now, just because he's on his feet?" She tried to pull away, and his grip tightened. "You just said you enjoy his bed. And he's no milksop out of it. He stole you, remember. Workable marriages have begun on far less. The Sabine women mothered a nation."

"Papa." She enunciated the words as if explaining to a slow child: "I told you, he *doesn't* want me."

"Have you ever thought he may not *let* himself want you?"

She stared at him as if he were some *sayah* suggesting a *nat* might change shape before her eyes. Behind Herriott, Harry Armistead with jaunty sailor's gait, a seabag slung over his shoulder, was crossing the lawn.

CHAPTER 19

An Exchange of Mistresses

Now lies the Earth all Danae to the stars,
And all thy heart lies open unto me.
                              ALFRED, LORD TENNYSON

"Passage to Shanghai? Why not. I'll take you to Papeete if you like." Ram leaned against the taffrail of the *Rani,* his white cotton Indian garb ruffling in the rising offshore breeze in the harbor. Although he was thin from his ordeal, his prison pallor was unnoticeable under a light sunburn from an afternoon on the *Rani*'s decks while readying her for sea. His old elegance had returned despite the plain dress. The old careless ease was evident as well, but with a hard edge, his cynicism near to the surface.

With a rueful grin, Harry eased the seabag to the deck. "I can't afford Papeete now that I've resigned my commission. Besides, I haven't had my fill of the Orient. I want to potter about a year or so. Maybe try Australia when I've pocketed a few pounds." Already, he had the easy look of a wanderer, with shirt undone at the neck and frayed sailor's cap tilted back from his forehead.

"Have they disowned you back home?" Ram asked quietly.

"More or less. The old man took it hard, but he has a sneaking fondness for rogue elephants. I think he'll take me back into the fold in time."

"A tusker among Suffolk sheep?" Ram smiled gently. "You won't fit in after a few years, Harry."

"No, maybe not. I suppose it's already too late. I've lost the knack of bleating."

"I hope I didn't contribute to your disaffection."

Harry shook his head. "Not to my disadvantage. I used to think soldiering was the most glorious fun I could have." His face lost some of its youth. "What we British are doing in Burma and a hundred other places isn't glorious and damned well isn't fun." His lips quirked with a touch of mischief. "I suppose I'll have to turn soldier of fortune to find amusement." He laughed suddenly. "Don't worry though; at this point in my career, I can still pay passage to Shanghai. This time next year, I may be down to my underwear in Brisbane."

Ram grinned. "No charge for this trip. If it weren't for you, I wouldn't be making it."

"Thanks, no. If I can support a servant"—Harry's head jerked toward a coolie squatting on the afterdeck—"I can pay my way. Besides, helping you out wasn't exactly my idea at first." He paused. "I gather Lysistrata isn't making the trip with you."

A shadow seemed to move over Ram's face. "By her choice, not mine."

"Oh?" Harry's eyes glinted. "Did you give her a choice this time? That's a step forward."

"I offered to marry her," Ram replied with dangerous quietness. "Did you make an equal offer, Harry?"

"Lord, I adore her; but without an income, I can hardly consider a wife, even one as lovely as Lysistrata. Besides, you must concede she's a trifle used." He watched Ram's lips tighten into a hard line. "I'd take her as a mistress in a twinkling, but she'd probably find me dull and stuffy after you." He smiled coolly. "I cannot imagine your ever being stuffy. Your proposal must have been the soul of passion and romance." His hand waved dramatically. "Come, my love, let me take you away from all this ordure they're hurling at you. From your loneliness and beggary. From all the slimy hounds who'll come sniffing about . . ."

"Shut up, Harry."

Harry blinked. "Sorry, old man. Did I say something wrong?" He peered at Ram's taut face with a clinical air. "I mean, who could know you gave a damn? You've taken care enough to hide it. You did finally mention love when you suggested marriage to her, didn't you?" At Ram's flat look, he let out an exasperated sigh. "God, you're sensitive. I could wring more emotion from a prune."

"If you want to stay on board, Harry," was the blunt reply, "stay out of my sight."

"I will," gaily cried the young Englishman after his departing back. "After all, I have someone to look after me."

From under the coolie's hat, smoky green eyes glared wickedly into Harry's laughing ones.

Four days out of Rangoon, the weather turned foul, Ram's mood fouler yet. The crew, unaccustomed to any show of temperament from him, went about their duties as if walking on eggshells. Still, no one could suit him. Harry did not try. Even the coolie who stayed glued to Harry's heels drew a sharp look when he slid awkwardly on the slippery deck and lurched into the Englishman, who quickly gave him a steadying arm. The fifth day saw the rain turn to gray drizzle and the ocean heave in sullen rolls. When Ram spotted the coolie limply clinging to the rail after relieving his nausea over the port side, he bore down on him. Seizing him by the scruff, he propelled him into the master cabin and angrily batted off his hat. A torrent of coppery gold spilled free in the dim light.

Lysistrata flinched weakly from his furious face. "How did you find out?"

"Harry doesn't treat you like a coolie and you don't exactly have the skinny shanks of one in those breeches," he snapped. "Just how long did you two plan to carry on this charade?"

"Until we were too far from Rangoon for you to turn back," she muttered. "God, I think I'm going to be sick again."

He eyed her unsympathetically. "You're a rotten sailor. You should have remembered that before you tied on with Harry."

"I'm not tied on with Harry"—she took a gulp of air—"and I only get sick to my stomach around you."

"I have nothing to do with it."

"You have everything to do with it! You—" Eyes rounding she waved a desperate hand. "Porthole."

Abruptly, he spun her about, pushed her to a washbasin, and shoved her head down. After a bout of dry heaves, she lifted her head and gasped. "Dammit, I'm pregnant, you know-it-all."

His eyes narrowed. "So that's it. Harry?"

"Harry!" Letting out a feeble screech, she hurled herself at him.

He caught her hands. "Why else would you be here? You turned *me* down definitely enough."

"I never should have come," she muttered. "I knew you'd be like this."

"Like what?" he demanded. "How am I, Lysistrata?"

"You . . . treat me like some . . . cracked crock that wants pasting!" To hide her wretchedness, she tried to jerk away. "Let go of me! I'll scream the innards out of this . . . scow!"

"For your adventurous leftenant? Why *did* you bring Harry along, Lysistrata? For reserve entertainment in case I proved unreceptive?"

"Harry was Papa's idea, too. He's supposed to keep you from bullying me into bed again," she snarled unevenly. "My father's full of ideas. I wouldn't have you for lunch."

"Well, that's a straight answer, at least!" Ram snapped, then pitched her onto his bed. "Stay there, or throw up again!" He strode to the door, shoved it open. "And if Harry has anything to say about it, I'll stuff the mattress with him!"

"Lysistrata's locked in my cabin. We'll share it until Shanghai," Ram flatly informed Harry after summoning him to the foredeck.

Harry smiled mildly. "Why tell me? Or were you planning to dictate your amorous memoirs?"

"Lysistrata says you have some agreement with Dr. Herriott." Ram's eyes bored into Harry's.

"Oh, I do," Harry said blithely. "If you don't marry her, I'm to cut you into tiny pieces."

"Think you're up to that?"

"Oh, I very much doubt it, but then"—Harry repeated his sweet smile—"if I thought I'd have to lift a finger, I wouldn't have come. I'm just along to take the sun."

"See you don't get heatstroke," Ram growled. "I'm going below."

Harry's fingers impudently waggled. "To her, you dog."

When Ram reached the cabin, he found Lysistrata restlessly dozing. She still appeared pale, but less ill as the sea had quieted at sunset. The coolie tunic had twisted under her, outlining the shape of her body. He looked away, torn between wanting to throttle her and make love to her. Intensely private by disposition and training, he recoiled from having near-strangers intimately meddle in his life, particularly his feelings for Lysistrata. Herriott and Harry were like a pair of mice nibbling at him. Even Lysistrata seemed as if she felt cornered, only her greatest bogey seemed to be him. Had Herriott *ordered* her to come? That might explain her reluctance to approach him. She would be ruled by no one else . . . but her father? The thought was intolerable, but if he and Lysistrata were to have any future peace, he had to know the truth.

He moved to the bed to look down at her. The signs of the trial, his illness, and her nights without sleep still shadowed her face. All because of him. His gaze shifted to her gently rounding stomach. That too: for him and of him. He had used precautions with casual mistresses and *bibees,* but had never even discussed prevention with Lysistrata. Had some secret part of him wanted to make a child with her, so that what was between them could never entirely be erased?

What *was* between them? Deliberately, he stroked a finger behind her ear, along her jaw. Her eyes opened, startled, then became wary at his speculative mood. "Am I so much the ogre that you couldn't tell me about our child before I left you in Rangoon?" he murmured.

The bleakness in his voice stanched Lysistrata's defensive anger. "I didn't think you'd want it."

"Did you imagine I'd refuse you passage to Shanghai, as well . . . that is, if Shanghai is where you really wish to go?"

"I didn't know how you'd react," she answered quietly. "In some ways, I don't know you at all; any more than you do me." She smiled faintly. "You're right about one thing: I couldn't care less about Shanghai.''

He sat on the bed. "Why did you come, then?"

Her smile became rueful. "One of Papa's crazy notions. He thought you might be in love with me."

Ram laughed softly. "One of Papa's crazy notions." He smoothed her hair on the pillow, then leaned over and kissed her deeply, lips lingering over hers.

"I'm not, you know," she whispered breathlessly. "I'm not going to marry you to be stuck away somewhere and ignored!"

"Am I ignoring you now?" As his lips moved along her throat, his finger slipped the tunic from her breasts.

"Don't!" She struggled, gasping as his mouth closed warmly over a stiffening peak. "I'm not going with you!"

"Then I'll just have to pirate you off again." He found the other breast.

"You can't . . . just . . ." Then, desperately, "Harry'll carve you up for curry!"

He nuzzled a soft undercurve as he removed her lower garments. "Harry's only along to take the sun; didn't he mention it?"

She strained away as he unfastened himself; then, despite his teasing tone, felt the impatient heat of him. His body firmly moved over hers, then his lips, demanding now, stifled her protests. They burned, making her crave him, his hands, moving urgently as if he was as starved for her flesh as she for his.

"Don't," she pleaded hopelessly. "It's cruel when you . . ."

"Have I ever been kind?" he whispered roughly.

His hands locked hers at the bulkhead, and she felt his slow piercing as if he were tightly holding himself in check. He poised, unmoving, breathing unevenly. "Tell me, do you love me, or do you just fuck as if you do?"

When she flinched, jerking her face away, he swore under his breath. Knowing what he could take from her, he took it. His body moved on her, in her, with skill she craved and dreaded. For all his seeming control, his neck was corded, sinews taut. Her hands closing convulsively against his, her body shuddered with an almost terrifying need.

"You're gutting me!" he muttered harshly, body quickening. "I can't give you any more. Love me, damn it!" As her desire splintered, the wild, silky heat of her under him became unbearable. His mouth hot against her neck, he found what he had to have from her.

With unexpected anger, his hands left hers to knot in her hair. "Why do you always make me crazy?" he said hoarsely. "Drag things from me I want buried. Make me crave the impossible. I hate you. I love you. If you leave me now, I think I may kill you." His hands tightened. "Do you like what you find in my darkest soul, my love?"

During the terrible days after the trial, Lysistrata had seen Ram suffer, but not like this. Not with this splintering rage and pain that pierced her soul. His eyes held hers with a diamond-hard glitter.

"Once you were willing to follow me from Eden . . . God, how quickly I would have snatched you away . . . and how you would have come to hate me and my shadow world. Now, I'm inside you; my life, my future is inside you and I've gone beyond caring whether you damn me for it." His mouth poised over hers as if his kiss would silence any denial.

Her eyes glazed with tears. "Oh, Ram," she whispered in anguish, "I'm sorry if . . ."

Abruptly, he sat up, rubbing his forehead as if it ached. "Don't worry, I won't force you this time. Harry was right. I should have tried persuasion, not rape. Remember, I warned you: out of his element, your merprince is something of a gnome." He looked at her, his black eyes luminous with longing, the uncertainty of the boy whose every dream had been wrenched away. "That first time I saw you, I felt as if I *were* some gnome peering up through a lake to see a vision woven from sunlight. Then you let fall your hair and began to dance, an innocent, fatal Delilah." Taking a deep, ragged breath, he threw back his head. "For all my struggles, I was lured and lost. Still, I cannot regret even the loss." As if waiting for her to fade like all his other lost, long-ago dreams, he gave her a whimsical, wistful smile. "What now for the unrepentant gnome, Delilah?"

With a smile as soft as the sunlight he dared not hope for, she drew him down. "He is doomed to lie in his love's arms forever." She ruffled his hair. "My devious gnome, who must know he is irresistible." Her smile grew softer yet. "Surely he knows as well that he is loved to his lady's like distraction."

Ram's eyes darkened. "I fear he may not. Truly, the poor, stupid creature must be shown like a child."

"I have limitless patience," she whispered.

"Life with me may be hell."

She laughed. "If it were heaven, I might begin to think we were dead." Her fingers feathered lightly on him in the first delicate invitation of love.

Harry tilted his cap down over his forehead as he gazed at the shimmering, moonlit trail the *Rani*'s wake painted on the sea. At the first muffled cry from the main cabin, his hand had gone to his pistol. Though he half hoped for another sound of distress, it did not come—as he had known it would not. With a sharp pang of loss, he shifted his gaze toward the China coast beyond the star-spangled horizon. His nostrils were pricked by a pungent scent of land: the jungles of Siam. He smiled philosophically. The East had not the particular lure of Lysistrata, but was not a bad alternative. God knows, he would probably not grow old enough to forget her. For a moment, as if teasing him or perhaps in farewell, memory recalled a grim, black bonnet sailing into the wake of another ship and stubbornly floating until its sodden weight pulled it down. Unregretted.